He lunged forward, trying to break the hold on him, trying
to escape that knife coming for his face. All it got him was
a cracking sound in his wrist and a boot in the back that
sent him sprawling, leaving him open to the knife that
glittered above him.

Weakness. You are weakness, Petri Egimont.

It was true, and he wanted – more than he wanted his
eye back, or his face back, more than he wanted to hold
a sword again in a good hand or to see Kacha just one
more time – he wanted that not to be true.

He kicked out, got the man a good one on the knee that
staggered him, and then Petri was up off the floor, back
to the wall, wrestling for one of the knives. A knee to the
man's gut, and he had one, wobbling in a weak hand, but
he had a knife and no compunction whatsoever about using
it. Let them all come, every last one, and he'd show them
what was pent up in his head. Let them taste it through
the knife.

By Julia Knight

The Duellists
Swords and Scoundrels
Legends and Liars
Warlords and Wastrels

By Francis Knight

Fade to Black
Before the Fall
Last to Rise

Warlords and Wastrels

Julia Knight

www.orbitbooks.net

ORBIT

First published in Great Britain in 2015 by Orbit

1 3 5 7 9 10 8 6 4 2

A CIP catalogue record for this book is available from the British Library.

ISBN 978-0-356-50411-7

Typeset in Apollo MT by Palimpsest Book Production Limited,
Falkirk, Stirlingshire
Printed and bound by CPI Group (UK) Ltd, Croydon CR0 4YY

Papers used by Orbit are from well-managed forests
and other responsible sources.

MIX
Paper from
responsible sources
FSC
www.fsc.org
FSC® C104740

Orbit
An imprint of
Little, Brown Book Group
Carmelite House
50 Victoria Embankment
London EC4Y 0DZ

An Hachette UK Company
www.hachette.co.uk

www.orbitbooks.net

Chapter One

Vocho took a crafty swig from his little bottle, wiped his lips and slid the jollop back into its hiding place in his tunic. It didn't take long for the familiar warm fearless sensation to flood through him, settling the pain at his hip and more subtle agonies inside.

Suitably fortified and numb enough that he wouldn't limp and ruin the effect, he strode along the cloister and out into the damp and misty courtyard ready for sparring practice. Lessers today, first-year students with lots of shiny little faces turning to watch Vocho the Great as he readied himself for the lesson. Just one more reason to keep taking the syrup, he told himself. Vocho the Great didn't limp or feel fear. He did everything with as much style as he could muster, and he was going to carry on being Vocho the Great if it killed him.

"Right, line up in twos," he said. "Footwork today, boys and girls, because you lot are a bloody disgrace."

Vocho the Great wasn't a natural teacher either. These lessers were so new and clumsy that he despaired. Had he ever been that useless? He didn't think so. Besides, he should be out doing great feats of derring-do as befitted his name. Not nursemaiding little children and trying to get them to not fall over their own feet when they used a sword, or watching them try not to cry when he raised his voice. He drew the line at wiping snotty noses.

"Cospel! Oh, there you are. Will you do something about that nose over there? It's making me feel ill."

Cospel rolled his eyes and advanced on the offending boy, muttering under his breath about "not being paid for this".

"I don't pay you to moan either, but you do that all right."

Truth be told, they were both bored rigid. No to mention this wasn't their job, not really. It should have been Kass out here. She was guild master – she'd cheated in the duel, he was sure of it, the only way to explain how she'd beaten him, even with his dodgy hip. As such, she should have been herding snotty children and trying to make them into duellists, not him. But after that brief spurt of action to win the title, a few weeks where she'd got stuck in, ordering the guild as she saw fit, grief had finally won, a battle even she couldn't win. She'd sunk further and further into herself, away from him. Away from life it seemed. And while he didn't mind helping out, he'd somehow ended up doing pretty much all of the guild master work with none of the prestige of the actual title.

He got the lessers doing a few basic exercises, which they still managed to cock up, and looked up at the outer wall that overlooked the harbour. There she was, again. Watching the ships go in and out like she'd never seen them before, like they hadn't been brought up on the docks. Watching her like that was one of the subtler pains that the jollop helped with. Every day there she was on a different section of the wall, ghosting along like a wraith. She barely spoke, and answered questions with a wan smile that worried him more and more as time spun on.

Worse, with her turned in upon herself like this, it left him to run the guild. He was making a pretty poor fist of it as well. It didn't help that he was itching to do a job himself, something where he could shine a bit, help keep up the name. But he and Kass always did their jobs together, everything together, and now she'd left him on his own, even though he could see her up on that wall.

Pining for Petri or not, it was time Kass got out of her own head. He'd tried, Cospel had tried, half the masters, fed up of Vocho, had tried, but she just smiled and nodded and went and sat on the wall. It'd been months now, and something drastic needed to be done before Vocho either murdered the next master who complained about some trivial little thing or drowned in the snot of the lessers. Speaking of which.

"God's bloody cogs, boy," he bellowed. "You're supposed to be a duellist, not a drunken sailor. Have a bit of style. Oh, for the love of . . . Cospel, will you get that one to stop snivelling?"

After what seemed like about three years, the lesson was over. The lessers scampered out of his bad-tempered way as he stalked out of the courtyard, away from the prying bronze gaze of the clockwork duellist. He'd once fondly thought she looked on him with pride. Just lately the look seemed more of gentle reproach.

He strode down a cloister and through a door, then allowed himself to sag against the wall for a moment. All the twisting and turning, showing the lessers just where to put their feet when they wanted to thrust, to turn an attack, to change a feint into a slash that would cut an opponent in half, all that footwork had taken its toll on his hip. Only one thing would help. He took a look out of a window, at the great clock that towered over the square in front of the Shrive. Not yet. Give it until, say, five o'clock. His hand shook a bit at that, but he told it not to be so stupid and carried on to the guild master's office. Which was nominally Kass's but appeared to have been turned over to him, along with all the paperwork that went with it.

His footsteps slowed as he neared the office, and not just because his hip was singing like a tortured choirboy. This was a guild of duellists, men and women who fought, honourably, for pay. It was all about the turn of the blade, the flash of sun off a well-timed attack, the glory and adulation that came with it. Glory and adulation, to his mind, should never involve so much paperwork. There'd been two tottering heaps of it on the desk when he'd left earlier. The Clockwork God alone knew how much there would be when he got back. Sometimes he thought it was his punishment, and he often dreamed about drowning in crackling sheaves of white, black ink flowing down his throat until he choked. He was Vocho the great duellist, not the great bloody signer of papers. It all made him want to lay about with his sword and sweep up the resulting bits later.

Cospel, having got the lessers back to their dorms for now, caught up with him.

"Have you got it?" Vocho asked. He wasn't sure why he was whispering, given he was supposedly in charge here, but he was.

Cospel brought out a little clockwork gizmo, a fire starter of a newer design that was all the rage. You wound it up and, when you released the catch, two little bronze duellists fought each other in a tiny arena, swords clashing so fast, *click-clack-click*, it was almost one sound. Each time their blades met, a fat yellow spark would fly off. Unsurprisingly, cases of arson had shot up in the weeks since they'd become popular, to the point where Bakar, the prelate, had instigated a full-time corps for fighting the resulting fires.

"Good," Vocho said. "I'm going to sort this paperwork once and for all."

Cospel didn't say anything to his face, but his eyebrows whirled like disapproving windmills, and there was a certain muttering behind Vocho as he made for the office.

There was a certain muttering in front too as they approached, if anything more disapproving than Cospel's efforts. Vocho recognised at least two of the voices that drifted out of his office and liked neither of them. His hip twinged in sympathy and he ground to a halt. The limp was back through the numbing syrup, slight but all too noticeable, to him at least. He wasn't facing what sounded like half the damned guild with a limp. A clock struck in the background, swiftly followed by all the others across the city until the only sound was bells and gongs and the tinkling of inner workings that told everyone who wasn't deaf, and possibly even those who were, that it was four o'clock.

With a furtive look at Cospel, who was busy muttering under his breath about wages, overtime and days off, Vocho slid his hand into his tunic. One quick snifter, just to settle his hip. Help him deal with the stupid stuck-up bastards he'd been lumbered with as masters. Just a nip. That's all.

He shut his eyes and waited the few moments before the jollop got to work, then took a deep breath and strode, without a trace of a limp, into the office.

He actually liked the room, when he got it to himself. Large and airy, appointed with only the best – a desk of shining dark wood from Five Islands with a whole host of little drawers, open and secret, plain and booby-trapped, that had kept Vocho busy with his lock pick for the best part of a month. A tapestry from the far-ago time of the now fallen Castan empire, showing some great battle which supposedly the guild had won for the emperor and had led to their currently exalted position. An upholstered Ikaran chest, chased in gold and ivory, a rug made from what was supposedly the hide of a unicorn but which Vocho deeply suspected was, or rather had been, just a very nice horse. A whole collection of swords through the ages from the crude but brutal via the experimental to the springing elegance that was currently in fashion. A splendid view over the docks and, depending on what change o' the clock the city was on, variously the palace, King's Row or Bescan Square, with its markets and stalls, truth sayers, storytellers and outright liars. No matter what change they were on, the Shrive still loomed to his left, the great clock in the square before it, but he tried not to look that way if he could help it.

Today he could hardly see the damned window, let alone the view. A master bore down on him from the left, waving yet another bit of paper and bleating about how so-and-so had better rooms than he did – he'd said so last week, and why hadn't Vocho sorted it *immediately*? Kass would have done. A second came from the right, one of the dorm masters. She was informing him that Bronze Dorm had a bad case of stomach flux, which was testing the cleaning skills of every maid they had, and that not only would Kass have known what to do, she would have done it without the dorm master having to ask. Another sat back in the chair behind the desk – his chair, damn it, well OK, not exactly but even so. She had her muddy boots up on the shining desk as she drawled on about some of the journeymen who'd been caught selling their nascent services to a street gang from Soot Town, which wasn't a problem only they weren't cutting the guild in and did he want her to teach the little buggers a lesson? If Kass had been herself she'd have had her down there a week ago, of course, but Vocho wasn't quite as good at this guild mastering, she supposed.

Her boots caught one of the towers of papers, sending them scudding over the floor, but she barely even paused. Vocho noted she had some of his best rum in a glass too but didn't have the chance to do more than open his mouth before another one started, complaining about such-and-such getting all the best jobs, and why wasn't he getting them, he wanted to know, because everyone knew what an idiot such-and-such was, and just when would Kass be doing something about all this, hmm, because Vocho was obviously not up to the job. Kass this, Kass that. Why aren't you doing what Kass would? When will Kass start leading this guild properly instead of the hash-up you're making of it? When *is* Kass going to start leading this guild? And all in the sort of annoying upper-class drawl that set his teeth on edge.

Later Vocho wasn't entirely sure what had happened, but the next thing he was aware of was that the woman who'd sat in his chair was on the floor, surrounded by a shower of falling paper, the complainer about so-and-so had a bloody nose, and the one who didn't like such-and-such was nursing what looked like was going to be a perfect shiner. The dorm master had the reflexes to get across the room fast enough and appeared to have escaped unscathed as she stood by the now half-open window, waiting to see what would happen next. The desk was clear of everything except Vocho's hands and his sword, and the other masters were staring at him with shock and a simmering anger that would likely boil over later. For now the silence was broken only by the tolling of the god-buoy out in the harbour and Cospel's sniggers.

"Well," the dorm master said with a raised eyebrow, "I suppose we can't expect anything else from *you*."

Vocho glowered at her and she had the grace to blush. He took a deep, steadying breath and made sure not to look at Cospel, who was struggling not to laugh. He wasn't struggling all that hard though, because it kept leaking out like steam from a kettle.

There was a lot Vocho could have said. He could have asked them just how well Kass was doing up on that wall every bloody day. Perfect Kacha wasn't being very perfect at running this guild now, was she? She wasn't being guild master at all. But no one seemed to see that, only remembered her as she had been not as she was, and blamed him because he was here and she wasn't. A lot he could have said but didn't because he thought Kass had enough of a knife inside her without him twisting it further.

Instead he took a death grip on the desk to avoid lashing out again and a deep breath. "Out, the lot of you. No, I don't care *what* he said, or what anyone has done. Out!"

They went, muttering about his lack of manners and breeding, and that Kass would hear of this and more besides. Vocho held on to his temper, barely, until Cospel had firmly shut the door and let loose the laughter that had almost given him a hernia.

"You're not helping." Vocho gave the now scattered documents a vengeful kick.

"Maybe not, but we got to take all the laughs we can at the moment," Cospel said when he'd got his breath back.

Vocho conceded he might have a point and limped about the room gathering the papers into a nice pile in the grate, where Cospel employed his fancy new gizmo and set the bloody things alight. At least it took the chill out of what passed for a Reyes city winter, which mostly consisted of a misty dampness that seemed to seep into Vocho's hip and make it creak like a clipper in a gale. He lowered himself gingerly into the chair and stared at the flames.

"I'm not sure I can take any more of this. We should be out doing . . . things! Heroic things! Feats! Tales of great bravery they'll be talking about a hundred years from now. Saving people, guarding hoards—"

"Getting recognition instead of doing paperwork and listening to moaning minnies?"

"Exactly!"

Cospel slid a sly look his way. "Of course, that means she won, don't it? That she'd be better at this than you?"

"Normally, I agree – admitting Kass is better at something would be bad. However, this time I'm prepared to let her be better than me."

"Very magnanimous of you, I'm sure. Thing is, how you going to get her to do the work?"

A good question. They'd all tried. Vocho had talked until he was blue in the face, even Cospel had tried wheedling with that kicked-spaniel look he did so well, but she just shrugged. Some of the masters had tried complaining directly to her and got the same. For all they were happy to tell him how he didn't compare to her, he knew the masters were running out of patience with her too – there'd been too many whispered conversations that stopped hurriedly if he or Kass came into view, too many looks askance. He needed to do something and soon, or Kass wouldn't be guild master even in name.

"What we need," he said now, "is some commission for her – for us. Not just guard duty or anything boring but something to get her teeth into. You know what she's like about mysteries. They get her all fired up. We need a commission like that, something to engage her gears, get her out of her own head and back into the world. I mean, you know, for her." Not for his sake in the slightest, oh no.

Cospel poked at the dying flames. "I think we just burned all the job requests."

"Bugger." Vocho thought about it some more as Cospel found what was left of the rum and poured them each a glass. There was only one person she might listen to, who might be able to find something to jolt her out of her misery. Vocho told himself he was doing it for her, really. Helping her because she clearly needed it and she was his sister, and he did kind of love her. Most of the time. Maybe he should talk to her again first. He wanted her to be happy, not drifting around the guild like a ghost of the woman she really was.

But a lack of snot in his life would help too.

Chapter Two

Six months ago

The freezing rain driving into his face made Petri Egimont's empty eye socket burn behind the sodden mask that hid it, but that was the least of his worries. Night came early as autumn spun on into winter, and with it came a blazing cold that threatened every bit of him that was exposed. If he wasn't careful, an eye and the use of a hand weren't all he'd be without.

The road was drowning in freezing mud, ankle deep and more, dragging at bones that were so weary they felt made of glass. His cloak, such as it was, gave no real protection against the rain that found every crevice and wriggled its bitter way onto his skin. He barely even knew why he was on this particular road, except that it felt like he'd tried every other and had yet to find a place where he was welcome. He'd traded every fine thing he'd had on him when he escaped the city – every trinket, every polished button, even his boots, until all he had left was a shirt, his breeches, the holed shoes he'd traded for the boots and a threadbare cloak that was no match for his old one. Traded them all for a bite to eat, a place to stay. For a surgeon who was so far gone on rum his hands wouldn't stay still, the only surgeon Petri had been able to afford to cut out the infection that had settled into the wounds on his face, and a mask to cover what was left when he was done. Even with the mask, there was no hiding the ruin of it, or hiding from the reaction it got, which meant sleeping under a lot of hedgerows, in a lot of stables. Weeks spent reeking of mud and horse piss and grinding his teeth.

The Reyes mountains in the coming winter were no place for a man with nothing, not even a pot to piss in. But the plains were full of villages, farms, fields and hedges that people owned and didn't want *him* in. A man whose face scared the horses, whose right hand was now useless, who was still learning to use his left, who couldn't do much of anything to pay his way. A man who dared not say his name because he'd betrayed the prelate, sent him mad, helped plunge the whole country into war. Who was dead, so the newssheets said, and was in any case dead inside. But the mountains were all that were left to him, no matter the stories of robbers and cut-throats and high-waymen, and even that reminder of Kass brought a sharp pain to his chest.

Two ponies trudged past, heads down against the weather, a man bundled up in furs on one, a woman on the other. Petri's heart gave a lurch, but it wasn't her. Not Kass. Couldn't be. Besides, her horse was a deadlier beast than either of those two ponies and doubtless would have taken a chunk out of his leg on the way past. If it had been her what would he have done? Slunk off into the shadows like the coward he used to be or taken out his newly forged rage on her? The old Petri was dead, but he hadn't discovered who the new one was yet, except he seemed to boil with anger, and that hadn't helped him much down on the plains either.

The ponies passing him and taking a tiny side track that wound around a sharp fold in the land did show him one thing. If he squinted with his one eye through the rain, past a stand of trees, there was a light. Several lights in fact. What might be a village and maybe, if he was lucky, an inn. One or two innkeepers had taken pity on him, mistaking him for a man wounded in the battle with Ikaras in the summer, whispering with their patrons at his scars, at the accent that marked him. Not pity for long, or for much, but they'd let him sleep in a clean bed, had given him the few jobs they had that he could do to repay them rather than take their charity. Other payments once or twice that he shuddered to recall, dark and sweating and furtive, giving the last, only thing he had to give, leaving him shamed and shameful, torn and tearful, but alive to know it.

But an inn was a good bet – and out of this freezing rain, where he'd die if he stayed much longer. He'd find something to trade, find some job he could do in return for something to eat, a dry place to sleep. Even stables were better than this. Maybe up here in the mountains things would be different.

He turned his numb feet in their holed shoes towards the lights and lurched through the mud after the ponies, hoping only for a warm place.

Light and warmth and the glorious half-forgotten smell of cooking food, of the meaty smell of stew, the yeast of new bread, stopped Petri dead as he stumbled in the inn door. He stood there, dripping freezing rain from his sodden cloak, and savoured it for half a heartbeat.

All he was allowed. The room didn't go silent, but it did fall to whispers punctuated by the loud laugh of a drunkard in the corner who hadn't seen him yet. Petri gritted his teeth against the stares, shook out his cloak one-handed – that caused a whole new set of whispers as they saw what was left of the other hand – and swept the rain from his hair, which was just growing back and was now long enough for it to be curled over his shoulder in a way that would mark him as a man of means. Long enough, but he left it wild because he was a man of means no more. The soaked mask had slipped, and he hurried to get it back into place, but the fabric was ruined and with a pang he ripped it off.

In his head he strode serenely towards the bar, ignoring the muttered comments of "Poor bastard" and "God's cogs, that's ugly" and "I feel sick" and "Should be ashamed to be out in public." But numb feet betrayed him, made him stagger, and the need to tell them all to go fuck themselves burned behind clenched teeth.

He curled what was left of a lip at the nearest customer, a heavyset man dressed in a thick smock and loose breeches above mud-caked boots, who flinched back into his chair. Petri didn't blame him – he'd looked in a mirror once down on the plains and had no wish to look again. His old face was dead, like the old him.

The lump of a man behind the makeshift bar gave him an appraising look from under a heavy brow, but shrugged. "As long as you've got coin I don't give a crap about your face," the shrug said, which was an improvement on the whispers behind Petri.

"Battle of the Red Brook," someone said in a voice loud enough to carry and was shushed. Red Brook – or as it had been before so many were slaughtered in it, Smith

Brook — fed the Soot Town waterwheels. That battle had taken place not two months ago during the war for Reyes while a regiment of clockwork gods fought off the Ikarans at the front gate of the city. Yet there had still been other battles to fight, and people to fight them. Ikarans had assaulted the brook hoping to breach the walls by Soot Town, and Reyen guards and duellists had defended it even as red-hot blood had fallen from the sky, burning the skin and hair and eyes of Reyens and Ikarans alike. So many had died on both sides that even the ground was stained red now, so they said, and most of those who survived had scars like Petri's.

He'd been nowhere near Red Brook, though at times he thought it had to have been better than where he was. Most of the survivors had been Ikaran; almost all the Reyens who'd lived had been deserters, and that was where he came unstuck. But up here, so close to the border, where families were Ikaran or Reyen almost by accident, maybe he'd get away with the pretence if he kept his mouth shut, kept his accent behind clenched teeth. He'd always thought more than he spoke, but that had changed, along with a lot else. Down on the plains talk was looser and angrier, and no matter how he told himself to keep quiet, someone would say some bullshit about Eneko, or Bakar, or Kass even, and his once-even temper would explode, for all the good it did him. But up here on the edges of the mountains that had so lately been a bone of contention between Reyes and Ikaras, where laws were something you kept to if you felt like it, things were kept closer to the chest.

"Petri? Petri Egimont, is that you?" A familiar voice came from behind him, shattering any hope he had of staying anonymous.

"Of course it's him, Berie, you idiot. Petri? Petri!"

They approached on his good side, from a corner where they'd been drunkenly oblivious to his entrance. Now they moved towards him in a flurry of powder and faded silks, hair curled over their shoulders like they were still nobles and ruled Reyes. The whispers about Petri stopped, to be replaced by other words.

"Fucking nobles, *ex*-nobles more like," a man said. "More money than brains, and less use than a custard truss. Came up here because they was too scared to fight for Reyes, and now they're stuck. I'd give 'em coin to bugger off, if I had any."

Berie didn't hear or maybe pretended not to — he'd always had a talent for that. He swooped down on Petri like a pigeon after scraps, with Flashy close behind. Petri caught a whiff of fear about their movements. Too sharp, too jerky for these two, who'd raised indolence to an art form. Stuck, the man had said, and it was certain they didn't fit in this rough inn in the middle of nowhere, with no one of their own imaginary stature. Maybe they'd run out of people to borrow money from.

"Petri, old boy, how the hell are—"

Petri turned to face him with what passed for a smile on his ruined mouth. Berie blanched and staggered back with a very uncharacteristic word. Flashy waved a handkerchief in front of suddenly white lips and swallowed hard.

Nothing for it now. No hope of escaping without talking, revealing what he was, that these scars were not the scars of a hero but more likely that of a Reyen deserter. He could protest he'd been nowhere near the brook, but he'd tried that down on the plain and no one had believed him. So he cranked the smile up a notch and felt the ropes of scar tissue that ended where bare bone began bend and twist.

"About as well as could be expected," he said. "Under the circumstances."

A hiss of indrawn breath from behind, a startled curse from further off. Petri had tried but couldn't get rid of the accent that gave away who he was, or rather what he had once been. Rich, noble, privileged. Hated by all the men and women who'd risen against the king and his favoured few two decades ago. Time changed many things but not hatred, Petri was beginning to understand. Battle of Red Brook or not – and with this accent it would be quite clear not – he was noble, and up here in the mountains things were different. *Very* different.

A glass smashed behind him, and another. Something metal *clonged* heavily against wood. Flashy keeled over backwards before anyone had even made a move towards him, while Berie clutched his clinking but skinny purse to himself.

"Them tosspots been up here a while," the voice behind said slowly. "Throwing around their cash like confetti, acting like they was still lords of the manor, giving people all the more reason to hate 'em. Didn't peg you for one of them though, not in that get-up. So are you?"

Petri shrugged. "Does it matter?"

"And the Battle of Red Brook?"

Another shrug.

"Here, isn't Petri the name of that bloke in the newspapers? Didn't he poison the prelate?"

With that, a bottle flew end over end and smashed on the unconscious form of Flashy. Something shiny slashed at Petri's good side, but he managed to dodge, barely. It wasn't going to stay that easy, not with only half his vision and half his hands working. He whipped round and got his back to a wall – at least he cut off one avenue of attack that way. Berie screamed like a child as a rugged set of fists slammed into his face.

"Petri," he gasped when he could. "Petri, help me."

Petri grabbed a bowl of hot soup and flung it in the face of the nearest man. Berie would have to fight his own battles because Petri had his hand full with his own.

The evening descended, as it so often did when people saw what was left of his face, heard his voice, into fists and chaos. It was a miracle he wasn't dead already, but while down on the plains they seemed eager for him to bugger off out of their nice village, they drew the line at killing him, although he sometimes wished they'd get over their scruples and do it.

It looked like he might get that wish here; the mountains were known for their scant regard for the finer points of law. This wasn't just barroom brawling, not just thrown pint pots and brass knuckles and the cracked ribs that seemed to follow him wherever he went across the plains. The people in this inn were as hard as the rock underneath them, and had knives and swords and even a clockwork gun or two.

Down on the plains Petri hadn't fought back. What could he do against men and women burly from farming and brave from numbers? Not much, except curl up, live and loathe himself for doing it. He hadn't fought anyone since he lost the use of his right hand, not drawn a sword he no longer had or thrown a punch with a left hand he was still unsure of using. Now the swords came out, the knives glinted under tables, guns clicked as they were wound, and it was fight or die.

He tried a punch to the burly man advancing on him with a long knife in each hand, but his left hand was too slow, the punch mistimed and weak. Someone else's hand grabbed his useless right wrist, squeezed hard enough to make him gasp, then twisted so that Petri ended on his knees with nothing to look forward to but the knives advancing on him. An image flashed in his mind – of a hot knife coming for his eye, of a voice telling him he was *weak, Petri Egimont, weaker than bad steel, softer than lead* before the blade had taken his eye.

That voice, that memory, had him lunging forward, trying to break the hold on him, trying to escape that knife coming for his face. All it got him was a cracking sound in his wrist and a boot in the back that sent him sprawling, leaving him open to the knife that glittered above him.

Weakness. You are weakness, Petri Egimont.

It was true, and he wanted – more than he wanted his eye back, or his face back, more than he wanted to hold a sword again in a good hand or to see Kacha just one more time – he wanted that not to be true.

He kicked out, got the man a good one on the knee that staggered him, and then Petri was up off the floor, back to the wall, wrestling for one of the knives. A knee to the man's gut, and he had one, wobbling in a weak hand, but he had a knife and no compunction whatsoever about using it. Let them all come, every last one, and he'd show them what was pent up in his head. Let them taste it through the knife. He stabbed forward with it just as a blow connected with his cheek, leaving him reeling with a dying man falling off the end of the knife and another ready to kill him.

A sudden silence rippled out from the doorway to the outside, and the man set on killing him backed away. Petri, unable to see what had caused the pause in the fighting, took the opportunity to shove the dead man off the knife and grip it harder, keeping himself ready in a modified duelling stance. Sod Ruffelo's gentleperson's rules for duel-ling; now it was kill or die, and with his back to the wall it became suddenly clear in his head that he had no inten-tion of dying, not here, not like this. If he had to, he'd kill every last one in the place.

Slow clicking boots across the flagstone floor from Petri's blind side, a general shuffling backwards and lowering of weapons from the mob, Berie quietly sobbing somewhere. Petri turned towards the steps so that his one eye could see and came face to face with the woman whose entrance had caused such a stir.

She was tall, half a hand taller than Petri, with corded muscles showing at cuffs and collar. Her fingers were criss-crossed with old scars, perhaps from the long knife that sat easily at her hip, or the sword, no duellist's blade but solid nonetheless, at the other side. She looked Petri up and down, cocked her head at the mess of his eye and cheek and never even flinched. Maybe she'd never flinched in her whole life – he'd believe it of that face, with its thin sharp nose and jutting chin, a face like a hatchet ready to split wood, with its own puckered scar that ran from lip through to hairline. He let out a breath when her glance went to Berie, where he cowered under a table, one hand to a nose that was leaking blood all over his once fine clothes, the other hand clutching his now empty purse.

"Well now," the woman said in a cracked husky voice like morning crows. "It looks like we've got a problem, doesn't it? These two –" one hand lazily indicated the sobbing Berie and the prostrate Flashy, who appeared to have lost his boots "– are the ones I've come for. I told you to leave them be until I got here and then we could all have a share. That's the deal."

Almost everyone looked to the lump behind the bar,

who still had a large chunk of wood in one hand, which he hastily put away when the woman glanced his way with a questioning eyebrow.

Given the man looked like he could bend steel with his teeth, the contrite "Yes, m'm" he came out with was the last thing Petri expected. "Well, not the one with no face, m'm."

The woman looked Petri's way again, and a cold shiver itched across his back at the appraising nature of her stare, as though assessing the value of everything he wore and him too. She turned back, dismissing him from her thoughts, and speared the barman with a look.

"Sorry, m'm." His lips twisted, and he shuffled his feet like a five-year-old caught stealing sweets before he whacked the gawping pot boy next to him into pulling Berie out from under the table while another propped Flashy up in a chair.

Berie resisted half-heartedly as the pot boy made him face the woman. Whatever she'd been after him for – and given the general lawlessness of the region coupled with Berie's habit of flashing his money about, it wasn't hard to guess – he wasn't looking a very good prospect, what with all the blood and tears and torn clothes, not to mention the empty purse.

The woman tutted under her breath, and a small shower of coins, which had presumably recently belonged to Berie, cascaded onto the floor at her feet as the inn's patrons shuffled and coughed and gave her what they'd stolen.

"Better," she said, and two men who'd been lurking, unseen by Petri, behind her went to pick up the money while delivering menacing looks to all and sundry. "And don't forget, you and this miserable inn are here under my sufferance. We have an agreement, and I expect you to stick to it."

She turned away from the barman and his muttered "Yes, m'm, sorry, m'm" and back to Petri. He gripped the knife and tried to figure his best way out. The door was on his blind side though, and any chance of being subtle had been lost with that eye.

"And who is this wretched little shit?" she asked the crowd.

They fell over themselves to tell her he was Petri Egimont – you know, that bloke what poisoned the prelate – it was in the papers from Reyes.

Her interest perked up. "Really? Isn't he supposed to be dead? Doesn't seem to have worked out so well for him anyway." Then to him, "Is it true? Are you this Petri? A man trained in the duellists' guild, if I recall. Did you poison the prelate?"

He screwed his courage into the knife in his hand, screwed all that pent-up rage and fear too. If he failed here, there was nowhere else to go. If he failed here . . . He was sick of failing, sick of being a coward, of people looking at him like a freak. "Maybe," he said, and she raised another eyebrow at the accent. "Who the hells are you and why should I care?"

Unexpectedly she laughed at that. "I am what you might call lady of this manor. In a manner of speaking. Valentian, at your service. And why should you care? You look like you need a job, someone to feed you, clothe you. I might be that person. In return, I get a duellist, someone with a guild education. My lads and lasses –" she indicated the men collecting Berie's money "– they're good boys and girls, and we do well enough in our own small way. But with a duellist to teach them we could be so much more. We could live rather than merely exist."

"Highwaymen?"

"Oh, not so high class as that. More sort of freebooters. My boys and girls need feeding is all. We don't take too much, and nothing that'll be much missed. A sheep here, some coin there. A couple of places, like here, we have a little arrangement that keeps these fine upstanding if drunken gentlemen from being dragged to the Shrive, in return for letting us know about likely-looking donors to our cause. We keep our heads down and don't cause enough trouble for the guards to bother with as a rule. Safer that way." She looked him up and down again and nodded to herself. "You look like shit; your sword hand is useless, and your left is weak, but there's something under that layer of crap. I can see by how you hold that knife, the way you stand, that you know what you're about. We'd never get someone guild trained else, not without kidnap, and how would we manage to kidnap a duellist without the guild coming down on our heads? Now here you are, guild trained, supposedly dead, and in dire need of a job and a bath. Barman! Quick as you can, or quicker. Give this man a good meal and as much beer as he wants."

Petri shook his head. "I can't pay."

The calculated smile that answered brought his stomach into his mouth. "Oh, but you will. One way or another. Sit down, unless you have somewhere else to be?"

A bowl of thick beef soup landed on the table next to him, with a plate of hot bread swimming in butter and a pint of foaming ale. His mind was dizzy with hunger, and his stomach told him to agree to any damned thing just to eat. His pride tried to say something but his bloody pride had got him into this mess in the first place.

He sat and shovelled in the soup as fast as he could with his left hand before anyone could take it away, only half listening to what she said. His priorities had changed somewhat over the last months. He'd wanted to be free but not free to starve to death, to be run out of every town and village and inn for the way his face looked, the way his voice sounded. Not free to be hated everywhere.

"So, Petri, what would you rather? A job with me or freezing to death out there, if this lot don't kill you first?"

He watched her face – the stillness of it, the intensity – and heard the seeming honesty of the offer.

"Come with me and they'll never dare touch you," she said as he hesitated. "Teach my lads and lasses how to fight properly. All the soup you can eat, and no one will ever dare lay a hand on you again. Because I bet they have, with that face, haven't they?"

Heat rushed to what was left of his face, shame for it, that he'd let them too, not fought back. "Yes" was all he said.

"Of course they have. I know, you see, because they used to for the scar on my face. People fear it, I find, fear disfigurement and those that show it, and people attack what they fear. But I found my place and a use for that fear, how to make it work for me. Maybe you can find your place, a use for their fear of you. You could have a chance to get back at all those pathetic peasants who wouldn't take you in, who ran you out, who hated you, abandoned you. A place among my little band of outcasts."

He stopped shovelling and stared at the soup. Oh, he was going to pay for this, one way or another, as she said. But there was nowhere else, no one else, and the chance to get some semblance of a life back, maybe even get his revenge, yes, that was tempting. Eneko was dead, but others weren't. Kass – the word came unbidden, boiling up on the top of a fountain of rage – she'd abandoned him to this, this face, this hand, this fate of being feared wherever he went, of being tolerated at best, beaten more often. The old Petri had been weak and soft. Maybe the new one could be strong, given half a chance.

He gave Valentian – Scar she said later, call me Scar – a terse nod that seemed all he could manage and set to the soup again, trying not to think about how he'd fallen so low a bowl of food was the price of his soul.

Chapter Three

Now

Kass watched dully as various masters stormed out of Eneko's – no *her* – office. Not that she used it at all, leaving everything to Vocho. Surprisingly, the guild hadn't fallen about their ears with him running the place, even if it was in her name. She felt a twinge of guilt that she'd left him to it, but it was short lived before other, deeper guilts that plagued her.

A newspaper lay, as yet unread, on her lap as she ostensibly looked out over Bescan Square. What was in the paper was often at odds with what the storytellers down there shouted out to anyone who'd listen. Of course, the storytellers weren't above being bribed, which was probably why she heard so many tall stories about Vocho drift up over the walls. She wondered whether he bribed the newspapers as well, or whether they got their news from Bescan Square, but only for a moment. She couldn't seem to take an interest in anything for long.

She tried the newspaper. At least she could keep up with what went on if nothing else, but it seemed like every page brought to mind old memories. Everything in Reyes did, and that was the trouble. A softly spoken word here, a glimpse of a dark head, hair curled over a shoulder there, the chimes across the city at midnight, even the mists that plagued the city of Reyes at this time of year. *Everything* reminded her of Petri.

The newspaper, she concentrated on that. The Battle of Red Brook again – even now, months later, it still cropped up. Some kind of hush-up, the paper said, though how they knew was anyone's guess. The writer went through the whole thing again – the rain of hot blood that had left men and women on both sides screaming, the unnamed clusterfuck that had left almost every Reyen dead. No one seemed to know exactly what had happened there other than two Reyen units had ended up attacking each other, but it didn't stop them speculating, often at great length. Wild theories, paranoid conspiracies, more measured thoughts – Red Brook was the battle that everyone talked about. Something had been covered up, the paper said, but it was distressingly vague about what that was, apart from the fact that the guild or Bakar had ordered it. The guild hadn't, as far as she knew, but a lot had happened in that battle and in the run-up to it that people wanted to forget, like they had been right behind Eneko when he tried to take over the city. As for Bakar, it seemed to her that the prelate probably had quite a lot that he wanted kept quiet from the whole debacle, things it wouldn't do any good at all for the city to know. How close Reyes had come to losing, for a start. What it had cost its citizens.

What it had cost her, and Vocho and all the rest; they never mentioned that in the papers, she noticed. She scrunched the paper up into a ball and threw it as far as she could over the wall. Bunch of suppositions and lies, all of it.

A sound behind her made her turn: Vocho coming up the steps, trying his best not to limp. Probably no one else noticed it, but she couldn't help but see. Another guilt to add to the rest. She'd been so fired up about getting Alicia and Eneko, she'd not even noticed he hadn't been right behind her. Left him to face that battle on his own, and now he had a lame leg, which he tried, so very hard, to hide. That he'd never said a word of blame about it only made it worse.

He plunked down next to her with a weary sigh. She knew what he was going to ask, to say, before he said it. What he always asked, and she couldn't give. Not now. Not yet.

"I'm going to kill one of them soon," he said. "Kass, you have to—"

"I'll talk to them." She could manage that at least.

"Kass, no. Look, you took the bloody title, you should be doing the mastering! Not me."

"I delegated. I'm allowed to do that."

"Well, yes, technically this is true. Technically you could have every damn one of us shot, if you wanted to. You're the guild master – what you say goes. Only you aren't saying anything."

She looked out over the city, then down at her hands in her lap rather than at him. "I can't, Voch. I tried. I did. I managed for a while, but I couldn't keep up the pretence. Soon perhaps, but I'm not ready yet."

He grabbed her shoulder and forced her round. Deadly serious for once. "Yes, you can. You have to, for the sake of my nerves if nothing else. Please, Kass. It's been months. I didn't mind to start with but I can't carry on like this. Seriously, I'll kill one of them. Maybe more than one."

She shook him off, angry at the both of them. "Not yet. I hear them talk, you know. I know what they say about me, about you. They say I killed him, Voch." No need to say who – they said she'd killed Petri. "They say it was my putting that piece of paper into the Clockwork God that was the evidence Bakar used. That without it he'd still be alive."

"So? Get down there and give them what for. Tell them good and proper that it was Eneko who killed him, not you, and, if they recall, they were taking their orders from that bastard and never said a bloody word. They're saying that to absolve themselves of blame."

She shook her head and ran a hand over her eyes. "I thought I could do it; that's why I took the title. Thought I could, thought it would help me forget, that I could lose myself in it. But I can't – the stares, the whispers – because they're right, Voch. And I can't forget. This place won't let me." Petri was in every echo of steel on stone, every change o' the clock, every movement of the Clockwork God, in every sight, every sound.

Vocho stood up and laid a hand on her shoulder before he left her to look out over the city she loved and wonder if she could bring herself to leave.

Vocho stared at his washstand. A bottle of jollop stood where one hadn't been when he'd left. Every time he came to the end of a bottle, he told himself he would stop, he'd give it up. It'd be easy, he lied to himself, though his hands shook at the thought. And every time another bottle would appear on his washstand, and he'd weaken and fall on it like a starving man reaching for bread, would take a first swig and let all his cares fly away into numbness.

The worst thing was he didn't even know where the stuff was coming from. He had to assume from Esti, who had magical ways with plants and concoctions made from them, and a certain sympathy for his wound and how he'd got it, but he didn't *know*. The bottles just turned up in his rooms, on his washstand, one a week. And he'd tried to be strong, tried to give it up, and maybe he'd have managed to if not for the limp. A sword thrust to a hip is not a pleasant experience, he'd come to discover, but it paled in comparison to the weeks-long, possibly lifelong pain that followed. So it was limp around like an old man and not be able to even spar never mind duel properly, or it was the syrup that he couldn't give up, which made his hands shake and his head throb when he was without it.

He stared at the bottle and willed himself to look away, to not pick it up. He didn't need it. He could be himself, be great without it. But his hands fumbled his shirt buttons, his head swam with need, his hip sang a raucous tune of pain, and he gave in. He always gave in. A swig of green-tasting jollop and he was himself again, dashing as ever and no trace of a limp as he made his way through the city to see the prelate.

There was *one* part of his surrogate position that Vocho appreciated: how every master stood a little straighter when he walked by, whether they were sniping at him in whispers or not. It was much the same at the prelate's palace. As he walked past the guards they snapped to attention and cut a salute sharp enough to draw blood. He could live with that.

Cospel had come with him, possibly just to avoid the next lot of lessers, but he didn't go in with Vocho. Instead he loitered outside, fishing for gossip among the hordes of servants, soldiers, traders and clerks as Vocho made his way to Bakar's rooms.

The room Vocho was ushered into had once been a sumptuous affair, a leftover from the days of kings and nobles. Velvet hangings, ornate little tables, chairs that Vocho had always worried he would break if he so much as looked at never mind sat on. Bakar hadn't removed many of the old king's extravagances but had added his own – clocks. Vocho had been here a few times before, and always he'd been all but deafened by the sound of clocks, the susurration of their cumulative tickings and tockings audible from halfway down the wide corridor. But the prelate's love of the things had almost been his undoing. Since Bakar had come back into his right mind, the clocks had gone – all but one, a truly hideous affair of what looked like bones and human skin. It couldn't possibly be, Vocho told himself, and then recalled his mostly slept-through history lessons about the old king and the magicians that had ruled in his name, and thought, Maybe it could.

"I keep it as a reminder," Bakar said into these thoughts, making Vocho jump.

He pulled himself together. *Be tactful, lad.* "Death comes to us all in time?"

A smile from Bakar, of the serene sort that made Vocho keep a close watch for any signs of madness or clock-talking. "To not trust what the clocks say, but to trust instead to people."

Vocho wasn't sure what to say to that without putting his foot in it in some way, so he said nothing, only returned the smile, though possibly his was less serene. Bakar extended a hand to a chair, inviting him to sit. He looked a different man to the one who'd lost his sanity months ago to a magician's poison. Then he'd been thin and furtive as well as completely mad, but now he looked back to his old, sleek self, if rather whiter in hair and more wrinkled in skin. The old poise was back, the confidence that had helped him lead a revolution against the old king and not only win but become the new head of state and keep that position in the face of all the rivalries that plagued the councillors.

"I'm glad you came." Bakar spread some of the dreaded paperwork on the table in front of him. Even upside down, Vocho recognised copies of a couple of bits he'd, er, disposed of.

"I've had three petitions this week. And that's not counting two rather upset pairs of parents. Last week I had six petitions, so I suppose that could be called an improvement?"

"Petitioning about what?" Vocho dragged his gaze away from the papers and their implied guilt.

"You mostly. You've upset a lot of people, and they are not shy about complaining to me about it. I know I have no real jurisdiction over the guild—"

"No jurisdiction at all, in fact."

"Indeed. But I was planning on asking, very politely, if the guild master would consent to come and visit me so we could talk. While I'm happy to help the guild when required, this is taking up more of my time than I can afford."

"She's, er, busy. Very busy. Lots of paperwork. You know how it is."

"I know a liar when I see one as well. No matter how well you forge her signature on the papers I get, Kass isn't running the guild; you are. And making a piss-poor job of it too, if these petitions are anything to go by."

They looked one another up and down for a long moment. Vocho could recall when the man in front of him had been, for want of a better term, a complete loony thanks to some artfully applied poison. There was no trace of that now though, only a firm and frank gaze.

"It's not a job I'm cut out for," he said at last, an admission that burned.

"Indeed. Your talents lie in other directions, as you have so ably demonstrated in the past. The guild may not be under my jurisdiction, but unrest there isn't something I can ignore either. We depend on each other. So you need to get on top of things, or Kass does."

"Exactly why I came. I think we can both agree that I'm really rubbish at being guild master. Kass got the job, and she's far better suited. If she'd do it. Only . . . Look, the whole thing with Alicia, Eneko . . . She took everything rather deeply. She always does. That business with Petri—"

"Ah yes." Bakar flushed slightly and looked out of the window towards the orrery that took up what had once been formal gardens. A planet whizzed past on its rail, spinning gently, and Bakar sighed. "I thought I was being kind to him, giving him to Eneko rather than the Shrive. Of course I had no idea, but still the fault was mine. Poor Petri."

Poor Petri indeed, but Vocho wasn't going to get led into that conversation.

"Which isn't what everyone is saying, or what she's thinking. And she's thinking too much. She needs *something*, something physical to expend her energy on. Something to wake her up, something she can get her teeth into, take her out of her own head and remind her that the rest of the world exists. She needs to get out of the guild for a bit, get out of Reyes and all its reminders."

"Ah, things become clear. Such a tragedy, and those newssheets do print some terrible things. Rumour and supposition for the most part. I can see how they might have affected her, but it's been months. Hasn't she . . . ?" A polite enquiring look.

"Not really." Vocho knew what it was, of course, because he knew his sister. She'd wanted to save Petri and had failed, had been less than perfect when it really mattered, and that was what was eating at her even if she never said it. But he wasn't going to tell Bakar that. "She needs something to remind her why she's in the guild. *What seems good to you*, protecting Reyes if it comes to it, and all that." Someone perhaps she *could* save.

"What do you suggest?"

Vocho leaned forward. "Well, as the prelate of Reyes, you are our foremost employer. Find her a job, a puzzle to figure out, one that others have tried and failed at. Appeal to her perfectionism and her professional pride. Ask her, personally, to take care of it, say she's your only hope. If you can make it sound like a good thing, so much the better. Honestly, I want her in charge of the guild more than you do." More than that, he wanted his sister back. What was the point of being bloody marvellous in a duel if you couldn't crow about it to your sister?

Bakar sat back and tapped his teeth with a pen, watching the grand orrery outside as it slid around. Planets and stars, fate and life and death, if what the priests said was true. Which it probably wasn't, Vocho reminded himself, because he was pretty sure Bakar had invented the Clockwork God out of thin air.

"Everything on its course in a clockwork universe," Bakar said at last. "Predetermined, like the course of the planets. I always preached it, though I didn't always believe it. But sometimes the clockwork surprises us all. I may have just the thing for you. I was considering asking for a few masters for it, but perhaps, yes, perhaps it is important enough for me to request the guild master to intervene personally. From what I can gather, there may be links to the guild. Besides, your sister isn't the only one needing a little help to forget last summer. Maybe the two of them can help each other."

He pulled out a fresh piece of paper from a drawer and wrote in a fluid hand, blotting carefully from the little pot of sand by the inkwell.

Vocho read it over once he'd finished.

"Oh, that should do the trick. If it doesn't, I'm moving to Five Islands."

Chapter Four

Five months ago

The valley was small and narrow, a slice in the mountains except for at one end, where it opened out and dropped away towards the Reyes plains, which lay dim and brown in the distance. Snow choked the passes, and by the time Petri reached Scar's camp, he was frozen to the bone despite the cloak and boots he'd been grudgingly lent.

Scar had made her offer and then ignored him, leaving him to the not-so-tender mercies of her followers. One, a bald-headed giant called Kepa, had given him the boots, still warm from whatever poor sod he'd stolen them from. Petri had a suspicion they had once been Flashy's, along with the cloak, given their complete unsuitability for a mountain winter. Flashy himself had been left alive, along with Berie, at the inn with nothing much left for themselves except their underwear. Again.

Without this poor largesse, it was doubtful Petri would have made it to the valley. What had started before the inn as freezing rain that scoured the scars on his face soon turned into the full icy blast of an early winter. They had shaggy little mountain ponies – Petri had been given a broken-down nag as grudgingly as he'd been given the boots – but now snow fell in great feathering waves, obscuring everything, drifting in places higher than a horse's head, so they'd been forced to stop.

Not for long though, because Scar would brook no stopping unless she had to. Two days after the inn had receded into the snow behind them they left the scant path and made their own trail up to the valley, the snow filling in their tracks behind them. Petri's face and fingers had long since gone numb, and on his useless hand the skin was white and hard.

"No Man's Land," Kepa had grunted, though Petri hadn't asked, hadn't spoken at all along the trail. Those were the only words offered to him the whole trip.

The valley was cold and hard with packed snow, dotted here and there with huts walled with badly hacked logs and topped with snow-covered turf. These men and women had been settled here a while, Petri thought – grass and lichen grew on the rough planks of some of the huts, and a small tree had taken root in the thatched roof of a barn – but several of the huts sported freshly cut logs, still bright with sap, making him think the band had grown lately.

A larger hut at the end was where Petri was taken. Inside it was dark, gloomy with smoke, lit only by a mean fire at one end that did little to dispel the cold. A few rough planks on sawn-off tree trunks served as tables, and the floor was nothing but hard-packed earth, not even any straw. A few men and women sat huddled in old furs and patched cloaks, slurping a thin soup. It was rough, but Petri recognised a mess hut when he saw it.

Kepa gave him a push, and Petri stumbled in. The door

closed behind, shutting out the last of the grey light with it. The people at the tables looked up, and there – he could never escape it – were the stares, the whispers, the sneers and snarls as people saw his face, thought they saw *him* in the bony shine of his cheek.

A hand shoved him down to sitting, and a bowl appeared in front of him filled with a greyish-brown liquid that was at least hot. His face began to tingle and burn as it warmed up, but he supposed that frostbite could hardly make it more of a mess.

Kepa sat down opposite with a bowl of his own. He took a few slurps, peered at Petri from under beetling brows, then he looked around, made sure he had an audience before he spoke.

"So, what's so special about you then, skull man?"

A few sniggers sounded around the hut, and a few of the bolder came to crowd him at the table. Petri shrugged and kept his eyes on his bowl. He knew how these things went.

"Scar don't take just anyone in," Kepa carried on. "Especially not a nob. She takes on those that no one else wants but not cripples. She wants fighters, artisans, makers and doers, *useful* people, does Scar. So what's so special about you?"

"Guild, wasn't he?" someone else said. "Didn't you hear Scar say? He's a guildsman."

"That true?" Kepa asked and shoved Petri's shoulder, spilling his soup. "You a guildsman?"

"He was," another voice chimed in. "Looks like someone fucked him up good and proper though, eh? And the guild didn't bother to save him, did they?"

"Nobby bastards," Kepa growled. "Well, I hope we won't be a disappointment to you, Mr Guildsman. Whoever did that to you has left you right in the shit along with the rest of us. See this here?" He waved his spoon around the mean hut. "Once you're this far out, it don't get any better. Ever. We're the dregs no one else wanted, and this is where we wind up."

"The shit on their shoe," another man said behind him, nodding morosely. "And that's all you are now."

The spoon jabbed towards Petri as Kepa went on: "No going back, no chance of a nice little house somewhere warmer, or a job, or anything. No one wants us, excepting Scar. You'll be out here scraping a living off the rocks for the rest of your life with the rest of the crap. They didn't just ruin your face, they took your life and stomped it into the mud. Whoever got you here, you hate them with all you got. It'll be the only thing keeping you warm at night."

He took another slurp of what Petri supposed must pass for soup before he carried on, seemingly encouraged by Petri saying nothing.

"We've been screwed over or ignored, hated – all of us – and don't go thinking you're any better than us, or had it worse just because you had further to fall. Now we screw back, just a bit. Fair's fair, after all. Just don't go thinking you're something special because once upon a time you had a fair crack at the whip and lost it. Because you ain't. Nothing special at all."

With that he got up, and the rest wandered back to their tables, their little knots of cronies and friends, leaving Petri alone once more to contemplate his cooling soup and the thought that this was as good as his life would be ever again.

Later, as he shuddered under his thin cloak on the cold dank floor of the mess hut, felt icy draughts reach every crevice, heard the soft murmurs and groans of others who at least had company in their misery, he thought again of how he'd got here, who had put him on this path, had betrayed him to a cold and lonely existence.

Hate — the only thing to keep him warm. He felt sure he could supply enough for everyone.

Chapter Five

Now

Vocho found Kass up on the walls. Not looking over the docks this time, but down towards the rebuilt Clockwork God, who stood over the bridge that kept the guild separate from the rest of the city.

She looked very far from being the sister he thought he knew. Kass had always been a bit of a whirlwind, always something moving, outside or in. He hadn't seen her fidget in months, and today she stood as still as the god she watched, so it was all going on in her head, and that worried him. He worried about being worried, because that wasn't like him either. Petri bloody Egimont, buggering up his life even when he was supposed to be dead. If he ever saw him again, Vocho might have to kill him.

"Do you suppose he's real, Voch?" she said without turning, startling him.

"Who?"

She looked sideways at him as he leaned on the wall next to her. "The Clockwork God. Bakar said he invented him, that he's not really real only . . ."

OK, now he was really starting to worry. "Only what?"

She hesitated, then came out with it: "I swear he winked at me once. And it's stupid. Bakar invented him to give people something to believe in, only I *do* believe it sometimes. Or I wish I did."

He looked at her like she'd grown a new head.

"Kass, you really need to sort yourself out. The guild needs you to. I need you to."

She shut her eyes, snapped them open again and sighed. He hated that sigh. Kass never sighed, or not until the last few months anyway.

"The place hasn't completely fallen apart under you. Much to my surprise,"

"My surprise too. Look, Petri's gone, and I know how much that hurts. But god's bloody cogs, Kass, you have to *do* something."

She twisted the ring on her finger. "I know. I just don't know how."

"Well, here's your chance." He thrust the envelope under her nose. "From the prelate, asking us to help. Asking *you* to help. See, it's got your name on."

She eyed it critically. "I also see it's been opened."

"Well yes, Kass, because you haven't been doing any opening yourself lately, have you? Just read the bloody thing, OK?"

She looked daggers at him but took the proffered envelope, opened it and read, frowning as she got further in. "It's that bad?"

"You haven't been paying attention. That's the problem, Kass. I can deal with recruits and training and all that, if I really have to. Quite fun knocking them all on their arses, actually. But this? I *can* do it. But you *need* to. And I'm going to make you, if I have to strap you onto that bastard you call a horse and drag you the whole way. I'm going to keep on at you until you threaten to cut my head off. That's when I'll know I've got my sister back properly. Tell you what: I *dare* you to do it, double-dare you. Bet you a bull even."

She snorted a laugh, but he could see the idea appealed. She never could stand being kept in the dark about something, even something as simple as what Bakar wanted. A last, longing, look at the Clockwork God, and she nodded. "You are so on."

Vocho was feeling much more cheerful as he went with Kass to see Bakar. At last she was doing something. Even if it was only answering a polite, if rather cryptic and intriguing, summons, that was more than she'd done in weeks. She eyed the now almost clockless room and grimaced at the one that was left. Its sonorous ticks were the only sound in the room as they entered.

Bakar got up from a little table by the window to greet them, and urged them to take a seat.

"The clocks were always a comfort, and I miss them," Bakar said to her unspoken question. "Now I prefer to watch from afar."

Kass didn't seem inclined to say anything – she was staring out of the window at the orrery, watching the clockwork with a distracted frown.

"So," Bakar began with an embarrassed cough. "You read my letter? Any thoughts, Kass?"

She stopped looking out of the window and finally gave him her attention, and a shrug. "Highwaymen in the mountains. Or rather mercenaries, and with them leftovers from the Red Brook – Ikarans and Reyens, both probably. Maybe, if you're really unlucky, maybe even a magician or two, since they shut the magical arm of the university in Ikaras and turned them all loose. Displaced men and women, looking to carve out a living by stealing, joined up most likely with the ones already there. Your men haven't got very far finding them, and they've grown bolder but still not especially troubling." A wan look appeared. "I've read the news, even if I haven't done much else. So, not especially troubling, which makes me wonder why you asked for me?"

Bakar hid the twitch of a smile quite well, Vocho thought. "Because they aren't just thieving any more. People are dying, many of them. Not to mention they're closing in on Kastroa. Quite an important town as trade goes, or it was. Things have suffered of late, what with all the trouble with Ikaras, but now the Ikarans have found themselves a queen we were hoping to hammer out some new trade agreements, and the town would benefit immensely. First town out of the coal and iron mines on the Reyes side, you see."

"I see that it's important to getting Reyes back to where she was." Kass frowned, which Vocho took to be a good sign – her brain was getting into gear.

Bakar took a sip of tea and nodded. "The area has had a bit of trouble with banditry in the past, nothing major, but now this new group is giving trouble all over the mountains and creeping ever closer to Kastroa. The Scar and the Skull, they call themselves. Been getting bolder by the day. The whole town's in uproar and petrified of this Skull person."

"And you want the guild to sort it all out?" Kass raised an eyebrow.

"Succinctly put," Bakar said dryly. "I want you to stop them, stop the killing. Will you?"

"For the right price, naturally," Vocho said.

She gave the pair of them a faintly amused look. "I've taken a bet that I would. But I don't see why it has to be me — us?"

Not the response Vocho had been looking for, but it was better than nothing.

"For the good of Reyes? Isn't that what you swear?" Kass bridled at that, but Bakar rolled right on. "Now Reyens are dying, and not just one or two. You're the guild, the best Reyes has to offer, but that isn't the only reason. You, the guild, weren't the only ones to suffer in the battle for Reyes. Others suffered very much and are only now recovering, maybe need a little nudge in that recovery. I am, shall we say, more kindly disposed than I may once have been towards those who have a little emotional difficulty."

His smile became strained at this veiled reference to his time of madness. Little emotional difficulty indeed.

"I hope you're not thinking of sending us out with a bunch of madmen?" Vocho asked. He didn't like the way Bakar had inserted this angle into the plan.

A flinch at that last word, but Bakar rallied. "Certainly not. As I say, many men and women suffered, as you have. Not all had the guild to fall back on. Perfectly good soldiers who just need . . . a little boost to their confidence. A little help from the two most renowned duellists perhaps. Besides, banditry is one thing, people dying is far more serious. I want it to stop, and who better to ask? Well, Kass? Will you do it? It would be an immeasurable help to me and to the towns currently terrorised."

She looked between the pair of them like she knew exactly what they were up to, took another glance outside at the orrery and sighed. "Why not? It's not like I have anything else planned."

Bakar acted as though nothing was amiss and he and Vocho had hatched no plots. "Excellent. Reyes is always happy to pay the guild as befits its station, and it will be rewarded handsomely for this. Now." He indicated a sheaf of papers strewn over his table. "Here's everything my men have been able to find out. I've sent for the captain who led them, who'll take you through it all, let you know everything they could discover. I've instructed him to do anything you tell him, Kass, and he and his troop will come with you. Latest reports put the band at about forty, possibly more, so you'll not want to be going on your own. Ah, here he is."

A rap on the door, which opened smartly when Bakar called.

He was tall, with a dark curl of hair over his left shoulder and a smooth way of holding himself that made Vocho sit up straighter and made Kass flinch – and no wonder because the resemblance to Petri was striking. His face was sort of blandly good-looking to Vocho's mind, but there was a hint of a sneering twist to the mouth that made him seem as though all the world was there for his wry cynicism to laugh at. Add to that a crisp uniform and the way he moved, and he was the sort of man who walked into a bar and had women fall over themselves to reach him. Vocho hated him instantly.

"Captain Eder, Kacha and Vocho of the guild. I'll leave you three to it, then," Bakar said and did so.

Eder sat smoothly in the chair Bakar vacated. "I suppose I shall have to go through everything again for your benefit?"

Kass ripped her gaze from the orrery and gave him the kind of look which had left braver people hiding behind cushions, which he blandly ignored.

"If it wouldn't be too much trouble?" she said, and Vocho was glad to note a spark of life in her tone, even if said life was mostly annoyance.

Eder huffed self-importantly but did so. Places scouted, villages robbed, lines of inquiry, estimates of numbers and tactics and various strange rumours. Vocho's eyes began to glaze over about two minutes in. Right up until Eder said in an odd tone of voice, "And I'm pretty sure there's at least one duellist with them."

Kass shrugged, half interested, half looking as bored as Vocho. "What makes you say that?"

Eder shifted in his seat and a frown creased his good looks, but some hard place in him seemed to soften. "It's nothing solid, you understand? A hunch, I suppose. But we talked extensively to the people who'd been robbed, those still living anyway. There've been highwaymen in that area for years. Small things mostly. A few sheep taken here, a couple of people held up there. Nothing organised and nothing too violent either. People accepted it – it's a hard life in the mountains, and they're a hard people, used to taking whatever the mountains fling at them. They were just as likely to lose a few sheep to the snow, or wolves, and the villagers felt a bit sorry for them, I think."

Kass came and sat at the table, leaning forward as though actually eager for once. "That was then. Now?"

Eder cocked his head. "Now they're afraid. Because things have changed. These bandits or whatever you want to call them are *organised*, and now they're killing people. Not just those defending their own either, but old men and women, children. Whoever gets in their way. They don't care. They seem to have suddenly adopted tactics more usually seen in military encounters and, added to that, they've started using their swords like duellists. I heard the villagers talk about it, and I've no doubt. Ruffelo's style, Icthian – I studied them as best I could outside the guild, for all the good that did me . . ." Here Eder paused a moment, as though embarrassed, but he plunged on. "Someone's been teaching them how to fight properly, and now they're killing people. Lots of people."

That made Kass sit up and really take notice – she looked more alert than Vocho had seen her in months.

"Any idea who it might be?" Vocho had missed a few faces around the guild house since the battle with Ikaras, but no one seemed absolutely sure who had died. Possibly because Vocho had burned the relevant bits of paper that would have told him. Possibly because in several areas bodies had been unidentifiable, and he was certain at least two had taken the opportunity to hightail it out of Reyes in the confusion, given their very strong links with Eneko and the fact he'd ended up with his head bouncing across the cobbles in front of the Shrive. "Any descriptions? Do we know who's in charge?"

Eder's wry smirk faded at that and he sat forwards. "A few that match. A tall man, almost a giant, with a shaved head. A woman in charge, by all accounts, huge scar on her face, not afraid to use her sword – these two have been about for years, but while they've proved elusive, they also haven't proved too much of a problem when it was just Scar's men. Now the Scar has a second. Maybe, anyway. The Skull."

"The Skull? That seems an odd name," Kass said.

"It does until you know why," Eder replied. "All we know about him, apart from thinking he's the duellist, is he wears a mask over one side of his face. On the other side . . . there *is* no face, only bone, a few remnants of muscle. Hence the Skull. It's enough to frighten the hell out of people. Other than that, he's fairly tall, dark hair. Could be almost anyone. Could be Vocho, or me, only without all our faces."

A little shiver at that, a remembrance of Petri in the Shrive, of his upper-class drawl, which always scraped across Vocho's nerves. But while Petri had been badly wounded in the face, he still had one – he wasn't down to the bone. Could be any number of ex-guildsmen, Vocho told himself. No point jumping at ghosts. He wished he'd brought his jollop nonetheless.

Eder laid his papers out across the table. "Apparently he supplies the threats; she carries them out if the victims don't immediately do as they are told. Oh, yes, and she's a mountain girl all the way, by the way she talks. He's not. Doesn't talk much but when he does . . . definitely not a mountain boy."

Kass pored over the papers and nodded. "Makes sense. All the ex-nobles and richer clockers send their precious children for a guild education, even if they pull them out before they take their master's. He could be any one of a hundred men – someone who left before he took his master's, a retiree who got bored, someone who went missing after the battle last summer." She stopped with a grimace but shook it away and carried on. "So, he's your tactician. Odd he's not doing the fighting though. Any ideas on where they might be based?"

Eder pulled a map out of the sheaf of papers. "Looks to me like somewhere around here. See, the attacks start close by, then radiate out."

"And what's there?"

"Not a lot. An inn where no one would even look our way let alone talk to us, a few ramshackle farms, one small manor house that's seen better days and is now empty.

Last time we managed to get there, anyway."

Kass cocked an eyebrow his way.

"More snow than the mountains have had in years, apparently. Lost three men to an avalanche, and then they attacked us." Eder looked down at the papers, folding the edge of one over and over. "We didn't even hear them coming, and I couldn't give you much more of a description either because they came, did what they set out to do in the dark and left. They aren't just a bunch of farmers gone to thieving. My men – well they aren't duellists but they aren't poor with a blade or gun either. They all fought last summer against Ikaras; they know what they're doing. Or they did. I left a dozen soldiers up on that mountain, buried wherever we could find some ground not totally frozen. I want to find the people who did that."

Kass looked at him with more animation than Vocho had seen in her for a long time. Bakar had been right about this. What seems good to you – the guild motto that Kass lived by, or had done for a long time. Now he could see the beginnings of it in her eyes again, the sister he thought he knew.

"We will," she said to Eder now. "I promise you we will."

Strange how that promise only made Eder's face all the darker.

Chapter Six

Five months ago
The barn wasn't large, but it was the largest building in the valley and the warmest by far. Petri eyed it on his second night, imagining how much warmer a soft cushion and blanket of hay would be than the cold floor of last night. He slipped through the door, out of the snow and into the warm animal fug, and knew immediately that he'd made a mistake.

Stalls ran down one side, most with a warm horse's or cow's back showing above the rough planks. The ponies had better blankets than he did. As the door shut behind him, swirling a fresh drift of snow over the straw, human heads poked out of the stalls, and from the pen to the other side, where more ponies stood, heads down, contented as they sleepily munched on wisps of hay.

He knew he was in trouble when Kepa stepped out of the foremost stall, knife already to hand and a scowl making creases that went halfway around the back of his bald head. Within heartbeats others moved in the dimness behind him, half seen in the light of the one fitful lamp.

Someone scampered down a rough ladder at the other end of the barn that led perhaps to a hayloft.

"You don't got sleeping rights here," Kepa said. "You have to earn them, and you ain't earned shit. Get back to the mess."

Petri stared at him, at the piggy little eyes in the centre of his moon-shaped face, at the gleam of the lamp off his shaven head. Instead of this man he saw others in that face. Eneko, perhaps, in he way he held the knife. A pudgy-faced innkeeper down on the plains who'd taunted Petri mercilessly, whose burly sons had done more than that and left him with cracked ribs and bruises that had taken weeks to heal. Bakar, who'd looked at him with gentle reproach as he sent Petri to the Shrive. He saw Kass, an unruly tangle of blonde hair flopping on her forehead, grinning at him crookedly before she abandoned him, left him to the cruel hot knife. He saw every man and woman who'd ever turned away from him, ever jeered at him, told him he was weaker than bad steel, softer than lead.

He was on Kepa before he'd even thought about it, good hand scrabbling for the knife, bad hand at least some use as a bludgeon. Kepa fell back, startled by the onslaught he hadn't expected, and Petri pressed his advantage, mindful of the others standing behind, around them, watching. Maybe waiting to see who won.

Petri had never brawled – duelled yes, sparred within the strict rules. His only experience of brawling had been trying, and failing, to throttle Vocho in a pokey little cell in the Shrive. He surprised himself with his own vicious-ness, at the savage glee when a blow told, when Kepa rocked back on his heels after a brutal headbutt the old Petri would never have countenanced, would have consid-ered unbecoming to a guildsman.

Petri grabbed a pitchfork and cracked it around the man's head, making him stumble, and then had his good hand around Kepa's neck, squeezing and squeezing. Weak, was he? Good for nothing? Worthless?

Hands yanked him upright, and he tried, flailed around him with good hand and bad, tried to fight them all because he was never going to be weak again. Not this man, not Petri who wasn't Petri any more. He thrashed with elbows, slashed with Kepa's knife, which was now in his hand, felt it catch at flesh, heard the warm patter of blood on the straw. The hands let go, and Petri stood back, panting, grinning with what was left of his lips.

He had a circle to himself now, Kepa groaning at his feet, another man holding a wound closed on his arm. Petri kicked at Kepa until he got to his knees, then to his feet, where he wobbled uncertainly, the red imprint of a hand around his neck darkening to purple, his lip swollen and leaking blood. Kepa wiped it away absently and looked at Petri from under lowered uncomprehending brows.

"Who don't got sleeping rights?" Petri growled.

A long silence, then, "Reckon there's room for one more tonight."

He spent that night in the hayloft, warmed from the ponies underneath, snug under a cover of sweet-smelling hay. He made sure to find a corner on the far side of creaking planks to warn him if anyone came close, but he didn't sleep except in snatches, for all the warmth.

The next night they were waiting for him, but he was ready. Only a practice blunt, a sword made from soft metal that wouldn't hold an edge which he'd found in the make-shift forge behind the mess. He had the knife he'd taken from Kepa, but his rage wasn't that far gone or had turned from heat to ice in the snow. He didn't want to start killing people, or else Scar would send him on his way at best, and he'd freeze or starve. He wasn't intending on doing either of those, nor being bottom of the pile once again. Not *this* Petri. This Petri was strong.

They came in a group this time, having learned their lesson. Two in front, the rest flanking, trying to get behind. Kepa, sporting a perfect purple handprint around his neck and a fat lip, led them. Petri let them come. Brawling had its place, but against a guild-trained duellist with a sword, even a blunt one in his off hand, was not the best place. The blade wobbled out, caught a flanker in the gut when Petri had been aiming for the chest, but it doubled the man over with a whoosh of breath. Half a second later the hilt smacked back into the face of the man trying to come up behind him.

Petri was weak with his left hand, not as accurate as he would have liked, but he'd spent the day practising and had the balance of it now, and balance was half the distance. Besides, he wasn't trying to kill, only to have them leave him be, and his left was enough for that against men and women never trained in fighting against a sword. Or it was now, with all this heat and ice running through him. He snarled at the man on his right, feinted with an elbow and brought the sword around in a clumsy arc that still managed to hit its mark, albeit his arse instead of the stomach.

A wild slash towards Kepa as he advanced, enough to make him leap back, and it was all coming back to Petri, old muscle memories and new realisations he'd never understood about duelling, never got to grips with. Use the length of your sword so that you take up all the available space, leaving none for your opponents. Be louder, taller, bigger, bolder, or seem to be. Petri had never managed it, too reined in, more likely to stand back and let the fight come to him. Now all the years of restraint fell away.

It was his reach with the sword that won in the end, as he'd suspected it would. These people brawled, got in close with a quiet knife or a set of knuckles. That he could swing for them, even wildly, clumsily, from a distance was his advantage, and he used it. The blunt smacked into flesh, with the flat of the blade where he'd meant the edge, or at the tip when he'd meant for the blow to come further up the blade, but his clumsiness didn't matter against people who knew only how to punch and stab.

When he'd finished, victorious, he was wet with sweat, while they stood warily in a wide circle about him, not one without a purpling bruise at best to show for it.

"You got a way with a sword," Kepa said grudgingly, and one or two murmurs agreed.

Petri stood a little taller. "And I'm here to show you, or so Scar said. If you can stand it."

Kepa grinned suddenly. "I can if you can. Aye, reckon it'd be a handy thing to know all that. There's room in the loft for tonight. But maybe not every night. It's every man for hisself in here, and some time you'll find yourself up against it when you ain't expecting it. Reckon you'll do all right, maybe."

Petri took his place among the sweet-smelling hay and slept soundly for the first time in months.

Chapter Seven

Now

Kass packed her knapsack with mixed feelings. It'd be good to get out of the guild, away from a place that had too many ghosts swirling through it, that never let her forget. She was pretty sure that Vocho and Bakar had asked her to do this for just that reason, and maybe, OK, maybe they were right, but it was hard. It had all seemed so clear once, what the good thing, the right thing was. Now she couldn't be certain they were the same.

Her horse, recalcitrant beast that it was, greeted her with a well aimed swipe with his teeth at her face that she dodged only barely. It settled when she put the saddle on, its whole stance indicating it was about bloody time she took it somewhere interesting, preferably with people to bite at the end of it.

Out in the courtyard four dozen of Eder's men and women stood ready, horses waiting in the early mist-swirled light. With them were Cospel lurking on his pony and Eder looking resplendent in a sharply pressed uniform atop a gleaming chestnut that her horse took an instant dislike to. Behind them a couple of guildsmen that Bakar had insisted they take, "for the look of the thing". Vocho stood beside his indolent nag, giving last-minute instructions to the master who'd given him the least trouble over the last few months, who he'd picked to run the guild in their absence. She wouldn't do a bad job either, Kass thought — dependable if nothing else, and not quite ambitious enough to try a coup while they were gone. Other masters lurked further back. Some had been voluble about Kass and Voch both leaving, others had been suspiciously quiet, but Kass found she didn't care overmuch about what they were planning while she was away.

Once they were out of the teeming city with its crowds of hawkers and beggars, clockers and tradesmen, the way grew quicker, and her heart lightened as she left memories behind her. A broad road wound its way up towards the mountains, a road she and Vocho had known well enough in their own brief days as highwaymen. Now that brought a wry smile — they had been pretty awful at it.

"Something amusing?" Eder asked with a sneering effort at being polite.

"Only if you think setting two ex-highwaymen to catch your band of cut-throats is amusing."

Eder looked taken aback. "Ex-highwaymen? But I thought—"

"There was a time we weren't very welcome at the guild," Vocho said from the other side. "Or in the city, come to that."

"Some might say you still aren't. Welcome in the city, that is." The curl at the corner of Eder's mouth turned up a sly notch. "You were *supposedly* cleared of that though."

"Sort of," Vocho said with an airy wave of his hand that

made Kass roll her eyes. "I mean, I did kill that priest; it's just that I didn't know a damned thing about it."

Eder looked to her to explain. "Magicians," was all she said, and that was enough. Magicians were blamed for everything that had gone wrong in Reyes last year, from the prelate going mad to Eneko trying a coup. And they had been to blame for a lot, but not all of it.

She spent the time looking around her at those who accompanied them. The guildsmen and -women she knew, solid duellists who'd seen action enough for this trip to seem like a nice, if rather chilly, outing. Vocho had picked them well – been a bit staid perhaps even, and the thought that it was because he'd shine better because of their stolidness made her snort a laugh. Eder's troop on the other hand were a mystery, and she didn't like to travel with mysteries. Eder too – a bit stern, very disapproving and rather held-in, but there was something underneath, there had to be. There always was.

She nudged her horse forward to ride next to him, though not too close because her horse was feeling frisky.

"You said you'd all fought against Ikaras," she started, and was surprised at the flinch in his previously bland face.

"You weren't the only ones fighting," he said. "Everyone fought, not just the guild, though it'd be hard to tell from the stories the bards tell in the square."

"I never thought—"

His face went to sneering in an instant. "Didn't you? Everyone else does. We didn't need you to come, but Bakar insisted. It's not what you're used to, all court manners and civilised duelling and people doing what you tell them. A bit rough for the likes of the guild, not half cultured enough. You'll just be a hindrance up here."

Kass glanced back at Vocho, got a puzzled shrug in return and looked up at Eder again. "We'll do our best not to be, I'm sure. You seemed glad enough of us in Bakar's palace."

He pulled his horse to a snorting stop, and the rest of the company flowed around them as he glared at her. "Bakar said you might be able to tell us who this guildsman is up there. He didn't mention you coming along, or not to start with. We're perfectly capable of dealing with this ourselves. It's not a guild matter."

"If it involves a guildsman then it's a guild matter. And I am guild master, so it's definitely my business. Bakar employed us to help in any case, so we will. Besides, if you were so capable, your men wouldn't be buried on the mountain." A cheap shot, and one she regretted the instant it left her mouth. "I'm sor—" she began, but he didn't wait to hear it, instead kicking his horse into a canter until he was at the head of the little procession.

"What the hell was that all about?" Vocho asked as he came level with her.

"Ever get the feeling you're not wanted?"

"Everyone wants me."

She gave her brother a look. "Only if they're blind. Eder seems to have a bit of a problem with us tagging along. Or with the guild in general. Wonder why."

Vocho grinned, a conspiratorial thing that was odd given he didn't have anyone to conspire with except her, and she hadn't a clue what was behind it.

"Well then, maybe we should find out?" he said.

By the time they were ready to stop, they'd left the rain-sodden plains behind and were heading up into the snow-line. Vocho's hip was not slow to inform him it did not like the cold. It protested all the way through pitching their tent in among a stand of firs that clattered above them in the wind, and was positively howling by the time he could find somewhere private to swig his jollop. After that it settled into a mellow nagging, and he joined Cospel by the fire he'd got going in a clear space among the trees. The air smelled of snow and pine needles.

Vocho could see down across the plains, dark now with little rings of light that would be hamlets and villages, a further, blurrier but bigger splotch that was Reyes. All of it was coated in the sleet that seemed ever present. Behind, the mountains loomed, all tipped with snow. It had been cold and wet enough on the plains for Vocho. He wasn't looking forward to worse than sleet.

"I don't see," Vocho said to Cospel, blowing on numbing fingers, "why we couldn't have found a nice, and above all warm, inn somewhere."

"Because Eder didn't want to," Cospel said. "Bit of a nut for doing everything hisself, so I hear." He poked at the fire until sparks whirled up into the trees and Vocho began to worry they'd catch light, but at least his fingers weren't numb any more.

"Well, I wish he'd picked a warmer night for it. I thought it was supposed to be spring."

"It might be in Reyes," a new voice said, "but up here winter lasts longer."

Vocho turned to see one of Eder's troop crouching by the fire, warming her hands. She had a sharp face under a dark crop of hair tinged orange by the fire and an almost permanent wry smile as though she'd caught the world out. Carrola, he recalled, one of Eder's seconds, a sergeant who was briskly efficient and seemed to hang on the captain's every word.

"Well," he said, thinking about Kass wanting to know what was behind Eder's manner, "I hope it decides to go away before we get too far up the mountains."

She laughed at that and got herself comfortable by the fire. Vocho wasted no time in settling next to her with a meaningful look at Cospel, who managed to leer with his eyebrows as he took the hint and left.

"It should be starting to thaw up there by now," she said. "Hopefully. It'll be a late spring if it doesn't, very late. Our gear might not be up to it otherwise, and we'll have to refit at one of the towns. Better than lugging it all up here and suddenly it's thaw."

"Got pretty chilly last time you went, so I hear."

"Pretty chilly," she agreed.

She gave him a sideways look that made him shiver, like she could see right through his bluff and bluster. He found his hand groping for his jollop and yanked it away.

"Eder's—"

"A fine man, and one you shouldn't ask me about," she said sharply.

"I'm sure he is, only—"

"Only nothing, Vocho the preening, with your fancy clothes and fancier sword. He's got no love for the guild, which is what I suspect you're fishing about, but he's my captain, and I'm not gossiping about him. OK?"

He watched her face in the firelight, the way her chin jutted determinedly, how her eyebrow rose as though she could see inside him and didn't think what she saw was worth a whole hell of a lot.

"OK," he said. "We can gossip about me though, right? If I'm honest, I prefer talking about me anyway."

Carrola shot him a sharp look, perhaps thinking he was making fun of her, but subsided with a laugh. "I'd heard that. All those stories about Vocho the Great, and I don't doubt you spread them. How much is true?"

"Not much," he admitted and wondered at that because normally wild horses wouldn't have dragged it out of him. But there was something about her, a sharpness to her glance that made him pretty sure she'd spot any lie of his, so there didn't seem a lot of point trying. Embellishments, well, that was a different matter. That was hardly lying at all.

By the time Eder came along she'd winkled out the almost true story about a notorious occasion involving him, the nuns with guns and the weasel, and they were giggling like drunkards.

Eder put a stop to all that like a bucket of iced water down the back.

"Carrola, I wondered where you'd got to." There was a sharp undercurrent to his tone. "See to the horses."

She looked about to protest – the horses had all been seen to long since – but his jaw tightened, and she got up and went.

"You leave my troop alone," Eder said to Vocho when she was out of earshot. "I don't want you infecting them with all your bullshit and lies."

"Now hold on a minute." Vocho struggled to his feet, his hip making complaining noises about being sat on the cold ground for too long.

"No, you hold on and listen. I know who and what you both are, and I don't want you here. But if you keep your comments to yourselves, both of you, then we can make the best of it. I'm not an unreasonable man."

"Could have fooled me."

Eder ignored him. "If you don't keep your mouth shut, then I am prepared to become very unreasonable. Clear?"

"Oh yes, absolutely."

Eder seemed content with that and stalked off down to the other fire, where his troop sat silently as sleet turned to snow and the wind deepened with cold. He passed Kass coming up on the way, though he never gave even a hint that he'd seen her.

"He looks like someone just pissed on his parade," she said. "What did you say to him?"

"Me? Nothing. Honestly!"

"Well someone has."

"Look, all I did was talk to that Carrola a bit. I was hoping to find out why he hated us so much, but she wasn't talking. About him anyway."

Kass frowned after Eder. "Something odd there. Very odd. Like why was he all sugar and sweetness while we were in Reyes, but now we're out he's pricklier than you with a hangover."

"Well, like the man said, he did lose some of his troop up here last time. Maybe he's just edgy about losing any more. He seems a very, er, intent and conscientious sort of man."

"Hmm" was Kass's only reply, and all she said before it was time to sleep.

Kass spent the next day watching Vocho alternately desperately trying to impress Carrola and winkle information about Eder out of her. By the despondent look on his face when they reached a village at noon, she guessed he wasn't getting very far or getting much except a few tart comments from Eder. While Vocho failed in his intent, Kass kept an eye on Eder.

He sat, ramrod straight in the saddle, occasionally barking out commands and reprimands for minor infractions of what looked to her like arbitrary rules he'd imposed on his troop. Horses to be exactly in line, two abreast. Eyes front at all times, like they were on parade, only they weren't on parade were they, and an eye or two to the sides might help up here, where laws were less set in stone than general pointers on how to be polite and not murder anyone if you could help it, please. They weren't in the mountains proper yet, but there could well be highwaymen up here, or worse.

No talking, another of his barked orders, his tongue lashing out when he caught one man whispering to the woman next to him. He'd been as bad when they'd mounted this morning, worse perhaps, inspecting every blanket, every bit, every braid in the horses' manes and tails. One woman had got a bawling out for starting her chestnut's braid a quarter-inch too high. Kass might have thought nothing of it if they were about to be inspected by Bakar perhaps, but out on the road? Heading towards lawlessness where braids wouldn't help, a quarter of an inch out or no?

She'd ridden out more times than she could recall, and could recall no other officer who didn't loosen up from regimental best while they were at it. Nothing wrong with being a bit particular about your gear when it might save you, but there was a gulf of difference between that and this pedantry.

The morning was biting cold as they reached the foot-hills, but the thin snow stopped just before noon. When they reached the small green at the centre of the village, Eder called for his troop to dismount, snarled at one who was half a second behind the command and set him the task of seeing to everyone's horse instead of joining them for food.

The village was much like any other – a straggle of houses puttering smoke from crooked chimneys, a smithy where it looked like half the men of the village gathered to keep warm by the forge, a bakery where the women did the same by the great oven, a gently rusting Clockwork God on the snow-crusted greensward at the centre.

A gaggle of gangling children came to stare at them, but soon left after a few sharp words from Eder. One of the bolder ones lingered, and Vocho, with half an eye on Carrola, threw her a bull, which she caught in fumbling, surprised hands before she ran off whooping and crowing. Carrola laughed and looked like she was about to say something, but Eder's sharp voice calling for her to attend him put paid to that. She smiled apologetically at Vocho and attended.

Kass slid off her horse, shooed away another bold child who was about to take the reins, and saw to him herself. The boy, undaunted, ran to take Cospel's reins for him instead, startling Cospel so much at being served rather than serving that he handed them over without a peep. Vocho, naturally, had immediately identified the crumbling house that served as the village inn and was already making for it before she'd finished with her mount. Kass followed more slowly, looking up at the sky, which promised more bad weather in the lowering clouds that obscured the looming peaks behind. They'd been promised a thaw, that the weather would turn, but the cold looked like it had settled in for good, as though this winter might last for ever. They'd have to see about better furs somewhere along the line – the only furs they'd managed to get in Reyes were more ornamental than warm because the city never got worse than a bit chilly even at winter's worst.

When she caught up with Vocho, he'd made a start on

the woman whose house it was – the tiny front room served
as the bar, while she ran up and down the stairs with jugs
to fetch the foaming beer. Eder came in behind Kass, his
disapproving glance chilling the already cold room by
several degrees.

The captain took off his gloves, laid them on a table and
motioned for Carrola to sit next to him while they waited.
They might wait a while because Vocho had the woman
fully engaged, winking and cajoling his best. When he
finally came and sat with Kass and Cospel, he had three
plates of bread, cheese and cold meats and a bottle of what
he said was "the best wine she had. I think it probably
won't take any skin off. But don't bet on it."

Eder's men and women entered in dribs and drabs behind
him, upright and silent before their officer's disapproval,
and the woman was hard pressed serving them all, but
finally everyone was fed and watered. A few locals had
come in too, to gawp or exchange gossip, though Eder gave
his troop a sharp order to shut up when one opened his
mouth.

One old man sidled up to Kass's table, crabbed and wrinkled like an old apple, his moth-eaten furs over a thick
tunic a mismatch of rabbit and fox and threadbare wolf
that had seen better days. And incidentally stank like a
week-dead cow. "My boy says you lot are off up the mountains, to find these bandits then?" he said. "The Scar and
Skull?"

"That's right," Vocho said around a mouthful of bread.

The old man sniffed derisively, making his skinny
drooping chins wobble. "You're going to need a lot more
riders in that case. Ain't you heard?"

"Heard what?" Kass said, acutely aware that Eder was
listening while trying to appear uninterested.

"Moving down the mountains they are. Further every time, and more vicious every time as well. Getting closer to us. Funny, ain't it, that they can move about all right in feet of snow and yet the prelate's men get stuck if there's half an inch? Ain't seen none of them lot up here for months and months, though I heard they went over eastwards. We've not seen the guards since before all that business down at the city. Not since this winter turned so hellish bad."

"Well, you've got a couple of guildsmen now, so—" Vocho began.

Eder stood up behind the old man with a scrape of his chair and with a cold glance ordered his crew out.

"He's starting to get on my nerves," Vocho muttered.

"Mine too," Kass said. The old man was still hanging about, looking like he had something else to say. She cocked a questioning eyebrow his way.

"If it's the guild," he said. "Well . . . we heard all sorts of things. Like they got a guildsman with them now, and there's magicians about, and—"

"A magician?" Vocho choked on his bread, and Cospel had to bang him hard on the back before he could breathe again.

"Aye. After all that down in the city, well, a lot of people run up into the mountains after, see? Ikarans, a few Reyens even. They didn't stop long here, like. But there was this fella, he was right odd. Always kept his gloves on, and the priest reckoned that was a sure sign. Funny things happened around this fella too. Or rather people acted funny around him."

"Like how?" Kass asked.

The old man sniffed meaningfully, and Cospel got the hint and gave him some wine.

"Very kind of you. Well, like old Barley, see. Now he was a lazy old sot, always was. His farm only just about fed him and his missus, because he never liked to do no work. Left it all to her, and she weren't much better neither. And all of a sudden he was up and doing things, like, to help this chap. Barley's wife made him some new clothes. Badly mind, she wasn't never no seamstress. And Barley himself ran around like a headless chicken to do all this chap's errands for him. Then he sold his pig."

"Sold his pig? What's that got to do with it?"

The old man laughed, slung the wine down his neck in one go, and at Kass's nod Cospel filled the cup again. "Aye. That pig was the one thing he ever spent any effort on. Champion pig, it was, and it wanted for nothing. Best food, better than Barley ate, I expect, and he gave the bloody thing beer. It fathered most of the bacon for a twenty-mile lick. Probably worth as much as the rest of his farm put together. He sold it for half that, less, to buy this chap a horse. Gave him the money left over, and all. Then the chap gets on the horse and rides off towards the mountains without so much as a by your leave in the clothes and furs they made for him. And as soon as he'd gone, old Barley was down here like a man with a three-month hangover, hollering that someone had stole his pig and threatening dire things to whoever done it. Didn't remember a damned thing about the chap, or selling his pig or nothing."

"Well that's certainly odd—"

"And when the priest tells him he sold the pig, what do you think he said?"

Kass eyed the man – he was getting a lot of satisfaction out of this, and she wondered if he was the person who'd bought a half-price champion pig. "I have no idea."

"He said the man's hands told him to. Now, what do you think of that?"

Kass shot Vocho a look, noticed how his knife had dropped back to the plate, and even his wine was untouched.

"Probably just going back to Ikaras," she said. "Escaping the battle like everyone else."

"Oh no, miss." The old man grinned, wrinkling his face like a demented walnut. "See, we had a refugee or two the other way, coming down the mountain these last weeks. Escaping the bandits, see? The university shut, didn't it, in Ikaras? New queen don't like magicians, told 'em all to sling their hooks. No place for 'em now, so where's he going to go? And the winter, it's been a terrible hard winter, worst I've ever known it and I've known it cold enough to make a man's nose snap clear off. Heard a lot of things from these people, I did, a lot of things."

"Yes?" Kass topped his wine up. She wished he'd just get on with it, but seeing as he was the only one talking, it wasn't prudent to say so. "Such as?"

"Well, see, like this chap, he went up into the mountains, but the snow started next day – early it was, and sudden. He'd have not got far, even with magic, in that storm. Then not long after that Scar starts getting right bold. Skull joined her about then too. And she had a magician with her, for sure. Drinks up all the blood she can get him, he does, fries a few people for her, boils their brains in their heads, that's what they say, and that he can melt snow and make it, that he's the one making the winter hang to the mountain with its fingertips. I reckon he's how come they can move around in all the snow, where good honest Reyen men are snowbound. I do hear say."

The sound of horses clattering off brought Kass back from pondering this suggestion.

"The cheeky bugger!" Vocho burst out. "He's gone without us!"

By the time they made it out of the makeshift inn, leaving half their lunch and a fair bit of wine to the gleeful old goat who'd been so forthcoming, Eder was long gone and pushing so hard it took them a good two hours to catch him.

Chapter Eight

Four months ago

Petri blinked sweat out of his eyes before the wind could freeze it and smacked the man straight in the mouth. Left hand or not, there was enough blind rage behind it to knock him flat on his arse.

"Say that again, and I'll do that with a blade," Petri said. "And it'll make this face look like a beauty by the time I'm done. Clear?"

The man struggled up out of the wind-blown snow that streaked the little valley, spat blood from his mouth, started to say something then seemed to think better of it as he glanced over Petri's shoulder. He nodded sullenly before he stalked off, followed by the other half-dozen or so Petri had spent the morning teaching swordplay to with mixed results.

Petri took a look at what had changed the man's mind and saw ponies coming, Scar at their head. The shaggy sure-footed beasts were trudging from the ramshackle barn that saved them from the worst of the weather and where Petri had taken to sleeping when he could bludgeon himself a place, which was most nights now.

Scar halted her pony by him and looked at the imprint in the snow, tinged in blood. "Making your mark, I see. And making a few enemies, if what I hear and the bruises I see are right. Get ready."

"For what?"

A smile lightened her face. "To see what good you're doing. A raid – a village down over the border in Ikaras. Oh, don't get too cocky. Today you watch, and tomorrow and the day after too probably because it'll take long enough to get there in this snow. Learn, see how we do things. Get yourself a pony and stay at the back. But it's time you saw who and what we are."

She turned away leaving Petri grinding his teeth, but he found the only mount left – a scraggy pony – and got himself ready. Kepa sat atop the biggest pony they had and still his legs dangled, but he was at the front, at Scar's right hand, and Petri was left to the back. Not for long, if he had his way.

It was a long trek through the snow, hip deep on the ponies in places so they had to stop and dig. The short day waned, and they still hadn't found the village, so finally Scar called for them to make camp. It was just over the Ikaran border, or so Kepa said – gods knew how they knew where it was under the snow. They spent a cold and cheerless night in caves they scraped out of the snow for themselves, laid blankets on the ponies. Kepa made a fire, but it only took the worst of the wind, didn't keep them warm only alive. They huddled around it, the rest talking in low voices about what they'd find tomorrow and about the meagre rations lately, though a look from Scar soon shut that talk up. Rations were meagre indeed though – their meal was watery barley broth and no bread. Kepa had grown friendlier since their set-to in the barn and now sat next to Petri and rubbed at his rumbling belly. "Better be something good in this village, or I'm going to waste away."

The night passed in cold hunger, and dawn saw them on their way again, the ponies with their heads down against the cold, Scar's crew no better.

It was almost noon the next day by the sun as it lurked behind a bank of dark clouds when they came to a track that had been cut into the snow. Scar halted them with a raised hand, and she and Kepa rode forward to scope the lie of the land.

"Easy enough," she said when she came back. "A soft little village, this. They'll hand over what they have without a squeak, I don't doubt, but take your usual care anyway." Her gaze sought Petri out. "Watch today. Don't interfere. I'm not sure yet whether I trust you."

Kepa rolled his eyes behind her, and when she'd ridden to the front of the line to ready herself said, "Not to worry. She says that to everyone. She wants to see how good your training is. Me, I think I could take on a duellist today!'

With a parting grin, he kicked his pony up to Scar, and they waited for her signal. Petri hung at the back – with no weapon bar a practice blunt he'd be little enough use anyway.

They rode up the track, silent but for the crunch of hooves in the snow and the huff of their breath as it clouded in front of them. Over a shallow rise, and there below them sat a little village – a dozen houses and a barn, two ramshackle pigsties behind it. Slim pickings, Petri thought, and not enough here to feed all they had back at camp for a week, if that.

Scar nudged her horse forward. The village was quiet.

No one moved between the houses though smoke puttered out of the chimneys. It wasn't until Scar reached the little space at the centre of the village and slid down from her pony that they saw anyone.

A door opened in one of the larger houses and a woman came out. Very young, she seemed, with ice-fair hair pulled back from a fresh face that looked hauntingly familiar to Petri. No daughter of the household, he thought, dressed in ragged clothing more fitting to a slave, but she wore it with an aplomb that pulled Scar up short.

The woman looked them all over, and more than one man sat up straighter in his saddle at that look, before she turned to Scar and said, in a strange mix of Reyen and Ikaran, "What is it that you want? We have nothing."

Other faces showed at doors that now opened in neighbouring houses. Faces shadowed and waiting.

Scar shrugged and laid a hand on her sword hilt. "We have less. Food is what we want. Meat, grain, whatever you have."

The faces at the doors shrank back, and Petri realised that they were all very old, or very young.

The woman smiled, trying a welcome that was clearly forced. A quick glance behind her at the shadowy faces before she said, "We have nothing to spare."

Scar stepped forward, Kepa at her side. "I think you misheard me. My name is Scar, and these are my crew. Perhaps you've heard of us?"

The young woman's smile faltered, and her face paled even further, but she didn't back down, making Scar lift a sneering lip.

"We don't have anything spare to give you," the woman said. "Or I would. We've barely enough for ourselves to see us all through the winter."

Scar slashed a hand close to the woman's face, her patience at an end, and nodded to Kepa.

The village was soft, Scar had been right about that. Only old men and women or children, except for two — the young woman who'd greeted them and another about the same age, also dressed in rags. Petri wondered about that, wondered where the rest were, but Scar said nothing and so neither did he.

Scar's crew spread through the village, taking what they wanted. Children cried, and an old man begged quietly for them to leave something, please, enough to get the children through the winter, and that was the only violence Petri saw, when Kepa shoved him out of the way and got on with unhooking a vast smoked ham from a ceiling. The swords Scar's crew had in their hands were enough to stop any resistance, it seemed. Until they came to the last house, where the young woman stood in the doorway and refused to move.

"You can't," she said, chin high though her hand shook on her skirts. "I won't let you."

"Can," Scar snapped. "And will."

She nodded to Kepa, who loomed over the young woman. "I don't want to hurt you, missy," he said. "But a man's got to eat, and I ain't got nothing *to* eat. You got more here than this little lot needs, so why not share?"

She struck, quick as a snake, with a kitchen knife she'd held hidden in her skirts. Not for Kepa — she was bright enough to go for the leader but not bright enough to realise she might die doing it.

The kitchen knife missed Scar's eye by a whisper, glanced off her brow in a blow that sent blood scudding down her cheek. The cut didn't even get the chance to drip before Scar gripped her wrist and twisted the knife out of her hand, making her scream.

"I can take this," she hissed at the woman. "I can take all of it, and I could make them kill all of you doing it, and you couldn't stop me. So tell me, why are you protecting that which you can't protect? Why is an Ikaran slave protecting what isn't hers anyway?"

The woman yanked her arm from Scar's grip and glared back at her but said nothing, only glowered in the doorway, one hand wiping Scar's blood from her arm.

Kepa stepped towards her, sword out for the first time. "You want I should stick her?"

The woman flinched at that, but she didn't back away.

"No," Scar said at last, gently feeling the cut to her head. "No, find her a pony and put her on it. Tie her on if you have to. Then leave what's in this house to the people in it. We've taken enough for one day."

She stalked back up the slope to where Petri waited with the ponies, snarled at him when he got in her way and mounted. The rest came, quickly now, stowing all they'd taken onto the pack ponies they'd brought for the purpose and tying two cows behind. Then they wheeled the ponies and left without another word, the girl on a pony just behind Scar. Not tied on, Petri noted.

Kepa dropped back to where Petri brought up the rear, deep in thought.

"She going to be scratchy as hells all the way back now," Kepa said.

"A nasty wound," Petri replied. It was too, stretching from one brow right up into her hair in a jagged line, and it had bled copiously.

"Oh, that's not what'll make her scratchy. She looks all scary on the outside, does our Scar, and she is. Bloody scary. But she don't like it when things go wrong on a raid. She was lax there. Should have herded them all up and kept an eye on them while we did our business. They put up with us around here, mostly. We don't give them too much trouble; they don't give us too much trouble. Like an agreement."

"An agreement? They let you rob them?"

Kepa laughed so his jowls wobbled. "Yes and no. They don't *like* it much, but they don't create too much of a fuss either as long as we don't take the piss, at least on the Reyen side of the mountain. But this winter, it's a bad one for everyone. Closed in worse than I've ever seen it, and it's early yet. That village weren't on the Reyen side neither, so maybe they don't know about our little contract. We're having to go further afield just to keep fed, especially with them refugees who came after the battle last year. And the villages have less to spare as well, with the weather as it is. It's hard all round. We take a bit, mostly, though this year we got to take more. But that there – that girl was brave, but she almost got herself killed, and that was because Scar was lax. She'd have been scratchier still if we'd had to kill the girl. No killing, that's the rule."

"You've never killed anyone? On your raids? Surely you must have to use violence sometimes?"

Kepa shrugged. "Oh, sometimes, yes. Bit of roughhousing to soften 'em up if they're getting uppity like, though mostly they ain't. Broke a man's jaw once, one that wouldn't lie down. Mostly we wave the swords around to scare 'em up a bit, and that's enough. But killing, well, if we start killing them, then like as not the guard outposts up here will start sitting up and taking a bit more notice. They can – and do – ignore a bit of thieving, a broken bone. They can't ignore killing."

"If you're only waving the swords around, why did Scar need me to train you?"

A sly look from Kepa. "She didn't, not really. Soft touch for lost causes, ain't she? Why else do you think all us dregs is here? It looks better if we can wave the swords like we know what we're doing, but it's best not to use them if we don't have to. But best too to know how to use them if we do. More'n one of us would go to the gallows if they found us."

So would Petri – treason just to start with.

"So what about her?" He nodded towards the young woman, who sat ramrod straight in the saddle.

"Told you. Soft touch for lost causes. She might tell you, she might not, but she was that girl once. Long time ago – when we first met. Both slaves in Ikaras, weren't we? A bit further down the mountain but not much. Always been outlaws up around here, skimming off the top, and one day they came to our village, and she went for one. Almost had him too. Rennal his name was. Big man in these parts for a long time, though he were getting old then. Me and her fought him tooth and bloody nail, and she caught him a good 'un, and you know what he did? He laughed and said he was taking us two as part of his day's prize."

"So you were still slaves?" Petri glanced ahead at Scar, thought of the hard planes on her face, the face of someone who'd seen a lot, too much maybe.

"Naw, he set us free, and we joined up! He's the one that taught us, see. Be quiet, be subtle, be kind when you can. The guards is lazy around here, so don't give them too much cause to come find you, because if you do, it'll be the gallows. They caught old Rennal in the end though – he killed a man accidental in a bar fight and even the guards around here couldn't ignore that. Rennal never did take his own advice."

They rode on in silence, into a clear cold that deepened

as the sun waned. Scar signalled to make camp, and while it was cheerier than the last — they had some food for a start — Scar sat deep in frowning thought, though her gaze softened when she looked at the young woman. Maitea was her name, she said at last, when Scar insisted, though she said nothing else, not even when Scar told her she was free now. She merely sat, haughty and separate as though even a captured slave was better than an outlaw.

They camped in a little hollow dotted with stunted trees to give a bit of shelter and cut the worst of the wind. Scar set sentries, but they were far from anywhere and mostly it was wolves they need worry on so she didn't set many. By the time the sun had spent its last, most of the crew were asleep under bundles of ragged furs as close to the fire as they could get. Maitea had been given furs of her own and hunkered under them, but Petri doubted she slept.

A soft sound disturbed him. He looked out into the darkness but couldn't see anything past the flickering halo from the fire. Another scuffing sound brought him to his feet.

"What's the matter with you?" Kepa asked sleepily.

"Shh!" The air seemed far too still, the silence far too deep. Shadows flickered in the trees, but Petri couldn't tell if it was the fire that made them or something else. Someone else.

Scar looked up as he took a few steps towards the trees, peering into the darkness. There was something there, perhaps, but it was too soon to look a fool by flinching at nothing.

A figure stepped out of the darkness, hands raised in thick fur mittens. Scar was on her feet in an instant.

"Who are you?"

"Morro," he said in a voice heavily accented by Ikaran birth. "The village you just raided . . . You took her. Take me too."

Morro wasn't a big man, nor well set up. Small, furtive-looking, with a cast to his eyes that suggested secrecy and lies. Petri's hand groped for his blunt weapon.

Scar lowered her sword and snorted a laugh. "You? What for?"

"I can help you." His glance skittered over Scar, Kepa as he got to sleepy feet, over Petri. Something about the man made Petri shiver and not with cold. "I can help you with whatever you want."

"In return for what?"

Morro shrugged. "Reyes wants me dead. So does Ikaras. I want only somewhere where I can live, like you. I was trying to get past Ikaras, out into the states beyond. But I can't on my own, not in this snow. Not even me, not on my own. The village agreed to shelter me for the winter, but they couldn't *help* me. You can. Help me get past Ikaras in the spring, help me find a home. Me and Maitea. And in return I can help you get what you really want."

Something hypnotic about that voice, lulling the senses, so when Kepa laughed and said, "What good's a little runt like you?" his words startled Petri with their harshness.

Morro only smiled and shook his head. His eyes kept going to Maitea, little skimming looks that might miss being noticed. She marked them though, had sat up straight at his mention of her name, her going with him, though Petri couldn't tell whether she was pleased or disgusted.

Those looks weren't missed by Scar either — she saw and smiled to herself. "Sit," she commanded. "Explain. Make it good, and maybe I'll listen."

He bowed a gracious head and sat where she pointed,
close to the fire and by her crew, who slept or lay half
awake from the noise and watched.

"Well?"

Morro peeked at Maitea, who ignored him, before he
said, "I'm no use with a weapon, as such. But I know
things. Lots of things. You're starving, I see that well
enough." Hard to deny, given the pinched state of all their
cheeks. "This amount of snow has made it harder for
everyone, and the winter looks to deepen yet. You can't
move easily through it to raid, and when you get to them
villages have less or try to keep more for themselves."

"And?" Scar asked, but her voice had softened a touch.

"And I can help you move when they can't. The snow
will not trouble you if you help me."

Petri looked down at where the man kept his hands in
his lap. He'd taken the mittens off, and the gloves underneath, and black markings writhed there, pulling the eye,
turning the mind. He opened his mouth to shout a warning
but didn't get the chance.

Someone roared past him – a man in rags with a long
slim blade out, mouth agape as he knocked Petri aside and
plunged for Scar.

Petri fell to the snow and rolled, his blunt sword already
coming out as he got to his feet. Scar was on her back,
the man atop her with his blade held aloft, ready to stab
down into her eye. The rest of the camp was in uproar –
half asleep, jerking out of their bedrolls. Kepa was ahead
of the rest by a good dozen paces as he threw himself at
their attacker and knocked him from Scar's chest, sending
him sprawling into a low snow bank. Kepa pounced, but
the man was no longer there to receive him. Petri whirled,
but all he could see were Scar's crew, all awake now. No

sign of those Scar had set as sentries, and Petri thought all they would find would be blood and bodies.

Scar got to her feet, her hand on her sword.

"That village had no adult men and women in it," Petri said. "Only very old and very young."

Scar swore under her breath.

"Out hunting," Morro said. "They'll have found what you left by now. And now they've found you."

"Or one of them has." Petri scanned the shadows again but saw no trace of anything untoward. "But they come for a slave?"

A shadow flickered, and Petri turned a half-second too slow as the man came again in a rush from behind Scar. But that rush, or perhaps the rage that boiled out of him, sounded in his snarl, made him too reckless. He leaped for Scar, but the newcomer, Morro, stood up in a blink and waved a hand. A faint tang of blood stained the air.

Petri didn't get to Scar before the attacker flew backwards to land in a tangled heap in the snow. The man tried to get up, but Morro smiled and twitched a hand and he stayed where he was as though struck to stone. It was only a moment before Kepa was on him in any case, and then he moved, thrashed and struggled and bit and spat. Kepa struck at the arm holding the knife, a hammer blow that might be enough to break it, but the bone stayed whole, and the knife spiralled off towards the fire. Another smack from Kepa's great fist into the man's face, but he didn't still, not until Kepa was astride his chest like he was riding a pony, and Petri came to help, to hang on to one arm as someone else grabbed the sword from the man's waist and a third got his legs. A last smack in the face, and the man was finally limp under Kepa's weight.

Scar stood by the fire, a hand on her sword but looking shaken. Kepa sat on the ragged attacker until the rest had managed to bind him as firmly as they could, take all the weapons they could find and give them to Scar.

"Leave him be for now," she said. "Just tie him and watch him. Kepa, take a few crew, make sure it was only him."

Kepa nodded and picked a woman and two men who had done better than most with their blades, and they slunk off into the night.

"Who is he? From that village, you think?" Scar asked Petri when they'd gone.

"Where else?"

Maitea spoke at last. "He turned up a few days ago. He says he's my father."

Scar glanced at her sharply, a frown dividing her face, splitting it around her scar. "And you don't believe him."

A delicate shrug. No expression marred her features — she looked down on the crumpled form of the man who called himself her father with no feeling at all. "Even if he is, why should I care? He left me to slavery."

"Maitea, as I said, you are now free." Scar smiled, softening. "Once I was as you are, and a good man set me free and told me to do as I would. You were brave back at the village. You deserve the chance I'm giving you, same as that man gave me. I set you free — it's up to you what to do with that freedom."

Maitea sat as unmoving as a stone, even when Morro came to sit next to her and talk in soothing words that Petri didn't trust for a moment.

He moved over to Scar as she checked the mystery man's weapons. "Morro's a magician," Petri said in a murmur. "He should be bound as well."

She glanced over at Morro and back to Petri. "He's right – we're starving, and it'll get worse before winter is done with us. We need all the help we can get."

Petri gripped her wrist, and she turned, startled and snarling. He didn't let go. "He's a *magician*. Not to be trusted. Ever. Kill him now, before he kills us."

She yanked her arm from his grip and laughed. "Him? He's a runt, like Kepa said, magician or not. Why should I listen to you?"

"Look at me, Scar. I know them, dealt with them before to my cost. Magicians use people for what they want. They don't care who dies because of it. They tried to take Reyes last year and almost managed it. Rumour has it that Ikaras had to find its new queen because a magician slit the throat of their old king, for blood. A magician killed my father, left him as nothing but ashes blowing in the wind. They serve no one, not kings and queens, and not you. His offer is for his benefit, not yours. I've seen what they can do, know what they're capable of, and I say we kill him now, while we have the chance."

Scar gestured at the unconscious bound man. "He saved my life from whoever this is. And I know you no better than I know him, do I?" She glanced over at Morro and Maitea where they sat heads together and talking quietly, looking as dangerous as any courting couple. "We'll leave him, for now. But . . . Petri, you keep an eye on him. Watch him. We'll see who we can trust."

Chapter Nine

Now

Once they caught up with Eder, they slowed to let the horses cool while Kass stared at the captain's back and Vocho tried, and failed, to catch Carrola's eye. The way became icy, then dusted with snow, and then no longer dusted but thick with it. It wasn't long before the early sunset, what they saw of it behind looming black mountains scarved in snow under bellying clouds that promised more. Kass didn't care about the cold. It seemed to slice away the fog in her head, leave her thinking more clearly, out of Reyes where there were no memories to haunt her.

They found a place to camp that was at least out of the wind – a crack of a valley with steep slopes and stunted trees. Kass and Vocho along with the few guildsmen they'd brought set to pitching their tents close to one slope that curled about in an arm which they hoped might break the worst of the wind. Cospel saw to the horses, hobbling them in a stand of trees not much bigger than they were.

Kass watched Eder's troop as they pitched their own tents and wondered that they didn't make use of the shelter of the slope. Eder caught her watching and strode her way, and she had to steel herself against how very like Petri he seemed – not in looks so much, but how he moved, the tenseness of him as Petri had been when she'd first met him. So tightly wound he might snap. She had to look away, concentrating instead on a guy line that was being stubborn.

She heard the crunch of his boots in the snow behind her but didn't turn.

"You should pitch away from the slope," he said, and his voice had lost its strident edge.

She risked a look and wished she hadn't, or that the sight of him, the thought of Petri alive still, didn't rob her of breath.

"Why's that?" she managed.

"That's how we got caught in an avalanche last time."

She took a proper look at him now, shut up the little voice in her head that kept whispering about Petri. Maybe Eder was trying a friendly overture.

"There's not much snow yet," she said. "We'll chance it." He shrugged and went to turn away but stopped when she said, "What seems to be your problem? With us, I mean? Because we're going to have the hells of a time of it if you keep on as you have been."

A twitch about his eyes at that, but he inclined his head in a cool manner. "My apologies. My problem, not yours." He hesitated, seeming suddenly unsure of himself. "Maybe . . . maybe we could discuss it. In private. Without your brother."

She glanced over at Voch to find him trying surreptitiously to watch Carrola, and suppressed a sudden grin.

"I always try to do everything without him, but rarely manage it. All right."

His tent was as she'd expected it – immaculate with

everything in its place. He sat on his pallet, and she took the saddle that was against one wall.

"Well, then," she said.

Why did she think he was going to come unwound? Something was going on in there that she couldn't fathom and found she wanted to.

Finally Eder blew out his cheeks, and some of the tenseness left him. "I'm no fan of the guild."

"I gathered."

"I'm sure you did. I have my reasons, though I won't bore you with those. But you two especially. Bakar sent you to nursemaid me. I . . . don't take kindly to the idea."

"Nursemaid?" She took in the pallor of his face, remembered Bakar saying something about them not being the only ones to have suffered last summer. "He's more likely to have sent you and Voch to nursemaid me. I haven't been myself just lately." And didn't that hurt to admit to anyone other than Voch? She'd told everyone who asked that she was fine when she'd been anything but. It was a relief to say it, made some part of her inside burst and drain away. "Not myself at all."

When he looked up at her words, the rigidness had gone from his face, left it soft and vulnerable. It took all her willpower not to lean forward and lay a hand on his.

"I've not been much myself lately too," he said softly. "I don't accept help very gladly, I'm afraid."

"I gathered that too." She tried a smile and got a tight one in return. She got off the saddle and crouched in front of him. "I don't accept help all that well either. But I'm beginning to realise I may have to. I'm not here to do anything but what Bakar said. People are dying out there, and we're here to stop it. Both of us. It'll be easier if we at least don't want to kill each other. Agreed?"

He shifted awkwardly and a flush crept up his neck. "It's not killing I was thinking of. Look, I don't want your help because I need to know that I can do this. A test for myself after . . ." A deep breath as though he was about to tell her some great secret and had to gear himself up to it. "I want *you* to see that I can do this. That the guards aren't some pathetic second-rate substitute for the guild, that we are as efficient as you. That I am worth your attention, even if I am just of the guards. Because of this."

With that he leaned forward and kissed her. She froze a second in shock, and he seemed to take her hesitation as consent. His hand found hers, and he leaned into the kiss, and she didn't stop him. With her eyes half closed it could be Petri's mouth on hers, his breath now on her neck, his hand on her waist. With her eyes half closed the last long months of guilt and recrimination might never have happened.

The kiss went on until her breath was hot in her throat, until she wasn't sure where she was or who it was kissing her. Then his mouth was on her neck, whispering sweet words into her hair, and her own words were coming without any thought. "Petri," she said into his neck, and he went rigid, yanked himself away, and she realised what she'd done. The might-have-beens vanished. She jerked back, shaking her head, leaving Eder gape-mouthed in anger.

He stared at her, the gape twisting into something else before he leaped to his feet in a burst of energy that startled her. He got no further than that because a sudden noise outside brought her up too. A shout from over where they'd picketed the horses, Cospel's voice. Close on the heels of that, a jumble of sounds as Eder's troop jumped up from their places at the fire and Vocho shouted for Kass to "Get the hells out here, quick."

She was already half out of the tent, into a deep gloom lit only by the troop's fire. Voch and Carrola were standing on one side and jumped apart when Eder followed her out of the tent. A glance towards the stand of stunted trees, where Cospel's voice had come from, told her all she needed to know.

Wolves, a score of them, more, flowing under the stunted trees, going for the hobbled horses. She ran, joined Voch and Carrola, Eder half a step behind. One of the horses was down and screamed briefly before a mouth took its throat. Blood splashed the snow as the wolves darted in to yank away what flesh they could before they ran off. Cospel flailed uselessly at them with a branch. They ignored him, intent on feeding.

The rest of the horses plunged and reared, trying to escape but unable to due to the hobbles. Except Kass's horse, which had caught a wolf in the back as it ghosted past, had broken the wolf's spine and was now snorting and stamping to finish it off.

Everything came clear to Kass then, in the pump of her blood. She felt wiped clean of everything that had plagued her, reduced to the sword in her hand, recalling the joy in it when that joy had been much dimmed for longer than a few months. Eder's kiss seemed to have broken the spell she'd kept herself in, made things come clear.

The wolves – thin pathetic things she saw now, starved from an overlong winter – scattered as they approached, took some last lumps of meat and loped out of view. One, a larger male with an eye missing, turned and snarled as Eder's troop followed before he too disappeared into the gloom.

A couple of Eder's troop followed to make sure they stayed gone. Cospel, breathing hard, laid down his branch and looked at what was left of the luckless horse. Not a lot. At least three others had bite wounds too. Carrola swore under her brcath and hurried over to Cospel and the dead horse, Vocho on her heels.

Kass and Eder inspected the wounded horses – two had superficial cuts, the third wouldn't be fit to ride for a few days. Eder soothed the horse with the more serious wound, a pat to the neck, a few soft words and a hand on its nose that settled it some.

He studiously avoiding meeting her gaze, and his jaw clenched and unclenched before his words came out in a measured tone. "That's a nasty wound to its leg, poor bastard. This is going to slow us down. One horse short is bad enough. If that wound goes bad . . ."

She'd have thought the kiss had never happened, that his twisting shock when she spoke the wrong name had never been if not for a tremor under his words, so faint she might have missed it. Like he was wound so tight he might snap, and she had only wound him tighter, closer to breaking.

"Eder, I'm—" His look of sudden panic stopped her words in her throat, and instead after a moment she followed his lead and made no more mention of it. "We should count our blessings it was only horses. We're going to have to be more careful. Where there's starving wolves there may well be starving bandits too. We'll get Cospel to look at the wounds. He's got some stuff somewhere that helps."

Kass looked over to where Carrola had her hand over her mouth, looking down at what was left of her horse. Vocho chanced an arm around her shoulder, and she took it. Eder noticed too, and that darkened his face, made all the muscles tense even more, so Kass was surprised he didn't whirl apart there and then. He spun on his heel, and Kass had to wonder at herself, that she'd ballsed it up when he'd offered a softer side. It took everything Kass had not to follow him and ask to try again, try to unwind him as she had once before, unravel the mystery to find the man inside.

Vocho looked down at what was left of Carrola's horse, his arm around her shoulders – to his surprise. Also to his surprise, she hadn't objected.

"We can get another in the next village, I expect," he said and realised how callous that sounded as soon as it left his mouth.

"True," she said and turned away. Cospel began to do his best to cover the beast up – to discourage the wolves from coming back more than anything. "It wasn't a very good horse, but it was mine."

Vocho looked back down the slope. Eder stalked off towards his tent, and Kass was looking after him wistfully. Vocho hadn't failed to note she'd looked somewhat dishevelled when she'd burst out of his tent. Oh, god's cogs, no. Not Eder. Petri had been bad enough.

"He's going to be pissed as hells," Carrola said. "It'll slow us down."

"You can ride double with me, if you like."

A smile at that, anyway. "All right. Look, I'd best get back before he erupts. Thanks."

She slipped out from under his arm and hurried towards the troop tents, passing Kass on her way up.

"Going to have to be more careful," Kass said to Vocho. "Should have been more careful before now, really. We aren't on the plains any more." She turned to look down towards Eder's tent with a thoughtful frown.

"Find out what his problem is?"

She hesitated. "Yes and no. He thinks Bakar sent us to nursemaid him and he doesn't like it."

"Why would Bakar do that?"

"That is precisely what I didn't find out."

"Yeah, well don't go getting too wrapped up in trying to, Kass."

She gave him a sharp look that at least was better than the wistful sighs. But if it was Eder who was making her sharp, he'd rather the sighs. "Don't you worry about me. I'm not going to make the same mistake twice. I learned my lesson."

With that she set off for their fire. Vocho followed more slowly. She wasn't going to make the same mistake? He rather thought she was halfway there already.

Chapter Ten

Four months ago

The morning after Morro joined them, Petri woke to Scar's growl at the mystery man who'd attacked her, or tried to. Petri got up and found her dangling him from the bunch of his rags in her fist as Maitea watched impassively.

Kepa stood next to Petri and winked at him. "Got a new guildsman now," he said. "Ain't so special after all, are you?"

Petri took a step forward. A guildsman? Who?

Scar dropped the man. He regained his feet slowly before he bowed with an insolent flourish that got him a double-handed blow to the face for his trouble, knocking him straight onto his back, where he laughed.

"She's right pissed with him though. Won't tell her who he is, he ain't even given his supposed daughter much of a name."

Petri only half heard Kepa as he went on. Something about the man in daylight. His dark hair, just beginning to frost with grey, was long and tangled but still had a remnant of a mare's tail, which might once have curled artfully over his shoulder. The clothes were finely stitched, immaculately cut where they hadn't been tattered into shreds. Not clothes for a mountain winter but a court somewhere, or the heat of Reyes down on the plains in the summer. What meagre furs the man had were scraps here and there, tied together with string. Petri was surprised he still had fingers.

A pair of eyes peered out above the beginnings of a raggedy beard greyer than the hair, and there was something about them, about the man, that nagged at Petri. Something familiar behind the beard and rags, the laugh when she'd knocked him down. The man struggled back up to sitting, caught Petri's eye and winked.

Scar noticed the movement and whipped around to face Petri. "You know this bastard?"

"I . . ." He couldn't be sure. He took another step.

"Come on, Silent Petri," she snarled. "You know him or not? Here, I got his sword. Ring any bells for you?"

She threw a sword his way, which he caught awkwardly in his left hand, dropping the baldric. A duelling sword right enough, the style of the hilt was a giveaway. This one wasn't immediately familiar but, like the face, nagged at the back of his mind.

Scar glared at Petri. "Well? I want to know the name of this laughing bastard before I gut him."

Her tone was off, and he looked up sharply. Something behind those hard eyes, that scar. If she wanted just to gut him, why hadn't she already? A soft touch, Kepa had said, underneath the bravado.

It came to him when he wasn't trying. He moved closer so that the reek of the man's rags was all he could smell and looked down at the hilt again. The twist of the basket, the stylised duellist that stalked around the pommel. He'd seen this sword before.

"Domenech?"

As soon as he said the name, the man's features became apparent behind the beard – the cut of the cheekbones, the lines around clear eyes.

"The very same!" Dom said and laughed again. "You're looking well, for being dead. Any chance of helping an old man up?"

"You know him? Good. Kepa, get him on a pony and tied back up. There's something odd about him."

"Tie him twice," Petri said. "Extra tight."

Scar cocked him a questioning look, and Maitea turned her unnerving gaze on him.

"He's an assassin. A very good one. You're lucky to be alive, if he really wanted you dead."

Kepa and a couple of his friends took extra special care with the still grinning Domenech.

Scar sauntered into view from behind Petri on his blind side. "How well do you know him?"

"I fought him a couple of times. Regretted it both times, and I know of his reputation." And who his allies are.

"Good. Maitea here wants to know all about her supposed father. You can tell her on the way back. We'll hold off on deciding what to do with the little shit until she decides whether she wants him alive or not." Scar caught Maitea's eye, and they shared a smile that faltered on Scar's face when Morro hove into view. She lowered her voice as she turned back to Petri. "All the better to keep your eyes on him. Find out all you can and come to me when we're home."

Scar's house sat at the centre of the valley, a crude thing made from bound-together logs and turf like all the rest only better made, snugger with no gaps in the planking and no leaks in the roof. The warmth of the hut was enough to stagger Petri, make toes and fingers come back to painful life for the first time in what seemed like weeks, made his own spot in the hayloft seem like ice in comparison. She sauntered in, dropped her baldric over the back of a chair and poked an already good fire. A pot of something hung over it, and not the watery soup that would be his in the mess later. A rich rolling smell puffed out with the steam when she lifted the lid, making his stomach growl audibly.

She looked up at him, frowned and jerked her head towards the rough table and chairs pulled up close to the fire. Petri took the hint and sat, wary, hiding his right hand in the fold of a worn fur cloak he'd fought off some man a week ago in the barn.

Scar walked over to the table and sat opposite him, one hand playing with a long knife. Petri realised he was still carrying Dom's sword and he put it down on the table.

"Don't talk much do you, Silent Petri?"

Something about her made him squirm – the intensity of her look, the way her hand moved over the hilt of her own sword, the hook that he was sure was barbed into that question.

"Not much," he agreed.

The reproach in her look chided him. She'd saved him from the gods knew what fate, fed him, found him somewhere warm to sleep.

"Never did talk much," he said with an effort, to appease her, maybe stifle some of that unnerving energy. "And people seem less inclined to talk to this face."

"I'm not less inclined," she said. "And dinner's waiting, if you don't mind sharing. I hear you had a little trouble in the barn."

He looked up from the sword and found her watching him with a forthright look and a cock of her head. He looked down again because he must be mistaking that look.

"Come on," she said, handing him a bowl that brimmed with hot mutton stew. "It'll get cold, else."

He didn't seem to have much choice, and the memory of no food for days on end was still fresh in mind and stomach. His pride stung at charity taken, but his stomach told his pride to quieten down when it came to eating what little came through the mess just lately.

"Stolen food always tastes better, I find," she said with a grin. "And they'll be getting the good stuff in the mess today too, if that's what's sticking in your craw."

He dug in, and so did she. They sat and ate in silence for a while before she threw down her spoon. "God's cogs, you really don't talk much, do you?"

"I said as much."

"You're hard work, Petri. But I know a bit more about you now, whether you tell me or not. Maybe it's true and maybe it isn't. And maybe you'll want to tell me which is which. Because that assassin had a lot to say on our way back." The grin had gone, and her face grew serious, hard as the mountain they sat on. The knife was laid, very precisely, between them on the table. "Tell me about him. Because he's a man I never expected to find in these mountains, much less trying to kill me. As out of place as a shark up here, and almost as silent on the why as you are. Talk, Petri. It's time to talk. Show me I was right to bring you here."

She moved the knife upright so that its point pierced the wood of the table and twirled it.

He watched the light flicker along the blade as she toyed with it, swallowed down the shivers that image brought with it. A hot knife and a dark cell, and pain and betrayal – his own. The knife had made a coward of him, and that one man could do that to him coiled inside and fermented into rage. And Eneko had done that, because Petri watched Scar's knife now, glittering in the light, and he was piss scared, and he hated her for that, wanted to stand up and shake it out of her, whatever she was doing to him.

"Domenech," he said at last, his voice sounding strangled as though his brain tried to throttle the words before they could come. "One of his many names. Used to be a guildsman, a long time ago. Eneko . . ." He shut his eye but couldn't shut out the glimmer of the blade, the knowledge that he was weak in front of it, in front of her. No, not this Petri, this Petri was strong. "Domenech was the guildmaster's assassin once, I know that much, and he was thrown out of the guild. Years ago. He appeared again last year." With Kass. The roiling in his gut grew worse, so that he thought he might throw up the stew or maybe pick up the sword and stab something with it.

"And what might an assassin want with me? A guild-trained assassin at that?"

"That you kidnapped his daughter would seem a fair bet."

"If she is his daughter. She doesn't think so, does she?" Scar laughed, flipped the knife up and laid it back on the table so that Petri could breathe again. "Maybe someone hired him to kill me. Someone I've robbed, probably. There's a certain freedom to knowing everyone hates you, have you ever thought of that? You never have to worry what anyone thinks of you because you already know."

He couldn't say that he had, but then again he'd never seen someone so utterly carefree, who seemed to give not a crap about what anyone thought of her.

Her grin became feral as she looked askance at him. "What should we do with him, this Domenech? Dangerous, he could be. Very dangerous to keep around."

Petri shrugged. "Maitea wants him alive for now. I've told her all I know, which isn't much."

"No, she wants to try to find out what she can about him and her supposed mother, but he's dangerous, I think. Maybe too dangerous. But killing – I don't like that much either, especially not in cold blood."

"It depends on what you want. His father is very rich, so I'm told."

"Is he now?" She looked thoughtful. "A ransom?"

"Maybe. Or maybe Maitea would be the heir if Domenech were to die."

"Ransom's not usually our style; we like to keep quiet, out of sight as much as possible. Survival, that's our watchword. Like you, Silent Petri. We want to just be, and be left alone. The smart way. Small and subtle and we live. Stupid and loud and we die, it's as simple as that. And I will not have these people die if I can help it. They are mine, and I will look after them. You included."

She stared at something inward with a frown, and Petri was struck again by her energy, her drive, though it was only now he realised what she was driving for. Survival, the smart way for her and every other outcast here, him included. The way she looked at him, talked to him – she didn't care about his face, or what he'd done to deserve it. She didn't care about where he'd come from except how it could help the people up in this thrice-forsaken valley.

"Maybe I can get him to see sense, help teach your crew a few tricks," he said. "Subtle is what he does, what he's trained for, and he's as rootless as anyone, as far as I know.

Maybe if he really wants his daughter to trust him, he'll help you."

"An assassin on my crew, now that would be handy if you could manage it, if I could trust him. Waifs and strays the lot of us." A slow mouthful of stew, and then she said, "What about Morro?"

Petri shook his head. He'd tried, dug with all the subtle words he could manage, and the magician had said almost nothing, and Maitea with him. "Just want to be somewhere safe, both of us" had been all he could get out of the pair of them.

"Strange Morro and Domenech should both be at that village, isn't it? Neither is a mountain man, that's for sure. And that Morro, he's an odd one. Persuasive with it too. We'll see. Perhaps." She picked up Dom's sword and laid it in front of him. "Well now, Silent Petri, how would you like this very fine sword I have procured for you? Fitting a guildsman such as yourself."

He looked at it, glittering on the table. Scar's men had swords, a few made here, some stolen, and they were passable enough but crude and heavy, not given to quick work. Not easy for his weaker left hand to heft. This, though, this was perhaps the finest example of a duelling sword he'd ever seen. He picked it up in his left hand. Not too heavy and not too light. With this maybe he'd be able to teach himself to use his weak hand properly, like he used to use his right.

"Go talk to your Domenech. Find out why he's here, what he wants, why he really tried to kill me, if Maitea really is his daughter. Take her with you too, because she has questions of her own. See if he can be persuaded to join us, as you suggest. If not, he's going to be exceedingly uncomfortable until I decide what to do with him. Spend a few words, Silent Petri, and take the sword."

She meant it, he thought, and meant something else he couldn't quite work out. Still, there were perhaps a few words he wanted to spend with Domenech for himself.

The hut they'd taken Domenech to was the worst of the lot, barely better than being outside. The turf was starting to slide off one side of the roof, letting in little puffs of snow, and the logs in the walls hadn't been caulked so the knife wind moved through the space in icy slices. The floor was a mess of half-frozen mud and rancid straw that stank of pig.

Domenech sat in one corner, double tied as Petri had suggested, at wrist, elbow, ankle and knee. Even so, even tied like a hog waiting to be butchered, sat in filthy rags that showed only a hint of the splendour they'd once had under furs not fit for a dog, Domenech gave off the air of a man who could walk free whenever he chose. He just wasn't choosing to right now.

Maitea stood beside Petri and looked down impassively at the man who said he was her father.

Domenech was rather less impassive as he looked back. "Maitea? Maitea, please."

She turned away sharply, and that movement made Domenech's face twitch as though in pain, but he soon gathered himself though he stared longingly at Maitea's back.

"The tables turned then, Petri?" Domenech said, at last sparing Petri a glance when Maitea stayed turned away. "I seem to recall the last time we met: it was you in the cell and me, magnanimously, letting you go. I hope you don't feel you need to cut my face off to even things up at all. You could let me go though."

Petri leaned back against the door jamb and watched

him carefully. The hilt of Domenech's sword was cold in his hand – everything seemed colder than ever, inside and out. But his hand worked on the hilt, itched to be used. Sudden rage made him want to slice that face, as his had been. For someone else to know what it was to be faceless, friendless, betrayed and alone. He gripped the hilt harder. Yet he wasn't alone now, was he? He'd found a place, rough though it might be.

"Not yet," he said at last. "What are you doing here?"

"She wants to know, does she? Luckily for her, there was a slight tactical error on my part due to an emotional overinvestment. If she doesn't get on with long words, tell her I tried to kill her because I, personally, wanted her dead."

"That's all?"

"Isn't that enough? That's all. No one hired me, no one paid me. I merely wanted to kill her for daring to kidnap my daughter. Almost twenty years I've been looking for her; I finally find her, and your friend takes her away from me. So, in a moment of rash emotionality I decided to do what I was trained for, but wanted it too much and buggered it up."

A long silence then, before Domenech shifted uncomfortably in his bonds. "I suppose there's no chance . . .?"

"None. Unless you were to agree to work with Scar."

Domenech raised an eyebrow. "Scar? Is that her name? Seems to me I've heard of her, taking in waifs and strays, thieving to keep them fed. Very noble of her, and she's smart too. Keeps a bunch of cut-throats and thugs in line, which isn't easy. A graceful tightrope to walk, and she does. But to work with her? Doubtful. Would she trust me enough?"

"She might. I won't."

"No, and you'd be right – I'll be honest about that. You're working for her though?"

Petri shrugged. It seemed obvious enough.

"Interesting she took you on. Does she know who you are? I see she does. Why? Why take on a half-handed ex-guildsman whose name is known for cowardice in every newssheet in Reyes? Just another waif and stray? I've heard much about her, and being soft-hearted doesn't fit. She's got a use for everyone, and she's got a use for you."

Words wanted to explode out of him, the right ones that would flay Domenech where he sat, but Petri couldn't seem to conjure them. His hand worked on the hilt.

Domenech shifted again. "Small-time robbery? I mean, it doesn't seem enough for you, really. Scar has plans, though, I bet. I also bet that the snow hampers her, to Reyes's benefit." He looked at Petri sideways. "Of course, if Scar were to become bolder, then she'd have to be dealt with. Bold enough, the guild would become involved. But I don't think she's that stupid. Are you?"

"She's no plans that way. She just wants to keep everyone fed."

Domenech looked up slyly. "If the guild were to become involved . . . You know who the guild master is now, do you? No? We kept our word, me and Vocho. Told her, told everyone you were dead. She hasn't taken it well."

"She should have thought of that earlier," Petri growled.

"Maybe. And maybe you should think about it now. She tried, you know, tried to get to you with everything she had. It just wasn't enough."

Petri stood back, thoughts knotted in his head. Maitea stirred, her glance ice-cold as she regarded Domenech. Petri welcomed the distraction.

"You say you're my father," she said. "You say that I

was stolen from you a long time ago. You say a lot of things, but Morro tells me there's a lot you don't say too."

All of a sudden Domenech didn't seem half so sure of himself. He shuffled onto his knees, looking like a man begging for his life.

"I am your father, and you were stolen from me – us – by the man who did that to Petri's face. I've spent all the years since looking for you. I've *killed* to find you. I tried to kill Scar because she took you away, stole you from me again just when I'd found you."

Maitea seemed unconvinced. "What about my mother?"

Domenech flinched at that, then steeled himself to look Maitea in the eye. "Your mother tried to kill me because she blamed your loss on me, and rightly. She spent years trying to find you too. She started a war to find you, pitted Ikaras against Reyes just for that. Neither of us wanted to let you go."

Petri stared at Maitea – now he could see it, what was so familiar about her. Ice-fair hair and ice-fair face. Alicia's daughter.

"And where is she now?" Maitea said.

"She . . . she died in the war she started."

Finally an expression on that cold face, a smile, but not one Petri would ever want directed at him. "Morro tells me it was you who killed her. That you ran her through from behind, like a coward. That killing is all you know how to do."

Domenech sagged back at that, his hands opening and closing uselessly on nothing, his face behind its ragged beard suddenly very old. It was all the answer Maitea needed. She leaned forward and spat in his face, her cool features full of sudden and all-consuming hatred. "I never had a father, and I don't need one now."

With that, she spun on her heel and strode out of the door, back straight and head held high. Dom stayed statue still. He seemed crumpled, smaller than when they had come into the hut. Petri turned to go and only just caught Domenech's whisper behind him: "Just like her mother. Just like her."

Maitea stalked across the snow, and Petri hurried to catch up. She spared him a glance that told him nothing, just ice behind the eyes.

"Did you know my mother?" she asked.

"Yes," he said. "Not well. She was a magician, like Morro." And had a snake for a heart. Just like her mother, Dom had said. Petri wondered just how like her she was.

"Did he kill her, like Morro said?"

"I don't know. I was . . . otherwise engaged at the time. But if he hadn't he would have denied it."

She stopped and turned to face him. "The man who did that to you – he says that it's the same man who stole me."

Slavery, Petri recalled from the day his world shattered, when Eneko had thrown him to the wolf of Bakar. Petri's brother had discovered their father and Eneko had been involved in slavery and had been killed for that discovery. "It would not surprise me in the slightest."

A short nod, a delicate frown that creased her clear forehead. "My mother, what was she like?"

Petri hesitated, but her cold eyes demanded the truth. "I have no love for magicians, and she was one reason why."

Maitea looked back at the hovel where Dom was trussed like a pig to be slaughtered. "Morro tells me many things. That I can do magic, that I'm to be his apprentice, that my mother was powerful and so might I be. Is it wise, do you think, to deny a magician what they want?"

What to say to that? His life had unravelled from the day he'd become involved with them, and the thread of that unravelling had ended in Eneko's room.

"Look at my face," he said, "and then decide."

Scar paced up and down in front of her fire as Petri told her about Maitea and her mother. "What about the assassin?"

"He won't work with or for you. If he agreed, he'd be lying."

"Worth keeping?"

Petri shrugged. "For the ransom you might get, maybe. It depends on what you intend to do."

The pacing increased, and Petri was reminded of a caged lion he'd seen once, forever pacing, chaffing at its inability to hunt, to pounce, to do anything but pace. The snow had stopped Scar's plans, though what those plans were beyond thieving enough to live on, Petri wasn't sure. Though even that had become a struggle this winter, with snow up to the eaves. Even on horseback a five-mile trip was an ordeal, and they needed to range further if they weren't to attract too much attention.

"Do? Same as I've always done. Keep my crew fed and safe. Outcasts the lot of us. Looks to me like a magician is as outcast as the rest, now the university has closed in Ikaras, and Reyes has never been fond of them since Bakar took his seat in the palace. Morro might do very well for us. You can go, Petri." She dismissed him with a distracted wave of her hand and called for Kepa. Petri went and fought for his place in the barn, and the sword at least made that easier, if not the thoughts that circled his head like vultures.

Bold enough, and the guild will become involved. His insides roiled and cramped. Kass thought he was dead, and Petri was. The old Petri had wanted nothing more than to hide away, but this new one was bolder and thought perhaps showing her just how strong he could be would be sweet as strawberries.

Chapter Eleven

Four months ago
Petri obeyed the summons, which came in the grey light of a coming snowstorm. Scar's hut was as welcomingly warm as before; she paced as she had done, looked up when he came in. She wasn't alone.

Maitea hovered in the background, as impassive and regal-looking as her mother had once been. Kepa stood behind Morro, one meaty hand holding the magician firmly in place, a casual knife ready should it be required.

A cold hand gripped Petri when he saw the magician's gloves laid neatly in his lap, leaving his hands for all to see, and the markings that writhed over them, dark and ominous. Now swords, now half a face, now a severed head.

"Petri, sit," Scar said, and he did. "Kepa, take them both to the mess, get them some food. And keep an eye on him."

"Make him put his gloves on first," Petri said.

Kepa pulled the magician to his feet, shoved his mittens on him and hustled him out of the door, the knife never far away from the man's back. Maitea followed slowly, with a glance for Petri as she went.

Scar stopped her pacing, sat at the table and ladled out some food for Petri. Something behind her look, he thought again.

"Eat," she said.

So he did, trying not to bolt it, savouring the hot rush of it in his stomach. She leaned forward, and the scent of her overpowered him. Metal, leather, another darker scent. Ambition, he though obscurely, where he'd never noted it in her before.

"You've dealt with magicians before, Morro said."

A nod from him.

"And it didn't end well. I understand that. But Morro can help us, and he will if he knows what's good for him. If I make sure he knows who his mistress is."

Petri fidgeted with the spoon, but all appetite had fled. "Magicians are their own masters, and he'll make himself your master too. He'll have you in his net as soon as you can spit."

Scar waved a derisive hand. "This one will work for me or find himself at the bottom of the mountain with his throat cut. They still die like any other man. They have cares too, points to lever them on, just like any other."

"Maitea?"

"Exactly. She's minded to help us, is grateful to me. I can use that – her – to keep him in check." She sat back and looked at Petri critically. "Do you ever wonder, Petri, what it is we're doing here?"

"Surviving. Keeping your waifs and strays fed."

A bark of a laugh at that. "Yes, and barely at that. Don't you think we deserve more, these poor wretches whose life has been shat upon? Don't we deserve lives like those fat old sots in the villages, the towns, deserve their warm houses, tucked up against the snow? Enough food to eat?

Almost every man and woman here fought last summer – whether for Reyes or Ikaras – and was then thrown aside when the need for their help was past, when they were too broken, too scarred. Aren't you the same? Discarded when no longer of use?"

Her face glowed with the need to make him see, her eyes flickering orange in the firelight. They weren't like her eyes at all, and the words weren't like hers either. Her ambitions before had never gone further than keeping her "boys and girls" safe and fed. Now a magician had appeared, and she had changed in a way that made his skin clammy.

"Let me tell you something." She fingered the scar on her face. "Everyone always asks, except you, so I'm going to tell you. I got this when a man got upset that I wouldn't fuck him, like he had some right to it. Thought he'd make sure no one else would want to, or some such stupidity. It worked, his stupid plan. Plenty of people can't see past the scars, men and women both. Then again there's some who can, if you give them reason enough. You have to let those people have a chance."

Petri swirled his stew with the spoon. "Do I?"

She ran a finger along the blade of the knife. "Oh, I think you do, Petri. I think you want to tell me at least a bit of it. All I see now is a man with a fucked-up face and a fucked-up heart, full of hate for the world and rage at everything in it, who doesn't care who he hits, who he threatens, even if it's just for a bed for the night. Oh yes, I know how it's gone in the barn. I see the scars of those who cross you, see how even Kepa looks at you as though you're a snake waiting to strike. A man like you could turn quite happily on the hand that is feeding him, I see that right enough. I've given you time, and food. I've given you something to do, and maybe, just maybe, I might give you what you're really after, payback for whatever kindled that hate. But you'll have to tell me. Because I won't have a man in my camp who might turn on me, or any of the people here. A man like that is as good as dead, just like that magician if he tries to cross me."

The knife wavered in front of him, but he wasn't scared now. He was tired of being scared, sick of the terror that littered his dreams. Instead of visions of a hot knife, now came hot rage, dimming his vision, blinding him, energising him. He wanted to take the world by the scruff of the neck and show it that it was wrong.

His good hand shot out and grabbed her wrist, twisted it until she dropped the knife, kept twisting until her shouts, and a stiff cuff around the ear, penetrated his head. He dropped her wrist like it burned him and shoved his chair back, shaking and sweaty.

The door opened behind him, let in a blast of frigid air that cleared his head. Two men ran in, two of the company's rare guns drawn and ready to blow his head off at Scar's word.

Scar sat half out of her chair, rubbing her wrist, the knife already back in her hand. Pointing at him. A shake of her head, and the two men left, grumbling under their breath. They didn't go far though – Petri could hear them take up stations just outside the door.

He wanted to say something, anything, but he couldn't seem to get words past his lips, past the fear pent up in his throat, past the icy rage that seemed to burn his skin.

Scar sat back in her chair as though nothing had happened, changed her grip on the knife and drove it into the wood of the table.

"Not many men would dare to do that," she said. "And none in this camp, though I value a man who would dare it, might dare to tell me when I'm wrong. Tell me now. Tell me how I'm wrong about you, about who made you like this and what you want to do to them."

He shut his eye, but that didn't stop him seeing the hot knife, hearing Eneko tell him he was weakness, stop him hoping for Kass, that she'd come. She hadn't, she never would; she'd look at him and turn away from what he'd become, at how weak he'd been. Eneko was dead, and Petri couldn't get his revenge on the dead, but Kass . . . He'd started this all that time ago because he loved her, because she'd shown him things he'd never seen before. He'd betrayed because of her, lost his old life for good, would be hung for treason now if ever they found out where he was. Then, when he'd needed her, Kass hadn't been there. She hadn't been there, but now everyone knew what a coward he'd been, how he'd spilled his guts while he waited in vain for her.

"She abandoned you," Scar said, and he realised he'd spoken aloud. "She left him to do that to you. She didn't care enough to stop it or what came later. She discarded you like so much rubbish, like all of us were discarded. And you hate her."

The knife blurred in his vision, and his throat seemed to close up, but he nodded. Nothing in his head made much sense right now, but Scar's words cut through all that.

"Yes" was all he said, and that came out a whisper.

"Poor Petri," she said and came closer. "But all that changed you for the better, didn't it? I see it in half my crew, more. They've all been forged in the heat of every hell and come out the other side stronger for it. Like you. Stick with me and you can show her, show all of them, what they threw away."

His head swirled with her words until he felt dizzy. "I thought . . . I thought you wanted to keep your head down, stay safe, not do anything to attract the guards' notice?" Stay free, not invite a trip back to the Shrive, or worse. His skin shivered at the thought of another cell. Free, that was all he'd ever wanted, and he had it now. Free and strong. Why jeopardise that?

She frowned and stared at the fire for a while, as though she wasn't sure where her words had come from or if she meant them. When she spoke, it was slowly, as though reciting something she'd had to commit to memory.

"Too many of us now. When there were only a dozen, we were easy to hide. Now, after the battle with Ikaras, our numbers have grown. All good men and women, fighters, discarded like the rest of us, too scarred to be of use to anyone but me. We can't hide any more, and why should we?" Her tone grew belligerent, as though he'd argued with her. "Plans change, Petri. Now I have a magician to use, and use him I will. To make us stronger than anyone ever thought. I have you to use as well, and an assassin to either get on my side or ransom."

He looked at her, at the sudden sheen behind her eyes that reminded him too much of Bakar when he'd first started his odd ravings. Only she wasn't raving; it made sense. Only . . . only it was a sudden change, as though these thoughts weren't hers.

"Morro, did you look at his hands?"

She started at that and almost dropped the knife. "No! No, I know better than that. I told you, I'll use him not have him use me. I've heard the stories. It's just his turning up has given me ideas. Never had the opportunity to do anything but survive before. Now I have, and I intend to get what I can for my boys and girls. I could use a man like you though. Guild trained, experienced in things I've never known, like magicians and assassins. Join me, properly. Not just to train my men to use their swords, but be part of us. I intend to show all those who threw us away, thought we were nothing once they'd had their use of us. I intend to show them they were wrong about us. All of us. Will you?"

Discarded when no longer of use – that described it perfectly, what seethed inside him. Dom said his name was known as that of a coward in Reyes, and Kass . . . Kass had thrown him away, left him to rot because she didn't need him any more, because he was useless, weaker than bad steel, softer than lead. But he wasn't. No, he was sharper than knives, stronger than mountains. He would relish showing her that.

"If you grow bold enough," he said slowly, remembering Dom's words, "the guild will come."

Scar grinned at him. "She'll come, you mean. And then you can show her, and all the rest, what fools they were to throw you away. So you'll join me?"

His skin still felt clammy at the thought of the magician, of the damage he could do. "Yes. But be careful of Morro – warn everyone not to look at his hands at the very least."

Later, after Scar had come and kissed the mess of his cheek, had told him she could see the worth of the man behind it, had taken him to bed, he wondered why even so it was Kass's face he saw on hers.

Chapter Twelve

Now

Vocho hadn't slept well — he thought probably none of them had, what with the sound of the wolves, sometimes nearer, sometimes further away. When Kass had come to wake him for his turn on watch, he was already awake.

The campsite was still and cold, the sky full of frost-sharp stars. He limped to the stand of trees, took a quick look about and, when he was sure no one was watching, took a slug of jollop. His deep sigh puffed out in front of him as the stuff took hold, stilled the damnable shake of his hands that only went when he got his fix. He almost dropped the bottle when Cospel came around a tree.

"Cogs, you almost killed me," he said when he'd managed to get his heart back from out of his mouth.

Cospel glanced at the bottle as Vocho surreptitiously tried to stash it, but he didn't say anything about it. "Wolves are getting close again," he said instead. Vocho listened, but the howls had stopped. "They split up after we chased 'em off. Reckon that's why they howl — to find each other again. Now they has. Look, up there."

Vocho peered through the pre-dawn gloom. Dark shapes separated from the shadows at the end of the valley, slunk silently over the snow there and back into the shadows.

"Been talking to some of Eder's lot – they been up here before. Reckon them wolves'll try one more time before it gets light. But they won't get too close to a man. Smart, they are. They know we'll kill 'em. But if they's hungry enough, they won't care about that, and I reckon they's hungry enough."

"Thank you for that comforting speech," Vocho said.

Cospel leered a grin in the darkness. "Wolves won't be no problem for Vocho the Great. Will they? Might make you look especially impressive to a certain young lady."

A fine point, Vocho had to begrudge him that. "Come on then. Wait, get some brands from the fire."

"I wondered if you'd think of that. Eder has too. Look."

Of course he had – five of his troop already had flaming branches in hand and were moving up the slope. Vocho and Cospel hurried to join them, Eder close on their heels, radiating contempt. Vocho wasn't unduly disappointed when he saw Carrola's sleepy face at a tent flap, watching them go. He straightened his shoulders and made sure not to limp.

The wolves coiled among the trees at the end of the valley, working up the courage to attack again. As Vocho and the rest approached, brandishing flames, they shrank back until all he could see was the spark of their eyes as they reflected the light.

They didn't hold back for long – one, a bigger wolf with a shaggy silver mane, seemed bolder than the rest and crept forward out of the shadows despite all the brands. Vocho leaped forward, brand in one hand and sword in the other, but while the wolf retreated every time he got close, it didn't stay back. Neither did the rest. They oiled in and out of the shadows, inched left and right, wherever Vocho and the rest weren't, flanking them, keeping just out of sword reach for now. Maybe not for long. They were hungry enough, desperate enough, Vocho supposed.

One of Eder's troop strayed too far from the others. The lead wolf leaped at her with a snarl, and she darted back only just in time to avoid the teeth that snapped at her face. That seemed to embolden the wolves, and they flowed forward, two dozen or more silent grey forms. Half headed for the horses, and two of Eder's troop followed, shouting and waving their branches. One shot his gun wildly into the air, and the noise paused the wolves, but not for long.

The lead wolf and what was left of the pack swirled around Vocho, Eder, Cospel and the three remaining guards. Vocho tried a few lunges with his sword, but quick as he was, the wolves were quicker. He couldn't even get close. Their tongues lolled almost like they were laughing at him.

Behind Vocho the horses began screaming, and the stamp of hooves echoed around the little valley. They couldn't afford to lose any more mounts. In front of him the lead wolf leaped straight at Cospel, ignoring the flaming brand he thrashed about in front of him.

Vocho whipped a glance to Eder, who raised his gun and fired wildly. The bullet hit nothing but air. No time to lose – Vocho never stopped to think about it, he was too far away, the wolf had knocked Cospel to the ground, and Eder's shot had done nothing. Vocho grabbed the gun from the man standing next to him, and with a prayer ringing in his head – *I hope to crap this works* – he fired, hoping the noise would scare the beast.

It did better than that. The wolf fell dead from a bullet to the back of the head, leaving Cospel to clamber out from underneath, awash in blood. Vocho ran to him, helped him up and checked him over. A couple of scratches and a longer gouge along an arm, but it could have been worse. Much worse.

The death of the lead wolf had more of an effect than all their flaming brands, flashing swords and fired shots. The wolves circling Vocho and Cospel shrank back until they were just eyes among the lessening shadows again. The ones by the horses needed more effort, but soon they too had been driven off or downed, just as dawn began to lighten the sky.

Eder came over, face darker than ever as Carrola came bounding over the snow and looked down at the dead wolf.

"That was a shot and a half," Cospel said. "Didn't know you was any good with guns."

Neither did Vocho, but he wasn't about to admit that.

"A *great* shot," Carrola echoed and gave him a smile that could have melted every snowflake on the mountain.

"Luck," Eder snapped. "Sergeant, the rest of you –" Vocho belatedly realised it hadn't been just Carrola watching, but most of Eder's troop, along with Kass and their guildsmen "– get to your tents. Ready to leave in fifteen minutes."

Carrola shot Voch a look that spoke volumes he wasn't sure he understood, and then Eder's troop broke for their tents to get them down and packed on the horses in time. Vocho headed for their own tents, Cospel not far behind, muttering about some ointment he had that would help his scratches. Kass was already there. Neither of them wanted to be left behind again for a captain's stupid pride, especially with a hungry wolf pack on the prowl.

"We could just——" Vocho began.

"Just nothing, Voch," Kass said. "You saved Cospel, and that was good – great even, and a fantastic shot. Unfortunately you just upstaged Eder. Or that's how he'll see it. Like he didn't need another reason to hate you. Well done, Voch. Well done."

"I should have left Cospel to get eaten?"

She stopped her frenzied tent packing. "No. Of course not. But you couldn't have found another way?"

"No other way presented itself at the time."

"Great," she said. "Just cogging great."

Vocho wondered what was going through her head and gave up in the end – it could be anything, but he didn't think she was telling him what the real problem was. He got through the ensuing silence by relishing the thought of Carrola riding double with him later. An excellent chance to dig further into the puzzle that was Eder, not to mention it would be cosy and a chance to dig into what was Carrola. Maybe he could make her laugh.

Laughing seemed to be off the agenda as they packed the last of the tents. Over in Eder's camp raised voices leaked towards Vocho. Eder and Carrola, if he wasn't mistaken.

He tried to ignore the voices and got his horse ready for the trek ahead before mounting and, to a grin of Cospel's, riding down to Eder's troop.

"What the hells do you want?" the captain snarled.

Vocho took a breath and tried to remember what Kass had said as they'd packed – do our best not to antagonise. Do not rub in that we are guild. Try not to make him hate us worse than he already does. Please, Voch. Just this once.

It was a lot harder than it looked.

"I promised Carrola she could ride double with me, seeing as how her horse isn't available."

Eder snorted. "Not yours to promise. She rides with me."

"But—" Eder's glare cut Carrola off before she got started, though Vocho thought it was a fair bet she'd be saying plenty later.

Vocho took a look at Eder's horse – one that had been wounded by the wolves, if not seriously. A second rider would do it no favours. Vocho glanced back at Kass, got a shake of the head and reined his horse about. Fine. If Eder wanted to be a dick, he could be one. Vocho could find Carrola later.

They rode out, and Vocho was not slow to notice the way Eder harangued Carrola as they left, though not loud enough for him to catch the words.

The day was otherwise uneventful, except for the worsening weather as they climbed. They stopped at noon, and Eder's troop wouldn't even look at the duellists. Kass managed to get a few words out of Eder in the afternoon, though when she turned her back he gave her a look like bloody murder. Vocho began to wonder if it wasn't him pissing off Eder that was the problem. What had Kass done while they were in that tent to warrant a look like that? At least she got him to agree to find somewhere indoors for the night.

The village lay curled into a little valley away from the worst of the weather. Which was just as well because, despite the supposed thaw, a frigid wind whipped down from the mountains and across Vocho's face as they approached it. Their little band sat ahorse, heads down against the first flurries of snow, but it got everywhere. At least it was warmer now than it would have been two months ago, when this Scar and Skull band had begun branching out. They must have cast-iron skin, Vocho thought. Or cast-iron balls. Maybe they had better gear – with the thaw supposedly well on the way, the guards and duellists had packed maybe a little too lightly. He knew that his hip had seized up like sand in clockwork, and it made him short-tempered and want, with an aching need that worried him, to find somewhere quiet to slip a bit of jollop. Until that happened he found occasion to be sarcastic to everyone within earshot.

The village was small, more a bleeding-together of houses than a group, so that it seemed one long rambling building with a myriad of doors that thumbed a collective nose at the snow.

Eder had sent a scout ahead, and the inn was ready for them. It couldn't take them all, so the owner had arranged lodgings for some of the troop in a neighbouring house, or possibly just an extension of the inn, it was hard to tell. The horses were stabled in a barn just up the little stream that lay half frozen and miserable in the centre of the narrow valley, and some of the troop elected to stay there and haggle for a horse to replace Carrola's. At least it'd be warm in with the horses. The rest of them got the inn.

Vocho, ever a connoisseur of places where ale was drunk, gave it the once-over. It wasn't big – the nearby road was the main route through to Ikaras, but not many stopped off in this little out-of-the-way place when there was a larger, and much more pleasant, inn a few miles up the road. In fact this was more a tavern than an inn, with only a few rooms available.

Someone had taken some care trying to make the place look cheerful, with colourful upholstery on the benches that was now terminally beer stained, and the walls washed a pale yellow that had turned an ugly brown in the corners. But there were some odd touches that this careful cheer only brought into sharper relief. Gaps on the wall surrounded by soot stains where things had been taken down. A small pile of bright cogs and mangled gears by the fire, as though someone had recently pulled apart a clock and then stamped on it for good measure.

For the village's only inn, and one welcoming an unusual group of travellers, where the locals might expect to make a bit of money or at least get the chance to flirt outrageously with someone new, the main bar was almost empty. When he peered out of the windows into the gathering dark, only one or two houses had any lights. The woman who stood behind the bar was matronly and welcoming as you'd expect, but had a massive yellowing bruise across one side of her face.

"What a shit hole," was Cospel's muttered comment, accompanied by a grimace of distaste.

Vocho couldn't really disagree, and became even surer of it when dinner arrived and proved to be grey, greasy and almost cold. The bread that came with it could have made a half-decent cosh.

Eder kept himself to himself over in one corner with a few of his troop, Carrola included. He'd been on edge since their stop at noon, had hardly spoken a word to either Kass or Vocho, and barely even looked their way, except to snap at Carrola when he caught her grinning at Vocho. Now it looked like she was getting the full treatment. Eder leaned across the table with a twisted scowl and a jabbing, accusing forefinger while Carrola looked him dead in the eye and kept her face blank.

Kass persuaded the woman behind the bar to come and talk to them. "This is Vedora. They got raided two weeks or so ago, right in the middle of a snowstorm," she said to Vocho. "This is my brother Vocho. We've come to—"

The woman interrupted her with a frown. "Vocho, isn't he the one what killed that priest?"

God's cogs, would that never stop following him around? Couldn't people remember him saving the bloody city instead? "Yes, madam. And under the right provocation I might put on a repeat performance. Not necessarily a priest next time. I'm thinking of diversifying."

Vedora glared at him like she'd caught him stealing her underwear and then ignored him in favour of Kass. For once he didn't mind.

"Came out of nowhere, they did," she said. "Or leastways seemed like it. We was all battened down for the storm, a good half the village in here. Next thing we know, the storm went all funny."

"Funny?" Vocho asked. His hip ground in its socket every time he shifted, and he couldn't help himself. "It told a joke?"

Kass sliced him a warning glare and Vedora ignored him. "Was snowing fit to bust, a good ten, twelve inches we'd had since noon, and it were still coming down. We was all tucked up nice and cosy though, like I say, and then the snow stopped."

"I was under the impression it didn't snow *all* the time here. Only twenty-three hours a day."

"*Voch*."

He shifted, winced, tried a sneaky pass at the jollop bottle, but Kass was looking at him like her eyes could bore through his and out the back of his skull. He buried his face in his beer and kept all his thoughts to himself.

"The snow stopped," Kass prompted, and Vedora ceased glaring at Vocho and carried on.

"Was still cold enough to freeze a man where he stood, seemed like, and the wind still whipped around the

chimney like a hell-witch, but the snow weren't snow no
more. Rain and plenty of it, so it puddled under the door
and I used all my best towels trying to mop it. Then, all
of a sudden, by the door it weren't cold, it was hot like
spring, like summer, and the rain stopped like someone
was pouring a bucket and it ran out. I'd just said a word
I probably shouldn't have, and then there's bunch of men
and women at back door and front, all armed with swords
and them new-fangled gun things standing in a bunch
of fog."

Vocho snuck a look at Kass, and she was thinking the
same thing as he was – magicians, like that old bugger at
the previous village had said. There had to be a way Scar
was gettng around in the snow and the prelate's men
couldn't, and here it was. They were moving around because
they had a bloody magician to do something to the weather.

"Took damn near everything we got," Vedora went on,
seemingly not noticing their sudden interest. "And then
everything froze back up after, worse than afore, drifts six
foot deep and more and frozen solid. Took us days to dig
everything out, what with more snow coming down. Not
enough food to see us through until spring now, or not
the whole village anyways, so most of them went off up
the way to Kastroa. Bigger town, got a wall and everything."

"Just tell us what happened here."

Vedroa looked up as Eder loomed over the table. "I told
him already."

"It was in my report," he said. "Though I don't suppose
you cared to read it."

"I certainly did," Kass snapped back, and Vocho was
glad she had, because he'd not bothered. "But hearing it
from the people who experienced it can't hurt, can it?
Unless you don't want us to help? Besides there's a detail

or two you neglected to mention." She turned back to the landlady. "Vedora, could you describe any of them?"

"Not rightly, no, not most of them. Scarves and whatnot over their faces, some of them. Most of the rest just looked like men and women. One bloke were right big though. Banged his head on the beam over there, almost knocked hisself out on it. Bald as a coot, he was, with a big fat face and a nose like a potato."

Eder cocked a cool eyebrow Kacha's way. "This *was* all in my report."

She ignored him. "Any others?"

"Well, like I say, most of them just looked like regular people. Except two — couldn't mistake those two. Scars, see? She had a knife mark up her face. Shame really — she'd be handsome without — but it's a great big puckered thing starting at her chin and going right up over her eye and into her hair. Can't miss it. O' course, that was nothing to the fella. *His* scars were enough to give me nightmares."

Vocho shuddered in sympathy and in recollection of the last time he'd seen Petri Egimont, which had given him a nightmare or two as well. That his first thought had been Petri made another shudder ripple across his shoulders, so that Kass frowned. But Petri had still had his face left, even if it wasn't pretty. Besides, Petri was probably only second to Vocho in never wanting to see a magician again. He'd not work with one again if he could help it, Vocho was pretty sure. He waved at Kass for her to carry on.

"One side of his face was all but missing," Vedora went on. "Lost an eye, and not much left of his cheek, and that now nothing but bone, and scarred bone at that. The edges that are left are all twisted and pink like. Shiny in places. Wore a mask over the rest of his face so I couldn't tell you about that. Ever such a posh accent he had; you could have etched glass with it. Anyway, I told him his family would be ashamed of him, and what he was doing now that all his ancestors would be a-turning in their posh graves. You know what he said? He said, 'I think my father would applaud me. He never could abide weakness.'"

Vocho stared at her, aware that Kacha was giving him an odd look. "Did you notice anything else about him? Height, hair colour, anything?" he asked.

Vedora gave him a sideways glance. "About your height. Maybe not so broad. And for all his posh accent he didn't have his hair done in that curly mare's tail you got on your shoulder – you know, like all the nobs do. Dark hair it was, but he'd left it all wild. Odd though, he was. He was growling and snapping like a baited bear, but . . . you get to my age, you can see when someone's heart ain't in it. He was like a man who didn't want to be there, but if he *had* to be then he was going to play the part." She blew out her cheeks and her hands waved as though despairing. "They took or smashed near everything. Lot of people have upped sticks, gone down to relatives on the plains or to the city, and I don't blame them neither."

She shivered theatrically and went off to see about pulling some more pints.

"He can't *really* have half his face missing. Can he?" Vocho kept thinking of Petri's face, which had been bad enough. There had been some terrible business in the city during the battle for Reyes as well – adding magicians to a battle didn't do anything but make it worse seemed to be the lesson – and Vocho had seen more than one man with bits missing, but a face down to the bone?

"I did see one man who survived the Red Brook," Eder said grudgingly. "An Ikaran. He didn't have any skin or muscle left on one hand. It rained hot blood, hot enough to strip skin from bone. This Ikaran was wounded that way, and it got infected later. The surgeon didn't want to amputate – the man was in such a state he didn't think he'd survive it – so he cut away all the infection, the skin and muscle that were left, right down to the bone. He lived, but his hand . . . He'll never do anything with it again, but at least he lived. Plenty of us didn't."

"You were at Red Brook?" Kass asked.

"Yes" was all Eder said before he shoved back his chair with a scrape of wood on stone and stalked off towards the door that led to the stables, muttering about checking on the horses.

"Touchy subject," Vocho said when he was out of earshot.

"I'm not surprised," Kass replied, frowning after the captain. "Could explain him being so twitchy. You hear what happened?"

"I have been rather busy running your guild, Kass. I haven't had time to read the gossip sheets." Except when they mentioned him, naturally. "So, what did happen?" He knew the basics – Red Brook had been a clusterfuck, in a nutshell – but that was about it.

She shrugged. "Same thing that happens every time people fight battles. Things go wrong. A series of screw-ups leads to, well, one monster screw-up. All that magic flying about, it was probably bound to happen – sections get separated, turned about, ordered the wrong way. Then it rained hot blood, which would be enough to send anyone screwy. It ended up with two sections of Reyens, under specific orders from their commanders, attacking each other, each thinking the others were Ikarans. It was dark, it was the middle of a battle, and by the time they realised their mistake – saw the uniforms perhaps or recognised a face – it was too late. One crazy screw-up that pretty much wiped out the Reyens there, those who hadn't run away by then. Didn't know he was in it though."

Kass stared after Eder with a sharp line between her brows, one that meant she was thinking hard. At least her thoughts were no longer spiralling around Petri, had moved on to what was happening outside her head, for which Vocho could be grateful. And not just because all the time she was pondering Eder and magicians she wasn't watching him sliding up to his room for a nip of jollop.

Chapter Thirteen

Three months ago

The valley lay under a thick blanket of snow. Others, men who'd lived in these mountains all their lives, said it was the harshest winter they could recall. Every day when Petri left Scar's hut, the snow lay thicker, the air struck his face colder. Every day it snowed, now big fat flakes that swirled the senses so a man could become lost between this hut and the next, and then an hour later small stinging bullets that seemed to flay what flesh he had left on his face.

Scar paced and chafed; Petri watched through one half-lidded eye; Kepa grunted his observations, which were often surprisingly astute, and they planned how they would go forward. Scar worried about food, or the lack of it, about how to best serve these men and women who looked to her now to save them. Two men died, of cold or hunger, no one was sure which. Others weren't far behind. Even Kepa was beginning to look gaunt, and it would be weeks yet, maybe months, until the thaw set in enough for them to move around the mountains.

Scar insisted he keep up the training, which was held inside the mess hut now.

"The sooner they can fight properly, the better. The easier it will be. We need to think bigger, go further, if we're to survive. And more than survive."

She said nothing about how they'd reach wherever to fight whoever, though he could see her thinking on Morro's words, that snow would be no problem for them if they let him help. Snow blocked every pass, every nook and cranny, drifted in great mounds, scoured by the ever-present wind. Unless they could deal with the snow, they were doomed. They had the means perhaps, if they were willing to use a magician, but he said nothing, and neither did she. Morro and Maitea slept in the mess hall, where there was always someone to keep an eye on them. Scar wasn't trusting him just yet.

In the mess Kepa had moved the tables against the walls of the hut, and two dozen men and women shivered in front of the mean fire – food wasn't all that was running low. Every tree within reach had been burned or sat chopped under eaves, but what was left wasn't even close to enough to see them through.

Petri got out the practice swords and had them all warming up, a phrase that had taken on a whole new meaning in the last weeks.

One man didn't join in – Morro. He sat huddled in the corner as though afraid to show the world too much of himself. He sat and watched while he ate what little there was to eat, Kepa close by with a knife ready. Scar had some plan, but she wasn't so stupid as to let Morro get an edge, which comforted Petri.

The training went well enough. Three or four seemed to have picked up the knack of swordplay almost by instinct.

With a little more practice they'd be the match of most men they'd find in the towns, though against trained guards they'd still need to be careful. The rest at least were showing progress. Kepa handed over his knife, and his watch on the magician, to another and came for his turn.

The practice sword seemed far too small for his hands, which seemed like bludgeons all on their own. Still, he'd picked up the way of it quick enough, and Petri had to pull out a trick or two to save himself the indignity of being put on his arse. At least his own technique with his off hand was also improving, along with the strength in his wrist and arm. Finally, he managed to disarm Kepa with a crafty dodge that would have had him out of the guild in a heartbeat. But he wasn't teaching them guild fighting. Sportsmanship would get anyone killed outside the guild walls and the sandy arena where elaborate duels to strict laws were waged, and wagered upon. Even a guildsman had to bend those laws once he got through the gates.

Kepa gave him a rueful grin and got the rest of them picking up the swords, moving the tables back while he got Morro to his feet. A jerk of Kepa's head and Maitea joined them, her eyes cold on Kepa's neck.

"Got to take them to Scar," Kepa said to Petri, and they moved out into the abrading wind, heads down against the flurry of snow it brought to add to the rest. They trudged along the path that back-breaking and constant digging kept clear between the mess and all the other huts.

Inside Scar's hut Petri flung off his furs and headed to the pot of stew hanging over the fire. Even Scar's had little in it today. Kepa took the magician over to the table, where Scar waited for him. One meaty hand shoved the magician down in the chair opposite her, while Maitea hovered in the shadows by the door and watched.

"Well then," Scar said. "You told me, when we met, that you could be useful to me, that the snow would not bother me. Tell me how, if you want to keep eating."

Morro shot a glance at Maitea as she stood silent in the shadows. Petri hardly caught the movement, a mere flicker of an eyelid, but Morro nodded as though she'd spoken.

"What do you want me to do?"

"Oh, that's much better. I had Kepa show you around a bit today. What did you see?"

Morro's gaze flicked about the hut, looking for escape perhaps. It slid over Petri like oil before it stopped. Some thought seemed to strike him, and the smile it brought was quickly hidden. Petri shifted, loosened the sword at his side. Never trust a magician. Never.

"You're dying," Morro said, voice growing stronger now. "Cold, cut off, little wood, less food. You need me to help you live."

Scar twitched at that, but there was no denying the truth of it. "Go on."

"A bowl of that over there first, and one for Maitea too."

Morro shovelled the food in like he hadn't eaten in weeks, let out a contented sigh at the end and sat up straight.

"Snow," he said. "The snow is trapping you, and everyone else. But they're all cosy in their well stocked homes and you are not."

"And?"

"And I can help you with that."

"So you said. In return for?"

Once again his gaze oiled over Petri. "For the moment, in return for not starving, me and Maitea. A place we can be. When spring comes, we'll see."

"When you help us, we'll see," Scar said. "Because maybe you can and maybe you can't."

"Oh, I can. Let me show you. I'll need a drop of blood." He reached for Scar's knife, next to her hand on the table, but Petri got there first.

"No."

Scar looked between the two of them, frowned and gave the knife to Morro. "But you keep your sword at his back. Just in case. I don't trust him any more than you do, Petri."

Morro took the knife with a secret little grin, spun it in his hands and stood up, making Petri jerk the sword in his still wobbling hand to keep it at his back.

"Snow," Morro said. "Simple to win against, if you had enough wood to burn, eh? You could melt a path to wherever you wanted to go, and all the prelate's guards and guildsmen couldn't stop you. But never enough wood. Do you have paper?"

"What for?" Scar said with a snort. "Most of us can't read so it's all just pretty squiggles. Only thing paper is good for around here is wiping your arse."

Morro sighed as though Scar's bluntness scraped jangled nerves too highly strung for normal men to know. "Maybe I won't ask for any then, in case I get some that's pre-used. The crude way it is."

He made to take off his gloves, but Petri's growl stopped him and produced a sigh, so he rolled up a sleeve instead. The knife flashed, and a line appeared on Morro's arm, leaking slow red blood that he dabbed his fingers into and drew a crude symbol on his arm. Scar bent forward to look, but a twitch of Petri's sword backed her up. The symbols, always changing, never still, were how magicians trapped men into their wills. Morro looked at them both and laughed. "As if I would try something so . . . crass on you. Petri here at least has the sense to look away. And you, Scar, would I use magic on my benefactor?"

The voice was as oiled as the look, or tried to be, but without the work of the changing symbols the words sounded merely ludicrous.

"Get on with it," she snapped, "before I have Petri stick you."

A mocking little bow. "But of course. If your friendly giant could open the door you'll see what I've already done."

Kepa opened the door, but Petri had an inkling before it was even fully open as a puddle leaked beneath the wood. Scar stood wide-eyed and grinning when she saw the neat path melted into the drift of snow between her hut and the mess. It didn't go far, only a few feet, but the implications were clear.

Morro turned back to her with a sidelong look of triumph at Petri. "As you see, I can make it easy for you to move around. No being stuck up here for the winter, you can raid and thieve. Or even go to town and buy things."

"In return for how much blood?" Petri asked, bringing a scowl from Morro and Scar alike. "Because it seems you could take yourself to Ikaras doing that without much trouble. Unless you didn't have enough blood."

Morro sat again, primly arranging his tattered robes around him. "Not enough blood, exactly. Me and Maitea are stuck in these mountains until thaw, or until I can gather enough blood. In the meantime I can help you, Scar. Whatever it is you want, and I think it's more than just a raid here and there, I can help. All the *best* warlords have magicians, you know."

The faint scent of cooking blood turned Petri's stomach, but Scar didn't seem to notice or realise that she kept shooting little glances at the symbol Morro had painted on his arm. Petri moved between them, and she snapped back to the room from whatever dream Morro had tried to give her.

"Take them back to the mess hut," Petri told Kepa. "Dry all that blood off first and make sure he can't open up that wound again. Keep a sharp eye on him."

Morro said nothing to this, merely bowed his head as though he humbly acquiesced to anything they wanted. But his eyes on Scar were very bright, his smile only for her.

Chapter Fourteen

Now
Vocho was glad when he could sneak off to his room without it seeming odd. This last hour he'd had trouble stopping his hand from shaking, and as soon as he was in the room and had locked the door behind him, he rummaged in his pack.

He took the jollop out with trembling hands and had a swig. The twinges in his hip subsided, as did the inner voices. A sudden knock on the door made him drop the bottle, and he only just caught it before it hit the floor and smashed, and then where would he be? The thought made clammy sweat pop out all over. He stashed the syrup and answered the door.

Carrola gave him a bright grin before she frowned and gave a cautious sniff. "What's that smell? You're not secretly getting drunk, are you?"

She didn't seem to notice the strain behind his own smile. "Absolutely. A couple of gallons of rum a day or I can't even get out of bed, then I snort mead until bedtime." She raised an eyebrow, and he went on with, "Medicinal.

What the surgeon gives me for my hip. Got a terrible wound in the line of duty and while being brave, handsome and dashing, as it happens. Plays up when it's cold. Eder let you out to play then?"

Her lips pinched, and she gave a tiny shake of her head as though despairing of him. "I can deal with Eder. Your sister wants you downstairs."

"All right."

By the time he made his way back into the bar, Kass had rolled out a map marked with all the places the bandits had attacked over the last few months, at least the ones they knew about – some villages were all but cut off during the winter, and more reports had only just started to filter in now the thaw was nominally under way. Eder watched her pore over it with a curl of his lip that could not quite hide his interest. Even as Vocho joined them, another messenger, diverted from a longer trip to Reyes by Eder's commands left at the guard outposts, turned up mud splattered, snow frosted and freezing.

"Took a whole village!" the man said after a smart salute. "When we finally got your orders, sir, we did what you said, checked every village and smallholding we could reach. One or two had trouble in my area, and then we went to a tiny little place right up near the border but off the main road. Well, we got there in the end, though it was hard going. But when we did make it – nothing left, sir."

"Nothing?" Eder's incredulity mirrored Vocho's own. "Houses? Goats?"

"Nothing, sir. It's only half a dozen houses anyway, but they was all burned down. Everything was gone – what livestock they had, the communal barn emptied before it was burned if I'm any judge. Even the bridge over the stream was gone. All that was left was bodies."

Eder swore viciously under his breath, then blushed as he realised the landlady was giving him a stern look.

"Any indication how long ago?"

The messenger thought for a while and rubbed his three-day growth of beard. "Well, sir, we came on it a week ago, and I reckon it can't have been much longer than that. The ashes were cold, but we'd had a big storm before that and they weren't snow covered. Not to mention the tracks, sir. They looked fresh enough. Between a week ago and a fortnight, I'd say."

"You spent a lot of time in the mountains?" Kass peered at the flash on the man's tunic, which was partly obscured by a dark swatch of mud. "Sergeant is it?"

"Sergeant Danel. Born and bred, miss. Brought up in a village just like that one. They only put mountain men on the higher outposts, miss. Lowlanders can't take the winters, see."

"And did anyone follow the tracks?"

"Of course, miss. Petered out not far away – there's a big old slope where the wind scours the rock of snow, makes it tricky to track anyone. But they were headed up towards No Man's Land. Where else would they hide? Any mountain man could tell you that. Snow up there for all but the hottest days. They reckon there's two seasons up there, miss. Winter and Midsummer's Day."

No Man's Land. Where it snowed all year. Well, that sounded friendly. Vocho's hip twinged just thinking about it.

"Of course, they don't call it No Man's Land no more. Skull's it is. Staked his claim on it, and I don't reckon there's a man in a hundred that'll go near it."

Eder had the sergeant mark the village on their map, and he added a few more places they'd checked that'd had trouble, along with this No Man's Land.

"What do you think then, Eder?" Kass said in the end.

It looked pretty obvious to Vocho, but the jollop was still humming in his veins, and he couldn't be sure Kass wouldn't notice what it was doing to him.

Eder frowned over the map, for once seeming to ignore the fact he didn't want Kass or Vocho there. "I think Danel here is right. If you look at everywhere attacked, all are within a day's ride or so of this edge of No Man's Land, though it'd take longer in the snow. They're getting bolder too. Whether that's because they're hungry, or they have some ultimate plan, I couldn't say. But I will say I expect them to get bolder still."

"But how are they moving around?" Vocho enquired when it looked like no one else was going to ask the obvious question. "Your sergeant here says they can't reach every-where, and yet this Scar wanders wherever she feels like it through snow and wind and the Clockwork God knows what like it isn't there."

Kass gave him a look he knew well enough, the "Shut up" look, but it was too late.

"Got a magician, we think," Danel said. "Heard enough rumours to that effect, anyways. They say he—"

"*Thank* you, Sergeant," Eder snapped.

"That definitely wasn't in your report," Kass said. "And yet it's not the first time I've heard it since we started our merry little trip."

"It's rumour and supposition, that's all." Eder shrugged. "And I don't include those in my reports. People up here'll believe anything."

"Especially if it might be true," Danel muttered and snapped off a salute when Eder turned a glaring eye on him. "Superstitious lot, to be certain, sir," he said louder. "Can't believe half of it."

"It might be as well to assume they have some edge," Kass said, earning her a formidable frown all her own from Eder. "Magician or something else, they're moving where we can't."

"You may not be able to—"

"Unless you've got some spare wings stashed away, you've no better way of moving through snow than we have. All we've heard, all the way up here, is this winter has been the harshest anyone can remember, by far. But Scar and her lot don't seem to have a problem with it. Also, according to the people I've been talking to, the thaw is supposed to have started, in fact did start but is now retreating in a way unheard of. That doesn't suggest anything to you?"

"Plenty that involves actual facts. Not rumour or superstitious daydreaming. These mountains are treacherous in winter at the best of times, the timing of the thaw unpredictable. But if Scar can move through it, so can we, without any heretical magic. Sergeant, how well do you know No Man's Land?"

"Me, sir?" The sergeant looked suddenly stricken as he looked wildly about for some excuse not to volunteer himself. "Oh, I know where it is, sir, but that's about it. That and folk tales and such. You know, trolls living in caves, snow fairies, frost giants ready to rip all your arms and legs off for lunch. Nothing really real, sir. The point is, no one really knows because no one goes there. That's why it's called No Man's Land, sir," he said desperately. "Because of the name. No one goes to No Man's Land."

Eder's mouth twitched in a smile. "Then you're the best we're likely to get, us all being soft lowlanders and likely to get lost when we see our first proper snowflake. Good of you to volunteer, Danel. Well done."

Kass shot the man a sympathetic look – she and Voch

had been "volunteered" once or twice themselves — but she didn't naysay Eder, and the two of them turned back to the map in some sort of temporary truce, leaving Danel to slump in a woe-is-me attitude.

Voch felt a stab of sympathy himself and took the man by the arm. "Look at the bright side," he said. "You're in an inn, with free beer for Eder's select few and a friendly landlady about your age who I am pretty certain is single. At least you'll get to enjoy yourself before you go."

Speaking of which, while Kass was distracted by Eder and his map it would be a fine time for Vocho to enjoy himself before they left. There must be lots of people here who'd never heard him tell any of his tall tales. Like Carrola perhaps, seeing as Eder was otherwise occupied for the moment. He picked up a jug of beer, took a heroic swallow and set out to enjoy himself with as much dedication as he could manage.

Vocho found Carrola eventually, in the stables, making sure her new horse was fit for the next day's ride. He watched as she checked hooves, ran a hand over legs, fiddled with the blanket to make sure it was snug, all the while talking softly to the beast.

"I don't see why," she said to it, "everyone has to be so difficult."

"I think that's called life," Vocho said from where he leaned over the stall door.

Carrola turned sharply, startled. When she saw it was him her face couldn't seem to decide between a smile and a disapproving frown.

"Really?" she said tartly, giving the horse a final pat. "I thought it was more idiots."

"That's no way to talk about your commanding officer."

The frown won. "He's not the only one in the vicinity."

"Hey, I've hardly been idiotic at all. Barely even rash."

He moved out of the way as Carrola came out, shut the stall door behind her and went past him with a sniff. "I'm not supposed to be talking to you."

"I gathered. But you are anyway."

That stopped her. She turned and regarded him with a sideways look that seemed to go right through him. Funny, he hadn't noticed her eyes were grey before, but he saw it now, the deep dark grey of snow clouds. He was so busy noticing it, he failed to realise she was standing with her hands on her hips and in the middle of saying something.

"I'm sorry, could you say that again?"

A brief roll of her eyes. "I *said* Eder's warned me, all of us, off talking to you or Kass, especially you. I was also just about to say that I was inclined not to follow those orders. I can change my mind if you aren't going to listen."

Something strange was going on inside Vocho's head. He always wanted to impress, it was his reason for living, but he found he wanted, very much, to make an extra special effort with Carrola. That wanting seemed to tangle his tongue up in knots though, and he couldn't think of a damned thing to say that didn't sound stupid, so he fell back on the banal.

"Did he say why?"

"Who? Eder?" The hands fell away from her hips and waved about in a "Who knows?" sort of way. "He said I'm too young and impressionable and should keep away from people likely to warp me. Especially you. It didn't make a lot of sense, which is why I was inclined to ignore it. At least when he's not around. Besides, you're quite funny, and I could do with some laughs on this trip."

"Only quite funny?"

Carrola perched on a saddle rack and Vocho perched next to her, taking care to arrange his hip so that it wouldn't seize up. They really were very grey eyes, even better when she was grinning at him.

"I miss my old troop, really. Or rather, this troop's old captain. He retired a couple of months ago, and we got Eder instead, along with a few new guards. Eder's a good captain, a bit humourless at times, a bit of—"

"A bit of a dick?"

The grey eyes darkened with disapproval. "A bit of a stickler, I was going to say. For protocol."

"Same thing. And that's all he said, that we might warp you?"

"Well, it took a lot more words for him to say, but that's what it boiled down to. The guards are better than the guild, more moral, less fly-by-night. We should remember who we are and not go pining after what we aren't, not let ourselves be seduced by the flash, remember that we're worth more than that. And especially remember that the guild tried to take over the city, is not to be trusted and so on and so forth, at length. I don't think he rates you very highly in particular, especially after that stunt you pulled with the wolf. He said some very *intense* things in that regard."

"Technically it was Eneko who tried to take over the city, and I for one hated the bastard as much as anyone. As for not rating me highly, the feeling is mutual, I'm sure. And the rest . . . Well? What do you think?"

She looked at him in silence for a long time, long enough he was tempted to break it, but as he could still only think of inanities, he kept his mouth uncharacteristically shut.

"I think," she said at last, "that all the things he told

me just made me think you were at least someone interesting to talk to on this godforsaken trip. Also, Eder has
a problem with the guild. With perhaps you in particular.
And Kass too since the wolves – don't know why. He was
beginning to like her, trying to impress her with how
efficient we were, and then, poof, hates her. And you for
upstaging him. So now, no talking to you. I know I'm not
especially impressionable, and you're not especially warped.
Unless you're hiding something?"

He grinned at her and tried to look heroic. "Oh, all
kinds of things."

Sitting on the saddle rack was doing his hip no favours,
and he shifted awkwardly to try to relieve the pain. No
use.

"Really? You seem more the type to shout it across the
rooftops."

"Only when it makes me look good."

They talked on, and it seemed to be going well – she
laughed in all the right places when he told one of his
stories, and she told one of her own that made him laugh
in return – but the rack was doing him no favours.

"I did notice," she said into this, "you looked a bit pale
when that landlady mentioned the Skull."

"That? Oh well, you know. Just a stray thought." Only
it wasn't all that stray, was it? "It's just . . . OK, look, I
thought for a second I might know . . . only it can't be
him. He still had most of his face, and he's even more
unlikely to work with a magician than I am, and that's
saying a lot."

"Eder never mentioned a magician," she said doubtfully.

"No, well, it seems he's not inclined to believe in them.
On the basis of personal experience however, I am."

"And the Skull?"

Yes, what about him? "It could be anyone. Half the guild match his description – well, apart from the face bit – and a fair few went missing after the battle for Reyes. This guy's face was pretty messed up, but he still *had* one." A pause as he considered whether the jollop was starting to make him paranoid. "I've probably just got his name on the brain. He's not the brave sort or likely to start robbing people. Likes to think he's all noble, you see. And he's far too sly to get involved with this sort of thing. Besides . . ." A sudden remembrance of the lies he'd told, and a sudden shame for them, when he'd never really been ashamed before. What was she doing to him? How? "Besides, he's supposedly dead. The Skull might be, probably is, someone I've never met, even if they were in the guild. It just niggles me a touch."

It was no good – he had to move. He tried to make out that he was getting up to inspect a bridle, but her frown was back, though less disapproving. God's cogs, why couldn't they have gone somewhere warm? His whole leg was throbbing, and for a second he thought he might end up on his arse, which would do him no good in impressing Carrola. His hand found the bottle of syrup before he'd even thought about it. He hesitated, took a look at Carrola as she paused in what she was saying – that he shouldn't worry about it; no one thought he had to know who the Skull was. She wouldn't know what the bottle was either, why Kass didn't like him having it. He pulled the bottle out and had a swig, shut his eyes for a moment as he waited for it to work. It didn't take long, and he sat back down with a sigh, feeling less tongue-tied as a happy bonus.

"What was that?" Carrola asked.

"Oh, nothing much. You recall me saying about a grievous wound received in battle while being dashing and heroic?"

He settled back down, his hip quiet for now, relishing the opportunity to tell a tale in which he sounded fantastic but could also play up the humble angle. Saved the city, defeated a formidable foe, been heroically wounded but managed to struggle on and win the day. Single-handedly in his story, but hey, that's why it was a story.

Carrola was quiet when he'd finished, before she laid a hand on his. "So your hip . . . You can't duel?"

The hand was welcome but not the words. "Of course I can. Good as ever. No problem. Just need a bit of the jollop in the cold weather, that's all."

And then because . . . he didn't know why. Just that he had to tell someone the truth, just the once and why not her? Yes, why not, because he felt like he could say it to her and not get flayed, and while she might snort a laugh, might tell him he was a prat, it was . . . it was different. He lied because he could, as a rule, but something about her made him think that "could" was relative, that she'd see through all his lies and half-truths, so he might as well lay it all out. It made him feel both peculiarly naked and oddly comforted.

"Look, I haven't told Kass about me drinking this because, well, she's had other things on her mind. So, er, if you could not tell her too?" Strange how all the years of lying made telling the truth really difficult to do. He'd left most of it out without even thinking about it. Truth was something he might have to work on in stages.

She narrowed her eyes. "Why not? She knows you got hurt, doesn't she?"

"Yes, but look." He took a deep and not entirely steady breath. It must be the beer talking, he thought. Or the jollop, and that must be what made him keep thinking of Petri too. "This isn't what the surgeon gave me. In fact I'm not even sure where it comes from. Only that a magician made it for me to start with."

"You drink a magician's brew? Willingly?"

"Yes. Sort of. It's a bit complicated. And Kass doesn't like me drinking it, but I'm not me without it, so I hide it."

She shook her head, and the smile that came was tinged with sadness. "Come on, then. Let's get back where it's warmer and your hip can unfreeze and you can explain a bit better."

Vocho had the most unsettling feeling that instead of being impressed, she felt sorry for him.

Chapter Fifteen

Two months ago

Scar came at Petri from his blind side, slicing up inside his guard just as he'd taught her, taught all of them. The blade flashed close by his face — too close, but it was getting easier now.

He dropped the practice blunt from his left hand, grabbed at her overextended wrist and brought his other weapon to bear — a hidden stiletto strapped to the wrist of his useless hand. Not so useless now as he brought the blade to a halt at her neck.

The group of men and women watching laughed at the look of utter rage on her face as Petri pushed her away and picked up his sword again.

"The next lesson," he said. "For every move, *every* move I teach you, there is a counter-move. Learn it and learn how to counter that too. That'll do for today."

They started picking up all the equipment that today's practice had strewn across the snow-streaked valley. The wind whipped tiny stinging flakes in his eye, but Petri was becoming accustomed to the harshness of the weather up here, where snow wasn't the problem, it was the knife-like wind that scoured the snow from the ground, piled it up into drifts. Scar's fighters weren't the only ones learning; Petri had learned that snow could keep you warm if you got a good blanket of it on the roof of your hut, or if you found yourself lost and carved yourself a cave in it. It was the wind that killed.

He'd learned too that Scar had been right. Some people were willing to look past his face, and he was becoming more willing to look back. He still wore a mask over the fleshless cheek and empty eye socket, but the looks and whispers had stopped as they'd learned more and more about how to fight well. Most of them were natural thugs, had spent a lifetime clubbing people in dark alleys or exploiting a momentary weakness with a surprise knife. Now they were actually fighting rather than brawling.

Petri held out his good hand to help Scar up, but she glared at him and got to her feet without his help, then her sharp hatchet face broke into a grin that made her scar pucker even more.

"They're doing very well," Petri said.

"So arc you, learning with your off hand."

"I'm ready. You know that."

"For what?" A teasing grin that twisted her scar into enigmatic shapes.

"Let me come on your next raid." He hadn't thought he'd want to, but with better swordplay came more confidence. "Not just to watch this time."

"Why? You're comfortable enough here, aren't you? Why come with us?"

He looked down at the knife, pushed it back into the little contraption one of the smiths, or what passed for smiths here, had made for him. *Because I thought I was supposed to be your equal, and right now I'm your pet, and I'm sick of*

being people's pet. Because Dom had been right: bold enough
and the guild would come – maybe *she* would come – and
he wanted to show her who he could have been.

Not just that either, he thought. He glanced up at a
snow bank where Morro steamed gently in the cold, water
pooling around his feet, Maitea huddled close by. The
magician inclined his head as though he could see every
thought in Petri's head and thought them all worthy of a
five-year-old.

"I want to see how well they do in a real fight. How
well I do too."

"Petri . . ." She pinched her lips together, clearly torn.

He gathered up some of the blunts. For a time he'd
thought it had been enough to finally start to feel like he
belonged somewhere. Like he'd forgotten who he'd been,
what he'd wanted. For a time that had been enough, but
it wasn't now.

"*They* didn't want you," Scar said at last. "But we do.
They left you out to dry, but we won't. We *need* you. My
little boys and girls are starting to respect you even. I've
been waiting for you to say you'll come. Give them something to respect even more. Give you a reason to belong
a little more."

He stared around the camp, at the log and turf huts, the
windswept scree that fell away from the edge of the valley.
It had crept up on him in the last month or so, but it felt
like home, and the people he shared it with had started
to feel like friends. Friends who looked to him to show
them how to fight, who didn't see half a face and think it
meant half a man. *Bold enough, and she'll come, and you
can show her.*

"When do we leave?"

*   *   *

They hit the village just as another snowstorm crept in along the ridge that hung over the little houses and the inn. Scar led them, scarf over nose and mouth to keep out the wind, bundled up in furs, with a close-watched Morro ahead to clear a dripping foggy path. The inn, she'd said. When the weather turned bad, the villagers all sat it out in the inn, leaving their homes vulnerable. She sent half her crew to see what they could find there, set some more on watch, and yet others to stay with the shaggy mountain ponies they rode and the mules that would carry whatever they managed to steal. The rest, including Petri and Morro, headed for the inn.

Petri fidgeted with the new mask that Scar'd had made for him. Not to hide his ruined face this time, but to show it and hide the good side.

"No sense in anyone else recognising you. Tried for treason will be the least of your worries if that happens," she said. "Besides, you'll scare the crap out of them."

It worked even better than shc'd hoped.

Kepa threw open the door and Scar strode in, Petri half a pace behind, both with swords out. Behind, a ragged moan from Morro as he sank against a wall, spent from his exertions melting snow – he'd been using his own blood only, as Scar would allow none from her crew. The sound of his exhaustion was a comfort to Petri. A magician behind him was more usually a needle of worry in his head, but a magician without the energy to stand less so.

The crowded inn sat in stunned silence for all of ten seconds while Scar stood, swathed in furs, dripping slush over the flagstones, as though proclaiming herself queen. A clock ticked loudly on one wall, making Petri flinch with each click of the second hand. Kepa came up behind

Petri, almost braining himself on a low beam, a dozen more crew crowding in after.

Finally, an older woman, comfortably broad across the beam and with a red-cheeked quizzical look about her, stood up in front of the scant two dozen people huddled by the fire. She glanced down at Scar's sword and back up to her swathed face as though trying to place it.

"A bad night to be out," she said in the end. "We got room and to spare, and ale to make the time go faster."

Scar pulled down the scarves that had kept the knife wind from cutting her, and the woman blanched. A signal from Scar, and Petri stepped forward and after a moment's hesitation pulled his own scarf down.

"Oh, god's cogs and gears," the woman breathed. Someone behind her swore, and a thump shuddered through the flagstones as someone else fainted. A dropped knife clattered on the floor.

The clock ticked into the new silence, slicing seconds off Petri's life. He tried to shut the sound out but couldn't.

"You know who I am now?" Scar said.

"Yes, m'm," the woman whispered. Behind her men and women shuffled about, searching for weapons or valuables or children. A baby cried and was hastily shushed.

Scar's smiled twisted in the firelight. "I think you can see that we are men and women with nothing left to lose. Not even our faces. Food and money. Now."

"And ale," Kepa said from behind Petri. "I'd quite happily gut any one of you for a pint."

The woman looked around at the people crowded behind her. One or two looked belligerent, ready to defend them and theirs, but the rest – the rest wouldn't meet the woman's eye, and not one would look in Petri's direction.

The woman finally nodded, drew herself up and turned

back to face Scar. "If we give you that, you leave us in peace?"

Scar inclined her head in gracious assent.

The woman slumped back, shrivelled like last year's apple, and Scar didn't wait for any more words. A wave and her crew got going. Some raided the kitchens; Kepa headed a brace of men rifling behind the meagre bar; more went to the cellar. Others, weapons out and ready, grabbed what they could from the men and women here. There was little resistance – what good would that do when they had only perhaps eight men and women old enough, or young enough, to try, and none with anything more vicious than a knife?

Scar's crew came back with arms overflowing, pockets bulging. Supplies from the kitchen were already being manhandled out of the door and onto the waiting mules. Good hams, sides of smoked bacon, enough salt beef for a month, sacks of flour, potatoes, apples. Pockets chinked with copper pennies and bracelets, earrings and pocket watches, poor things mostly. Petri could hear the muffled voices of two men sent to check the icehouse for any meat stored there and the clink of men raiding the wood-pile stacked neatly beside the back door. Kepa had cleared the bar into a now tinkling sack and stood swigging rum from the bottle and growing redder in the face by the minute, his smile looking ready to lift the top of his head off.

The clock ticked on regardless.

Yet not everyone was willing to be robbed so easily. An older man at the back of the inn, half sat in shadows, yanked himself away from a probing crew member. The man's face was weathered and lined with years of working outdoors, his hair more snow than not, but Petri didn't mistake the gnarled iron look of hands after a lifetime of hard use, or the iron look in the man's eyes either.

But the bandit didn't have a clue, it seemed, because when the long knife flashed out he stumbled back, blood washing through his shirt. The iron man stood up, and another knife appeared in his other hand. Both knives were old, like the man, but well used and honed to a shimmering sharpness. The crew member grabbed a chair to pull himself back up, but a boot landed in his stomach, almost as an afterthought, sending him crashing back down, wheezing and bubbling from the wound in his chest.

Petri came forward without a thought. The right hand came up before he remembered, and then his sword presented. "Enough."

The iron eyes widened at his accent, flicked down to the sword and back again. No fear there, only a deadly reckoning. "Ah, one of them then. And a guildsman too? I see that sword and know it for what it is. Go on then. Run me through. Tell yourself it was the good thing. Like stealing from people who haven't got more than a loaf of bread to spare for the winter. Does that seem good to you?"

The knife came in a flash of firelit sparks, and again there was no thought from Petri, only reaction as his left hand smacked it out of the iron man's hand with his sword, his own right coming up with the twist that released the stiletto hidden in his sleeve.

The contempt on that iron face lit everything inside him, made it blaze behind his eye with a white-hot intensity that blinded him to anything else. To what he was doing with his sword, the sudden blood on the flags, the screams behind and around him. Only this mattered. Only slaking this thirst, this need. Fuck the good thing; it had brought him nothing but misery.

A cool hand on his arm brought him back to the tap room, silent except for the ticking of the clock. The iron man lay at his feet, his blood seeping along the wrinkles of the flagstones as though seeking absolution there. Petri's breath seemed hot in his throat, an iron band on his chest. Scar's hand on his arm again, but something . . . something . . . He lashed out at the clock on the wall, knocked it to the floor and stamped on it again and again, until cogs spurted like blood and the torturous ticking ceased. Until he could hear his own thoughts again, hear the rasp of his breath, the thud of his heart.

Scar said nothing, but a chuckle behind Petri sent the hairs on the back of his neck tingling. Morro came into view on his blind side, and the scent of cooking blood curdled the air. The room went from not mattering to being so vividly clear that it seemed imprinted on his brain – the older woman who'd spoken, face redder than ever, cheeks glossy and wet. A younger woman, shrunk back in tangled horror. A tow-headed boy hiding under the table, looking at the leaking blood with wide eyes that seemed pinned to the trickle of it, following it as it moved across the floor to the older woman's feet, where it puddled.

Scar turned aside, back to ordering her crew, telling them to gather what they had and go. Morro bent down and held a small glass vial to the blood that pooled at Petri's feet. Blood that confused him – that had briefly sated what coiled inside him and yet had also fed it, made him stronger, colder.

"How very brave," Morro murmured, "to kill an old man armed only with a knife. You must be proud. A true guildsman to be so brave."

Petri opened his mouth, to tell him to shut up, to curse him out. But in his anger he lost his caution, let his eyes catch on Morro's hands. On the marks there, writhing and dark.

"I defended myself," he said through numb lips, frowning over his own words. "That was all."

"Scar will be so appreciative, I'm sure. Her man being such a hero."

Everything boiled to a point inside Petri at that, at this man, this *magician*, dripping venom all over him.

Morro raised a marked hand that stopped him. "Ah, ah. So easily led, aren't you? First by Kacha of the guild, then by Sabates, now by Scar, telling you words you want to hear so that you'll do what they want. Just a bleating sheep you are."

Petri gritted his teeth but couldn't see past the markings on the magician's hands, now a sword, now a scar, now a slaughtered sheep.

"What does Scar want?" Morro whispered. "A crippled man who can take on an old one? She's twenty crew who could do the same, who could and would do more than the coward I see in front of me. But she has me now to help her, and you'd do best not to cross me. Not while I have blood at my fingers. He was an old man and poorly armed, but he hated you and everything you stood for once. I understand why he's dead. I wonder if you do."

Petri turned on his heel and stalked outside, into fog that dripped copper on his tongue and draped him in watery magic. Morro was right behind him, his soft voice oddly intimate. Maitea watched, wreathed in shadows. Watching, listening. Learning how to be a magician.

"It felt good, though, didn't it?" Morro said. "Even if it was just one old man, you enjoyed it, the brutality, the feeling of power for once in your miserable fucked-up life."

Petri whipped round to face him, and found they were

alone in the fog but for Maitea. Morro had his gloves off, and Petri strove not to look, not to look – if he looked he was lost – but there was nowhere else, nothing else to see but Morro and his hands.

"I can make it last longer than this scant winter, make it last a lifetime, that feeling. You can feel like that every day."

Petri dragged his eye away from the hands, from the markings that writhed there, and bit his tongue in the effort to keep looking at Morro's face. His voice came out strangled and strange, fell dead in the damp air. "What's in it for you?"

Morro shrugged, dripped his voice like oil to soothe Petri's troubled mind. "I'm like you, Petri. I'm hated everywhere, and I belong nowhere. Nowhere except here. I'm just doing the best I can for Scar. Like you."

He reached out, and Petri couldn't help but look, get caught up in pictures of swords, of scars, of pride and snow and victory.

"I could do so much for you too. If you'll let me. I could make you king of this mountain."

A stray breath of wind spun the fog into grey streamers that seemed to float inside his head as well as out. But . . . but no. He had been weak before, been seduced by black and red markings and the promises they seemed to bring. Every promise had brought with it lies and treachery, brought him misery and this face. He knocked the hand away, and a brief spark of something flared in him.

"Magicians die like anyone else," he managed to growl out.

"So you say," Morro said. "So you say, and I know that's true. But I also know that you've never felt as full of purpose, as *strong*, as you did back in that room, with a sword in your good hand. How much would you give to keep on feeling that?"

Petri had no chance to answer because Morro turned on his heel and left, little drops of blood on the ground following him. Little drops of blood and seeds of doubt.

That raid had been the start of it – the start of the Scar and the Skull.

Now, some weeks later, Petri was starting to get used to the stares, the whispers, the panic when he appeared. Truth be told he was starting to enjoy it too, the frantic rumours about the Skull. That he was dead but still walking, some long-ago bandit so bad even death wouldn't take him.

He rolled over and looked at Scar's back in the growing light, ran a hand over one shoulder with a dark and convoluted mark upon it, like a tattoo, that he'd not noticed before. She stirred and rolled towards him, still asleep, and laid her head on his shoulder. It still surprised him that she didn't care about any of it – the face, how that had happened, what he'd done to deserve it. There were times when he looked at her and couldn't fathom what went on behind her eyes, and times when she appalled him with her casual and brutal violence, and yet . . . and yet he was only human and had been alone too long. Too long, and she loved him with a fierceness that kept him warm on long cold nights.

Scar stirred again and woke with a smile for him before she rose and strode, naked and gleaming, to the couple of planks balanced on rough logs that served as a washstand. She had a supreme confidence in herself that he envied. She never doubted herself, or what she did.

By the time the sun began to struggle its way down behind the mountains they were ready, and Scar led them towards the main road, a place they'd never dared go before. There were outposts here, patrols of Reyes men, a few from every councillor and the prelate, doing what they could in the inhospitable mountains to stem the tide of lawlessness.

Morro rode with Scar and Petri at the head of the crew, doing his work with blood saved from the last raid mixed with some of his own and some donated willingly from Kepa and others happy to sacrifice a bit of blood if it made their lives easier, and warmer. Morro did his work to thin the falling snow, to make a path for them, much as he would cover their tracks after them once they'd raided. He'd made raiding ten times easier, had been nothing but courteous, quiet, doing as Scar asked, but still, having him there made Petri itch. He rode silently, as was his habit, and watched Morro and Scar.

She'd sworn to him that Morro had never ungloved his hands in her presence, but Petri wasn't sure that was enough. He caught little glances between them, a sly look from Morro back to him, an oily, smug smile before he turned forward again. Scar was oblivious, all fired up for her daring raid, not on a village but a proper town. Petri had his misgivings, but this was her crew and she had overruled him.

"What happened to survival?" he'd asked one night. "To feeding your own and keeping them safe, head down, subtle and alive?"

"This is survival," she'd said from where she nestled on his shoulder. "We *have* to think bigger if we're to feed everyone. We're too many now. Morro's right about that."

"I wouldn't look to him for advice."

"Why not, if it seems like good advice? I'm as suspicious as you are, but he has a point. We're too many now to feed just with the odd raid here and there. We need to think of bigger things, you and I. I always had ambition. Now I have the means to do something about it. *We* do. This is just a step up from what we've already been doing, and we need the food."

"Is that all it is?"

"Of course it is, Petri. Now be quiet and kiss me."

He saw the sense of that, but something niggled at the back of his mind nonetheless, more so when he saw how Morro looked at her when he thought no one was watching. Like a farmer weighing up a how much a cow was worth, what it could get him at market if he fattened it a little more. But Petri said nothing more, only watched and wondered because saying did no good.

The Scar and the Skull rode into Kastroa at nightfall like they owned it. It had a wall, but it was a poor thing and the gates weren't guarded. Despite the snow and wind, the main square was busy − some sort of old-time festival to herald the turn of midwinter. Against the coming night a hundred lamps hung from windows and balconies, were carried at the end of long poles in the centre of the square next to a poor imitation of the Clockwork God draped in firs and berries, a huge bonfire and the smell of potatoes baking in it.

Scar used her pony to push through the meagre crowds and into the square. She pulled down the scarf that protected her from the wind, nodded at Petri to do the same as the crew came in behind, in dribs and drabs so as not to attract attention until they wanted it attracted.

He pulled down his scarf, flipped back the hood of his good new wolf cloak, and they had all the attention they needed. The fire lit the side of his face not covered by the mask, what was left of it. The man nearest grabbed his two young children and tried to cover their eyes; a different child whose parents were less quick screamed, and the whispers started. Always the whispers, all his life – that was one thing that hadn't changed. Only what they said.

The "Did you see his face?" "God's cogs, that's ugly," "Has he no shame?" that had followed him across the plains, driven him out of fat little villages and sleepy towns into the lawless reaches of the mountains had faded away. The new whisper – "The Skull, it's the Skull!" – made his heart burn, and he couldn't be sure if it was pride or shame. The Skull because he looked dead, and because, they said, he couldn't die but had outwitted death himself. He grinned at them, and the grin stretched as people fell back before it. He had misgivings, but Morro was right about one thing: as the Skull he had power he'd never had before, and he liked it.

He nudged his pony further into the light from the fire. People scrambled away as he approached, dragged children out of the way or strained to see him and his face – from a safe distance. Scar's pony jogged next to his, her own puckered scar flickering in the firelight, until they reached the centre of the square. Petri looked up at the god and slowly, deliberately thumbed his nose at it, to outraged gasps from around the square before they fell silent as Scar stood in her stirrups and addressed them, reins in one hand, sword nonchalant in the other. On her other side Morro sat, shrouded and shadowy, doing something Petri couldn't quite see – and then all became clear as the snow stopped, seemed to hover above them like stars. The snow underfoot melted, and ran in little rivers across the muddy square.

"The Scar and the Skull are here," Scar said. "You have a choice, as always. Hand over your money, your valuables and what food you can pack on our mules. No one will be harmed. Or refuse, and they will."

Scar swung her sword, and Petri pulled his own, laying it across the neck of his pony with his one hand. Still clumsy with it, but a match for most any man here, he had no doubt. A certain amount of shuffling and whispered argument followed before a fat old man in a rich brocade coat trimmed with fur half walked, was half pushed forward.

"Sir, madam," he began, and some of Scar's crew behind them laughed at that, earning them a glare from the old man. "I'm mayor of this town. And you are nothing but brigands." Scar's sword rose, but he stayed her with an upstretched hand. "Your reputation precedes you for sure. But we won't be giving you anything willingly."

"Good," came a shout from one of the crew, Kepa most likely. "I've been itching to use this good new sword. Your face would be a fine start."

"I have to agree," Scar said. The firelight sent orange flickers along her sword and picked out the twist of a scar that changed her face from handsome to indomitable. The mayor grinned, quick as a flash and gone, and stepped back smartly into the crowd.

Who were suddenly not just a crowd any more. Cloaks were swept back, swords out, swords no backwater woodsman or ragged trader could ever afford. Then a clock-work gun, another, and Petri knew.

Scar figured it out at the same time. "Prelate's men!"

The night descended into chaos – gunshots and screams as bullets found homes, swords that glittered with blood. A tiny avalanche ripped from Morro on his pony towards the two men that threatened him, took their feet from under them and their breath as they landed hard on the cobbles. Maitea disappeared into a whirl of shadows. Kepa laid about him indiscriminately with his newly stolen sword, bellowing loud enough for a dozen men.

Three men charged Petri's pony and sought to drag him off. His clumsy left hand might be good enough by now to beat farmers, but not trained men. A wild thrust that missed its target by a mile, a slash from one of them that he dodged only by digging his heels in and sending his pony surging forward, trailing prelate's men behind it. Then one, two, had him, dragging him down off the pony and onto the cobbles of the square, smacking his head with enough force to blur his vision. One swung his sword down but was cut off when a blade thrust out of his stomach, washing Petri in the man's blood so that his one eye was blind. When he swiped it clear, Scar was standing over him with two dead men at her feet and a third reeling from a blow that would leave him a scar to match her own.

Under a cart the fat old mayor cowered, hands over his ears to drown out the screams. He caught Petri's eye, and his own went wide.

"Petri Egimont?"

Petri groped at his face and realised the mask that hid his recognisable side had been ripped off in the melee. He and the mayor stared at each other – he'd swear he didn't know the man, but how many mayors had he seen when he was aide to the prelate? How many had come to beg for this or that from the prelate, and Petri standing at his right shoulder?

Scar dragged Petri to his feet and shoved his mask, ripped but still wearable, at him.

"He knows me," Petri gasped. "Under the cart. I'll be hanged for treason if they find me."

They shared a look, and then she was shouting above the hubbub, "Fall back! Scar's crew, fall back!"

They didn't need telling twice. Scar grabbed at Kepa as he ran past, and between them they dragged the ashen and howling mayor from under the cart. "Bring him with us," Scar said, and Kepa threw the fat old bastard over his shoulder, then slung him over his pony's withers and mounted.

Scar and Petri were half a second behind, whirling their ponies and slashing about with their swords to try to prevent any of the prelate's men following. But they would.

Morro paused, two of Scar's men protecting him as he gathered blood from the fallen, face alight so that it turned Petri's stomach. When he was done, he climbed onto his pony and had one of the men lead it as he did his best with blood and precious stolen parchment from their raid the last week. Snow fell behind them like a curtain, obscuring the town as they left it, obliterating their tracks. Maitea appeared again out of her shadows and made more whirl behind them, obscure them. Finally, Morro sagged in his saddle, almost fell but held on, grim and white-faced but nodding his approval to Maitea.

They regrouped in the prearranged place, a lone and dying tree on a trackless and windswept mountainside. Snow fell, thick and fast thanks to Morro, the flakes almost blinding Petri and making him dizzy, but he followed Scar, sure in the knowledge she knew where they were headed.

Of the forty that had started out the evening, six never made the tree. Another five had wounds serious enough to have them risk bleeding out, and of the rest a dozen had wounds of varying seriousness, including Scar, who'd taken a cut to the arm that was more ugly than dangerous, and Petri, whose dizziness wasn't wholly from the whirling snow but also from the bang to the head as he'd landed on the cobbles.

Kepa threw the fat old mayor down at the foot of the tree, where he gasped and shivered in the cold like a landed fish. Scar had Petri dismount and got one of the crew to check the lump on his head while she nudged her pony forward to tower over the mayor for the second time this evening.

"Up," she snapped. "Up!'

He got up slowly at the end of four swords. "They won't ransom me, you know," he said querulously. "The prelate doesn't deal in blackmail."

"Well then, I shall have to think of something else," Scar said and nodded at the four crew holding swords on him.

Before Petri could shout out or say a word, they'd grabbed him and held him as Scar lashed out with her sword and split the man balls to ribcage, sending his guts to spill, steaming, into the snow. "String him up. They'll find him eventually, and a little message. We'll need to be more careful from here on in."

She looked over at Petri as he stared at the blood melting the snow by her pony's feet. Scar, who shared his bed and helped him forget who Petri Egimont had even been.

"No one threatens my man."

Petri sat and stared impassively and knew at last that Eneko had been right when he'd taken Petri's eye, his face, his hand. Petri was weakness, soft as lead, weak as bad steel. Petri Egimont had no place here. Luckily Petri Egimont had died back there in that cell with all his weaknesses and memories, and now there was only the Skull.

Chapter Sixteen

Now

When Vocho made it — barely — downstairs the next day, he found Cospel clattering around in the kitchens and Kass already up and poring over the map. While it was gratifying that his little plan to perk her up was working, the overloud greeting and sly grin when he winced were not.

The landlady wordlessly handed him a plate of spiced sausages and hot buttered bread, and he plonked down next to Kass and set to, feeding his face being the best hangover cure known to man. When he paused for breath and a swig of the apple tea that had come with the plate, he peered over her shoulder. He hadn't really been paying all that much attention before — Eder seemed more than capable of looking after all that — but . . .

"Kass, have you noticed what I've just noticed?"

"I don't know, Voch. Kind of depends on what you just noticed."

Ah. Well now he'd started . . . it wasn't like he wanted to remind her, but it looked like it was going to crop up whether he did the cropping or not. "Well look. Here's No Man's Land, or Skull's country or whatever we want to call it." He pointed with a bit of bread and then had to brush away the crumbs. "And here's where we know there have been attacks, right? Right. All in a semicircle out from No Man's Land, with Kastroa right on the furthest edge. Draw a line between the two and then go further. If they carry on as they have been, where are they going to end up?"

Kass frowned and turned her head to follow what he was saying on the map. Then, slowly, her voice sounding blurred, "Elona . . . Oh."

Oh indeed. Vocho didn't say anything but finished off his bread in silence as it sank in. Elona, where once upon a time the duke'd had a son called Petri. Of course there weren't any dukes any more, and the duchy was probably split up into half a dozen estates for the richer clockers who'd replaced the nobles. He didn't suppose there was an Egimont within fifty miles of the place. But still, just the name was enough to bring a shadow back to Kass's face. And why did he keep thinking of Petri? It couldn't be him. He was a sly double-dealing bastard, but the nerve to be the Skull? Never. Jollop paranoia certainly, perhaps a signal to pull back on drinking it so much. That and the look of pity on Carrola's face last night. He needed to learn to be him without it. Just as soon as he'd finished this bottle.

"Well, lovely as Elona is supposed to be," Kass said finally, "I don't think that's where we're headed for now. Come on, we're supposed to be getting ready to go."

Vocho glanced out of the window and suppressed a groan. The still grey air was thick with falling snow. "We're going out in that? I'm not sure our gear is up to a mountain winter. I thought things were supposed to be warming up. It *is* spring."

"Spring works differently up here, it seems. Eder certainly intends to go out in that, and if he goes, it won't do for the guild to stay behind."

He stood up and brushed crumbs from all the crevices they'd managed to invade. "And what do we think of Eder?"

Kass rolled up the map and stashed it in her pack, which was ready under the table. "I don't think about him much at all."

Vocho studied her. She was being entirely too nonchalant about Eder, which made him highly suspicious, but he left it for now.

Danel had managed to beg, borrow or threaten some furs for them and the rest. Cospel sat looking at a forlorn pile of ex-rabbit and ex-wolf sulking on the floor of the stable. He picked one piece up gingerly as they walked in.

"It stinks like it only died last week," he said.

"That'll be your one then," Vocho replied.

Cospel smirked in a most irritating fashion. "Fair enough. The rest stinks even worse. Anybody'd think they were keeping meat in these."

"Maybe they were." Sergeant Danel came in from the yard, stamping snow off his boots and looking resigned. "Salt's expensive here – too far from the salt mines – and smoking's all right, but for a mountain man the best way to keep meat is out in the snow. Mountain speciality, that is, proper cold-aged beef, like my mum used to make. Nothing like it. You cut your meat and let it age in autumn, then it freezes as the winter comes in. Only you don't want any critters taking to pinching it, and not everyone has room for a meat house. They sews it up in old furs and hangs it from trees."

Cospel dropped the fur with a grimace. "Nice."

"All I could get at short notice. We're going to need it too. Colder than a snow troll's balls out there. Pardon my Ikaran, miss."

Kass looked round from where she'd been absent-mindedly running a hand along a fur. "What? Oh don't be bloody silly. A bit of language never killed anyone."

The door to the inn opened, and Eder, Carrola and the rest of those billeted there came in and set about readying themselves and the horses. Most of them, like Vocho and Kass, hadn't ridden in weather like this very often, or indeed ever. Weather like this, to Vocho's mind, was for staying indoors near a fire, not actually going out in.

"Eder, are you sure that—" Kass began.

"Perfectly sure," he snapped out, voice clipped and cold. "I've my orders from the prelate to apprehend this Skull as quickly as possible, and I intend to carry them out."

"At the risk of frostbite or worse? Avalanche? You said you'd already lost men to that. You angling to lose some more?"

One or two of the guards gave Kass a look, the sort that said "*precisely* the wrong thing to say".

"I thought I'd made myself clear?" He turned away sharply and made for his horse.

Kass stepped between him and it, and yes, there she was, the sister he knew. One hand on a hip, the other on the stiletto that often graced her off hand when she fought, eyes bright and chin jutting.

"And I am making myself clear. Bakar put you under *my* orders on our little jaunt here, in case you'd forgotten, and you and your troop are going nowhere unless you convince me it's best."

Eder ground his teeth, but a glance at the way she was

playing with that stiletto, another at Vocho, who shook his head very slightly in return, and he turned on his heel and headed for the bar. "Very well," he threw over his shoulder before he addressed two of his troop on the way. "You and you, get the horses ready. We'll be leaving as soon as I can make her see sense."

Vocho would have told Kass that annoying Eder was a bit of a stupid move on her part, but the way she was smiling, like she hadn't in months, like she meant it – he didn't have the heart. Instead he faced the prospect of saddling Kass's evil beast of a horse for her and set about getting Cospel to do it for him.

Kass followed Eder back into the bar, where he threw himself into a chair by the fire and tapped a foot as he waited. She shouldn't have needled him, she knew that, but she wasn't taking men and women out in that snow without assurances. Besides which . . . besides which there were things that needed talking out.

Eder waited for her to sit and gestured impatiently when she leaned up against the fireplace instead, elaborately casual.

"We can't wait," he said at last. "We know they were at that village a week ago, and even they can't move fast in this. Maybe they'll be holed up, waiting it out. It's our chance to catch up with them."

"It's our chance to die of exposure," she said in return. "Which I don't much fancy. They've got a magician, whether you believe in that or not, and I doubt they're holed up anywhere except in their own beds. We, however, will be facing a snowstorm in tents, wearing barely adequate gear. After Red Brook and that avalanche, that surprise attack, I wouldn't have thought you'd want to risk losing any of your soldiers again. Yet you seem hell-bent on it."

His whole body seemed to twitch at that, and his teeth clacked shut. "What you think of Red Brook or the rest, or me — and you made that perfectly clear — makes no difference. Bakar gave us both our orders. Catch the Skull as quickly as possible. Once the thaw comes, there'll be no stopping him."

She regarded him solemnly. If he wasn't going to bring it up, neither was she. It might only make him worse, and he was angry enough as it was. Get through this job, stop people dying, that's what she had to be thinking of. Not whether she'd react differently if he tried to kiss her again, even whether she wanted him to. Whether it was just because of how much like Petri he was . . .

"Not so much orders in my case, more of a commission," she said at last. "He didn't order you to get all your troop killed, did he?"

It was as though he was a fully wound clock and she'd just turned the key another half a wind too far. He exploded out of the chair and slammed a hand on the table, the other reaching for his sword out of habit. Then his eyes cleared, he seemed to realise what he'd been just about to do, and he sank back into the chair with shaking hands.

"We need to go," he said at last, without looking at her. A brick-red flush worked its way up his neck. "No matter how little you think of me. Go, and as soon as we can."

"If you're doing this in a weird attempt to impress me—"

His lip lifted like that of a beaten dog. "Why would I want to do that?" he snarled. "I no longer care what you think."

A retort sprang to her lips, but she clamped down on it. She'd made a stupid mistake, and he was rightly pissed off with her for it, but this was something else, ran far deeper than a misplaced kiss. She'd do best to keep her peace for now.

Finally, Eder got himself under icy control. "Sergeant Danel says this will be no more than a flurry — clearer weather is expected; the thaw should be here any day. It's colder than we were expecting or have provisioned for, but Danel's found plenty of extra furs; each horse is going to carry as much wood as possible, and the tents we've brought are more than up to the job. I will go, even if the guild stays behind. Maybe it should. It might be better all round."

"It might," she said and noted the daggered look he shot her at that. "But it's not an option. I'm telling you this is a mistake. It could be a very costly one."

"Then it's my mistake to make, my troop, my men and women. The weather is set to clear, and we've prepared as best we can. You lot stay here if you like, but we're going whether you agree or not."

He glared at her from under a furrowed knot of eyebrows, waiting perhaps for her to argue the point. Instead, tired of argument, tired suddenly of everything, she said, "All right. But we go via Kastroa. It's not far out of the way. Find out what we can there, find some better gear, see how the weather is before we head up into the wilds. Agreed?"

The bewildered look he gave her brought back a sudden slew of memories so sharp she could taste the spiced wine Petri had bought her, feel his breath on her neck, his hand on her naked back, watch him unwind from an uptight, upright man into . . .

Petri would have been better off staying that upright, uptight man. And she'd be better off right now not thinking

about how Eder was like Petri and whether she wanted
Eder to kiss her again, because she thought she might,
might want him to show her what was under all that anger,
all that doubt. Later, she thought she might want him to
do more than that.

"Agreed," he said at last, and thank the Clockwork God
for small mercies.

"Let's just hope we don't regret this later when our
hands fall off due to frostbite."

Sergeant Danel had been right — the snow didn't fall for
long, although long enough for Kass to wish she'd not
agreed to this. While the snow stopped after half a day on
the road, the wind still came keening down over the tumbled
ridges of the mountains, sharp enough to cut through even
the furs and loud enough to ensure she'd barely slept that
night. Now, in a day that seemed cold enough to freeze
her to her marrow, Vocho fidgeted awkwardly in his saddle
next to her, lips thin and hands clutched on the saddle-
horn. His horse protested as his weight shifted, throwing
its head back and snorting, breath puffing out like fog.

"Voch—"

"It's fine," he snapped, though it clearly wasn't. But
Vocho was never going to admit that hip wound gave him
any trouble. Not when there were people to impress. Like
Carrola, who rode a couple of steps back along the trail.
A blind man could see how hard he was trying to impress
her, but Kass got the feeling that anyone would find that
tricky.

"Where are we heading and are we likely to get there
soon?" Vocho asked. "Like, before my face freezes off?"

"Kastroa, weren't you paying attention? Find out any
more we can, gear up if possible, and besides it's on the

way, sort of. I suspect your face will be fine. If you can call your normal face fine."

He gave her a startled sideways look, then grinned. "This face, I'll have you know, has been the downfall of many a lady."

"If by downfall you mean they have to shut their eyes to avoid it, I suppose."

He threw back his head and laughed, before it was cut short by a grimace of pain. "Kass, you have no idea how much I have missed you bitching at me. Go on, do it again."

All of a sudden they were easy again, like they had been before – before dead priests and robbing coaches and magicians trying to kill them. Before Petri. Even that thought couldn't cloud her mood, the weight lifting from her head, the fog flying out of her eyes so that she noticed, for perhaps the first time in months, the taste of the air, the smell of the wind that lashed her face. He cheeks ached from her own grin, from muscles too long unused.

"Your face would make the Clockwork God rust."

Vocho tried one of his poses, one which he liked to think made him look heroic but actually made him seem cross-eyed. "This face is the face of a great duellist, *the* great duellist, and don't you forget it."

"How could I when you spend all your time reminding me?"

The way went quicker after that, and warmer, for all the frosty looks that Eder threw their way as they joked and bickered along the road.

Kastroa was a higgledy-piggledy collection of houses that seemed to bleed into one another, a wall around them and a cobbled slushy square in the middle with a representation of the Clockwork God standing sentinel, a snow-clad trade house overlooking it. The roofs were steeper here than down on the plain to prevent a build-up of snow, decorated with fancy woodwork along the eaves and peppered with more chimneys than seemed practicable. The people dressed in furs rather than wool, making them the grey of wolves rather than the splashes of colour they would be in Reyes, but the god was the same, the clocker stalls in the square, the smells of spicy sausage coming from another at the back, the stories the bards were telling at the corners. One of the more astute of those saw the guild colours under their ragtag furs and promptly started telling how Kacha and Vocho had saved Bakar, Reyes and the guild single-handedly. Supposedly anyway. Kass noted an embellishment or two that she suspected had originated in Reyes, quite possibly under Vocho's instruction. She also noticed the way Eder kicked his horse past with unnecessary vigour and the worried look that Carrola gave his back.

"Did you hear that?" Vocho said now to Carrola. "Outstanding courage, the man said. Dashing elan and style."

"I heard it," Carrola said as she swung down from her horse and looked about, before her eyes slid colder than the snow over him. "I'm not sure I believe it." She left Vocho gawping after her as she made her way over to Eder.

"Smart lady." Kass made sure her horse was firmly tied up and away from anyone it might take a dislike to.

"You can take a good thing too far, you know." Vocho dismounted carefully and massaged one thigh before he tried a step that made him hiss. "God's cogs, the cold has done dire things to me. Very dire."

Eder held court by the rather rusty Clockwork God in the centre of the square. The prelate's colours on his flash got him deference, and a small crowd of people huddled around in their cloaks. Until Kass strode up, furs thrown back to show the guild tabard underneath.

A thin, ascetic-looking man in sumptuous furs and brocade that appeared to double his breadth, ignored Eder, making his face go puce with rage, and grabbed her hand in his cold one. "The guild! You must be Kacha, and . . . and yes, that must be Vocho. I couldn't mistake you two; we've heard so much about everything you've done! Please, come inside, come inside."

Eder looked daggers at her, but she ignored him and followed the man inside the trade house. The main room was sweltering from four fireplaces, one on each wall, and the man – "Call me Imanol, please. I'm the mayor now for my sins, after that terrible night" – took her and Vocho's fur cloaks and handed them to a smiling wide-eyed boy who couldn't seem to stop looking at them until Imanol gave him a gentle prod. Cospel hurried after the boy – he'd be in the kitchens with a plateful of food in no time, picking up all the gossip.

Imanol led them to the largest of the fires. The mantel was fully as high as Vocho was tall and carved into intricate patterns interspersed with little clockwork figures picked out in blues and reds and golds. A click of Imanol's fingers, and more boys and girls came with plates and steaming cups, bowls of fragrant steaming water to wash in, hot towels to dry them after. As an afterthought, he waved Eder to a sumptuously stuffed chair before he pulled another over to sit right by Kass and Vocho.

"Such an honour, such an honour," he said as he watched them wipe the grime of the road from their faces with hot cloths. "Here, please, try this. It's the best thing when you've been out in the cold."

He handed Kass a cup of something that smelled like

molten sugar and tasted even better. Vocho fiddled about with his, slid a hand into his tunic and out again before he took a sip with a sigh, but Imanol had Kass's attention.

"So glad that you're here. It's been a terrible time, terrible. The Skull has everyone petrified from here to the border, maybe even further. Raids all over. They killed the mayor, you know."

"Killed him? When?"

"Yes, poor man, dragged him off a few weeks ago and gutted him as some sort of message. Has us all quite quaking. I thought that's why you'd come? Because of our message? I see not – so terribly difficult to get messages through in this snow. The bandits even robbed a mine, and that's a huge worry. If we can't protect the mines, if we have no iron and coal to trade . . . The prelate's men have done what they could, but they aren't the guild, are they? Pretty useless, really, though better than nothing, I suppose. But now you're here, we should see something done."

A clank of a plate from Eder behind him.

"And of course just your reputation should have this Skull quaking in his boots," Imanol ran on over her attempt to interject. "Everyone is very excited. Kacha and Vocho of the guild in our poor trade house! I hope that you'll consent to dine here tonight, and also consent to tell us some of the stories first hand, as it were. So excited, so excited. I feel sure you'll succeed where the prelate's men failed."

Eder's cup rattled on the table. He stood up, turned on his heel and left. Kass watched him go with a twinge of sympathy.

Imanol waffled on some more before, at last, he got a boy to lead them to their room. Two beds about the size of boats, covered in wools and furs and down-stuffed bolsters and bedspreads so that Kacha wondered if she might drown in hers when she slept, the cold of the winter kept out with voluminous drapes that she could hardly shift. It was stuffy, musty and overhot from the too-generous fire, but a damn sight better than another night under canvas, being kept awake by her own shivers.

Maybe Voch had been right about it just being the cold that was bothering his leg – he was moving more smoothly now they were in the warm, and the pinch to his lips had gone, leaving him in fine fettle. He spent the next hour regaling her with stories of his exploits as though she'd never heard them. His eyes were bright, just a shade *too* bright, and his left eye had begun to twitch.

"Voch," she said when she could get a word in. "Are you all right?"

"Never better," he replied with an expansive wave of his arm. If she didn't know better, she'd say he was drunk. "Did you see the look on Eder's face when Imanol kept going on about the failure of the prelate's men? He looked like he'd swallowed a pig whole."

Yes, she had noticed, and she didn't think it boded well at all.

Chapter Seventeen

One month ago

Petri put the glass down with great care but still managed to spill what was left of the drink in it – some eye-watering concoction Kepa said was a mountain speciality for keeping warm in winter which he'd liberated during their last raid. Petri wasn't sure about keeping warm, but his toes seemed very far away so that was all right. He blinked owlishly at Kepa, sitting across from him in the mess.

"Sorry?"

Kepa, being more of a drinker than was Petri's usual habit, was far steadier despite the dent they'd made in the bottle. "I said that Morro fella's got some good ideas, for all he's a magician."

"Can't trust them," Petri replied, banging the table with his glass to make his point. "Not ever. Bunch of snakes, all of them. Almost finished Reyes, didn't they? Tried to kill Bakar, tried to assault the city. Tried everything. Bunch of snakes."

"I don't know." Kepa took a thoughtful sip that turned into a grimace as the stuff hit his tongue. "Like I say, he's got some good ideas. You got to admit he's helped us out with the raids and all, clearing the snow, sending more to stop 'em tracking us after. We've got bigger, and better."

"In return for what? He'll be after something, mark my words, and if it screws you into the ground, he won't care."

"Makes him no different to anyone else then, does it? I been screwed into the ground my whole life. But him, his plans . . . he could unscrew the lot of us. Make us kings of this mountain!"

That splashed across Petri's face like a bucket of icy meltwater. King of the mountain – hadn't Morro offered him that? Petri had been watching, as always, keeping quiet and seeing how things played out. He'd been keeping an especial eye on the magician but had yet to see the man do anything untoward, yet to see him bare his hands to anyone except Petri. But he was doing something. He had to be.

"Did he show you his hands? Show you any pictures while he was spinning this nice future for you?"

"Naw," Kepa said. "He just made sense. We got the power up here, if we want it. All them mines all around, cut off now – can stay cut off too with us having Morro and his snow. We got the power. Why not use it? Can't go on the way we was, we'll starve. So we got to try something new. Bigger, better, for all of us."

"And I bet he's just the man to help you, correct?"

Kepa and his cronies nodded happily, more or less gone on the spirit that fumed out of the bottle on the table. Kings of the mountain, got to try something new, bigger, better. Words that had been creeping into Scar's talk these last weeks. And she swore, they all did, that Morro had never shown his hands, never made pictures dance in front of their eyes. Yet Petri was ever surer that he was working something on them, some twisted magic for his own ends. Nowhere left for a magician to go beyond either Reyes or Ikaras, and neither was a safe home for magicians just now. Nowhere except here, where the only law was theirs, because who else wanted this godforsaken bit of snow-scoured rock that didn't even have the decency to have a seam of coal? A place as unloved, as unwanted as they were. Only they wanted it, needed it because there was nowhere else to go. Them, only them. And now Morro.

The spirit bubbled in his stomach, and he lurched to his feet, suddenly sure he was going to be sick and just as sure he didn't want to do it in front of Kepa or the rest. They'd forged an uneasy truce these last weeks, built on their fear of his sword and, since Petri had started raiding, a grudging admiration from both sides. The valley felt like his first true home, just in time for a magician to rip it to shreds.

He made it outside the mess before it all came up in a hot rush, leaving him dizzy and stumbling. Scar'd have words with him when he got back, but not many. Too pleased that he was getting on with her crew at last, too engrossed in planning what she was going to do next. And what was that, exactly?

Kepa staggered outside after him and pissed, holding himself up against the wall with one outstretched hand. When the pair of them had done, they fell into step along the pathway that magic had cleared for them. No snow fell now, not here. Elsewhere it piled up in mountains of its own, draped itself in pristine ranges that on a sunny day could spear the eye with white blindness. But while snow still lay about, a thin crust over frozen churned-up ground, it no longer snowed in the valley.

"Him did that," Kepa said, and no need to say who.

"And he dulls the wind too, sure of it, so's the barn is warm as spring. Going further tomorrow, right down near the plain."

A prickle of alarm through the warming spirit. "Near the plain?" The first he'd heard of that. The plain – Reyes proper, where farmers had more and clutched it harder to themselves. Where no one much had any sympathy for men and women fallen by the wayside, who didn't reckon they'd likely lose a sheep to the wolves anyway so, if they were going to, why not to the human wolves? Where people didn't freeze to death and guards were in abundance and more likely to catch anyone fool enough to raid there. "Since when?"

Kepa stopped dead, a hand clapped over his mouth as though trying to drag the words back. "I . . . er . . . maybe I didn't hear right?" In the face of Petri's stare, he faltered. "Wasn't supposed to say nothing, was I? A surprise. She'll tell you soon enough. You won't tell her I let the cat out of the bag?"

"No."

Kepa seemed reassured by his terse answer and stumbled off to find his place in the barn, leaving Petri churned up and walking his slow way to Scar's hut. She'd not be so stupid, surely? Be subtle and live, that had been her watchword. Take a bit here, a bit there, not so much the guards need bother with her crew overmuch. Now they'd raided a town, not just a gathering of rambling farms or isolated hamlets. They'd stolen all they could carry from a mine, which might almost be enough to get Bakar worried and send guards all on its own. Now the plain, crowded with fat farms, little market towns that bustled and thrummed with life. The plain, full of people and guards, and no hope to move unseen, magician and his snow or not. *Bold enough, and she'll come.* His hand shook as he lifted the latch to Scar's hut, but whether from fear or anger or just the spirit he'd drunk not even he could say.

He opened the door and shut it quick before all the precious warmth could leak out. He shook out his new good wolf fur and turned to the fire and where Scar would be . . .

And found Maitea instead, sitting still as stone. Scar was nowhere.

He came forward slowly, watching Maitea watch him, and sat down opposite her. If anything, she was quieter than he was, had said almost nothing to anyone that he'd heard. Just those questions of him when they'd gone to see her father, and silence since. He wondered if she'd accepted Morro's plans for herself, or just pretended to.

He noted her hands were gloved, recalled Dom saying, "Just like her mother," and shivered. Maybe her mother had looked this bland once, this innocent.

"I'm supposed to try my magic on you," she said. "I've been practising on my father but now I'm supposed to practise on you too."

Petri raised an eyebrow at the baldness of it, even as his stomach shrivelled. "Practise doing what?"

She shrugged. "Trying to get you to do what I want."

"And will you?"

A delicate frown. "I don't think so. I'm supposed to try to influence you – that's what magic is *for*, Morro says. But I'm not very good at it, and besides it's wrong." She looked at him, face utterly calm and without feeling. "He's with Scar."

A curl of fear in Petri's stomach, but she had only confirmed what he suspected anyway. "Is he using his magic on her? To do what? What does he want?"

The faintest hint of disgust in a curl of her lip. "Maybe. I'm not certain. I've never *seen* him use his magic on her. And he wants somewhere to belong, he says. Here's where it is, along with all the other outcasts. Ikaras won't have him, and neither will Reyes. Nor me, if he makes me into a magician. But Scar will, this valley will. And if here is all that he can hope for, he wants it to be more than just living on scraps. He's had enough of living like that and he has . . . ambition. He doesn't care what it costs anyone else."

Petri leaned forward. "And why are you telling me?"

She cocked her head and looked him dead in the eye. "My father told me about you. Not much, but enough. He said you were an honourable man once but that you'd been led astray. I think so too, so it seemed right to tell you. Warn you. Morro sees you as the biggest threat to what he wants – a comfortable life here in this valley, or anywhere that will take him if this fails. He'll have no compunction doing something about you, if he has to."

She stood up and smoothed down the front of her skirts.

"Your father . . ." Petri began, but she cut him off with a look.

"My father kills people for a living. He killed my mother."

"But?"

A faint and troubling smile. "But he's my father. I can't love him but I can't deny him either." She threw her cloak around her shoulders. The dim scent of cooking blood wafted from her, and her cloak wasn't just made of fur, but of shadows too, which wrapped around her like lovers until Petri could scarcely see her. "Be careful," she said, and the shadows made for the door.

He sat and thought for a long time in front of the dying fire, wondering why she'd really come or if this was just some ruse of Morro's, some kind of warning. What was lurking behind Maitea's bland face? A magician, like her mother. Plans of her own, like her father?

The door opened and shut gently behind him, and Scar threw on a bright grin that didn't fool Petri for a moment.

"He kept his gloves on," she said when she caught his look. "I made sure of that."

He nodded and didn't know what to say. She was changing, was already changed, and he thought he knew why, but what could he say when he had nothing to show her to prove it? No proof at all except what Maitea had said, and he doubted she'd say anything to Scar or she'd have to face Morro over it.

"What did he want?" he asked instead.

"We were going over where we'd strike next." Scar, always so sure of herself, so confident in everything she did, now hesitated.

"Do we need to strike anywhere? We've food enough for weeks, wood, even coal from the mine we raided over the mountain. We've enough, more than enough to see us to the thaw and easier living."

She began her pacing, the familiar rhythm of it a soothing sound against troubling thoughts that chased each other around his head.

"Why stop now?" she said, one hand balled into a fist. "Why stop just when fear of us is at its peak? There are things out there for the taking, names for making, Petri. Do you want to stay in this pathetic valley the rest of your life when we could have so much more? *Be* so much more? We could be king and queen of this mountain."

Those words again, a dreadful repetition that shook Petri's bones. "You didn't used to want that. You used to want to be subtle and live. If we keep on, Bakar will have no choice but to send guards, as many as he thinks he needs, and he's no shortage. We've no hope against that."

"We have a magician, Pet. We have someone who can conjure the weather to his will, who can burn men with cold and bury them with snow. We've *every* hope." The pacing stopped, and she knelt by him, a hand on his trembling with some inner drive. Some need to make him see, perhaps. "We're heading down towards the plain tomorrow. Fat little villages ready to be picked, down towards Elona."

"No," he said. "That's too much. Too far. You're over-reaching." Something the old Scar would never have done – too canny for that, too concerned with keeping her crew safe.

The hand was removed, and Scar moved to sit in the chair opposite him, cold of a sudden where an instant ago she'd been warm.

"I thought you'd like that, raiding your old estates – show them all, take back a little of what was once yours. I thought we were in this together."

"We are." *Or we were. Now I'm looking just to survive the only way I know how.*

"Then be with me." She looked away, into the fire, her face as still and blank as he'd ever seen it. "Do you think of her?"

"What?"

"Kacha." She spat the word into the flames and turned to face him. "Do you think of her still? Do you hate her? Or miss her?"

The questions caught him off guard, so unexpected he flinched, and something died in Scar's eyes at that. What could he say? That sometimes, when he woke in a bleak dawn, for a moment he thought he was back in Reyes, that he was whole again and the warm woman beside him was Kass. That when he shifted and felt the rope of scars outlining one cheek, or opened his eyes to find he had only one . . . when he realised, it would leave him speechless for long minutes, fighting an aching longing for what had been and a consuming rage that it wasn't now. That sometimes he saw Kass's face on hers and was floored by the hatred that coursed in every vein. That sometimes he dreamed of her, saw her standing before him, always just out of reach, but when he tried to scald her with his raging words, hold himself up and say "This is who I am now, this is the man you threw away" his throat was choked with ice, and she would turn away without ever seeing him.

"I think of her sometimes," he said at last. "Not kindly."

"I'm doing this for you, for us, all of us. Bold enough and the guild will come. She will." Scar watched him with her usual intensity, which he now found hard to stand. "Morro said to me that you think of her, and not unkindly. That you're only here, only with me because no one else will have you. That you're using me, using all of us, and that if the guild comes – she comes – you'll turn on me like a beaten dog turned savage. I don't want to believe him."

"Then don't."

A faint smile, a rueful shake of her head. "Not so simple, Pet. It never is, is it?"

She sat quiet after that, her intensity banked like a neglected fire quenched in a doubt that made something turn over inside him. Maybe he could undo whatever Morro was doing to her. He owed her that. This time it was he who laid a gentle hand on an arm.

"I am here, with you, because I want to be. You showed

me who I could be when I doubted I could be anything. If they come – she comes – then I can show her what you made me and be glad of it. But I think of her less and less, and you more and more. But not the plains tomorrow, not for me. Not for anyone."

A sudden beatific smile that turned his insides again, but in a different way. And new thoughts to tangle into the old ones. Morro was changing things his way, slowly and subtly but changing them nonetheless. Time to be careful. But not right now, when that smile was turned on him, the warmth of it melting the edges of the ice inside.

Chapter Eighteen

Now

By the time it came to dinner, the syrup Vocho had sneaked into his drink had begun to wear off. With that came the feeling that he was sinking and a growing ache in his hip. Not to mention he now noticed the looks Kass kept giving him, like she knew he was up to something; it was just she couldn't figure out what it was.

Still, a decent dinner was something to look forward to, and his hip wasn't too bad now they were out of the cold. As he went down the stairs he was feeling pretty good.

Right up until halfway through dinner. Imanol sat at the head of the table, naturally, being the leader of the traders who ran the house as well as being stand-in mayor. To his right was Kass, and to her right Eder, both their faces sour like they were sucking on lemons. Vocho was placed to Imanol's left, which was perfect. Except to *his* left was Carrola, and . . . and . . . and he felt a bit odd about that. She hadn't been the same since they'd spoken in the stables: she'd done her best to keep away from him, had striven not to catch his eye since they'd left the inn, had been strikingly cold and aloof. Perhaps Eder had stuck his oar in again. Still, it was nothing Vocho the Great couldn't handle, and maybe he could catch her away from Eder later on and find out. He turned up the charm, gave her a beaming smile that brought not much more than narrowed eyes and settled in.

The dinner went well enough to start with, despite Carrola's muttered "Really?" or "Huh!" whenever he told one of his stories, which made him stumble once or twice. But all the rest, Imanol and the other traders, lapped it up, and Vocho was feeling warm and cosy inside when it all went wrong.

Of course it didn't feel wrong when Imanol stood up, dinged a knife on his glass to call for quiet and proposed a toast to "Kacha, Vocho and the guild, who will most surely rid of us the problem that has plagued us and the prelate's men these last months. May their reputation be not unearned, and may their swords be ever accurate!"

A hearty agreement from all the traders, the odd "Hear! Hear!" a harrumph and a sniff from Carrola and a look that might have curdled milk from Eder.

"So," Eder said with a polite chill in his voice when Imanol sat down with a raised glass in Kass's direction. "Can you tell us what happened? It would help us to determine where we should be looking perhaps, and what we might expect when we get there. And of course what help you are prepared to give us."

The table fell still; traders swapped nervous glances, and there was the general impression that if they'd been standing they would have shuffled their feet.

Imanol didn't appear to notice. He cleared his throat, took a sip of wine and started. Most of it was in the report. Bands of thieves had always been a problem, but more so after last year's battle. This band was led by a woman called Scar. Whenever her name was mentioned, Vocho noticed that everyone looked to Kass, as though she was going to pull this Scar woman out of her arse or something. Most of what Imanol said was so dull, Vocho wondered if anyone would notice him having a little doze, but a pointed look from Kass made him think again.

"We tried to send to Reyes," Imanol was saying, "tell them what was going on, but it was clear that all the men experienced in these conditions are already here. Inexperienced people he might send would be a liability. It was also clear that the Scar had many men and women who knew what they were about, especially after she picked up the Skull."

"And when was that?" Kass asked.

"Just at the tail end of the year, at least that's when we first heard about him. And it wasn't that he was more feared than her, it was what his arrival did to her. She was always quick to lose her temper, but while she thieved it was mostly non-violent. When he starting joining them on their raids, she got worse. Much, much worse. People started dying, many of them. And the Scar and the Skull got closer and bolder, and we called in help from the prelate's men at the outposts. It was clear that the Scar and Skull were coming our way. So the prelate's men decided on a trap. A poor decision, it turned out."

"And not theirs." Eder's voice came quietly into Imanol's words. Quietly but not without force. "Yours. Isn't that the truth of it? Because I've talked to those men today, and what they say doesn't tally with what you're saying."

"Well someone had to decide something, didn't they?" Imanol went from unctuous to snappishly blunt in a second. "And that lot of useless watchmen weren't about to – they have trouble deciding what to have for dinner. So all right, yes. Me and the mayor decided that if the Scar and the Skull were coming, then we'd be waiting. It might have even worked if those guards had been half the swordspeople that Kacha and Vocho here are – that any lowly guild member is – instead of half-asleep and clumsy with it. Our mayor would still be alive, not dragged away—"

"From under a cart, where he was hiding like some helpless blubbering child," Eder said.

"Dragged away and taken off with barely a hint of trouble from the prelate's so-called guards. Taken off and murdered by the people we'd asked them to protect us from. If they'd been half—"

"Yes, yes, half the men and women the duellists are." Eder twirled the wine in his glass, lips back from his teeth like a dog tormented to the point of ripping a throat out. "Or perhaps if they'd not been ordered into a fool of a scheme by two men who'd read too many tall stories about Vocho and his exploits."

"Hey. Now that—" Vocho began, but Eder wasn't stopping for him. He wasn't stopping for anyone.

"But did you read them all? How about the one where Vocho caused Licio to burn in his house and planned to assassinate the prelate? Or the one in which Vocho had to run to hide in Ikaras like a scared rabbit? Or Vocho the Great having to be saved by his sister? Or how he once tried to kill that sister because she persisted in beating him at sparring?"

"Oh, now hold on. Wait a minute – how did you know that?" Even through the dying dregs of the jollop, there was a worm of panic in Vocho's gut.

Eder smiled, but it wasn't a pleasant experience from Vocho's end. "Oh, I know a great many things. Like what it is you keep in your tunic you don't want your sister to know about, and that you think you might know who the Skull is."

Vocho turned to Carrola, who blushed and refused to meet his eye. He'd told her about the syrup, about Petri too, and only her. Told her his big secrets, and she'd turned round and told Eder. He felt oddly crushed, not because Kass would find out about the jollop – that would happen eventually and he had his arguments ready – but that it was Carrola who had told him.

"Vocho the Great is a sham," Eder was saying. "And you, Imanol, killed your mayor by reading too many stories about him and, worse, believing that half of them are true. Kacha here runs the guild, and she's barely able to concentrate on what's in front of her, leaving it all to her second, Vocho the liar, murderer and all-round bloody liability, and you think they'll help you? You think they *can*?"

Vocho and Kass both opened their mouths to speak at the same time but Imanol beat them to it. "Then what should we have done? Rolled over like beaten dogs? Died? Handed them everything we have and then starved for the rest of the winter?"

Eder's smile was small and tight with victory as he spared Kass a disparaging glance. "Listened to the prelate's men you had is what you should have done. Or handed over a portion in return for not being plundered, as several other places have."

"Hand over our *profits*?" Imanol gasped out, and a murmur of agreement ran around the table.

Eder shrugged. "Guild here or not, this is not a band to be trifled with. Yes, hand over your profits and listen to the men and women you have asked to protect you."

"Listen to the ones who let the bloody bandits roam

free in the first place?" Imanol's glare snapped off and a beaming smile took its place as he turned to Kass. "Now we have the guild, men and women specially trained for exactly this. No matter what you may think of them, Captain Eder, we here hold them in the highest regard. The *highest*. So, my dear Kacha, now that you've heard what happened, do you have any thoughts?"

Kass took a sideways look at Eder that promised a lot of words later, not many of them friendly, and turned on a sweet smile of her own. "Oh, plenty of thoughts now, Imanol. I will also talk to any guards who were here on the night. And can we borrow Sergeant Danel for a while longer? We'll need someone who knows his way around up here, and he's shown himself to be a resourceful man."

Imanol inclined his head, shot a dark look at Eder and returned to her. "Anything you wish is at your disposal. I'm sure the *guild* will have this cleared up in a flash. While the prelate's guards aren't ours to command, I'm sure we can spare one . . .?" He looked around the table, got a chorus of nods and murmurs of agreement. "Quite so. If it pleases you, I'll have the guards sent to you in the morning. They'll confirm what I said."

"I'm sure they will," Kass said smoothly. "But maybe they noticed something you couldn't have seen. You've been most helpful."

Imanol preened at that while Eder glowered, and soon enough the meal broke up. Vocho hurried after Carrola. He caught her by the main doors, and she wouldn't look at him.

He wanted to say something cutting, something rakish and sarcastic, but just about managed a pathetic "Why?"

She looked at him then all right, and he wished she

hadn't. It was like being sliced with a knife. "All those things they said, are they true?"

"Well, er, I . . . Yes. I mean sort of. I can explain—"

"That's what I thought. Goodnight." She hurried off at Eder's abrupt command.

Imanol came over, unctuous again, his former bluntness well hidden. "I'm sure that was just sour grapes talking," he said low enough that only Vocho could hear. "We all know you were cleared of any wrongdoing about the priest. Magicians! Could happen to any man." He shivered theatrically. "And the rest . . . well, jealousy is a terrible thing, isn't it?"

"Certainly is," Kass interjected before Vocho could say anything. "Could I just steal my brother for a few moments?"

Imanol subsided, and Kass and Vocho left.

"Well that was interesting, don't you think?" she said.

"What, my character being assassinated?" He stared after Carrola, but she didn't look his way.

"He didn't say anything that wasn't true," Kass said. "Except maybe that bit about what you're hiding from me and how you suspect you know who the Skull is?"

He'd hoped she'd missed that. "Kass, when have I ever hidden anything from you? You're my sister."

"Don't give me that tripe. All the time, is the answer, and you know it. Besides, your eye is twitching."

God's bloody cogs and gears. He'd wished for his sister back, properly, but he was starting to regret that now. "Fine. I've been trying to think who the Skull is, because we probably know him, but I don't *know* any more than you do." Though if half his suspicions proved to be correct, making sure he was a good distance from Kass when she found out would be a grand plan. Or maybe he could somehow persuade her not to go up the mountain . . . No, that was never going to happen. He was starting to wish he'd left her mooning about up on the guild walls, because all the masters of the guild berating him at once would be nothing compared to the Skull being Petri and Kass finding out. *Dear Clockwork God, please don't let it be Petri, OK? For her sake. Honest.* It wasn't Petri, it couldn't be. Pathetic Petri would rather die than do half what the Skull was supposed to be doing.

"And the surgeon gave me something for the pain in my hip," he carried on. Which wasn't actually a lie, because she had. It just wasn't what he was hiding in his tunic.

"And your hip is worse than you let on. Oh, don't look at me like that − I'm not blind."

"It's fine. *I'm* fine. Up to beating your sorry arse at sparring in fact, now that you seem back to your normal annoying self. The cold bothers it is all."

She didn't look like she believed a word of any of it but said no more.

Vocho hopped from one foot to the other outside a midnight door, wondering what he had to be so nervous about. All right, he'd embellished the truth a bit and omitted several other truths, but when didn't he? It had never bothered him before, which didn't really help with the fact it was bothering him now.

He knocked on the door before he could talk himself out of it and regretted it half a dozen times before the door opened. One of Eder's troop peered out, looked him up and down with a barely hidden sneer and said, "What?"

Vocho had a bizarre urge to ask if Carrola wanted to come and play but restrained himself. "Is Sergeant Carrola there?"

She raised a cool eyebrow. "Yes."

A short silence which almost undid Vocho. "Well, can I see her then?"

"I can ask, I suppose." She turned away as though doing Vocho a huge favour she expected to be paid back double, and he got a peek into the large room that was serving as the dorm for the women in the troop. Bits of uniform lay strewn everywhere, furs and tunics and swords and tabards, along with various little contraptions that held him spellbound as he wondered what they were, or were for. Someone shut the door in his face as he wondered, saying, "I don't want an audience while I get undressed, thank you!" He hesitated, unsure of himself for perhaps the first time ever, but the door opened again half a minute later and Carrola shut it behind her.

"What the hells do you want?" she said. "Are you trying to get me demoted or something?"

"No, I just wanted to—"

"I don't care! Go on, bugger off. I'm in enough trouble with Eder as it is, and why in the world would I want to talk to someone who's done half those things? And you even admit they're true!"

"Well, sort of."

"How do you 'sort of' try to kill your own sister? Or 'sort of' burn the old king in his own house? If I listen hard enough, what other things are going to pop up, hmm? What other shitwittery have you committed? No, no, I don't want to know. It'd be lies anyway, wouldn't it? Or your version would be. I thought you were funny and a bit silly, half as dashing and possibly about a tenth as brave as you tell everyone, which is still fairly dashing and brave. Now I find out you're just a bastard like all the rest. I'm in trouble up to my ears with my captain for talking to you, and I'll likely get thrown out of the guards if he catches me doing it again. Eder's fit to bloody split by the way. If he goes off half-cocked, it'll be because of you, and we'll be the ones getting it in the neck, so thanks for that. Now bugger off. I've got the middle watch shift and I need some sleep first."

With that the door was slammed in his face so hard the vibrations shuddered his feet. He'd come intending, in a most un-Vocho-like way, to be truthful for once. Properly truthful. Now he recalled why he didn't usually bother. He stared at the door for a while, like that would help, until another door behind him opened and Cospel appeared, a foaming mug in one hand and a sandwich thick with beef in the other.

It was a relief to be able to say "How in hells do you do that every time?"

Cospel looked at what his hands were filled with and grinned. "Natural talent. You look like someone just shoved a poker somewhere intimate."

"That is exactly how it feels."

Cospel sniggered but then took another look at Vocho, and a hint of sympathy crept into his voice. "I got a flask too, don't ask where from. It'll put hairs on your chest. Come on."

Vocho was too deflated to debate it, so followed Cospel down stairs and around corners until he was thoroughly lost. Finally Cospel opened a door into what was little more than a cupboard with a bed in it.

"This is the room they gave you?"

"Aye, well, I've slept in worse. It's got a bed and it hasn't got rats." He put his mug and sandwich on the windowsill and rummaged around in his pack, which lay by the end of the bed. "Got a few things to tell you anyways, so we might as well enjoy it. Not like I paid for this after all."

With the flourish of a conjurer pulling a fake bouquet of flowers out of a hat, he produced a bottle. "Your best rum, this is. I thought we might be wanting some against the cold."

"*My* best rum? Can I ask why it's already half empty?"

Cospel shrugged. "Like I say, against the cold. You want some or not?"

Vocho took a swig and sat down on the bed, handing the bottle to Cospel, who took a generous gulp of his own.

"That Eder is bonkers, by the sounds of it," Cospel ventured, looking his sandwich over like he was inspecting it for soundness. "I been speaking to some of his troop."

"Oh, *you* can then? It seems I'm cause for getting demoted if they talk to me."

"Yeah, well, you have that effect on people. Me though – just your bloke, aren't I? A servant. Huh. Men like Eder don't even see me, never mind worry about who I'm talking to. Useful, that is. Captain Eder is slowly undoing the screws that hold his head on, if you ask me. Got a right bunch of ants in his pants about you and Kass, I know that. More than he's let on to you two. Standing orders: anyone caught talking to you or her gets it. He's given 'em all a good talking-to about, what were it? Oh, yes, fraternising. None of that there fraternising with any guild members. If the guards is good enough for him, then it's good enough for them, and all that bollocks, and they are to make double sure everything they do is to regulation and top notch, so as not to let the guild show them up. Get the idea he's got a little plan up his sleeve too."

"What sort of plan?"

"That I do not yet know, but I will. I also get the idea
. . ." Here he broke off for a solid swig of rum, while
considering Vocho out of the side of his eyes. "Likes that
Carrola, he does. Quite a bit."

"Yes? And?" What was he supposed to say to that? He
didn't even know how he felt about it, or why he should
feel anything. If he had known, he wouldn't have told
Cospel anyway.

Cospel snorted and shook a disbelieving head. "Oh,
nothing. Nothing at all. From the sounds of it, she liked
him too, in a way. Until that last trip up here, as it happens,
and the avalanche. Turns out he tried it on; she told him
she didn't like him *that* way, she felt sorry for him and
that, and they had a massive row what half the troop heard.
Since then they've been all jumpy like scalded cats, but
he was trying to talk her round. And of course then you
come along being your usual grandstanding self, and then
you show him up bad over that wolf business on top, and
well. Just adds to his previous dislike of the guild, and
with the temper you've put him in you've both made him
hell to serve, Carrola in particular getting it in the neck
about talking to you."

"I don't see—"

"Oh don't give me that. You been sniffing around her
since we started, and he knows it and don't like it, or
you."

"I have not been sniffing! I have been engaging with
my fellow travellers."

A knowing grin scrunched Cospel's pliable face. "You
don't normally look like a sick sheep when engaging with
your fellow travellers. Anyway, might be why he was
sniffing back, at Kass, to make Carrola jealous. Got short
shrift there too, I reckon. I'm surprised he can still walk

properly. Didn't work making Carrola jealous, obviously, and Kass knocking him back probably put his nose all out of joint, so now he's started throwing his weight around. And also now he *really* hates the guild, even worse than he did before."

"Yes, well." Determined to steer the conversation as far away from Carrola as possible, Vocho said, "And do we know why he hated the guild to start with?"

"Red Brook, something to do with that – all I or anyone else seems to know. Shattered him pretty bad, that did, and it's only in the last couple of months he's been back on duty and got this troop. Left him very twitchy by all accounts."

"I could tell that by myself."

"Yeah, well you be careful. He's bandying about threats, empty or otherwise, and all sorts. He's got it in for you, make no mistake. Kass too, though I think that's more complicated."

"I gathered. Cospel . . ." Vocho hesitated, which made twice in one day, and that was unheard of. He thought of Carrola and her grey eyes and the way she'd spat her words at him before slamming the door. He thought about the jollop hidden in his tunic and Petri's ravaged face, Kass waking up and the Skull and all the lies he'd told and was still telling. What telling even part of the truth had got him and what telling the whole truth now would unleash. "Never mind. Hand over that rum, will you?"

Chapter Nineteen

"So the prelate has sent extra men?" Scar grinned at the news, twisting her scar in new directions. "Excellent."

Petri sat at the back of the tiny hut, wreathed in darkness, watching and wondering.

Morro cracked a smile. "Exactly what you wanted, yes. We – you – can show them they were wrong to write off all these men and women."

Scar's grin faltered as though she suddenly wasn't so sure, but it soon came back.

Only this wasn't what Scar had hoped for once. Now, with Morro clearing the way, making sure no one could track them, things had changed, and so had she. She was worse this last month, seeing obstacles everywhere, questioning Petri constantly about Kass, about his loyalty. Sometimes he thought she was sinking into herself, spiralling inwards at an ever-increasing rate. The rest too. Kepa had begun to mutter to himself; others were acting strangely, and where Petri had been at least friendly with some, and more so with Kepa, now they spoke to him less and less, yet whispered in corners just on the edges of his hearing.

No matter how he tried, Petri could never catch Morro using magic on any of them. He never took off his gloves; the smell of cooking blood never tainted the air of the valley except when he used it to melt snow. Just his voice, telling Scar this was what she wanted, what she'd always wanted.

"Just what we wanted. Isn't it?" Scar said, this time to Petri.

"Yes." What else to say when she was so excited, so fired up? When Morro sat and smiled at Petri like he was imagining how cutting Petri's throat would feel.

"God's cogs, Pet, you could sound more enthusiastic." Scar waved away her messenger and came to crouch next to him, put a gentle scarred hand on his arm.

Careful, that's what he had to be. Strong or not, careful was the way to go. And did it matter, if he got what he wanted? He glanced behind Morro to where Maitea stood, wreathed in the shadows that seemed to follow her every-where. Like her father, Petri thought suddenly, shadowed and unexplained, waiting for the right time. She was holding herself with careful patience until she got whatever it was she wanted. A timely reminder to do the same.

"What next?" he said. "Where next?"

"That's better. Well, I think we need to deal with this new batch of prelate's men, don't you? Show him he made the wrong choice about you."

The wrong choice – yes. He could feel it all bubbling up now behind what was left of his face. The rails and gears behind the world didn't rule him; he was going to make his own fate. He was going to be, finally, free – that had been his thought when she'd begun this. He could still do it.

He looked at Morro, at the smug little smile as he watched

the two of them. Petri needed to know if what Maitea had told him about Morro was true. Until then he needed no suspicion from either of them. He had to play his new part as well as he could, be canny with it. The disturbing bit was, part of him wanted what Scar now did, wanted to show every last fucking one of them. Maybe he could use Morro until that was done.

"We have to do this now," she said, perhaps sensing his reticence. "In winter, with Morro helping us, we have a chance. If we can beat them now, maybe the prelate will let us be for a time. Until the thaw, which will come when Morro lets it come. Or at least until the towns agree to treat with us, pay us tribute. Food and wood and whatever we need. If we want them to do that, then we need to show them they have no choice, no protection. Not even from the prelate."

"Which way will they come?" Petri asked her eventually, his hand on hers now, a thumb gently along the skin that recalled another hand, other days, other nights, long ago and when he was a different person.

"Up the Razor Gorge, I expect."

"Then let's be ready for them. Let's show them who we are."

Chapter Twenty

Kass looked up at a fall of snow so thick she could barely see the other side of the square and wondered if perhaps a day or two would make any difference. Eder would argue it, of course, but she was in charge of this mission. A sideways glance at Vocho as he stood next to her, pretending that his hip wasn't bothering him at all.

He paced jerkily up and down, seeming purposeful, but if you looked there was a care to that stride, a swing of the good leg to disguise the hitch in the bad. She was about to say the weather would hold them here until it cleared, as much for him as anything else, when Danel bowled up, out of breath and red faced behind the fringe of fur that almost obscured him.

"Is this snow going to last?" she asked. Then, because she caught a glimpse of what looked like panic, "What is it?"

"Eder, miss. I *told* him, I did, last night I told him the weather was unpredictable and we probably wouldn't be going anywhere for a day or so. But he went anyway. Him and all his troop."

"Gone? Where? When?"

"Before first light, miss. And up the mountain, where else? Skull country, No Man's Land, whatever you want to call it. Bad country, that's what it is, even with no Skull. They left before the snow started. Any mountain man could have told him how the weather was going to close in, but he didn't *take* no mountain man, or none of us is missing."

Kass swore viciously under her breath.

Vocho strode over, all false bluster and pretence. "Why would he do that?"

"Why do you think, Voch? Because he's got an axe to grind against the guild. He wants to prove, to us and everyone else, that he doesn't need the guild. Come on."

Danel showed them the rapidly filling tracks by the gate.

"It's going to be a proper blow, and no mistake," he said. "Looked like it was warming up too, that maybe we'd seen the back of this winter barring a flurry or two. But mountains always like to have the last laugh. You can't trust them. *He* wouldn't know that. Told one of my men that we was worrying over nothing, being too cautious; it'd blow out like the last one. I could have told him not to trust to that, or lowlander thinking, not up here, miss, but there you are. He's gone, and him and all his troop are up on the mountain in that, and probably getting lost with it."

Well, fuck. Bakar had been most insistent about everyone coming back from this little expedition, and her responsibility to his men and women as well. "What about their gear?"

"Well, it'd do if it were thaw or this was just a little flurry, but for this? He's only got what they brought with them, lowlander stuff like yours and them poncy little furs from the inn. The traders offered to lend them better gear, but he said no."

"Lend?"

"Well, more like rent, I expect." Danel grinned nervously. "Get money out of snow itself, they could. But Eder turned them down. Not authorised to spend that kind of money or something."

"Stupid bastard," Kass said. Eder, driven by pride, even if it was all tangled up. Trying to be the good man, do his duty, but it twisted in on itself. She looked at the tracks, which by now were the faintest hint of depressions in the pristine expanse of snow, and up at the mountain behind the curtain of the weather. It seemed to fill her whole vision. Eder was out there, and pride wouldn't keep him and his troop warm, or alive. She shut her eyes against a memory that flashed up. She hadn't been able to save Petri because she'd hesitated, been too slow. No making that mistake twice. Eder wasn't him, didn't own the voice in her memories, but she'd failed to save Petri. She wasn't going to fail again.

"Well then," she said. "Looks like we're going whether we like it or not."

"Are we?" Vocho said with a hint of desperation. "I mean if Danel says the weather's too harsh . . ."

"Then they'll freeze to death if we don't find them and bring them back."

A long drawn-out sigh from her brother. "The good thing, huh?"

"Yes, the good thing. I thought that was what this was all about, you and Bakar making me be me again and thinking you were being so secret about it? Well, this is part of that − me being me."

"I knew there was something I didn't miss about you, and now I recall what it was."

"Get your fur knickers on, Voch. You're going to need them."

Vocho struggled into the thicker furs that Imanol had loaned to them at a "reasonable" rate. Solid wolf furs in good condition and not smelling of dead meat, which was a vast improvement. Better than the gear they had anyway, but so they should be for the price. At least, Danel had promised him, they were windproof, near as anything could be. They also had handy pockets. A quick nip to steady his shaky hands while hiding in the shadow of his horse and he was ready.

A last plea for sanity. "Kass, are you sure—"

"Yes" was all she said in the tone of voice that meant she was going whether he liked it or not. She gave some last-minute instructions to the couple of fellow guildsmen they were leaving in Kastroa. Vocho wished he could be one of them – they were grinning like fools because naturally they saw a future that held warm fires and possibly a few light games of chance – for wagers of course – while Vocho's future appeared to involve freezing his cogs off on a sodding mountain rescuing someone who didn't want rescuing because of his stupid pride.

"As soon as the snow clears," Kass said, "one of you is to go down to the nearest outpost, get a message sent on to Bakar, and I want my position on his fool of a captain made quite clear."

"I don't see why they get to be left behind, Kass."

"Because there's no point risking all of us out in that, and if we need to get a message to Bakar I wouldn't trust it to that snake Imanol. We take Danel because he knows his way about, and once we find Eder, maybe he can stop us all freezing to death. You and I and Cospel are going because I won't ask anyone to do something I won't do myself." She wouldn't catch his eye on that last point, but he knew he wouldn't stay if she was going. "The rest can stay here – any more people won't help and might hinder." She turned back to the guildsmen. "If we aren't back in three days, a message to Bakar, and you get some guides and come looking with as many people as you can, OK? Kick Imanol's arse until he agrees to help because if anything goes wrong I don't want to be stranded with no one to watch our backs."

Snow fell in great feathered clumps as they left the stables, sticking to Vocho's face, his horse's mane, everywhere it could get. The wind had picked up since they'd looked at the tracks by the north gate and now it howled and tore at his wolfskin cloak, but Danel was right: the furs were very nearly windproof. Which didn't stop Vocho's face going numb.

The snow slackened soon enough, but the storm didn't, whipping up snow and ice and driving it at them with ever-increasing force. It was bad enough in the good furs – the Clockwork God knew how bad it must be for Eder and his crew. Maybe Kass was right. Vocho thought about Carrola freezing to death out here in not much more than woollens and thin furs that stank of old meat. The good thing. Hey, he could save Carrola and be a hero, right, just as Kass could save Eder? Maybe then Carrola would speak to him again; he could explain, and she'd laugh at one of his stories. Vocho the Great Saves Guards with Stupid Captain from Freezing to Death. That thought cheered him immensely.

The tracks were, to Vocho's eyes, invisible, but Danel

said he could follow them, though he made them stop twice while he dismounted and cast about for signs. They came to a narrow winding valley that protected them from the worst of the wind, and the tracks were still clear – to Danel anyway.

"Straight on to Skull country," Cospel said gloomily.

By the afternoon they were sure they were gaining on Eder, but the weather began to turn again.

"I thought you said—" Kass eyed the lowering clouds.

"I also said the mountains like a laugh," Danel replied. "You can't never be sure what they'll do, which is why you got to be prepared. That's what Eder didn't understand."

"Wonderful," Cospel muttered in the background. "Sounds like the story of my life, that. Having to be prepared for all manner of shit."

"Ah, a mountain man?"

"No, I just work for these two."

"I resent that!" Vocho said.

"No, you resemble it." Kass nudged her horse closer. "What now, Danel?"

"Well if we were sensible, we'd find somewhere out of the wind to camp until it blows over."

Kass gave Vocho a look he knew well enough just as the snow started again, great lazy flakes that flipped and danced in the wind. "Are we being sensible?"

He thought about Carrola, and the good thing, and how much jollop he had left, and Kass needing to prove something to herself. "I doubt it. We aren't usually."

"See?" Cospel said. "See what I have to put up with?"

They stopped twice more along the way, once to rest the horses and check their feet and leg wrappings – ice had formed on the snow crust and with every step they risked a cut. Danel had made sure they all had leg wrappings before they started, but they were in danger of working loose. They rewrapped them and gave the horses each a share of the grain they carried. While Kass was busy trying not to get kicked in the head, Vocho managed a slug of the jollop. It kept him warmer than any fur could, and made the rest of the slog, through driving snow and a worsening wind, possible to bear.

As light started to grow dim in the short day, they came to a narrowing of the way with steep upward slopes on either side. As they passed into the defile, the wind dropped abruptly, as though someone had turned it off. The snow that had been whizzing past their heads and into their faces and every bloody cranny it could find dropped lazily before it too stopped, leaving behind an unnatural stillness, a silence that seemed to echo in his head. Vocho was reminded all too forcibly of the rumours about magicians and weather.

The first hint of anything untoward was a dark splotch in the snow ahead surrounded by a great billowing depression as though someone had delighted in kicking the snow about. When they got closer, the dark splotch was red, the depression horse-made – in at least two places hoof marks were clearly visible.

No one said anything, but they all pushed their by-now-tired horses on. Around a shallow bend, and a dead horse lay in a patch of red snow, darkly fletched arrows sticking out from neck and rump. Their own horses grew skittish, and Kass's briefly threatened to have her off.

Danel swore under his breath and looked up. Kass and Vocho did the same. The walls of the defile narrowed above them, almost met in places, leaving handy gaps to shoot a gun or bow through.

"Just about as perfect a place for an ambush as you could wish for," Kass said.

"Then let's not go any further, because it only gets more so." Vocho nodded to where the trail narrowed to a track that would only take one horse at a time. The defile ended, and the cliff on one side disappeared, becoming a drop that descended with dizzying swiftness far below them. The snow on the trail was all churned into spikes, and one or two arrows and crossbow bolts stuck out like spines on a hedgehog.

"Any way up there from here?" Kass asked Danel, pointing to the top of the cliff.

"Not easily, miss. If we go back about five miles, perhaps. Or you can get to it from higher up on the trail, I suppose. If you could climb like a goat there might be a way."

Kass muttered about stupid bloody captains having stupid bloody ideas. "What in hell did he think he was going to achieve?"

"Catching the Skull without our help, I expect. Doesn't look like it's turned out too well." Vocho had just spotted what was up at the next corner – a dark bundle half covered by snow with more arrows sticking out of it. Not big enough to be a horse. A sudden sweat under his furs, and he didn't think about ambush or narrowing tracks with sudden drops. He didn't think about anything except wanting, needing, to know who that was up there.

His horse shied as he gave it an unexpected kick, but it shifted, picking its way along the slippery track. Kass called out from behind, telling him another person being stupid wouldn't help, but he ignored her.

Besides, "There's no one up there now," he called back over his shoulder. No shadows at the edge above, no telltale clumps of snow falling as men moved around. If anyone was there, they'd have shot as soon as Vocho and the rest had turned the corner, not waited for them to stand around and look at a dead horse.

He half climbed, half fell off his horse, staggered in knee-deep snow and knelt awkwardly by the bundle. Blood soaked the snow underneath it, but he could see movement – whoever it was they were still breathing.

His hand shook as he reached out to brush the wind-blown snow from the face, and not from the cold. Dark hair, like hers, cropped short, like hers. But – the snow fell away – not hers. Relief made him bark out a laugh, until the woman's eyes fluttered open at the sound. One of Eder's people; he recognised her even if he couldn't recall the woman's name.

"I . . ." he began, wanting to apologise for laughing, but the eyes shut, the chest stopped moving with a final hiss of breath. "Shit."

He looked up, swiping snow from his eyes, and looked around the corner, where the narrow path opened up into a small plateau edged still with that dizzying drop. A glance was all it took, then he was on his feet, hand reaching for his sword, all thoughts of dead women or aching hips forgotten.

Petri grinned under the mask that hid the good side of his face, parried a poor thrust and returned the favour with more accuracy.

Blood splattered the snow all over the small plateau where they'd herded the prelate's guards. No room for them to manoeuvre, no way back that wasn't covered by archers and crossbowmen, no way forward except through Petri and a dozen others, and a precipitous drop to one side if they were careless.

Morro had driven them into the defile with vicious wind

and snow. The captain had been cautious where the trail narrowed, but not cautious enough. Arrows had taken the captain's scout; a flurry of crossbow bolts had driven the rest of them on, taken horses from under them and left them floundering in the snow ready for Petri and the rest to finish off.

Scar whirled across the snow, face fixed in a rigid grin as she fought. Kepa threw a man over the side and looked on as he bounced down the drop, and Petri watched, and wondered who it was that was watching.

They had them now, this band of poorly prepared men and women. They'd leave one or two alive, to tell the tale and spread the fear even further, back to Reyes and the prelate, but not one of Scar's crew had a qualm – these guards had been sent to kill them. Petri had no illusions about that and no hesitation in returning the intent.

Four of the guards stood, backs to the cliff that bounded one side of the plateau, fending off anyone who tried for them. Four people, including the captain. Scar's crew stepped back and let Petri through.

"God's cogs," he heard the captain mutter when he caught sight of Petri's face.

"The Clockwork God has nothing to do with it," he snapped back. "Weapons down."

The captain grimaced at that but looked about and saw the hopelessness of it. "Do it." He flung his sword into the snow with a look of twisted disgust, as though he might try to do something stupid anyway.

Three more dropped. The woman hurled something at Petri, at his blind side, but Scar knocked it away and smacked the woman in the face for her trouble, told her she'd get the sword next time.

A scream echoed off the mountain behind him, and Petri

whipped round. They'd missed one, must have, because a man was slicing through Scar's crew from behind with alarming ease. Two men had fallen dead even before Petri had turned, and as he did a third man pitched screaming over the edge from a well timed boot to the gut.

Petri couldn't see the man's face behind the frost-crusted furs, but he didn't need to. The preening style, the over-elaborate flourishes, even the style of footwork. His face flashed hot and then cold, and an icy hand gripped his stomach. Not just a prelate's guard. Vocho. And where there was Vocho, there'd be Kass, maybe more guildsmen too. Scar's crew might be improving but they had no chance against the guild.

And there Kass was, no mistaking her, not ever. He found his hand had slackened its grip on his sword, found he'd taken half a step towards her before he even thought about it. Scar's voice brought him up short, made him remember.

He'd wanted to show Kass, worst of all. Show her who he really was, that he wasn't weak, never weak. Wanted to show her too how little he cared that she'd abandoned him, that he could be someone without her in his life. Kepa went for her, but Petri's growl stopped him, stopped Morro too, who had drawn out a slip of paper and a brush and was preparing who knew what.

"No," Petri said. "Not this one." Morro and Kepa both cocked a look at Scar, who nodded, and they stood back.

Vocho headed Petri's way, but his eyes were on the woman guard, distracted. Petri was never going to have a better chance at the grandstanding little prick and dived forward, sword out. Killing Vocho the Great would be a fitting way to gain a name and a grand message to send to Bakar, along with Vocho's head perhaps. A show of strength to Morro too, who hovered at his back like a malignant cloud.

Vocho's sword came up in the nick of time, but he staggered, and now Petri could see he was favouring one leg. Petri drove forward again, kept Vocho with his weight all on the back leg, the bad one. But that was never going to be enough for Petri to beat him, not left-handed. Vocho ducked away from the thrust, and then they were in the thick of it, just the two of them. Petri kept up the pressure on the leg, but Vocho used every trick he could against Petri's blind side, against the inexperience of his left hand. Played with him because even with a halt leg he should have been able to beat Petri. But after every flashy thrust or lightning-quick parry, his eyes would dart sideways to the guards and back again, as though making sure they were watching.

It was unlike Vocho, who usually just assumed everyone would be watching him, and left him open, but even so Petri wasn't going to beat him, not this time, not with his off hand. Not unless he did something drastic.

He stood back, raised his sword in the guild way of asking for a halt. Vocho cocked his head but did likewise, though he kept himself ready for whatever trick Petri might pull.

Petri peeled off the mask that covered the good side of his face, and the way Vocho gaped and sagged backwards was worth almost everything. Almost. The look on Kass's face as she moved up behind her brother was better, and satisfyingly sweet. She dropped the stiletto from her off hand, raising her fingers to her horror-struck mouth.

"Hello, Kass," he said. "It seems I'm not as dead as you thought."

Kass couldn't seem to think straight. A man with one side of Petri's face, with his voice, stood in front of her, and she couldn't think past the thundering in her ears. Petri was dead, hadn't Vocho told her . . .

Vocho had told her. A man for whom lying was as natural as breathing. But even Vocho wouldn't lie about . . . would he? Her head whirled to keep up, as everything she thought she knew was suddenly like quicksand under her feet. But it didn't matter because Petri was here and alive and she hadn't failed. She started towards him, not knowing what she'd do when she got there but with a bubble of laughter in her throat.

A woman spoke, not a voice she recognised, and then someone barrelled into her, a blade flashed in front of her face, and they were rolling in the snow. Kass flailed for her dropped stiletto but all she found was snow.

"Leave him alone," a woman's voice snarled into her ear. "Haven't you made him suffer enough? He's mine now."

Kass managed to heave herself over, threw the other woman off to sprawl in the snow. Now Kass could see the scar that ripped over her face, puckered and twisted at one end like frayed rope, and knew her for who she was.

No time to get the stiletto from where she saw it in the snow, but time enough to get her own sword out before Scar scrambled to her feet. Someone shouted off to one side, a voice she recognised this time, but she didn't take the time to listen to what it was they said. Scar was on her in a flash, the puckered flesh twisting even further with a grimace.

No finesse to her, no guile, just all-out brute force and anger so that Kass could barely keep her feet for the rain of blows she had to parry. A glimpse of movement before something, someone, crashed into the pair of them and sent Kass tumbling, end over end, over the edge of the path and down into the chasm on the other side.

*   *   *

Vocho was halfway to Kass when the well timed swipe of a sword in front of his face brought him up short, and he was confronted with the half-dead half-alive face of Petri bloody Egimont. Of course, it *had* to be, didn't it? Just Vocho's luck. Couldn't have been any of the other possibilities, oh no, just the one that would earn him a hole in his gut from his sister when she got hold of him.

Petri's one eye gleamed deep in a shadowed socket, a taunting smile across ruined lips, and for the first time Vocho considered that maybe Petri might be a dangerous man to cross.

He might have discovered right then whether that was true if Eder hadn't chosen that moment to let out a wild yell, punch out the man holding him and dive towards where Kass was trying her best to parry what looked like a windmill made of swords. Vocho had time to shout a word of warning – to Eder, not Kass, because she'd skin him alive if he interfered – but not soon enough.

Eder slammed into Scar just as she turned and knocked her flying before he barrelled past and on into Kass, his speed and weight carrying the two of them over the edge.

A long moment of silence followed. Vocho didn't know about anyone else, but he was frozen in place. The cold had finally, irrevocably seeped into his bones and seized him up, or so it seemed. Then everyone started moving. A big bald-headed man ran to the edge and peered over. Scar got to her feet, brushing snow from her legs and looking like she wanted to murder someone. A couple of others decided to take things out on their prisoners. More turned to Petri, their looks questioning.

Only one man looked anything like composed, and the way he looked at Petri made even Vocho's shoulders twitch. Worse when he saw the man hastily drag on gloves, and the smell of cooking blood wafted over. Magicians. Vocho had hoped to live his life without ever meeting one again, and he couldn't see Petri working with one willingly either. Yet here one was, smug as a well fed cat and looking at Petri like he was some kind of experiment.

"Kepa?" Petri called to the bald man over by the chasm. His voice sounded odd to Vocho, but everything was odd – his face was numb and not from cold, his hands were shaking and every muscle felt made of water. It was all he could do to stand up and hold on to his lunch.

"Not sure yet," came the muffled reply as the bald man lay down and stretched out over the edge.

Others went to look, or called out "helpful" comments.

"They ain't moving," the bald giant called out eventually, and the bottom dropped out of Vocho's world. Only the fact that Petri was there stopped him from falling down – he wouldn't give the bastard the satisfaction. Vocho groped around blindly, not knowing what for, not caring, only wanting something to do with his hands, something to hang on to and stop him being pulled away by the black hole inside him.

His sword, he still had his sword, always dependable, never let him down. He held on to it with everything he had and thought about running Petri through, making him as dead as he was supposed to be. If Kass was gone, there was nothing to stop him, no explanations required, no need to feel guilty because he'd killed the one thing she'd loved. He blinked back to the snowy mountain, to the sight of Petri's ruined face and the magician watching them both, hand ready on a redly dripping brush. Half a dozen men and women with swords drawn, more than one with a gun, and him with a gimped leg. Not now then. Bide his time, yes, make it worth all the more.

Out of the corner of his eye he spotted Cospel and Danel lurking almost out of sight. Cospel waggled his eyebrows in a way that Vocho took to mean, "Maybe time to go?"

He'd have been right, except for the prick of a sword at the back of Vocho's neck, the low growl in his ear from Petri that raised every hair on his nape and the way that half a dozen men were eyeing him with something like gleeful anticipation.

"Weapon down, please," Petri said in that cultured drawl that annoyed Vocho no end. "Or you can follow your lovely sister over that cliff. It won't be a bother. Kepa is more than capable of throwing you a good distance. In fact, I'd rather enjoy that."

Kass came back to the here and now and wondered what in hell she was lying on, and why. A drawn-out groan gave her a clue to the first.

There was snow everywhere – in front of her, above, in her eyes, mouth, ears. There should be snow under her too, but if so it was very lumpy. She sat up gingerly against the sudden throb in her head that made the snow zigzag in front of her eyes. Whatever she was on, it was very lumpy indeed, and something sharp was digging into her.

The groan again, somewhat indistinct but definitely from underneath. She rolled away from – off – whatever was sticking in her and checked herself over. Apart from a head that felt like it was fit to burst and an accompanying dizziness that made angles look funny, she thought she'd got away with only a multitude of bruises. Which meant she'd got off pretty lightly, considering. She looked up again, wincing at the throb in her neck and head, and felt dizzy all over again at how far she'd fallen. And how far the sun had moved since then, gone from the small wedge of sky she could make out in the gloom.

What the hell had happened to send her over the edge? Had Scar come too? That thought – that Scar might well be down here – made her hand go to her sword, only to find an empty scabbard. It had been in her hand when she fell but wasn't now. It had been in her hand, and she'd been fighting Scar, and then something had barrelled into her, and then all she recalled was an empty space underneath her, snow all around falling with her.

Another groan caught her attention more sharply this time, because maybe she wasn't the only one to have fallen down here and lived.

The heap of snow and clothes she'd just rolled off – what she'd landed on, which had probably saved her from broken bones or worse – groaned again and shifted. Kass cast about and saw her sword, hilt jutting from a great jumbled pile of snow. She felt a lot braver with it than without.

On closer inspection, the heap appeared to be a small pile of bodies liberally strewn with snow. Only one was moving, the one on top – she wasn't the only one to have had her fall broken, it seemed. At least one of the others had a broken neck, if the way its head flopped at an unnatural angle was anything to go by.

The groaner moved, a shifting veil of snow slid off its face, and Kass let out a breath she wasn't aware she'd been holding. Not Scar – at least this particular body wasn't her. Eder wiped snow from his mouth, tried to sit up and fell back onto his elbows with a hiss of pain.

Kass moved towards him, still keeping a weather eye out for Scar. She tried to figure out the tangle of arms and legs that poked out of the snow at odd angles. A foot here, a knee there at a right angle to it, and it almost made her eyes cross when she realised they belonged to the same leg.

"Who's there?" Eder whispered, his eyes still unfocused. She must have caught him a hell of a whack when she landed on him – with her own head, it felt like.

She looked around again, watching for any movement that would give away Scar, and crept towards him.

"It's Kass. Lie still. You've had a crack to the head, and I think your leg's broken."

"I think so too." Eder tried again to push himself upright and failed as dismally as before.

"Eder, I don't know where Scar is."

He squinted at her, grimaced at the movement and shut his eyes. "I . . . I'm not sure if she came down with us. Someone appears to be under me? That feels very much like an elbow in my kidneys."

It was indeed an elbow, but not Scar's. "He's probably why we aren't both dead. But I can't see her, under you or anywhere else. Or any tracks or anything."

She looked back up. The drop was almost sheer apart from a couple of outcrops near the top which were shedding clumps of snow that burst at the bottom like feathery bombs. If Kass squinted, she could perhaps see a face far above against the fading light. Maybe. Then again maybe it was a bird. And Voch was up there, him and Cospel and Danel on their own against Scar and Petri and all their crew. Voch might very well be dead already. She looked away from the lip and tried to concentrate on here, now. Vocho would be fine. He always was. Always. He'd go on being fine if she told herself enough. Anything else didn't bear thinking about, so she didn't. Not yet. Later, in the dark, those thoughts would chase each other around her skull, but not now.

Eder made it to sitting on the third try, though the effort left him white and shaking. "Well that takes care of one problem, I hope. She'd didn't fall with us, or not all the way."

"Speaking of which, what in hell did you think you were doing?" Kass moved over to take a closer look at the leg and wished she hadn't. So did Eder, who shut his eyes and swallowed hard, spat and swallowed again.

"Not this, I assure you. I thought to knock her over the side, but you both shifted at the last second."

"I had it all under control."

Eder tried a shaky laugh that tailed off into a hitching gasp. "Typical guild arrogance. No, you didn't. She'd have beaten you, and you'd be down here with a broken, if stiff with supercilious pride, neck. You can thank me later. For now, how bad is it?"

Kass bit back the retort that sprang to mind – if she was any judge they were trapped down here together, especially if she didn't abandon him, which was tempting but no, not the good thing. They were trapped, and the Clockwork God alone knew what trouble Voch was in up there. So instead of snapping back, she wiped her sword of the snow that dripped from it, sheathed it and braced herself to look at the leg.

Her stiletto had gone, left far above, so Eder dragged out his knife and handed it wordlessly to her so that she could cut away the breeches below his knee.

"That's, er, that's not good." Through the skin she could see where the bone had snapped, leaving the ankle at a stomach-churning angle to the leg above. Below the break his leg and foot were already starting to darken.

Eder snorted in disgust. "Really? How surprising. Maybe you could not patronise me and elaborate instead?"

"Fine," she snapped back. "You're fucked. Happy?"

A long silence before Eder began to laugh, all ragged at the edges like he was coming apart at the seams. "One extreme to another," he said at last. "Shouldn't have expected anything else from you, I suppose. Damn you and damn your bloody guild as well."

"I might be able to get it back into position or at least make it not as screwed, but you are still fucked without me and the guild to help you out. Or I suppose I could just leave you here to either starve or freeze to death, whichever happens first. I get why you don't like me. But why do you hate the guild so much?"

"So do it then. Leave me behind like the guild always leaves behind anyone who isn't one of its precious masters. And why? Isn't it obvious? Bunch of arrogant bast—" He broke off with a hiss as Kass touched his leg as gently as she could. "Think they're better than everyone else, worth more than everyone else. Look at your brother."

"I'd rather not. Keep still. And try not to give away the fact we aren't dead by screaming if you can. This is going to hurt. A lot."

In fact she wasn't sure she wasn't going to make it worse, but she'd seen breaks like this before – a fall from a horse usually – and she'd seen what happened if no attempt was made to straighten the limb. If she recalled her lessons in basic field care, and she might not, the foot going that colour meant an artery or large vein was trapped in the break. Possibly. She had to get it straight though, she definitely remembered that part. It was do this or, if they actually managed to get out of the ravine, he'd lose the leg, or worse. Even if nothing was trapped, getting it back into its proper position was going to make things a lot easier when it came time to move.

She took a deep breath and a firm grip on his ankle that brought a clenched yelp from Eder. She thanked her lucky stars that all that sword work had left her with a decent set of muscles and pulled, slowly but steadily.

The scrape of bone on bone vibrating up her arm made her shudder and Eder bite on his arm to try to hold in the scream. Slowly, too bloody slowly for either of their likings, the leg came straight. The trick was to make sure she pulled so there was a gap between the ends of the bone before she eased it back into position and hoped like hell nothing got caught. She kept on pulling until she was sure the ends were clear and then let go. Eder flopped back, sweat soaked and shaking, but almost immediately the ominous swelling began to go down.

As did the sun. It winked out behind a bank of clouds on the far side of the narrow slice of sky above them, leaving snow and shadow in its wake, and the beginnings of fear of how they were going to get out of there. Kass turned to say something to Eder about it, but he'd passed out, which was probably a mercy.

Chapter Twenty-one

"Can't you at least take another look?" Vocho said to the man holding a blade to the back of his neck.

The bald giant Kepa poked him with a finger the size and shape of a well stuffed sausage and said, "If they get to the bottom, they ain't alive. And I seen 'em at the bottom, and they weren't moving. Sent plenty down there before now. Even if they get to the bottom and live, they can't get out again without help. So they're dead, or soon will be. Get used to it."

"Kepa's quite right," Petri said from somewhere behind him. "Several people have fallen there before. They never come back."

He might have been talking about paperweights for all the emotion in his voice, but Vocho refused to believe him. It was going to take more than a little tumble to kill Kass. He hoped. He really, really hoped. She'd survived worse, survived being shot at, being stabbed − more than once − and any number of other things. Take more than a little tumble to kill Kass. Probably. He didn't like the way his eye kept twitching when he told himself that.

To cover up the rancid pit of fear his stomach had become, he said, "I realise I probably don't want to know the answer to this, but I'm not going to end up in there as well, am I?"

"Only if you don't shut up."

Vocho shut up. It didn't stop him thinking though. He was going to assume she was alive. He had to because otherwise he'd crumble, and he was buggered if he'd do that in front of Petri. She wasn't dead. Just like Petri hadn't been dead. It was catching, not being dead.

Of course she'd probably kill Vocho first chance she got, for not telling her that small thing about Petri not being dead, for in fact lying outright about it. Probably rip him open balls to chin. But it'd be worth it because she'd be alive. Of course, he had to survive for her to be able to kill him.

First things first. Get the hell away from Petri and his cohorts. Only that didn't seem all that achievable. There were a dozen of them that Vocho could see, some making sure their prisoners didn't escape and of course there was that handy drop into nothing, should any of them get bolshy.

Some of Petri's people were rounding up their new horses, Kass's bastard of a thing gave a couple of them some new scars in the making before they ganged up on it, and it took four of them to manage it in the end. First a nosebag on it to muzzle its teeth, and then, after much swearing and what looked to Vocho like a broken arm, it was loosely hobbled so it could walk but kicking would be near on impossible, though he was sure it'd try anyway.

Another dozen or more men and women lurking, weapons ready, and the magician around too – he kept making little snide comments to Petri about how brave he was, but Petri seemed as oblivious as a plank.

I know it doesn't come easy, Vocho my lad, but I think you may need to bide your time here.

Sensible advice from himself, but hard to follow nonetheless, especially with Carrola watching, slogging along in the snow next to him, silent, bruised and battered but slogging along nonetheless. His hand slid into his tunic and came out with an almost empty bottle. Cogs damn it. And where was he going to get any more? Whoever had taken to leaving it on his washstand – he liked to think of them as the Jollop Fairy – probably wasn't up to clambering up a mountain in hip-deep snow in order to do it. He was going to have to ration himself, so he took a last sorrowful look at the bottle, stashed it back in his tunic and tried to take stock.

The only bright spot was that Cospel wasn't among the captives. Neither was his new best friend, Sergeant Danel. Vocho had a faint hope that they'd kept out of the way and would now either help him escape or go and get Kass, who would then help him escape. He could rely on Cospel at least. It looked like he might have to.

The day grew colder, and his hip grew stiffer as a cruel wind whipped ice-edged snow around their ears. The magician at least made it easier – now it was obvious how Scar and her crew had managed to get around the mountain when everyone else was snowed in. He was melting the snow to clear a path, then making more snow behind to cover their tracks.

Carrola and the two men from Eder's troop shivered in their too-thin furs. Vocho offered his thicker wolfskin cloak to Carrola, but she waved it away with a frown. His hip grew worse until he was certain he could hear the muscles twang with every step, but there was only a mouthful of the syrup left. He concentrated on how bloody great it would taste when they got to where they were going.

By the time night fell – sharply behind jumbled peaks – they'd reached a small hidden valley dotted with little snowy humps that on closer inspection turned out to be buildings, and Vocho was lurching along like a badly made doll.

Kepa shoved them into one of the meaner huts with nothing more than a smirk from Petri that twisted his features into something nightmarish before the door banged shut. At least it shut out his face too.

The hut was unlit except for torchlight coming through the many cracks in the log walls, so that Vocho could just about see his breath fogging in front of him. They all slumped to the frozen mud floor, Vocho with his bad leg stiffly out in front. No matter how he sat, his hip burned with cold, the muscles so tight he could probably use them as a drum.

His fellow captives settled down with worried murmurs, trying to rub some life back into frozen hands.

Suddenly a voice he recognised shot out of the dark: "Vocho? Is that you?"

He couldn't make out much, but what he could see was the opposite of what he'd expected from the voice. He'd expected impeccable clothes, powdered silks and ridiculous brooches, a dark curl of hair over one shoulder. Maybe a smile as sharp as daggers on a man who looked like he was walking on oiled springs.

Instead he could make out a straggled beard shot through with grey, clothes so torn they looked like rags held together with string and covered with strips of mangy-looking fur. The ornaments were gone, along with all the poise, replaced by a god-awful smell and a cracked voice.

"*Dom?*"

"I'd bow but I seem to be rather restricted."

An understatement. Dom hadn't just had his wrists tied, but also his elbows, ankles and knees, not to mention the noose around his throat that was tied to a beam, leaving him just enough room not to hang himself as long as he stayed upright. Someone was taking no chances.

Vocho shuffled over. "What the hell are you doing here?"

"A slight tactical error involving being a bit overconfident and having a burning need to shove a knife right through someone's eyeball, a need so burning in fact that I was oblivious to all else. You?"

Vocho raised an eyebrow, even if Dom couldn't see it. Dom, usually so indolent it was a surprise he stayed awake, angry enough for that? It didn't seem possible.

"A slight tactical error," he replied, "involving being a bit overconfident, and then Kass seeing Petri alive. I suspect she may want to shove a knife through our eyeballs. If she's still alive."

"Ah," Dom said through his tangled beard. "Knife through the eyeballs seems rather restrained in that case. I suspect more slicing us balls to chin?"

"I suspect you may be right." Vocho tried to undo the knots that held Dom's wrists, fumbled them and wiped a shaking hand across his eyes. Must be tired. Or missing his jollop. That was all. He kept on trying, more for something to concentrate on than anything else.

"And 'If she's still alive'?" Dom asked.

So Vocho told him the lot, ending with "And when she saw Petri . . . Balls to bloody chin, you're right. And she was so busy staring at the ghost we made for her, she didn't see Scar until it was too late, and then Eder tried to get in the middle, only Scar moved at the last second so Kass and Eder went over the edge."

A long silence greeted that. Vocho gave up on the bonds that held Dom. Someone knew what they were about, enough to confound his numb fingers anyway.

"Do you *know* they're dead?" Dom said at last. "No. Unless you know for sure, I wouldn't write Kass off. Not ever. Not least because balls to chin would be nothing compared to what she'd do if we did that. However, perhaps more to the point, she's hardly likely to come and rescue you if she hates your guts."

"What is going on?" Carrola whispered from the far corner. "Vocho, who is this? And what in hells have you done *now*?"

"Ah," Dom said. "There speaks someone who knows Vocho well."

"Better than I'd like to, if half what my captain told me is true. And to think I was taken in by his 'I'm just a naughty boy, but I don't mean it' act. Huh. Now I know better. Come on, Vocho, what new shitwittery of yours is this?"

"I meant it for a kindness," Vocho said, unable to take any more reproaches, from himself as much as anyone else. "Petri bloody Egimont. I told her he was dead, we both did, me and Dom. We told everyone but especially her. Petri *asked* me to tell her that, and I did because . . . because I gave my word, and I thought it would be a kindness, for both of them. She'd have only blamed herself if she'd seen him. Of course she did anyway, but she didn't need to see that, see what he'd become. It wasn't just the face, it was him, inside. He wasn't − isn't − Petri any more, and she'd have blamed herself for that when it wasn't her fault. Funny, I didn't think he could be worse than the pompous sod he used to be, but I was wrong."

Carrola moved close enough that he could see the disapproval twitching her face into a frown that struck fear into his heart. "You *lied* to her that he was dead?"

"He asked me to! Dom, tell her. He asked me to. I gave my word."

Carrola looked at him aghast. "Vocho, Eder was right when he warned me about you."

"Yes, but if I could just ex—"

"I don't want to hear your excuses. There *are* no excuses. You really are the most—"

"I know," he said, slumping back against the freezing wall in defeat. "I try not to be but I am. I very, very am."

Carrola pointedly turned her back on him, and he couldn't say he blamed her. He took the bottle out again, squinted at it in the light and put it away with a sigh. His hip had totally seized so that any movement became a slow grind of muscles and bones, but he couldn't have any, he told himself. Not even a nip, not a little something against the cold and pain. Things were *bound* to get worse than this. Even if things improved and Cospel or, even better, Kass turned up, he might need to run.

A sudden extra blast of cold as the door opened, and there was Petri, no mask now, half his face just . . . gone. He smiled, but there was nothing pleasant about what it did to the face that was left. Nothing pleasant in the eye that was left either, not a hint of the man Petri had been. Vocho might have reasoned with Petri once upon a time, but he had the feeling this man was no longer anything close to reasonable.

Petri strolled into the hut, outlined in torchlight from behind him. Left hand casually on a sword, right dangling uselessly. A certain swagger to him, a strident confidence that had never been there before. Shadows moved in front of the torchlight – the bald giant – and a racheting sound signalled a gun being wound.

"Just in case you feel like doing anything foolish," Petri drawled. "Because we all know a fool is exactly what you are."

"It does look that way, doesn't it?" Vocho said. "I'd get up, but it's only you so I can't be arsed."

Half a mouth twisted into a snarl, and Vocho wasn't unduly surprised when the sword tip came to rest, oh so gently, under his eye. "Perhaps I should tell you how all my patience was burned away with hot metal, along with my eye, my face, my hand. My life, in fact. I don't especially need you alive, remember that."

"So what do you need?"

"Hostages. I've killed the guild master—"

"She's not dead." Vocho wasn't sure he believed it, but he had to keep telling himself that or he'd fall to pieces. He found his hands shook at the thought Petri might be lying, shoved them away where no one could see and laid on all the bravado he could muster. "Take more than that to kill her, and you know it as well as I do. Or you used to."

That twisted, nightmare smile again. "Do you know, I rather hope that's the case, that she's alive knowing her shit stain of a brother was lying to her, and not just a small lie either. Dearest, brotherly Vocho, I do hope she's still alive to kill you for it. We'll find out soon enough. I've sent a few men with climbing equipment to discover that very thing. Maybe bring back her head on a plate."

Before, Vocho had privately – OK, not all *that* privately – thought Petri had milk for blood. He'd thought today that Petri had changed, but now he was sure. This wasn't Petri bloody Egimont, quiet, sneaky rather than brave, a double-dealing little shit hiding under a sheen of nobility. If he'd loved Kass with half the passion he seemed to putting into her death – into hating her – maybe Vocho wouldn't have minded him half so much. Maybe. He hoped like hell not only that Kass was alive, but that she'd manage to carry on being alive with this loathing directed at her.

"Why is it you want her dead so much?" Vocho asked. "I did think you were supposed to be fond of her. You certainly seemed so in that letter you wrote."

Petri leaned forward so the horror of his face was clear even in the gloom. "She let you read it." The drawl was gone, replaced by a tone colder than Vocho's fingers.

"Well, not *let* exactly. And I didn't see all of it. Enough though. Very flowery, all those protestations of undying devotion."

"Did she tell you, then, of how I put all myself into that letter. Into her. And then she left me. Abandoned me to this." A cock of his head so that Vocho could see the devastation more clearly. "Left me to Eneko and a hot knife, to having the old me cut away like a disease."

"Abandoned?" Vocho laughed and was gratified by the flinch that got from Petri. "God's cogs, she half killed me trying to get to you. She didn't abandon you. She didn't do that to you. *Eneko* did that to your face, but what's behind it . . . that's all you. Pathetic little Petri, who was never man enough for my sister. I for one am glad she never saw what a little chicken shit you are. Always were even. So why don't you fuck off, my dearest duke, and leave us be?"

Petri straightened, and the smile on his lips made Vocho's skin crawl. "Cut away the old me like a disease and left the strong part. She was the reason Bakar had his proof, sent me to Eneko for this and then she left me to it, left me to rot. She threw me away, but I'm not so easily got rid of. Her head, on a plate, that's what I'm after. Then I'm going to send that head to Bakar with a little note. Eneko is dead; Kass may or may not be, but I've still Bakar to send my message to. Show him what he too threw away. That, idiot Vocho, is why hostages, and guild ones at that, are useful. If I can't find her head, then yours will suffice. Until then, until we know for sure if she lives, you, alive, are tempting bait for her to come and rescue."

"Well, it's nice of you to—"

"Enough!" The sword pricked at the skin under Vocho's eye, and he could feel the tremor in the blade, the rage of the hand that held it, all pent up and waiting to explode. Maybe now wasn't the time to say something smart-arse. "If it could have been anyone but you. But no, I get Vocho the preening arsehole who speaks only banalities. Keep your idiocy to yourself or I might forgo the need to keep you alive. I might, in fact, thoroughly enjoy cutting your throat right now. Tell me, where's Cospel?"

Vocho had been wondering much the same himself, but he wasn't about to tell Petri that. "Had to leave him behind in Kastroa. Broke a leg falling off a horse. Silly bugger never did ride very well. Probably lucky for him this time, though, eh?"

That nightmare grin again. The tip of the blade twisted and broke the skin, leaving a trickle of blood on Vocho's cheek.

"Your eye's twitching," Petri said, "and I think that tells me what I need to know."

Abruptly the sword was gone, for which Vocho was profoundly thankful. There had never been any love lost between the two of them, and Vocho wasn't rating his chances of living through the night very highly.

"You two," Petri snapped out at the men hovering in the doorway. "I want four guards on this hut at all times. A couple of snipers watching too, and extra patrols. It wouldn't surprise me if a one-man rescue party turned up. If it does, kill him."

He turned back to Vocho, who if he'd thought Petri couldn't get any colder, had been wrong. "You might do well to remember that I need my hostages only alive. Not intact." A mirthless laugh at that. "Think on that and be grateful I don't have a hot knife to hand."

Petri shut the door into Scar's hut behind him, threw the sword onto the table and sank into a chair. So close to just slitting the bastard's throat and having done with him for good. He had half a mind to go back and do it. He stared at the sword, Dom's sword, all duellist's flash and glitter, but the finest blade beneath belying that. It wasn't Vocho he wanted sitting there, not Vocho he wanted to rage at, demand answers from, though he'd do.

Preening bastard was right though – Petri didn't think Kass was dead either. Not yet at least. Maybe she was bleeding to death at the bottom of that ravine. Maybe she'd freeze in the night. Maybe she'd live. She hadn't abandoned him, Vocho had said. Had come for him but not in time. A complex tumble of thoughts at that, ones he couldn't untangle. But it was Vocho who'd said it, and so none of it to be trusted.

Scar came in, stomping snow off her boots. She stooped to kiss the top of his head and started to shake her furs off. He watched her, the vital intensity of every movement, the quick, smiling glances she shared with him. So sure of everything when he was sure of nothing but a hollow pit of rage sitting in his stomach that made him colder than the wind whipping over the mountains.

She sat opposite him at the table and reached for his hands, the good and the useless. Her thumb stroked at fingers that couldn't feel it.

"Talk to me, Petri. You're the Skull, and they're all afraid of you! Isn't that what you wanted?"

He looked at her, at the way she watched him, waiting for his answer, and wondered why it was he always felt so cold, even here by a fire. Like there was nothing left inside but the crack of ice.

"Petri?"

"Morro," he said at last. "Has he . . . Is he using us?"

Her hands slipped from his. "No, Petri, we're using him to get what we wanted. *This*."

"He's not tried his magic on you? Shown you his hands?"

The briefest of hesitations. "No! And I wouldn't look if he had – you've talked about it enough. I'm not stupid, I know the dangers." But she wouldn't look at him while she said it. Instead she got up and applied her energy to stoking the fire with unnecessary vigour. "I know what I'm doing. I'm using Morro to do what we wanted, that's all. If you still want it?"

Using him too, he thought now. The ice inside him cracked, but underneath there was nothing but hate, blinding him with its white-hot glare. "Yes. Yes, it's what I wanted. What I still want."

But when she went to kiss him, he turned away, stood and made his way out into the cold, towards his place in the barn.

* * *

Kass had spent a long time looking at the bodies that had broken their fall, poor shattered things with faces black from cold. She'd debated a long time, then said some prayers over them before she gathered up as many cloaks as she could, though she left some to cover those faces. She'd scraped out a sort of cave in the snow and piled it with cloaks, but the cold penetrated everything. Her fingers fumbled trying to light a fire, though there wasn't much to burn except what other clothes she could find and a few cheap wooden scabbards that had fallen with their owners but were frozen and hard to light. In the end, under Eder's sneering gaze, she gave up.

It was, at least, slightly warmer in the little cave. Not much, but they might not freeze to death just yet. Water wasn't a problem – she'd put some snow into her canteen and put it under her arm to melt – but food was going to be a problem very shortly, along with Eder.

So was the fact she knew why she was thinking on those things, because it was keeping her mind from other more painful thoughts. Ones which Eder seemed intent on bringing to the surface, exactly where she didn't want them.

He shifted under the pile of cloaks she'd given him and grimaced at the movement. "Petri," he said dryly. "Seems to me I've heard that name recently. And strange, I could have sworn your brother told everyone he was dead."

She didn't answer, instead trying to arrange her own pile of cloaks better.

"Which begs the question," Eder went on. "How did Vocho not suspect that the Skull was him? Or maybe he did – he told Carrola he thought he might know who it was. Why didn't he say anything to you?"

"Why ask me?" she snapped. God's cogs, she was going

to murder Voch when she found him. *If* she found him. She didn't want to be thinking what she was thinking. That Vocho had lied, once again. He'd told her that Petri was dead, that he knew that for sure. He'd told her that and, unusually for Vocho, had been careful with her ever since – he'd looked after the guild she was supposed to be running when she'd been staring out over the walls and remembering, trying to work out where it had all gone wrong. It had twisted in her gut, the thought that somehow, unknowingly, she'd pushed Petri into the course that had led him to Eneko's room. And Vocho had been there to listen when she couldn't keep that pent up any more, had reassured her, comforted her, been an actual brother to her.

That should of course have been a dead giveaway that he was feeling guilty about something.

If she'd known Petri was alive, she'd have . . . she'd have . . .

What would she have done? Gutted that old fuck Eneko for doing that to Petri, for starters. Killed him like the animal he was, not let Vocho persuade her to leave it to the courts to find him guilty of all sorts and send his head bouncing over the cobbles. Maybe she'd have even got away with it, not ended on the block herself. Then she'd have found Petri, wherever he was. And then . . . and then she didn't know. She didn't know what she was going to do now. When she got out of this bloody ravine anyway.

The words on a ragged scrap of paper came back to her. *Remember everything, regret nothing.*

She wrenched at a cloak that wasn't doing what she wanted, and was rewarded with the sound of ripping cloth.

"I'm asking you," Eder said when she'd settled down, "because your brother isn't here. I'd love to be asking him. Preferably at the end of a sword."

That made her laugh, at least. "Yes, he does have that effect on people. I don't know why he said nothing, except I suppose he was hoping it wouldn't be true. I don't know why he lied, apart from lying is what he does. The point is, he did, and now we're stuck at the bottom of a very cold ravine with no food, no fire, and you have a broken leg. 'Why' is beside the very real point – we might die here."

A long silence broken only by the sound of Kass trying to stop her teeth from chattering. The cloaks weren't going to be enough, especially with no fire to help keep them warm. Eder's face looming towards her in the dark startled her.

"I might. No need for you to."

"What? Don't be ridiculous."

He shuffled over with a hiss of pain, bringing his cloaks with him, so that they were shoulder to shoulder, and laid a cloak over both their shoulders so they were cocooned together. "Warmer this way. Don't worry, I'm not likely to try to kiss you again. And I'm not being ridiculous. I've got a broken leg, as you point out. You haven't. You can get out."

He was deadly serious, she could tell that even in the dark. "No. No, I can't, not without you. We'll both get out."

"Guild arrogance again?"

"Guild honour. The motto, you recall?"

"Guild honour. Huh. Where was that for Petri when Eneko took his eye? Did Eneko ever have any? Or Vocho when he did all those things? I'd be surprised if he had morals, never mind honour. The guild almost took control of the city, tried to kill Bakar, fucked up Red Brook good and proper and didn't even care about all the men and women who died there. And you talk about honour. The guild has outlived its usefulness. You're stuck in the past, living on old glories. *Fake* old glories, in Vocho's case."

"The guild defended Reyes too, saved Bakar. Why is it that you hate it so much?"

She felt him tighten at that, his shoulder twitch against hers. "Who wouldn't? Bunch of arrogant arseholes who think they know better than anyone. Well, they're just as fallible as everyone else, they just won't admit it."

He wouldn't say any more, and she was struck once again by how like Petri he was. Even more so here in the dark. The curl of hair, tangled now, falling over his shoulder, the pent-up everything showing in the hunch of his shoulders, the burn of *something* behind his eyes that he wouldn't, couldn't say. Only he was a Petri who still had his face.

He caught her watching him, maybe caught the wistful look that must be on her face because it was surely in her head. The whip of his voice killed those thoughts. "You called me Petri."

She couldn't look at him any more, not at the hurt that twisted his face, made it worse even than Petri's horror. "Yes, and I'm sorry for it too."

"Why?"

She stared off into the swirling darkness of the night, shrugged the pain of it away, unable to answer in any truthful way that wouldn't make things worse.

"Because you wanted me to be him?" The question snaked out to stab her. "Is that it? You wanted me to be the man we came here to stop, who's killed and robbed who knows how many people? Outlaw, murderer, betrayer. Was it a tragic disappointment when I wasn't him?"

The bitterness in his voice seemed hot enough to melt

a mountain's-worth of snow, and when she finally looked there was nothing in that face to remind her of Petri. There was no answer that wouldn't twist the knife in him further, so she said nothing – and that was an answer in itself. He pushed himself away to the other side of the little cave, but she could feel the heat of his glare even so.

They were silent for a long time, until at last his breathing slowed into sleep. The real Petri was out there somewhere, alive, and with a woman who'd been prepared to kill Kass for him. He'd moved on, and she'd stayed where she was, eaten with guilt, turning away other men even while wishing they were him. He was alive, but she wondered if he needed saving more than ever, or whether she needed saving from her own head. Whether she should move on too. She pulled her knees up, wrapped her arms around them and stared at Eder as he slept.

By the time Eder shuddered awake, woken by trying to move his leg in his sleep, the gloom of night was starting to lighten into grey snow clouds above and she'd been hard at work for an hour.

Eder eyed her suspiciously. "What's that?"

"This is how I'm going to get you out of here."

It wasn't going to last long, but she hoped long enough. Scabbards strapped together with ripped-up strips of cloth and a short length of rope some unlucky faller had with him to serve as poles. Cloaks wrapped and tied around to form a sort of bed, the scabbards poking out so that she could drag it.

Eder scrubbed a hand up his face, the scratch of his stubble loud in the snow-swept silence. "Kass—"

She crouched down beside him and essayed a conciliatory hand that he shook off. "You are going to get on this thing, and we are going to get you out of here. You don't have a bloody say in the matter, all right?"

He frowned and laughed at the same time, setting her teeth on edge. "No."

"Yes, I think you'll find." She pulled together as many of the things she'd found that might be useful – rummaging in dead men's frozen pockets of a dawn wasn't her favourite way to start the day, she'd found – and made a bundle of them. A fire strike and stone in case they found something to burn, some travel rations she'd found crushed under a body, a couple of knives because you could never have too many, a gun and some bullets that she'd rather not use, all wrapped in the warmest cloaks she could salvage. She shoved the bundle onto the makeshift travois and headed for Eder.

A night out in the freezing cold had done him no favours, but she suspected she looked little better. His hair was awry, the black curl over his shoulder tangled and wet with snow. Skin pale, eyes dark with pain, stubble on his chin surprisingly streaked with grey, which made him look a dozen years older than she'd supposed.

"Don't make me argue about it," she said as he opened his mouth. "We need our energy for getting out of here and staying warm. It's almost light, and when it is there's going to be people coming down this ravine. Petri isn't stupid, and he knows me. He's got a load of men and women up there with him somewhere, and quite probably a magician. If he wants me dead, they'll be coming down to make sure I am. If he doesn't . . ." She took a deep breath because, what would that mean? What would either way mean? She shook her head. "If he doesn't then there will still be people coming down here to check. They will have swords and bows and most likely guns. Do you really want to be here when that happens? Because he's probably not going to give a shit if you're alive or dead."

Eder stared up at the lip of the ravine, far above, where the sun was just starting to make its presence felt behind banks of grey clouds that promised more snow. She waited for him to think it through — she really didn't want to have to wrestle the stupid sod if she could help it.

After a time, when she couldn't wait any more and it was say something or hit something, she said, "It's not the guild I'm doing this for. Salve your conscience with that. It's not the guild saving you, or even me saving you. It's you and me, down here, both wanting to stay alive and needing each other to do it. I'm not leaving you to die. That's it."

"All right," he said at last. "All right. But help me up. If you have to drag me on that thing too far, you'll be in no shape to do anything when they catch us up. And they will."

Chapter Twenty-two

Usually after a bad night dawn was something to be looked forward to. Not so this bad night, Vocho thought, because the coming day looked set to get worse.

To start with, he could see the true state of Dom. Vocho had always envied him his poise, his effortless way of being pristine even when surrounded by shit. Not today. Today Dom looked worse than Vocho felt, which was pretty bad.

Dank light coming in through the cracks in the walls showed up everything – every grey hair in Dom's beard, every stain on his now ragged clothes, every crack in his boots, every red thread in the whites of his eyes. Once Vocho would have gloated, just a bit, at the thought of being better presented than the immaculate Dom, but today he found he didn't have the energy.

He shifted his weight, remembered his seized-up hip a second too late and yelped.

"What the hell happened to you?" they both said at the same time.

Vocho tried a frozen grin. "You first. You look like shit."

"Feel it," Dom said quietly. He stared down at his bound

hands, which lay in his lap, opening and closing, opening and closing. "And every one of my years. Went looking for my daughter – you recall I was trying to find her?"

"How could I forget? Your and the, er . . . what's the word? Terrifying, yes, that's it. Your and the terrifying Alicia's daughter."

A soft plume of laughter filled with wistful wishing. "She wasn't so terrifying once. She was young and so was I, and youth makes people stupid. Made me stupid anyway. But . . . but . . . a daughter. Esti managed to winkle out where Eneko had last seen her, and I went to find her. Had it all worked out – what I was going to say, how I was going to tell her I'd never stopped thinking about her, never stopped trying to find her. I tracked her from that last place to where she was living. She looks like her mother. Just like her."

Vocho was mesmerised by Dom's hands, open and closed, open and closed. Like he was trying to hold on to something but couldn't keep his grip, his life slipping through his groping fingers.

"And?" Vocho said when it looked like that was all he was going to get.

Dom blinked hard and looked up as though only now remembering Vocho was there. "A magician was already there, though I didn't know that's what he was then. I think he'd worked out whose daughter she was, or at least that she likely had some magical ability. He'd had weeks to work on her, and he whispered in her ear, all poison about me. He wanted her help, I think, to escape the village."

"Escape the village? Couldn't he just walk off?"

"Not really. Even a magician like him would need bodies full of blood to get himself off the mountain in this snow. With an apprentice . . . Or maybe they were planning to slaughter the village for the blood they needed, I don't know."

"So she didn't believe you?"

"Or didn't want to. She — my daughter — her name was Maitea, did I say? She wasn't easy to convince, but I was trying. I'd only been there a few days, you know, trying to be friendly, show I was worth knowing. So when the village decided a hunting party was in order, I volunteered to help. When we got back, Scar had raided the village, taken most of the stores. Maitea had stood up to her though. And Scar took her, kidnapped her. Just when I'd found her again." A deep, harsh breath as though he was on the edge of an abyss and was trying not to fall in. "So, I thought, what good is it being trained as a bloody assassin if I can't catch the person who did that? Rescue my own daughter? Then I made a mistake. Several actually. All that time I wasn't thinking straight, *couldn't* think straight. I tried to kill Scar, get back Maitea, thought she might look on me more favourably then. Didn't realise Morro had already found her. Had a hell of a shock when I saw Petri. Not as much as he did when he realised Scar had picked up her own personal magician. So, all my plans failed, and me a prisoner. And now Maitea knows who killed her mother, and she's as unforgiving as Alicia ever was, with as much cause."

He wouldn't look at Vocho, just stared down at his bound hands and watched them move for a long time.

"I'm sorry," Vocho said when he couldn't take the silence any more.

"So am I, Voch. So am I." Dom sat up straight and made an effort to still his hands, stop them twitching. "What was your tactical error?"

So Vocho told him the lot: about Kass mooning about,

and him and Bakar trying to get some life back into her, about Vocho's niggling little doubts about who the Skull was, which had proved to be distressingly accurate. About Eder.

Dom interrupted: "Eder? Captain Eder, prelate's guards? Supercilious-looking chap? Looks like Bakar's played you for a mug, Voch. Or at least is trying to help Eder the same way you were trying to help Kass, though it might amount to the same thing. Bit of a risk, though."

"Why?"

"Why? Cogs, man, don't you know anything? Half the continent's heard about Red Brook."

"I did hear vaguely . . ."

Dom shook his head and laughed, and at least sounded a bit more like himself, which was a comfort, even if his words weren't. "Captain Eder, who lost every single man and woman under his command in the brook. Well, *he* didn't, and that's the trouble. Bakar told him, told all of the guards, to listen to the guildsmen in the coming battle and take their orders. But guildsmen are only great at single combat or in small teams. Big battles? Tell me, Voch, how much training did you have in the tactics of two armies coming together?"

"Not a lot. Not that I paid attention to anyway."

"How about two armies, each with a magician at its head?"

"Ah, I'm on firmer ground there. Bugger all."

"Exactly. And the guildsman giving Eder his orders probably had less than that, and certainly less than Eder, who was a star soldier, one of Bakar's best and brightest. It's all a bit vague – not too many witnesses left, obviously – but the guildsman gave Eder his orders, and Eder argued the toss, and the guildsman pulled rank, got a couple of others to back him up, and Eder had to follow those orders or get a sword through the gut because it was a fraught night and no one had time to argue, they just had to fight. And if he carried on arguing his men and women would have to follow those orders, only without their captain. So, discretion being the better part of valour, he followed those orders to the letter. I *think* – again, hard to know for sure – I think he realised that they were attacking their own but too late, and all his troop died. Nastily. Eder went a bit odd afterwards."

Well, that had the ring of truth to it. Vocho could imagine some of the masters being just that stupid. Explained a thing or two about Eder as well. "I'm not surprised."

"No, neither am I. After the battle Eder tried his damnedest to murder at least three duellists, and managed it with two, including the one who'd given him his orders. The guild, presumably out of guilt or not wanting to look like a bunch of arseholes, hushed it up – duellists died in battle, saving Reyes and so forth."

"Hang on. How don't I know this? I've been running the guild for months."

"Hushed up even from you and Kass. Afraid of looking even worse than they already did, what with having followed Eneko in his failed coup. Can you imagine what ʃould have done to whoever owned up? They didn't ʃar, I don't think, except to say Eder needed ʃ the horror of the brook and until he was fine and dandy and back in ʃntil then anything he might ʃ being a bit strange in the ʃnd so forth. So now here Eder ʃery thought of the guild, under ʃnd where did you say Kass was?"

That explained everything. Only, only it was worse than that, wasn't it?

"Kass is down a ravine. Hopefully alive. With Eder."

Petri lay silent in the dawn, staring up at the low ceiling of the hayloft. This was what he wanted, wasn't it? To show them all what he could have been, if he'd had the chance. What better way than this? The guild master bested, perhaps dead. Morro and some men even now on their way with climbing gear to discover exactly that, and he grew restive thinking about what they'd find, what they'd bring back. What he wanted them to find. Maybe it wasn't that he wanted to show them all. He wanted to show *her*. Even if Vocho was telling the truth – unlikely – about Kass not abandoning him, that she'd tried . . . here he was, still with half a face.

He had her brother captive too. A smile ghosted across what was left of Petri's lips. How better to show her? Vocho the Great brought low in a duel, that was how. Petri had never beaten him, never had a hope before because while the prick had a vastly inflated sense of his own skills, he was a damned good swordsman. Vocho beaten, fair and square. That would show everyone, or everyone that mattered. Now, with Vocho's leg seized so badly that he'd lurched along at the last yesterday, and after a night on a frozen floor it'd be worse, he migh have a chance.

The day was grey with clouds, pregnant with mo Morro's snow. Petri's breath puffed out into a sea crystals, and he took a deep draught of it, let the ness spear his head. His heart hammered hot b his temples. If he did this there was no going bac Kass was alive or not, there would be no g them after this; it would slice his old life away for good, as the surgeon had sliced away his old face.

The men guarding the hut stood back as he approached, moved out of earshot at the wave of his hand. The hut stank, a fetid, rotting smell that made his stomach roll over, recalling a small dark cell under the guild. He was never going to be that person again.

He blinked away the ghosts and went in. The prelate's guards sat huddled in one corner against the cold. Vocho and Dom were at the far end, but Petri was surprised to see Maitea standing over them, a knife in one hand. She whirled as Petri came in, lifted a lip in a brief sneer, then she was gone in whirl of grey shadows.

Petri gestured at Vocho. "You. Up."

Vocho rolled his eyes. "Really? If I must." He lurched to his feet, catching hold of a beam to steady himself. Favouring his left leg heavily, but that was all right because Petri would be fighting with his off hand. No one could say it wasn't a fair fight. "Found Kass yet?"

Said with a nonchalance that didn't hide the worry behind his eyes.

"Not yet," Petri replied. "But we will. In the meantime I haven't had anyone decent to spar against in months. I'm not fool enough to try against your friend there or let him free of his bonds even for a second. Come on, out."

A quick glance between Vocho and Dom that Petri couldn't fathom and didn't care much about anyway. All he cared about was, here was Vocho the Great at his mercy. Here was his chance.

He held Vocho at the point of his sword, flanked by two of the men who'd guarded the hut, until they reached the circle that they used to practise – sheltered at least somewhat from the wind by an arm of rock, swept clear of snow to show dead grass underfoot. Plenty of places for people to sit and watch and learn.

As word flew around the camp, those places soon filled. Not to watch Petri, of that he was sure, and he ground his teeth with the old resentment. Vocho of the bloody guild, who'd had everything fall in his lap, who found life an effortless fun-filled jaunt. Vocho hadn't been hemmed in, chained to clockwork for the rest of his miserable life. Vocho hadn't been betrayed, abandoned to a grisly fate by the only person who'd ever mattered, the only person who'd ever cared, or seemed to until she left him to his fate and made that seeming a lie.

Petri watched Vocho now as someone handed him his sword, watched him check it was still true, test the edge, heft it like an old friend. Vocho, who coasted through life as though he was owed everything. Vocho who had everything Petri had ever wanted but didn't even know he had it.

"Are you sure about this, Petri? Kass isn't going to be happy with me if I kill you. Accidentally, obviously."

That had to be a lie. "If she cared, she would have come."

"I told you, she did. Just too late. Been mooning about after you for months. Cogs know why. It's not like you were ever much of a catch." Vocho gave the sword a practice swish. "In fact it's only this jolly jaunt to find the Skull that's got her out of herself, so I suppose I can thank you for that."

He had to be lying — he always was. Petri didn't give him the dignity of an answer but raised his sword in the proper guild manner to start a duel.

Vocho cocked his head. "I could give you a point on

account, seeing as you're using your off hand, Petri. Seems only sporting."

Vocho, who even now grated on every nerve he had left.

"Petri's dead," he growled out. "And I don't need a point from you."

With no more notice than that, he went for the heart. Vocho, who'd had everything Petri hadn't, wasn't going to have it for long.

By the time it was fully light, Kass and Eder had put some distance between them and the pile of bodies that had saved their lives, but progress was painfully slow. Eder's weight leaning on her grew heavier with every step, and snow drifted across the way, knee deep and worse. She'd tied a cloak behind the travois to muddle their trail, but it probably wasn't going to fool anyone for long. Not long enough anyway.

The bottom of the ravine began to slope up, making progress even slower. She wished desperately for a tree, an abandoned piece of something Eder could use as a crutch, but there was nothing but snow, rock, ice. It began to snow, slow swirling flakes that stuck to her face, her eyelashes, that melted down her neck. So much for the thaw.

"Stop," Eder gasped out, and Kass didn't need telling twice. They sank down under a small overhang and caught their breath. The back of her throat tasted like copper, and sweat had soaked the inside of her furs even as her nose had gone numb from cold.

Eder shut his eyes, and again she was struck by how old he looked, even though she knew he was younger than she was. His hands seemed struck with palsy, shaking so hard he couldn't get them inside his tunic, to whatever it was he was after, and he swore viciously under his breath.

"Can't," he said. "Can't go any more. Not yet."

"Have to." She could barely get the words out past her panting, but she was buggered if this was how she was going to die, waiting for Petri's crew to find them like rats in a trap.

He opened his eyes a crack and regarded her from under the lids in a way that set her shoulder blades wriggling. "We can't do this. Face it. We're caught, and you know it. Why keep on?"

She set her jaw. *Because I have to save you, to make up for not saving him. Because it stops me thinking about the fact he's still alive. Because if I don't, I'm going to sit here and put my head in my hands and cry.* "Because."

"Because it's the good thing?"

The sneer in his voice snapped something inside her. "And why not? What's wrong with that?"

"Tell me, how do you know what the good thing is? Do you ever think you picked wrong? Or do the guild always do right? Do you?"

She lurched to her feet and brushed snow from her face. "Get on the travois. I can pull you faster than you can walk."

"Do you?" he said again.

She fussed with the cloaks, with the straps, rather than look at him. "No. And that's why we're going on. I *can't* give in now."

"Can't? Or won't? Did you ever think being stubborn isn't a virtue?"

She rounded on him at that. "Fine, it's won't, all right? And if it pleases you, no, the guild doesn't always get it right, because it has people in it and people screw up. But

I'm not giving in. Do you want to know why I called you Petri? Because I didn't get there in time, before. Because I couldn't save him and I thought he was dead, and you looked to me like a man who needed saving. I wanted to pretend he was still alive, and I used you for it and I'm sorry for that. But now Petri isn't dead but he does want *me* dead, and my brother's up there somewhere too, probably getting into all sorts of trouble without me. If he's still alive, that is, because Petri hates me – I saw it in the way he looked at me – he hates me because I didn't get there in time, and he's going to take it out on Voch and . . . and . . . and get on the fucking thing before I brain you and strap your unconscious body to it."

They glared at each other for a long heartbeat before he looked away. "What do you think happened to the rest? Carrola, everyone?"

"I don't know and I'm surprised you care enough to ask. But I do know I can't help them sitting at the bottom of this bloody ravine, and neither can you. Get on."

He didn't move but sat in the thickening snow, which obscured his face so his voice seemed to come out of nowhere, cracked and thin.

"You think I don't care? That some of those bodies we landed on were men and women I knew? That I rode with and ate with, and there they are, nothing more than a cushion to save us? That we had to leave them there? You think I don't care about what's happened to the rest of them? That I don't care that you think nothing of me except someone to save? Someone who needs saving?"

Wind whipped the snow away for a moment, and she could see his face, grey and gaunt, wet with tears that he wiped away hurriedly as the wind dropped, letting more snow veil the space between them.

She took a step towards him. "I—"

"I always cared," he said, voice low and tight now. "I cared when the guild turned me away, when all the duellists sneered at me. I cared when my whole troop died because of the guild. I cared when Carrola turned me away, and when you did too. Because of the guild, because I'm not one of you, because they wouldn't give me the chance. Everyone turns me away."

He exploded out of the snow, knocking her onto her back and the breath out of her. Red and blue cartwheeled across her vision, and she vaguely realised she'd hit her head. Hands tightened on her throat, and there was Eder's face, an inch from hers, as he bashed her head against the rock-strewn snow. She scrabbled uselessly at his furs, found no purchase, thrashed and kicked and caught his broken leg so that he howled and let her go, flailing backwards. She scrambled to her feet, hand on the hilt of her sword as she got there. It was halfway out when a cold gun muzzle found her cheek. She stood very still and looked into Eder's twisted face. He was still crying, though he didn't seem to be aware of it.

"Guild," he snarled, pressing the gun into her skin. "*Fucking* guild. Killed all my troop, all of them but me. Red Brook . . . We could have lived but for the orders the guild gave me, which I had no choice but to obey. Afterwards, it was all Kass the heroine this and Vocho the bloody great that, and it's all *shit*. No one cared that we died. Everyone looks to you, fawns over the two of you like you're god's bloody gift to the world. And it's all lies, nothing but lies. More of my men and women dead at the bottom of a ravine but, hey, the fucking guild is all right, the guild will be the heroes of the hour. Who cares about a few guardsmen dying as long as Kass and Vocho live, as long as there's a dashing tale to tell about the guild saving Reyes once again? Who cares about those poor dead bastards, whose only grave will be snow? No one. No one gives a crap except me. *I* care. I always cared, and they always turned me away, everyone."

Slowly, carefully, she raised her empty hands. "Eder, I—"

Eder cocked the gun, and she could feel the tremble of it against her cheek. "Shut up. Shut up with your stupid bleating. Petri has it right, I think. Oh, he hates you, the guild Why not? I read all of it in the papers, heard the rumours, and more informed rumours than the papers got too. I heard what happened to him, and then, up there, I saw the state of his face, and I thought, I can see why he did what he did. The guild screwed him over; you screwed him over, left him to that horror, and he had enough. Maybe he'll have a use for a captain of the guard, broken leg or no. If I show him that I'm on his side. On your knees. I said, on your fucking knees, so I can shoot you in the back, which is all you deserve for a death."

The gun jabbed into her cheek, his finger tight and twitching on the trigger. She dropped to her knees, hands out, breath tight as she struggled to think. The muzzle left her cheek and there was no thinking, there was only instinct. Her shoulder into his gut, his scream as he slammed onto his back. Her hands on the gun, trying to wrestle it out of his grip, but he was stronger than she was. The grip smacked into her face and blood came, searing her skin, smelling of copper and death. Another smack, and blood was in her mouth now, making her gag. Eder's face swam in front of her, his breath hot, his wet eyes hotter as he bore down, all his weight on her so that her own breath was squeezed out. No room for a sword, but a knife, she had a pilfered knife, and it was in her hand before she'd even finished the thought.

A punch like being hit with a rock, and all thoughts fled. The weight came off her, and she lurched onto her knees, trying to get clear. She couldn't see anything except snow and her blood dripping into it. Eder's harsh breath right behind her. She fell, twisting as she did, trying to bring her knife to bear. A bang that seemed to drive her ears into her head, a smack into her chest like a bull had just charged, and more blood, oh god's cogs, there was blood everywhere, pooling under her, melting little rivers in the snow. Shot, she thought disjointedly, this is what it feels like to be shot. But it'd take him time to reload, rewind the gun, and she still had the knife in her hand.

She stood shakily to face Eder, slipped in her own blood and caught herself, knife raised and ready, just in time to see Cospel brain the bastard with his trusty tankard.

"Hello, miss. Glad to see I made it in time."

She looked down at herself, at the blood everywhere. Shot somewhere in her chest, by the looks. It didn't hurt yet, which seemed odd, but she was sure it would later.

"Me too, Cospel. Me too. How's your embroidery? I appear to have a small hole that needs darning."

That also appeared to be all she had the energy for, because everything went grey after that.

Vocho lay on his back on the dead grass and looked up. It might have been a pleasant enough view of snow-streaked mountains against a looming sky if not for what was left of Petri's face leaning over him, or the point of Petri's sword drawing blood at his left shoulder.

Petri smiled – well, it looked like it might be a smile, it was hard to tell – and stood back.

"Get up," he snapped, and Vocho did his best.

It took him a while because his hip wasn't cooperating in the slightest. In fact it was making very loud protests, but Vocho wasn't exactly in a position to listen.

Once he was up, Petri cocked his head. "You weren't even trying. You let me win."

"Yes," he agreed. "Didn't seem wise to antagonise a man who could have me killed at any moment. Despite popular opinion on the matter, I am occasionally sensible."

Besides, he preferred to think he'd had just let Petri beat him rather than that, with his hip as it was, he probably couldn't have won anyway. He was never going to think that, never.

Petri growled deep in his throat and came at Vocho again, forcing him back onto a leg that refused to work properly without some serious pain. Vocho parried, kept his point on line and thrust half-heartedly, but Petri wasn't having any of it. And Vocho was tired, dead tired.

"Come on," Petri said in his new voice. "Come on and do it properly. Kill me if you can."

"Oh yes, that's a grand plan. Kill you while surrounded by all your new friends. I think not. Which is a shame because I've often dreamed about it."

Petri came at him with renewed vigour, very nearly impaling him, and it looked like Vocho had a choice here – be killed by Petri, or kill him and be killed by the woman who was just coming up the slope, her puckered scar twisted by a frown. Petri got his attention again with a well aimed thrust that almost winkled his liver out, and he was under no illusions now. Whatever Petri's plans, they looked like they included Vocho being dead, but he'd be buggered if Vocho the Great was going to be remembered for dying to a pissant little shit like Petri.

He gritted his teeth and went on the attack, hip be damned. Attack, parry, thrust, riposte. Try to keep on the forward leg as much as he could, but not too much or his balance would be all off. He bore it because there was nothing else to be done.

He held his own, barely, and watched. Petri's style had changed, and not just because he was using his off hand. He'd always been one for following the proper rules of conduct in a duel – no going for the face or genitals, and blades only. But they weren't sparring now at the guild under the watchful gaze of the clockwork duellist, or out on the greensward where Vocho had once dumped Kass into the river in a fit of pique. A slash almost had Vocho's nose off, quickly followed by another that sliced along one cheek and promised Voch the scar he'd always managed to avoid. No time to dwell on that though because Petri was all over him, and Vocho couldn't do a damned thing about it because his leg wasn't moving now, even painfully, and he was weary to the bone so that he could barely hold the sword up never mind use it. An elbow into his cheek to open up the gash, a thud of a boot into his bad leg at the knee, and he was on the ground again, staring up at Petri's mangled face as he crunched a heel onto Vocho's wrist to make him drop his sword and brought his own sword down to rest on Vocho's chest. A twisted grin. Bastard was enjoying this.

"I think, dearest Vocho, this could be the end," Petri said. "I can't say I'll be sad to see you go."

"I'll be pissed it's you that finished it," Vocho managed in reply. "I was always hoping to relieve you of your head."

Scar came up behind Petri and stared down at Vocho like he was shit on her shoe.

"What the hell are you doing?" she demanded of Petri.

Petri said nothing, only smiled down at Vocho.

That probably would have been the end of it, of Vocho at least, if not for the sudden sound of a gun going off, a gurgling scream followed by another, the crunch of a broken bone reverberating up the slope. Scar and Petri both turned away, and that was all the distraction Vocho needed to get the hell up, grab his sword and put some distance between him and Petri. His hip throbbed so badly he almost fell, but he kept his feet, barely.

By the time he was upright, Scar was halfway down the slope, running towards the hut where Vocho had spent the night, half a dozen men following her, and Petri was turning back towards him.

"We'll finish our little chat later," he said and nodded to someone behind Vocho. Hands grabbed him, relieved him, after a brief but heartfelt struggle, of his sword and dumped him face first into the dead grass. A knee was planted in his back, his hands were tied, and then it seemed he was all on his own, except for whichever sadistic bastard was sitting on his back, squeezing the breath out of him.

Which was great. Just bloody great.

Petri ran after Scar, down the hill towards the hut, where he could make out two men lying in the snow in steaming pools of blood. A third stood upright, a stolen sword in each hand, grinning through his straggled beard as though he'd died and gone to heaven. Behind him were two of the people the bandits had brought back with Vocho, a man and a woman, both now armed with knives.

Dom stepped forward to meet Scar with a mocking bow.

"I made a tactical error before," he said. "But not this time. Your magician isn't here, is he?"

A tinny boom from away to Petri's left, and the crewman

in front of him went down, spinning into the snow with blood flying from a wound to his throat. A gun, up in the hills somewhere. One of his snipers had come to grief perhaps, their gun stolen and now shooting at his men. A pause while the sniper reloaded, rewound. Enough time to get his men to a point where the hut was between them and the shooter. Which left Scar and Dom circling each other, maybe in range of the gun, maybe not.

This wasn't how it was supposed to go.

Petri stepped towards the pair of them and stepped back just as quickly when Scar's sword almost took his head off.

"Mine," she snarled.

"Oh no," Dom said. "I beg to differ. You are mine. You first, then that bloody magician, poisoning Maitea's mind against me, both of you, making her hate me. She was all I had, and you had to take her."

Another crack, and a bullet passed Scar's head with an inch to spare and smacked into the lintel of the hut. Seconds later another – the bastard had a second gun.

More of Scar's men and women poured down the slope towards them. Dom spared them a glance, another at the two behind him, both looking piss scared, and came to a decision. A knife replaced one of the swords in his hands and spun towards Scar. She ducked to avoid it, and when she stood up again Dom was gone.

"What the—"

"He's an assassin," Petri said. "I told you to be more careful with him. Quick, back here, where the gun can't get you."

They stood with their backs to the hut as her crew drove the other two back inside with swords and guns and a few belts to the face, and Petri tried to think.

"Who is it up there?" Scar asked Petri like he knew. "Kass?"

She shook her head. "What I came to tell you. Morro sent back a message – their bodies aren't at the bottom of the cliff. They're going to follow the tracks, but she's still alive for now. The man rode back using the trail Morro cleared on their way. Kass is on foot and she might not be at the bottom of that cliff, but there's no easy way out of that ravine without rope. Even if she did get out, there's drifts higher than a man's head she'll have to wade through before she gets to Morro's path."

"Cospel then, come to rescue Vocho. Killed one of our men and stole a gun. A distraction when he thought Vocho was about to die."

"Maybe. But whoever it is, they've killed at least three of my men. We need to find them and soon."

Petri looked back up the hill. "Cospel or not, Dom's at large and he's going to be a problem. But we have his daughter and Vocho; he won't leave them behind. One way or another he'll come back, and we'll have to be waiting for him. And Kass too. If she's alive, she's coming this way."

Scar smiled. "I'm counting on it."

It was only later that Petri recalled how tightly Dom had been bound, remembered Maitea in the hut with a knife and thought maybe, just maybe, she was playing some game with all of them.

The grey lifted, and the light it let in brought a pain that almost made Kass wish she was back in the grey. Almost, because there were horrors in there, ones she dimly recalled, about Petri and Vocho and dead bodies.

She tried to piece together where she was and why in

hell it hurt to breathe so much. Cospel's face looming over
her brought most of it back.

"I sewn you up best I could, miss. Won't hold out against
much though. I don't suppose you'll be looking to take it
easy?"

"You suppose correctly." She tried to sit up and revised
her ideas. "Maybe we won't go straight away. Tell me."

Cospel's face twisted into the ugliest grin Kass had ever
seen. "Got the bugger good and proper, knocked him out
cold. Gave him a kick or two for you too, for good measure.
Tied him up and left him, covered our tracks best I could.
Petri's people will find him soon enough – they were getting
close anyway."

"How did you not get caught?"

"Easy, miss. A misspent youth. Spent *years* not getting
caught. Comes in dead handy. When we came across Scar
and Petri, me and Danel, we was like, you know, biding
our time, out of the way, and they missed us in all the
hullabaloo. So Danel followed them, Petri and all that lot,
when they took Vocho. And I stayed here to find you.
Good job I did, isn't it?"

"Yes. A very good job. Vocho, is he . . .?" She didn't
want to voice the thought that Petri might have killed him.

"Not so good, miss. Danel says he can hardly walk on
that gimpy leg of his, and they got him trussed up in a
hovel of a hut where he's currently freezing his bits off.
But he's alive, so that's a start. They ain't all that far away.
Danel came back once they reached their camp, so's I know
where it is, and then he went back to it to make sure Vocho
stays being alive. He said he'd do what he can to find a
way for us to get him out of there. Good news is, they got
our horses, so if we nick them it'll help, but with only
two of us, three now, it's not going to be easy."

Neither was getting up when every time she moved it felt like someone was twisting a knife up under her ribs. She lifted up her bloodied shirt, peeled away the sodden dressing —part of another shirt, one of hers naturally – Cospel had put on and cautiously took a peek. And that was a very bad idea, she decided when she saw the mess underneath. Cospel had done his best given they were in the middle of bloody nowhere. She dreaded to think – and was afraid to look too hard to find out – what he'd used to sew her up with. But he had, and while it looked like some demented artist had tried to carve a picture into her breast, at least she was no longer bleeding. On the outside anyway. She raised her eyebrows at the thought of Cospel patching her up just there and decided not to think about it.

Cospel seemed to read her not-thoughts. "I kept my eyes shut where I could, miss, and my hands to myself, because I like them where they are. The dressing's only temporary, best I could do, and so's the stitches, and I can't say what state your inside's going to be. You still got the bullet in there, somewhere. Hopefully it didn't go too far in, but I didn't want to start poking about, making things worse. I put some of this on." He handed her a small pot with something greasy and vile-smelling in it. "I use it on the horses for girth galls, clears them right up. It might help. But you were lucky, I reckon. You, er, you got a bit of padding about there; might have stopped you getting your insides torn up."

A cheerful thought but one that was going to have to wait.

"How far did Danel say they were?"

"About five mile, give or take. And we need to climb up out of here first. Danel was going to meet me up this way later, with the rope. Ain't no other way in or out so far as I can see, and I wasn't leaving the rope for them to find."

"Them? How many?"

A shrug that was almost as expressive as Cospel's eyebrows. "Enough. Think they got that magician of theirs with them as well — there was a path melted into the snow, pretty as you like. But he ain't on his own, and they ain't so far behind as all that. Speaking of which, we'd best get moving. I don't doubt they've found Eder by now, but he won't slow them down much, and trying not to leave a trail in snow when you're carrying someone about ready to bleed to death isn't easy, miss. Come on, up you get."

He helped her up to agonising standing, where it was all she could do to breathe properly and the back of her throat tasted metallic with blood. She probed her mouth with a gentle tongue and found her lip cracked and swollen and a missing tooth at the back from where Eder had cracked her with the gun. It could have been worse. A lot worse. She tried to console herself with that thought.

It was easier once they were moving, and she could sink into the pain so that it throbbed in the background as an accompaniment to every halting step and hitching breath.

It took longer than it should have to get to where Cospel had arranged to meet Danel, and Kass was sure she could hear sounds from back down the ravine, voices echoing from the cliffs, back and forth, faint with distance but getting closer.

Cospel helped her to sit, close under the wall of cliff, and rummaged in his pack. Kass never quite knew what he was going to pull out of it. This time he started with a small bottle that looked suspiciously familiar and a gun.

He gave the bottle to her, checked the gun over and began to wind it.

"Took this off Eder, miss, and if it's all the same to you, I think I should be the one using it."

"You're never going to let me forget that, are you? It was one silly mistake."

"Yes, and mistakes with guns get very messy, very quickly. Drink up."

She took the stopper from the bottle and sniffed at it warily. "Cospel . . ."

"Drink it, it'll help with the pain."

"Cospel, is this the same drink that Esti got Voch hooked on?"

He had the grace to look embarrassed. "Close enough. I had her teach me how to make it."

"And you just happened to have some on you? Any particular reason for that you'd like to share with me?"

The gun clicked as it wound to its fullest extent. "You ain't been watching, miss. You know what he's like: he wants everyone to think he's all great and everything. You noticed he had a bit of a limp, I know that. Well, with that hip wound, the pain of it, he can barely walk without that syrup, never mind sparring and all the rest. He thinks without being able to duel he's nothing, no one. Vocho the Limping, Vocho the Ex-Great. So's I've been giving it to him, secret like. He don't know it's me doing it; he just knows it keeps turning up. A bottle a week – I make sure to ration it. Then he can duel and everything and keep on being Vocho the Great. It makes him a bit funny sometimes, but he's always been that anyway, the great pillock, so I thought it was worth it if he could still think of himself like that. Anyway, I'd drink it if I were you, for the pain. It's good for that, and no better nor worse for you than a tot of rum, really. The only reason he's hooked is because without it he's not him, and he can't bear that."

Kass stared at him, everything else forgotten in a blinding flash of realisation. "Cospel," she said at last, "how is it you know my brother better than I do?"

Another shrug as he sighted down the gun. "You ain't been with us much recently, in the head. I'm hoping in the coming clusterfuck you'll remember who stuck with you and that Petri didn't. I'm hoping you start seeing things again, miss. No shooting them though. I like my ears where they are."

Kass's head whirled, and she stared at the bottle. Her head was swimming, probably from lack of blood; her breathing was little more than short red-hot pangs of agony. There was no way she would make it up to the top of the ravine without *something*. And how, how had she missed all that about Voch? Because she'd had her head stuffed up her own backside, thinking about Petri. She still did, or maybe that fall had shaken that loose in her. Petri had Voch, and there was no telling what he'd do to him. Nothing nice, she could pretty well guarantee that – no love lost between the two of them, ever, and this Petri wasn't the old one she'd known. He was very far from that lost man struggling to do the right thing.

The echoes grew closer. She could pick out individual voices just as the end of a rope landed next to her, and Danel's earnest face appeared, far, far above.

Clockwork God, help me now, she thought and took a good glug of Esti's jollop.

Chapter Twenty-three

Scar paced up and down, and Petri watched. Like watching a stranger who wore a familiar face, he thought. She was no longer the hard woman with the soft centre, the sucker for waifs and strays who'd taken pity on Petri. No longer the woman who'd told him she could see past the wreck of his face, had kissed what was left of his cheek and taken him to bed. When she looked at him now there was no pity in her glance, no softness for anyone. She had hardened all the way through.

Maitea came into the hut and shed her cloak. Every time Petri looked at her she seemed darker, more insubstantial, as though she was becoming a shadow of herself. She eyed Scar warily, and the look she gave Petri was unfathomable.

Scar stopped her pacing and turned on a beaming smile as she indicated Maitea should sit. The younger woman did so, smoothing her skirts underneath her and putting her gloved hands primly in her lap.

"You heard about your father?" Scar said as she sat opposite.

Maitea glanced Petri's way again before she answered. "He escaped."

"Tried to kill me on his way too." Scar cocked her head as though expecting something.

All she got was Maitea's shrug. "Killing is all he does. You and Morro have shown me that."

"And now you see that we were right. Morro says your magic is growing, that you're an apt pupil."

Another shrug, tense with some emotion Petri couldn't guess at.

"Good," Scar said. "Maybe you can use it to help us now. Time to repay what's been done for you. He'll still be out there – I think we can safely say he'll not leave you behind. He wants to take you away from here, from your home. He'll come back for Vocho too, no doubt. They're old friends, and that tells you all you need to know about Vocho. We need to try to draw your father out. Funnel him to where we want him to be. Shadows are your magic, Morro says. So we use shadows against an assassin, who works in them."

Finally Scar spared Petri a look that was hot and cold at the same time. "Petri, escort Maitea to her hut. Make it very plain to the guards that she's now a prisoner like the others. And Maitea, when you get there, you wait in your shadows. Your father will come, and then we'll have him."

Maitea's face pinched at that, but she nodded meekly and got up. Scar turned away, dismissing them both, and Petri followed Maitea from the hut.

She kept herself stiff and haughty, but Petri was no less so.

"You had a knife in that hut," he said to her relentless face.

"I was going to kill him. Dom, I mean."

"Your father, you mean."

"Yes." She stopped and turned to face him. Her gloves stayed on, he noted, and no hint of cooking blood stained the air. She was only talking to him, not trying to persuade him, manipulate him. "I . . . I kept asking him about my mother. Morro and Scar keep telling me what he is, but I wanted to be sure. He admitted he murdered her, in the end. So I was set to return the favour."

She seemed very young in the darkness, and very sure of herself. Like her father, he thought again. So very self-possessed. "Not cutting his bonds to free him then?"

The look she gave him came from under sly lids. "When you found out your father was a slaver, did you want to free him from his? Or did you stand by while he was killed?"

A stab of something at that – he'd watched his father die and hadn't felt more than a twinge. "Killed by a magician," he said at last. "And that was just the start of their involvement in my life. I don't trust Morro."

A secret little smile from her. "And you're wise not to. He's got no love for you, but it might be too late. He's got Scar under his paw, thinking as he wants. Being strong is all very well, Petri, but you need to be careful too."

They reached her hut. "I spent my life being careful," he said. "All it got me was this face and a home in these mountains. Now I intend to win."

At last a smile from Maitea, a hand on his arm before she covered herself in shadows and went into the hut.

"I hope you win, Petri. I really do."

Kass squinted at the bottle, sloshed the syrup about, said what the hells and took another slug. She was beginning to realise why Voch liked the stuff so much. It wasn't that the pain went away, as such. She just didn't give a crap about it, or anything else come to that.

"Up you get, miss." Cospel got her to her feet at the top of the ravine. Kass tried not to look down because it made everything go spinny, and everything down there was a long way away. "And I think you've had enough."

Cospel made a grab for the bottle, but she hung on. Dimly she was aware that it was helping with more than the physical pain. Even more dimly came the knowledge there was something she should be very unhappy about, more than one thing in fact, but she gave even less of a crap about them.

"This stuff's bloody marvellous," she said and took an extra slug.

Another hand grabbed for the bottle from the other side, and she was so surprised they managed to get it away from her.

"You had to get her drunk, didn't you?" Danel said from behind her. "Great timing, given you've got a ruddy magician almost up your arse, and the snow's about to get ten times worse before it gets better. All that, and you get her so she can't hardly stand up."

"She's only had a bit! Don't drink much as a rule, see? Expect it took her a bit harder than it does Vocho – he's got used to it. She'd never have made it up there without it anyway."

"No, well." Danel took in Kass's blood-soaked furs and muttered on some more. "Best we get going. Scar's crew aren't too far behind, and they've got climbing gear and that magician bloke. Thought it was bad enough lugging the rope all the way here; now we've got to lug her back as well."

"She'll sober up soon enough."

Kass was having a bit of trouble remembering what they were supposed to be doing, but with Cospel's help she managed to make her way up the slope while he argued with Danel. A cold wind scythed at them from the ravine, bringing new bombardments of snow with it. She barely noticed the cold and watched the pretty snowflakes as they danced about, until she had to stop because they were spinning so fast she almost fell over trying to follow them.

"Found a good gun," Danel was saying. "Well, I say found, more like nicked from the dead body I had just created. They had a few gunmen up in the hills around the village, but this one, he weren't very watchful. I managed to put the cat among the pigeons as well. Got them running about all over looking for me. Bunch of lowland eejits, couldn't find a mountain man up here if I had a flashing light on my head. Saw young Vocho and a couple of the others. Shot a couple of the buggers holding them, but they've still got him, and the rest. One bloke did get free, but I never saw who or where he went."

"So now they're expecting trouble?" Cospel said. "Great timing yourself. Petri's no fool. He'll have guessed that I'm about at least, and now he'll think he knows it, and he'll be waiting for us."

"Petri," she said, stung into remembering even through the fug in her brain by the sound of his name. "Petri's alive."

Cospel stopped and turned her, wobbling, to face him. "Yes he is, miss. But he ain't the Petri you remember; he's all twisted in the head, and it ain't a good sort of twist neither. He's got Voch and the rest, and I don't have no doubts at all he means to kill all of them. Vocho most of all though. And you, if he gets hold of you. We've got to be careful."

"But Petri wouldn't—"

Cospel shook her gently by the shoulders, so that the wound in her chest protested even through the haze. "Yes, he would. And he's going to. Don't hold on to any fancy notions otherwise, because they'd be a load of shit."

She looked at his face, the way the eyebrows drooped as though in defeat, and tried to think. It was quite hard when she kept being distracted by snowflakes and hiccupping, but she managed in the end. Cospel was a thieving genius with scant regard for the law, or much of anything, but he was as straightforward as people came when it came to things like this. But this wasn't – her and Petri and Vocho – straightforward at all. They were all tangled up in each other like old rope.

"I was going to save him," she said, and watched Cospel's face crumple as the words slurred out.

"Miss, you ain't got no cause to be blaming yourself—"

"I was going to save him, and then I couldn't because he was dead, but now he's alive so I can. So I'm going to."

Cospel turned away and pulled her on, making her stumble in the snow. "He don't need saving, miss. Except maybe from himself. Got himself all tucked up nice, he has, shacked up with that Scar woman, nice and cosy. He knows what he's doing, and what that is, is killing you and Voch if he can. Seen it on his face when they ambushed us. On his half a face, at least. He means to have you two dead."

"Made a start even," Danel put in from the other side. "Him and Vocho were duelling, sort of. That's why I got them all stirred up. Because it weren't much of a contest what with Vocho not being able to walk properly. Old Skull, he kept sticking him – in the shoulder, in the leg – playing with him. Gearing up to run him through if I'm any judge. So I let off a few shots just to get him distracted. Worked too. Vocho's still alive, even if he is mostly a lot of holes."

A short silence as Cospel and Kass digested this.

"Fair enough, I suppose," Cospel said. "Though it's going to make life even harder than it already is. But see, miss, Petri don't need saving. He needs bloody well stopping before he kills Vocho and the rest."

By the time the light started to fade, the jollop had mostly worn off, leaving the pain to wreak havoc. Despite the cold Kass was sweating freely, her breath coming in hot little hitches. She didn't miss the looks Danel and Cospel shared when they thought she wasn't looking, but ignored them.

Kass and Vocho and Petri.

Like it or not, the three of them seemed to revolve around one another, irretrievably. All the spinning was starting to make her sick. She shook herself and tried to think properly through the haze that Vocho's syrup had left in its wake.

Petri was alive, and the cramp in her chest wasn't just from the bullet wound. He was alive but changed, inside. But the old Petri, *her* Petri, he was in there somewhere, she was sure of it. Behind the mess of his face, behind the terror of the Skull he'd become, was Petri, caught up in things beyond him, struggling to make sense of himself, wanting to do what was right. He had to be in there somewhere, had to be savable. She had to believe that or she'd go crazy. In the meantime, he wanted Vocho dead and had the means to do it.

But if anyone was going to kill the annoying bugger, it would be her. That might mean, probably would mean, facing Petri. Her sword hand throbbed, and she couldn't be sure if she was itching to use it or desperate not to. *What seems good to you*. She'd thought she was getting to grips with that after a long time flailing, but now . . . When the choice seemed to be between saving your brother or the man you were once in love with, maybe still were, was any choice good?

Vocho staggered when a hand behind pushed him, only avoiding falling by the skin of his teeth. Something had happened, something that no one seemed very happy about, but he had no idea what it was. He was grateful to whoever had done it though, because he was fairly sure Petri would have happily skewered him any number of times before he got bored and killed him. They'd taken him back to the prison hut, where Dom was conspicuous by his absence, thanks to Maitea cutting his bonds. Escaped, Carrola said shortly when he asked, and three of Scar's men shot. That had made him grin.

Now it was much later, almost sundown, and all his bruises had had the chance to come out and really make themselves felt. There seemed to be more bruise than skin in many places, in fact, except where he had a nice collection of holes and gashes. His cheek was promising to sport a very fine scar, eventually.

The hand pushed again, and this time he did fall, his hip twisting under him and dumping him on the snow-covered rock. A yank on his hair got him upright, and then he saw where they were going.

At least it was warm inside this new hut. It was larger than the rest and had no cracks between the planks to let the ever-present wind and snow in. A fire burned in a hearth to one side of the main room with a kettle of something bubbling over it that smelled pretty damned good to a starving Vocho. Through a half-open door he could spot a bed thickly strewn with furs and blankets. Too much to hope these were his new quarters, especially when he saw who was with him. Petri sat at a table, sword laid across his knees, his face, what was left of it, pinched and pale as though he was furious but trying not to show it. Scar watched from behind him, her eyes darting everywhere, piercing everything. There was something about her that shivered Vocho's shoulder blades, an intensity that unsettled him.

Not half as much as seeing Eder on the floor in front of Petri, covered in blood.

"Glad you could join us," Petri drawled to Vocho. "You," he prodded Eder with a foot, "start again."

Eder looked around, face grey and clammy with sweat. It was only when he tried to move and hissed in pain that Vocho noticed his leg, the rough splint on it.

"We fell. A long way. I landed on some bodies, Kass landed on me. My leg broke in the fall."

"And Kass?" Petri and Vocho said together. Scar's eyes lit up at that, and not in a good way. If Vocho was Petri he'd be very careful about her being behind him.

"I broke my leg, and her fall. She was well enough."

"Was?" Vocho's voice came out as a croak.

Eder glared up at him from under lowered brows, and again Vocho was reminded of a dog pushed beyond endurance into going for the throat. "Was. I shot her. In the chest. Someone else was there though – Cospel, I think. He hit me, tied me up. But she was bleeding like a stuck pig. Right in the chest. She'll have bled to death long since."

Vocho's leg collapsed from under him, and he found himself on the floor next to Eder, with Petri's nightmare face looming over them both, every muscle frozen. Scar laughed behind Petri, laid a hand on his shoulder. He twitched it off.

"How sure are you?" Petri said, and his voice was as husky as Vocho's had been.

"Sure I shot her. Sure I got her in the chest, that all this blood is hers. She's miles from anywhere where she can get medical attention. She's dead, or dying, no matter who's with her, unless they're a first-rate doctor. Not many of those in these godforsaken mountains."

Vocho sat and stared at him until his eyes burned with it. Scar's voice snapped him back to now.

"We'll find her body soon enough then, because my men are still tracking her. She'll soon find out what it is to come across a magician on this mountain, a magician who can conjure snow and ice and wind, can melt it away to clear a path for himself and my men, who can call snow to fill it again afterwards when all she can do is flounder in the drifts. A magician who's keen to find her."

Vocho caught Petri's eye, expecting to see gloating to match Scar's voice, but there was something else entirely. Regret? Sorrow? He couldn't be sure but found he didn't care much either way. "If she is dead," he said slowly, his eyes on Petri all the while, "then you know I'll have to kill you too?"

Scar laughed again, and her foot shot out to catch Vocho on the shoulder, sending him sprawling. "Says the man who can't walk properly. *My* Petri will fillet you. Might be a bit of fun at least. And another head to send to Bakar."

Vocho didn't miss that heavy *my* or the look of victory glowing in her scarred face. She thought she'd won a prize.

Weirdly, Scar seemed to think Petri, one-handed, one-eyed, half-faced, pompous old back-stabbing blowhard Petri, was a prize.

Yet from the look on his face Petri wasn't at all happy about being won.

Chapter Twenty-four

Scar had Vocho and Eder taken off to the hut that served as the prison, shooed all the rest out and turned on Petri, mouth hooked into a smile, eyes shining. She slid onto his lap and kissed him soundly, seemed not to notice or care that he didn't kiss her back, as she hadn't seemed to care when he'd started sleeping in the barn again. She leaped up and paced the floor by the fire. In the flickering yellow light she looked more like a lion in a cage than ever, bursting with the need to fight, to hunt.

"We did it," she muttered, then louder, "We did it, Petri. Everyone will know our names now, know that Scar and Skull killed the guild master. No head to send back yet, more's the pity, but there's always Vocho's. But no one is ever going to fuck with me again. With any of us." She paused as though noticing him properly, and a frown shadowed some of her energy. "We'll be famous, don't you see? And safe. Who would dare take a knife to my face now? Or yours? When we took out the two most feared duellists in the country. You've got your revenge; we've got a grand name for ourselves – made ourselves safe, and king and queen of our little domain, feared wherever we're spoken of. Aren't you happy she's dead?"

She came to kneel in front of him, a tremor of excitement in her hand as she laid it on his shoulder. She'd sold him revenge, nursed his hatred, told him she'd loved him, wound him like a gun and aimed him. He blinked hard. Used him, like Bakar, like Sabates and Licio, like everyone had. Everyone except Kass, who'd abandoned him. Maybe he'd deserved that, he thought at last.

Scar's hand tightened on his shoulder, and her mouth twitched at one side. "Aren't you happy?" she repeated.

He didn't know how to answer, didn't trust his lips not to say the wrong thing, so he said nothing, only gently took her hand away, stood to put on his sword and said the only thing he thought he could be sure of: "She's not dead."

Scar looked at him sideways, gauging him. "Is that what you think, or what you want?"

He paused, did some gauging of his own and wondered if he even knew himself. "What I think. You know what I want." Although Petri was beginning to have doubts he knew what it was that he did want.

She didn't believe him, that was plain from the twitch of her lip, the way her eyes slid over him, cold all of a sudden, and he turned away to the door.

Her voice came out gravel rough behind him, and he knew he walked a knife-edge here. "Where are you going?"

His hand stopped on the latch. "To see if they've found the sniper. Or Dom. We aren't safe yet. We've got Dom's daughter under lock and key. We tried to kill Kass and took her brother hostage. We won't be safe until both Dom and Kass are dead, and that's not yet."

She said nothing more as he went out into the frostbitten

place that had become his home and now seemed utterly
strange. Snow crunched under his boots as he made his
way to the edge of the scarp that fell away sharply at one
end of the valley. The dregs of the day were grey, swirled
with white, like his mind had become.

He was alone – the sniper had gone perhaps, perhaps
not, but no one was taking chances at this end of the
valley. Except him. He looked up at the sharp ridges which
could hide a man, that had been scoured and found empty.
Not Cospel, he thought vaguely. Cospel was with Kass, had
been the one to tie up Eder, from what he'd said. Was
Cospel enough to keep her alive?

Maybe his gut was wrong: maybe Eder was the shot he
reckoned himself, and she was dead. Petri couldn't be sure
if he was happy or not, whether it was as Scar kept telling
him, or even what he wanted. Or whether Scar was just
repeating back what Morro fed to her.

He should take some of the crew in the morning, find
Kass. Bury her properly, if they could find a place that
wasn't frozen. She'd abandoned him when he needed her
the most but she shouldn't be left out in the cold. Maybe
take that Eder too, make the bastard walk all the way on
his broken leg. In the morning because it was getting dark,
and shadows filled the gaps between the mountains.

"I said once," a voice behind him said, "that before long
someone might ask me to kill you. And that I might,
depending on what you did next."

Petri didn't turn or even put a hand on his sword. It'd
do no good, not if Dom had a weapon, and he most likely
did. Petri couldn't have beaten him if he still had two
hands and both eyes.

"Do you think you might?" was all he said, and wondered
as he said it.

"It depends."

Dom moved around Petri's good side, his dark shape visible against the snow, and yes, he had a sword in hand. Of course. What assassin would be without one?

"Maitea cut your bonds," Petri said.

A sharp, dark smile from Dom that promised pain to follow. "She did. Cut my bonds and told me to fuck off out of her life. I consider myself lucky Morro hasn't taught her much in the way of magic yet, or I'd be a small and messy pile. He and now Scar are teaching her a lot about hating me."

"So why are you still here? Come to try again for Scar? You'll fail as surely as last time. Or is it Morro you want now?"

Dom gave a little one-shouldered shrug that might have meant anything. "My attempt on Scar was . . . a brief aberration while my mind was disturbed by grief, which is the only reason she's still alive. But hot-blooded revenge? I think I've seen enough of that to know it does no one any good. Seen too many people dash themselves against the rocks of it. Cold and canny is the way to go. Think first, then strike. Scar and Morro have my daughter, have turned her mind against me. I don't blame her for hating me, but I can't just walk away and leave her with them, leave her to her mother's fate. I assume that capturing Kass to put in that hovel with Vocho is part of the plan?"

"Eder shot her," Petri said. "Killed her, he's sure." But if that were true, Morro would have found her by now, would have brought back her head gloating over it.

A long silence, the gleam of light on steel, a faint crunch as Dom moved another step.

"How sure?"

"He shot her in the chest. There was a lot of blood."

"You must be very happy," Dom said. "After all your hard work to get her here. After she almost killed us all to get to you, try to save you?"

Petri gaped at him. "That's true? Vocho said, but . . ."

"But normally Vocho lies about anything and everything. Not this time. She tried, we all did, to get to Reyes in time. And later we told her you were dead, and it broke her – it's still breaking her. Is that why you told us to say it? So you could blindside her, kill her when she wasn't expecting you?"

"I—"

The blade whipped across his face perilously close to his one remaining eye, and he jerked back.

"Truthfully," Dom whispered. "For once in your miserable life, Petri Egimont, be truthful – with yourself, and me. We told her you were dead because you asked us to. Because we saw what he'd done to you and we thought it a kindness to you both. All we could do for you. Now this, keeping Vocho in a cell so that she'll come to get him, so you and your delightful Scar can take their heads and show them to Bakar in some fool plan that you think will get him to leave you be. So, why did you ask? Was it so you could kill her later? Were you thinking of that even then?"

Petri shut his one eye and tried to recall. He'd been a broken man, not thinking straight. He'd only wanted her not to see him like that. Like this. But the hate had been there already, bursting out, hot. It had cooled later – distilled, crystallised – and he'd put it aside, concentrated on just surviving. Until Scar, who had nurtured it for her own ends.

He shook his head to Dom's question, even as his words belied that denial. "I wanted them to pay. All of them:

Kass, her ridiculous brother, Bakar, Eneko. Eneko was executed, so that left three. I wanted to show them they were wrong about me, who I really am underneath, and then I wanted them to pay."

"Is this who you really are, Petri?" Dom stepped closer and cocked his head. "A scruffy little man in a rat-arsed village built of frozen mud, with delusions of grandeur and obsessed by revenge? I don't think so. Kass would never have the bad taste to love a man like that."

The old Petri would have stood and taken it, would have thought on it perhaps but would have stayed his hand. This Petri lashed out with his good hand, knocking the tip of Dom's sword off point. He reached for Dom's face with the other arm, flicking his wrist to bring out the knife that served instead of fingers.

It found only air as Dom danced away, his sword back on point in an instant, if further away. His smile was dangerous.

"Not bad. Not bad at all, for all the good it did. Now, do excuse me. Several people have mayhem in their near future, and I need to decide which people. First, I think I'll have my sword back, if you don't mind. I'll be generous and let you have this in return. It's not too bad, a bit rough, and the balance is slightly off, but it'll do you. There, throw mine at my feet. Thank you."

In return, the sword he held plopped at Petri's feet.

"Think of this as a friendly warning," Dom said. "Because my daughter thinks all I can do is kill. Because Kass would want me to give you notice. Don't expect another."

With a whisper of swirling snow he was gone, leaving Petri cold with rage and a sick, exultant thrill. She'd come for him. She had.

* * *

Vocho sat and shivered in the hovel, trying to massage his hip back into some sensible sort of arrangement instead of knotted to buggery. After a while Eder was brought in and hobbled over to sit in another corner. Despite the fact his leg was broken, that he'd no doubt never walk properly on it again, would never lead a prelate's guard again, would lose his commission and everything he'd ever earned for himself if Bakar found out what he'd done, despite all that, the smug sod seemed to be gloating, especially when Carrola made a fuss of his leg and set to trying to make him as comfortable as anyone could get in their icebox of a hut.

Vocho really wished Dom was still here but took a bit of hope from the fact he was around, and free. He wished he had some spare jollop too. But what he wished more than anything else was that Eder hadn't shot Kass. Vocho watched Carrola as she tried to do something with a splint on the captain's leg that had seen better days and wished his own leg worked so he could get up and strangle him.

"Why?" he said at last, noting how Carrola shot him a look. "Why did you shoot Kass? What did she—"

No mistaking the shock on Carrola's face, the way she flinched back, let her hands drop from the splint in horror. "What?" she whispered.

"She existed," Eder spat. "The guild exists. Both turned me away as though I was nothing. I'd shoot you too if I had a gun handy, but it looks like I won't need to. Seems like Petri wants you as dead as I do. Eventually. I shall probably cheer him on."

Carrola got up jerkily and moved away, her face unfathomable in the dimness of the hut as she peered through a crack in the door so as not to look at them.

"No surprises there, then," Vocho said to Eder. "Feeling's mutual, in fact. You are a surprise, though. I thought you were the prelate's man. You *are* the prelate's man. Then again, so was Petri once, and look how that turned out. I'm sure you'll be very happy together, until he decides he wants to kill you too. But my sister, let's get back to her. Did you kill her?"

"I do hope so. Got her right in the chest. Unless your flunky is a doctor in disguise, I'd say it's unlikely she's alive."

Vocho levered himself to his feet, where he stood for a moment to let his hip settle, at least a touch. Sod the hip, sod no jollop. Sod everything.

Vocho limped over and cracked Eder right in the face, to the detriment of his own knuckles. Someone yanked on his hair and pulled him away, and he rounded to see Carrola, hand up ready to belt him one in return. He managed to pull the punch he launched, but the effort cost him his balance and he dropped to the floor.

"You should let me at him," he gasped. "Bastard deserves more than that little love tap."

"What for? What good will punching him stupid do?"

"It'd make me feel better? He shot Kass!"

She stuck out a hand to help him up, and he was past feeling any sting to his pride when he took it.

"So he says. But punching him won't change that, or whether she's still alive or not. I understand, I do. I understand you're angry and worried, and so am I. But the little shit's not worth it. I'm not sure yet about you. Leave him where he is and come look, and maybe we might live to find out what happened to Kass."

He knew she was right, but it didn't stop him wanting to punch Eder until his knuckles bled. He took a deep breath, used it to push that down deep inside where he could maybe use it later. *Time to grow up, Voch, past time*

probably. So suck it up and starting thinking, not just reacting.
"All right. Anything as long as I don't have to look at him."

She helped him over to the door, where a wider crack not only let in a frigid blast of air but also allowed a limited view across the valley. Where all had been dark before, now half a hundred torches blazed and moved across the snow.

"What do you think's going on?" Carrola asked.

"Best guess Dom is going on, or soon will be. Well, he's not having all the fun. And there's whoever shot those men – my guess is either Danel or Cospel. But who knows where they are now, if they've been caught or are about to be? Petri made it clear I'm here as bait for Kass. If they no longer need me for that, then our usefulness ends. And so do we shortly afterwards. Petri's not stupid either. He'll go looking for her, find her one way or another. Alive or . . . or the other thing. And then, I am fairly certain, he will come to finish me off personally. Carrola, are you . . . are you with Eder or . . .?"

She looked over at him sprawled on the floor, and a frown aged her face as she weighed things up.

"He's still a bastard," Eder whispered. "You know that. I told you nothing untrue about him. He did all those things."

"I haven't denied it," Vocho said. Much, anyway. "But what you said wasn't the whole story, was it?"

"You did them, that's all anyone needs to know."

"I'm sure he did," Carrola snapped. "And you shot his sister for no more reason than she was part of the guild you hate so much. What does that make you?" She turned back to Vocho. "Now, no more of your buggering about. You can explain yourself later, and you will. For now what do you have in mind?"

Vocho grinned at her in the dark, and received a matching smile that made him feel all warm and cosy despite the chill of the air.

"A brave and dashing escape plan. What else?"

Petri was still standing at the lip of the scarp when Scar came. He turned towards her when she called his name, but when she put out a hand to touch his arm, he couldn't help but flinch. He could have sworn he heard his father laugh, heard someone whisper, *You are weakness*. Everything flooded back into his head — every action, every mistake that had led him here. Too late now to do anything about any of them. All he could do was live. Think. Survive. This was the life he'd made, for good or ill, and he had to live with those choices, take them as far as he had to. Now he had to be strong.

"There's still someone out there with a gun and a grudge who's a damned good shot," he said. "And Dom." He turned to look at her, the scar flickering in the dim light, the strength of the bones underneath, the way she gazed at him. She'd used him, but he'd used her too, hadn't he? He'd thought he'd loved her. Maybe he had once, but that had been the old Scar, who took in those no one else wanted and gave them a place to call their own. Who'd freed Maitea just because she'd been brave. Not this Scar, who thought nothing of killing, whose eyes shone whenever Morro was near.

A moment of softness in her again, replaced by a brittle hardness that seemed as fragile as snowfall.

"What are you doing out here?" she asked.

"Thinking," he said. "We've pissed off a very accomplished assassin. Cospel's still around, if Eder is to be believed. Maybe Kass is dead, maybe she isn't. But someone shot our men. Vocho has allies out there, and we'd do well to make sure they fail utterly when they come for him."

A brief nod and a sidelong look. "If any one of them gets back to say where we are . . . We want to reveal ourselves at out leisure, from a place of strength, not have him find us before we're ready."

He hesitated, and she didn't miss it so he rushed in with, "They won't get back." Not time to show his hand just yet. And what hand did he hold? Not a winning one. Time to bluff and hope.

"None of them?"

"None," and because she seemed to expect something more, "I promise you that."

When he led the way back from the lip to their ragtag village, saw men and women look to him for answers, for guidance, listen to his every word, he knew he wanted this. It was what he'd always wanted and had never dared to hope he'd get. He thrust all thoughts of Kass away, of the look on her face when she'd seen him up at the pass, the thought of her shot, and made his way to the cleared space at the centre of the huts.

Kepa had scared up as many men and women as he could find. Petri got them lighting torches and searching.

"Searching for what?" Scar asked.

"Not what – who. Kass, dead or not." A painful spasm in his heart at that, but he dismissed it as just more weakness. "Both Dom and Cospel are here. Those two will find Vocho and Maitea if they can, and just as likely kill anyone in their way. You, Kepa, take half and make sure no one gets Vocho or Maitea. The rest, we search everywhere. Start at this end of the valley and work outwards, in groups. If you find either Dom and Cospel, send for me. Go."

Men and women scattered, muttering. A few made pointed remarks to Scar, who sent them off with a snarl.

"They aren't happy," she said.

"Neither am I."

"If Dom or any of the rest get back to Kastroa . . ."

"I promised you, didn't I? And if they do, we'll move. Regroup. Hide until we're ready."

She shook her head and seemed more herself than she had in weeks. "No. No more hiding. I was done with running a long while back. And you're sick of running – from the man who did that to you, from yourself. We all ran here. But now we stand, we fight, we live. Now let the others find who they can. Morro's back, and you and me have other work."

Petri watched with a roiling stomach as Scar and Morro sat in his hut, heads together, planning what they'd do come morning.

"We couldn't find her, but she's here somewhere." Morro waved at the map. He'd returned from Razor Gorge, where they'd ambushed Eder and his troop in the first place, disgruntled at not finding Kass, and had taken it out on the first man he'd found, who likely would never have his mind back as his own now. "She's somewhere close," Morro carried on. "She'll be coming for her brother, and when she does we'll have her."

Scar looked up at Petri, caught his set look. "That's right. With all the snow you've sent perhaps she'll freeze. If not, there's enough to stop her going anywhere else. With your help, Petri is going to find and kill her. Isn't that so, Petri?" Scar had changed since Morro's return. Her voice was edged like her blade, like the shards of thin ice Petri was skating on, playing both sides, theirs and his, and he'd not done so well before at that. He had to now, the last throw of his dice. His only chance to be the man he always wanted to be.

"Yes."

"Good." She bent back to the map, and Morro smiled at him over her bent head, raised one bare hand with its writhing markings, showing swords and a severed head. His.

Not even trying to hide what he was doing with his hands, openly using his magic on her, Morro turned to Scar with a different sort of smile, and the markings changed as he murmured in her ear. The swords remained, but the head was replaced with a crown, a throne. The changes in Scar became blindingly obvious at last, not just suspicions.

Inside Petri grew ever colder. Trapped again, at the mercy of a magician's whim. He twisted his ruined lip into a silent snarl that brought a wider grin from Morro and more patterns that showed only death for himself.

"We know where she's headed," Scar was saying. "Here. We can make sure we're ready to meet them."

"Make sure she doesn't tell anyone where we are until we want them to know," Morro murmured. "Eder will do well for that when the time comes. The valiant captain, horrendously injured, battling his way down the mountain to raise the alarm."

"With us right behind him," Scar said.

"For what?" Petri asked.

Scar looked up at him, and he saw it, that shine of mania behind the eyes. Like Bakar, like Licio, like him, all manipulated into doing what a magician wanted, believing it to be their own desire.

Scar stood up, and the edge was gone from her voice, instead a softness. More her than she'd been for days, but he saw it now for the act it was. "For us, Petri. All of us. You and me and Kepa, all of us. They cast us off, threw us away. Aren't we worth more than that? Worth a place down there with the rest of them?"

"By killing them?"

A shrug. "Why not? We're doing this for us."

"For him." Petri nodded at Morro, who only sat, cat-like and smiling.

"No, Petri. For us, it was always for us."

He opened his mouth to say no, it wasn't, but a subtle twitch of Morro's hand and the waft of cooking blood stopped him.

"No doubt your fine brave man here will help me to search for her," Morro said. "I'm sure he wants to find her as much as we do, Scar. Though I think perhaps his reasons, and his wants, have changed."

Petri's mouth dried up as Scar's look pierced him, like she could see all the doubt inside.

"Have they, Petri?" she asked, suspicion in her voice, in the way her eyes narrowed, and her hand hovered over her sword hilt. *I won't have a man in my camp who might turn on me or any of the people here. A man like that is as good as dead.* She'd warned him once, and he didn't doubt her or that warning.

"My reasons haven't changed, nor my wants," he lied.

Her face cleared as quickly as it had clouded, and she gifted him with a smile while Morro sat back, mouth pursed.

"Good," he said. "Then you can prove it by helping me search, and I'll let you be the one to take her head and bring it back to your beloved Scar. A romantic gift, don't you think? To prove to Scar how much you love her. How much you believe in what she's doing."

Petri didn't trust himself to speak so only inclined his

head. He was dead – or would deserve to be – whatever
he did. Unless he killed Morro with no blame attaching
to him. Yet that seemed an impossible task. Morro was
never alone, and Petri couldn't trust any of the others,
who seemed as under his sway as Scar was. Petri would
be dead before his stroke fell.

"Excellent." Morro stood up and dusted down his thick
robes. "Now then, to see about that snow. Can you spare
Petri for a few moments?" When Scar nodded, seeming
happy that the two men in her life were friends, Morro
led the way and Petri trailed after.

The night outside was clear, the sky a close blackness,
the stars hardened points against it. Clear, and so cold it
took Petri's breath. Morro moved away from the two men
standing guard outside Scar's hut, out of earshot though
not out of sight or gunshot range. If Petri stabbed him
now, and he could, he'd be dead as soon as Morro.

"You forget yourself, and me," Morro murmured. "You
forget I can see inside your head. Oh, not every thought
but enough. Enough to know you want me dead. Want
Kass too, don't you? No, don't deny it. I see it even if you
don't. You want everything that you can't have."

"I could kill you and have everything I want," Petri said.

Morro laughed at that, long and loud, bringing curious
heads from doorways to see what the fuss was about. "Empty
threats are all you have. You cannot kill me and live –
you're at least sensible enough to realise that. I cannot kill
you openly and keep Scar's trust, but there are means at
my disposal. Men here who would die for me, kill for me,
if I just show them the right markings, whisper the right
words, spill the right blood."

Petri opened his mouth to argue, but Morro waved a
lazy hand that seemed to sap his will.

"Currently you are somewhat useful to me," he went on. "Keeping Scar's attention where I want it. Much as having Vocho alive is useful to draw Kass in. Useful for now. At some point he will no longer be useful and we'll kill him." A casual shrug that was more chilling than the weather. "If you stop being useful, then the same will happen. Now, shall we see about some snow?"

Morro pulled some paper from the sleeve of his robe, a brush from some inner pocket and a vial that ran thick and black with blood. It was the work of moments for him to paint some symbols that squirmed under the brush. The temperature fell even further, and the light dimmed as clouds boiled up from nothing to cover the moon. A last brushstroke, and wind scoured down from the mountain top, driving snow before it in great waves. The force of it staggered Petri, and it sounded to him as though the wind had voices in it, screams of the dying.

"Screams indeed," Morro said above the noise. "How I imagine you will sound if you try to harm me in any way."

Kass slumped down in the snow and massaged her aching head. The jollop had long since worn off, leaving her feeling twice as weak as before, with shooting pains in her wound that robbed her of breath and an accompanying throb in her head with every heartbeat.

Cospel and Danel sat in a loose huddle next to her. Danel had managed to find a crevice that he reckoned "no bloody lowlander" would spot in years. It was a squeeze for three, but at least it was warmer than outside, which had turned on a coin from cold but bearable to a howling storm.

"We've got to get to Voch," she said, again. "We've hardly managed any distance yet."

"We've got to avoid being killed as well," Cospel said,

again. "They're bound to be looking for whoever shot up their little camp. We got to be careful."

"So's Voch, and that's the problem."

Cospel let out a long and heartfelt sigh. "Ain't it always? Look, it's dark; snow's coming down, and Danel reckons it'll get worse afore it gets better. What do you want, to flounder about in that, getting lost or, even better, freezing to death while getting lost? What good will that do Vocho?"

Kass didn't want to admit it, but perhaps he was right.

"So what happened with you and Eder in that crevasse, then?" Danel asked Kass. "I thought Eder——"

"Was an arse? Didn't we all?" Cospel said.

"What in hell was Bakar thinking, sending him out with us?" Kass said.

"Who knows, with the way his mind is? Maybe he's still a bit screwy. Anyway, all the more reason to find Vocho and get the hell out of here. You said three days to the lads back in Kastroa, right? They'll be on their way soon."

"They won't know where we are though," Danel said. "And we know where Scar is now. We could go back to them, get reinforcements in Kastroa?"

"Scar won't be here by the time we get back. Not if she's got any sense. Whatever needs doing, we have to do it. But," Kass said, "perhaps not this second. Maybe you're right, Cospel."

She peered out into the darkness. Snow filled her vision. Snow on the ground, in the air, making the darkness behind even blacker. As she watched, a howl of wind came up from the valley, a shriek that had the sound of human screams in it, bringing a mountain's worth of snow behind it.

"What in——"

"Magician," Danel said over the howl. "Seen him melting snow down in the camp just by looking at it. Maybe if he can melt it, he can make it snow harder too."

Snow fell, not in dribs and drabs or veils, but in great billowing clouds that seemed to cut off their hiding place from the rest of the world. It wasn't long before the entrance was almost blocked, and Cospel worked to clear it so they could at least have fresh air to breathe. The snow, so deadly outside, in here kept them snug – that and their closeness. Danel soon nodded off, closely followed by Cospel, rolled into a ball like a very large dormouse.

Kass tried to get comfortable, but it was impossible. Cospel had taken the only comfy spot, she was sure, and besides, every time she shifted even slightly great throbs of pain pulsed through her. She delved past all the layers of fur, tunic and shirt, peeled off the by now drying and crusted dressing and took a look.

It was a mess. Although she had to be grateful that the bullet had not gone any deeper. Pain was something she could deal with, to an extent – in her line of work it was a weekly occurrence near enough, something to be lived through, endured up to a point. The pain would fade, after time. Until then she'd live with it as best she could. Blood loss was her major worry, along with infection.

Cospel always had something in his pack for emergencies. Kass tried not to look too hard at everything else as she rooted around for the salve she came up with, finally. She opened the little tub and smeared what looked very much like goose grease onto one finger. Cospel's all-round miracle cure for everything. She sniffed at it. She supposed it couldn't hurt. Which was belied about two seconds later when she put some on the outside edge of the wound, where it looked puffy and a bit too pink. It hurt, quite a bloody lot. No wonder her horse always tried to kick Cospel every time he walked past.

When she'd finished, and finished trying unsuccessfully to hold in the whimpers and swear words, she put the tub back into Cospel's pack and sat silent for a while, watching the snow fall in almost solid waves, hearing the shriek of the voices on the wind. A magician. Typical. Magicians had started all this, had brought them all to this lonely and desolate spot. To do what? Save Petri, or Vocho, or both?

Maybe she could, maybe she couldn't, but she was going to try. She had to. She shut her eyes but didn't sleep for a long time.

When Kass opened her eyes, grey light was filtering into the crevice that Danel had found for them and she was alone. She sat up, regretted the swiftness of the action immediately as a stab of pain lanced through her breast, and got up more slowly. Once upright, she almost fell back down again – her head felt too light for her body. A few deep if painful breaths, and the world came back into focus. She made her way outside. It seemed to take a lot longer to climb out than it should have done – there was a tunnel where last night there'd been an opening.

Cospel sat with his back to a drift of snow, scanning their surroundings warily, but she couldn't see Danel anywhere.

"There you are, miss," Cospel said when he spotted her. "Just about to come and wake you up." He frowned at her as she stumbled over, feet sinking up to her knees in fresh snow. "Miss, if you don't mind me asking, when did you last eat?"

"Not sure. What day is it?"

"Huh. Too long then. Here, let me find you something."

He rummaged around in his pack and finally came up with a lump of something wrapped in oiled paper. "Not much, miss. We lost most of the food with the horses. But I always have a bit of this, in case of emergencies."

He unwrapped the parcel to reveal something dark brown and squidgy. It didn't look very appetising to Kass.

"What is it?"

"Cake, good solid fruit cake. Keeps for weeks and full of energy. My old granny used to swear by this recipe." He broke off a chunk and handed it to her.

She bit in, chewed with effort and swallowed. Barely. "Your granny, Cospel—"

"A better con artist than a cook, to be sure. But food is food." He bit off a lump, grimaced at the taste but managed to get it down. "And we're going to need all the energy we can get."

They sat chewing stolidly until Kass's jaw muscles couldn't take any more.

"Danel's off having a little look-see," Cospel said, "but looks like we had about a year's worth of snow overnight. Up here anyway. It stops a bit further down."

True enough. When she looked where he pointed, she could see a wall of snow that dropped like a cliff onto the lower mountain in an entirely unnatural way. "Magician?"

"Reckon so. He wants us on this mountain whether we like it or not."

Danel floundered back over a ridge from where he'd been scouting. By the time he reached them he was red faced and panting.

"It'd take us days to get back down," he said when he'd got his breath back. "There's a point up there you can see most of the passes. Scar had a scout up there herself before, but looks like he's gone. Maybe buried under the snow.

Anyway, thing is, every one of those passes is choked with snow. And I mean choked — they's full to the brim. No getting through in less than a week without a dozen good men and some shovels."

"I wasn't planning on going back down just yet," Kass said.

"I didn't think so," Cospel said. "Only how we going to get through all this? There's drifts here higher than my head, even if I was on my pony."

"However we can. Look, we're stuck up here with no food. And we came here to do a job — sort out the Skull and the Scar, stop the killing. The only food is going to be in that camp. So whatever we do, we're going to have to get to it, along with Vocho and the rest."

"If we're clever, we could get to it while they're out looking for us," Cospel said distractedly. "We came to do a job, but things have changed, haven't they?"

Kass looked down along a narrow valley strangled with snow at the near end which widened out in the distance. If she looked hard she could see the puff of chimney smoke against the white of the mountainside. Things had changed, but the job was the same. She had to stop the raids by Scar and Skull. But maybe she could stop them in a different way to how they'd planned. She'd been too late to save Petri last time, but she was here now, and it wasn't going to be too late if she could help it.

"Things have changed. Not the job but . . yes, I suppose they have. One thing hasn't changed though."

"Oh yes, what's that then, miss?"

"We came to pick a fight. About time we got on with it, wouldn't you say?"

Cospel grinned. "I thought you'd never ask."

*   *   *

Petri kept silent and watched as Scar handed out her orders while Morro stood at her shoulder. He wasn't even trying to hide his hands now, the markings on them. Every few seconds Scar would look his way, glance at his hands and smile to herself before she gave another crew member their orders. She thought she was doing what she wanted, but from bitter experience Petri knew better.

Finally everything was to her satisfaction, and Morro left Petri and Scar alone. She wouldn't meet his eye, kept moving in an attempt to forestall what he was going to say perhaps.

"Scar, are you sure about this?" He grabbed her shoulder as she bustled past and turned her to face him.

"Of course I'm sure." She wriggled out of his grip and put some distance between them. "This is our chance to show them all. What we both wanted." The tiniest of creases marred her forehead. "Isn't it?"

"It didn't use to be. Once you just cared about us surviving, looking after the waifs and strays. How long has he been showing you the markings on his hands?"

"He . . ." She broke off, looking confused before she shook her head firmly. "I know what you're trying to say, but you're wrong. All he's done is show me the possibilities. Think about it, Petri! With a magician on our side, one who can control the weather, and you training our crew, me at their head, no one can stand against us. *No one*. Before, yes, I thought about survival, but think of what more we could be, Petri, if our reach goes further. This mountain, all the mountains could be ours; we could hold Reyes and Ikaras to ransom for the coal and iron they both desperately need. King and queen of our own little realm."

She was closer now, the heat of her ambition burning

behind her eyes, burning through her skin when she reached out a soft hand to his ruined cheek. "We show them we aren't to be trifled with, that they can't beat us on our own ground. That we can beat even their best. We show everyone."

"Us? Against whole *countries*?"

The smile was unfamiliar – sly and earnest at the same time. "We don't need to beat whole countries, Petri. The guild has won wars, fought in every major battle for the last hundred – thousand – years and always on the winning side. If we show we can beat them, half the battle is won. And we beat them by finding and killing your precious Kacha, if she's not dead already."

A grimace at that he couldn't hide. "You'll bring the whole guild down on us," he said weakly to cover it. "We can't—"

"With them dead, and with Morro, yes, we can. Hells, we can kill half of them with frostbite before they even reach here. We'll have taken their head, and then destroyed the body."

"Scar—"

"Unless you've changed your mind about her? Morro said you would, that you're a coward who'd lose his nerve, that you still want her. I said you wouldn't, after everything she's done to you." Her fingers crossed the bone of his ruined cheek and stroked it. "I believe in my man. She tried to ruin you and almost succeeded. Time to return the favour."

He couldn't quite seem to catch his breath. He became aware that Scar was whispering to him. "It was because of her that Bakar found you out. Because of her you were sent to that cell. Because of her you lost your face, your hand, your dignity. She cost you everything."

Another voice behind him, soft and sibilant, commanding. When he turned, he was caught by Morro's hands, by the markings that writhed there. He tried to fight, but old rage and new pride welled up inside.

"I can't do this without you, Petri," Scar said.

He wrenched his mind away from the markings. Scar was looking at him like she used to, like she believed in him. Hadn't that been what had saved him? Did it matter now what her plans were as long as she looked at him like that, kept thoughts of Kass's dishevelled hair and mocking grin out of his head? A wary glance at Morro and back again. The magician had made it all go wrong. Without him Petri could have stayed here and been happy, could have lived with friends no matter how they earned a living. Morro wanted to destroy all that because he wanted to go home. But Petri'd had practice at resisting magicians, at ignoring what the markings were saying. He'd been caught that way before.

Scar though, she had no such experience. Her eyes glowed with the thought of whatever plan Morro had put in her head, lost to it. They were all lost unless Petri did something, and he could do nothing if he was dead.

A flash of an old lesson from Eneko – whatever he'd been, he'd been a tough and canny fighter. *Don't go fighting when you can't win. Wait, bide your time, think, and fight when you* can *win.* "All right," he said, and toyed with a rare smile that didn't seem to sit right on his ragged lips.

Scar grinned at him, clapped her hands and made for where the horses were tied up. Petri moved to follow her and hesitated only half a heartbeat before he passed Morro. He was never comfortable with a magician behind him, especially now when a muffled snicker trailed him.

He found Scar trying, with the help of four of her crew,

to get on Kass's horse, which they'd liberated in the ambush. The beast, and beast it always had been, rolled its eyes and lashed out with a hind leg at the same time as its teeth arrowed for the nearest man. The hoof cracked a woman on the knee, sending her howling across the cleared area Morro had made in the snow, while the teeth gripped an unwary set of furs and lifted the wearer up before dropping him on his face. Petri would have sworn the damned horse was laughing.

Scar wasn't. She yanked on the bridle — no one had managed to get near enough to untack the thing, and they'd only barely managed to get it back to camp — and was rewarded only by its ears going back as it noticed something new to attack. Meanwhile, it stamped on a foot, seemingly without even noticing.

"Scar—" Petri began, but she wasn't having any of it.

"*She* rode it, so I will," she said. "Help me up."

Petri shook his head but moved forward anyway, just in time to dodge as the bastard thing broke free and made a break for the end of the valley, flashing teeth and hooves at anyone within distance.

Until Morro stepped out in front of it. He raised a hand and spoke some words that Petri didn't catch, and the horse stopped dead in its tracks, eyes rolling and nostrils wide and red, its breath coming in great foggy bursts in the cold air. Morro took a step towards it, within range of the teeth, and Petri suppressed a smile, thinking of the damage it would do to him. Maybe even kill him.

Only the horse just stood, flanks heaving, sweat foaming at its neck and froth at its mouth as it chewed so hard on the bit that Petri thought it must break. Morro reached out a hand, perfectly placed for the horse to relieve him of it, but it only trembled at the magician's touch, seemingly struck immobile. After a moment Morro swung awkwardly into the saddle, turned the shaking horse around and brought it back to them at a steady walk that looked like clockwork under skin.

"This horse needs more control than most," he said to Scar. "Perhaps you'd be better with one of the others."

Scar opened her mouth to protest, but something flickered between the two of them and she relented, taking Vocho's indolent if impeccably bred chestnut which shivered under a blanket.

Petri mounted too, a rangy bay that moved under him like a skittish crab but responded well enough to his one hand on the reins.

Without a backward glance, Morro kicked his mount into a shaky trot on the business of finding and killing Kacha for whatever twisted end was in his head. Petri had no allies now who were not under Morro's control, only people who had been friends and more but were now blinded by the markings on the magician's hands.

All he could do was follow and hope that he could do something before Morro spelled the end of all of them.

Chapter Twenty-five

Several hours into their trek across the snow-draped landscape Kass wished she hadn't said a damned thing about carrying on. They hadn't gone more than a mile or so, and she was ready to drop.

That magician had really done his job, if he wanted them kept close by. Drifts of snow were feet thick in places, and even moving a few yards was exhausting as every step resulted in sinking up to the knee or further.

Danel guided them towards a rock slope where the wind keened down and had scrubbed away the worst of the snow, but here the wind itself became the problem. "It's a killer and no mistake," he said as they halted for a rest behind an arm of rock that sheltered them from the worst of it.

At least they weren't far now, Danel reckoned. Just as well. Kass was hungry enough to actually want some more of Cospel's cake; her face alternated between numb and aching needles, and she couldn't recall when she could last feel her feet.

Her head snapped up as the wind dropped abruptly,

letting her hear the sound of hooves on rock. Danel signalled them to be quiet and stay where they were while he took a look.

"A dozen, riding this way," he said when he got back. "Can't see who though — they're all bundled up."

Kass looked about. If they rode past the arm of rock, they'd see the three of them without a doubt. The slope in front was open, with only a few strewn boulders to hide behind. Below lay only more snow, so thick she'd probably drown in it, where they'd show up a treat against the unremitting whiteness. Above . . . Above was almost a sheer climb, a steep slope rising maybe twenty feet. At its top she could just make out a thick covering of snow, the edges of which whirled in the wind that was suddenly absent below.

She peered around the rock sheltering them. Ahead, snow lay thick and unbroken, piled in rumpled dunes, sculpted by the wind. Except in front of the riders — there it steamed, melted into nothing, letting the riders move easily across the terrain surrounded in streamers of fog, that sadly wasn't thick enough to hide Kass and the others. The fog was proof enough that a magician was present. Hadn't Petri had enough of the bastards? She'd never thought him so stupid to throw in his lot with magic again. She'd rather hoped not to get entangled with it again herself.

She turned back to Cospel and Danel. "Nowhere to go except up that slope."

Danel swore under his breath, but Cospel rolled his eyes and got to it, pausing only to say quietly, "You sure you're up to it, miss?"

"No, but we don't have much choice, do we?" She took a look over her shoulder at how close the riders were getting. "Didn't Eder have a bit of trouble with an avalanche?"

Cospel looked up at the teetering banks of snow riding the lip of the slope and grinned. "Come on then, miss. Last one there's a ninny."

Petri kept his head down against Morro's mocking smile. They'd searched in a growing spiral around their camp, looking for any signs of movement, for tracks or trails of smoke, but had yet to come up with anything. Morro had taken the opportunity to show Petri just how powerful he'd become.

He and Scar passed the hours discussing their plans, plans that Petri had known little to nothing about, ones that the Scar of old, before Morro had come, would have laughed at, dismissed out of hand as grandiose and ridiculous. Now she looked at Morro with something approaching worship and said nothing to every poisoned barb he sent Petri's way.

"Of course," he was saying to Scar now, with the scent of cooking blood wafting through the fog that shrouded them before it tore to tatters on the wind. "Of course, we'll need to take care. But a resounding success here, a sign to Bakar and to the new Ikaran queen that we are not powerless, that we are not defenceless or useless, and then you can carve out your own niche here and I can be on my way in the thaw. You can take the mines by force if guile doesn't work. Hold both countries to ransom for the iron and coal they need to survive, threaten every village and town within reach. They'll regret shunning you and those like you."

Scar nodded at his every word. Not just her now either, as Morro had promised. Kepa muttered dire threats to some unnamed person he blamed for his presence here, out on the edge of nowhere. They'd have to take notice now, wouldn't they? Others listened with a sort of stunned attention that Petri had seen before on the faces of men and women seduced by soft words and cooking blood.

"You'll need to bring some sort of order to your crew," Morro went on in a voice so reasonable only a madman would doubt it. "A hierarchy – someone to look over your fighters, someone to take care of provisions, someone to advise you. Others beneath them, to do what needs to be done." His eyes slid to Petri. "And some you'll need to be rid of, those who threaten the order of your new realm, those who speak against it, against you."

Scar let her own gaze go to Petri, a slow and thoughtful glance, absorbing what Morro said, and what he inferred.

Petri held his peace and kept his eyes forward. Later he'd get Scar alone, he'd talk to her without Morro's influence, make her see. Try to get back the old Scar, who thought not for herself but for those in her charge. A magician's influence could be broken, though it was difficult. He had to try, despite what she'd become – had to make the attempt for the woman who'd given him a second chance. Else, what was there for him? A return to stares, to whispers, to beatings down on the plains, a lifetime of pain and regret. Not again.

The fog cleared, and he caught a movement in the corner of his eye. A tumble of boulders, a steep slope behind. Something had moved. A head, perhaps, darting back behind a boulder. Or maybe just a bird or one of the rabbits that changed colour with the seasons and fed the eagles that nested even further up the mountain.

"Scar!" Seemed like Petri hadn't been the only one to see it. Kepa had too. "Up ahead, I seen something moving. By them rocks."

Scar kicked her horse on recklessly into snow that Morro

had yet to clear from their path. More movement, this time along the slope above the boulders. Petri peered but could make out nothing definite. With the rest, he kicked his horse after Scar.

By the time they reached the boulders all movement had ceased, but tracks scarred the snow, depressions where someone – or at the least something – had clearly rested for a while. Kepa dismounted to take a look, Scar peering intently at his side. Petri watched from his horse.

"How many, do you think?" Scar said.

"Three, maybe four."

Morro nudged his twitching horse forward. It tried to resist, flared its nostrils and stood stilt-legged and braced against his urgings, but in the end even it had to relent. As many had previously found to their cost, stubbornness was no defence against magic. Morro slid down next to Scar and took no more notice of the beast. Petri did.

While they debated whether the marks had been made by Kass and Cospel and looked to see where they led, Petri watched the horse, released now from the torment on its back. It trembled, and froth fell from its neck and lips; it knew something they didn't. The beast took a hesitant step forward, and another, put its head down and whiffled its lips over the disturbed snow before it gave a soft whicker of greeting.

"Up that slope," Kepa said. "I think I can see—"

He got no further. The horse brought its head up sharply, kicked its heels – catching some poor bastard in the back – and bolted. It wasn't the only one. Petri's horse spun, reared, dumping him off its back into the snow, and followed it, along with most of the rest whether they had riders still atop or not. Half a heartbeat later a white wall of snow thundered down the slope towards them, crashing over Petri like a wave that refused to end. Snow encased him like a tomb, crushed the air from his lungs and swept him away.

Chapter Twenty-six

The camp was almost empty, but Vocho had found no way to use that to their advantage. He and Carrola had watched as Scar tried, and failed, to mount Kass's horse, and Vocho had thought she'd been lucky to get away with her skin. Someone else had mounted it though, had made it docile if twitchy, which made Vocho even twitchier.

"What's so strange about that?" Carrola asked. "I mean, I noticed it was a bad-tempered beast, but that's what you get with these finely bred animals sometimes. A bit like finely bred people, I've always thought. All that inbreeding makes them go funny in the head." They both turned to look at Eder as he lay, sweating and shivering in turns, in the corner. "Sometimes, of course, people are just like that anyway, and horses are mad down to the last one."

"Bad tempered doesn't even come close to describing this particular horse." Vocho shifted position, swore a blue streak when his hip didn't move with the rest of him, just twanged its pain up his body and seemingly into his eyeballs, and shifted back to where he had been. "That horse is bloody-well possessed. I've known it for the whole five years Kass has owned it, and if I come within half a yard it acts like I'm about to murder it so it has to get in first. Even Cospel treats it warily, and he feeds it, which usually makes animals like you a bit better. The only person who's ever managed to get on, and stay on, is Kass. And that's down to sheer bloody-mindedness, which being a trait they share is why she and the horse get on. No, I reckon that there is our magician, and he's magicked the bastard thing into submission." A thought which gave Vocho a shiver right between his shoulder blades.

They'd watched in mingled horror and wonder last night when the storm had started. A howl of wind that sounded like the screaming souls of the damned, bringing with it what looked like a whole mountain's worth of snow. It had been no normal, if violent, storm. Normal storms didn't avoid one valley, so that not even a breath of wind invaded their hut, not a single flake fell on the camp. Yet, beyond some invisible border, snow had fallen in deadly sheets, piled up in monstrous drifts, sculpted into outlandish shapes by the screaming wind. It had cut this valley off – to anyone with more mundane talents anyway – and dashed any hopes Vocho had held about either being rescued or managing to escape. If they did make it out of the hut, they'd not make it out of the valley. Unless they could find some very long stilts.

They were left in no doubt about the magician when he had led the way, and snow had melted in front of him, wreathing the whole search party – Vocho had to assume that's what it was – in foggy tendrils.

"Now he's frozen them to death," Eder said from his sweaty pallet, "he's going to find them and gloat over them before he sends their heads to Bakar. Then he'll have no use for you, because all you're good for is bait. It's all you've ever been good for. You're a dead man, Vocho. You should have taken their side when you had the chance."

"Shut up," Carrola and Vocho said in unison.

Now the camp was all but empty. Just not empty enough, because Petri had been very explicit about how many men and women should guard this hut. Vocho sat back, carefully. "There has to be a way. I just don't know what it is." He took a look at Carrola, who was still studying the camp's comings and goings, such as they were. "I'm more of a let's-go-and-hit-things-with-a-sword type of person, but we need a plan, and plans aren't my forte."

She snorted her agreement with his assessment of himself. "What to do once out of the hut, that's the problem," she said. "Eder's right. We're no use to them now. I'm surprised they let us live this long. We have to get out, and soon, and chance our luck with the snow." She peered over at what was left of the breakfast they'd been given. It hadn't been much to start with, and now it was just crumbs. "We save whatever food they bring today. We'll need it. And they took my sword, but I've got my fire strike." She pulled out a little clockwork gizmo like Cospel had, only instead of duellists a cantering horse struck sparks with its hooves as it galloped. "We take whatever small things will burn, for tinder."

"Planning ahead. I like it. I can't do it, but I like it when others do. But how do we get out of this hut and past the guards? I can't fight worth a damn like this, or run very fast if at all. Let's face it, I can barely manage a stagger."

He liked watching her think, imagining he could see cogs and gears whirring behind those grey eyes of hers. Actually, he just liked watching her.

"Why are you looking at me like a lost puppy?" she asked.

He could feel himself blush and shifted again so that he could cover it with a yelp of not-faked-at-all pain. The almost empty bottle pressed against his chest, and he took it out and looked at it longingly to distract her. "I suppose I might have enough here for one short burst of being marvellous."

"Vocho . . ." She hesitated, and that didn't seem very like her. "You said what Eder told me about you was true. All of it?"

He looked over at Eder, who gave him a sneer in return. "Sort of. Yes. Only not exactly like that. I killed the priest, but I didn't know I was doing it. Under the influence of a magician, see. Didn't have a clue what I was doing."

"And trying to drown your sister?"

"I wish I knew how he found that out. I tripped her. I didn't mean for her to fall in the river. She was just so bloody *perfect* all the time. We were young, and her being the oldest, she was better than me. I wanted to beat her, just the once. It's the only thing I've ever had, that I could be better than her at one thing." He sloshed the dregs of the jollop sadly. "Can't even do that now, not without this stuff."

"Which you're hiding from her."

"Yes, though I don't doubt she's figured it out by now. She's irritatingly good at that."

"I'm sorry I told Eder about that – I mean he sort of knew anyway, I think, spotted you drinking it probably. He was watching you all the time, him or one of the others for him. But he's my captain, and when he said all those things . . ."

"You believed him. Quite rightly, because they are true, and besides you believe what your captain says usually, because your life might depend on it. One reason Eneko got away with so much in the guild, I think, was that unthinking obedience was pretty much built into the training. Kass and me were rubbish at that, her the unthinking bit and me the obedience part. And I am every one of those things he said about me, though I do try not to be. I'm just not very good at that part. I'm not very good at anything now, really, without this."

Her frown grew indignant. It quite suited her.

Vocho glanced out of the crack in the door. "Well now, I wonder what she wants?"

Maitea was walking up the path to the hut, back straight and head high. It was impossible not to see her mother in her studied poise, that cool face. Vocho thought back to when she'd cut Dom's bonds and cut him too with her words, told him she hated him and to get out. He didn't think she took after her mother only in looks.

The guards let her in without a murmur of protest, and she came through the door like a queen attending her coronation.

"Gosh, well this is an honour," Vocho said and got a sharp poke in the ribs from Carrola's elbow.

"Petri's going to kill you," Maitea said. Her voice was loud and oddly inflectionless.

"I was rather hoping he wouldn't."

"He's going to take your head and send it to Bakar along with Kass's. As a message. And good riddance."

Vocho opened his mouth to say something smart-arsed, but Maitea dropped to a crouch in front of him and leaned in.

"He's going to do it personally," she whispered. "In a duel. I've seen it in the shadows, seen him bring you out to kill you. It might be your chance to escape."

She took a furtive look over her shoulder and Vocho took her meaning.

"I wish people would stop talking about my head on a plate. I like it on my shoulders," he said.

Maitea nodded at his understanding. "And I'm going to enjoy watching very much. *Everyone's* going to watch our man beat Vocho the Great," she said loud enough for the guards to hear, then, whispering again, "A distraction so the others can escape. I'll help you. Be ready."

She stood up suddenly, her face bland again. "It's going to be ever such a thrill," she said and left.

When the door shut behind her, Vocho let out a low whistle. "I have no idea what just happened. I thought she hated all our guts."

Carrola watched Maitea walk away before she came and sat next to Vocho. "She cut Dom's ties, didn't she?"

"Well, yes, but she also said a lot of not very nice things while she did it."

"That's not the point — the point is she helped him escape, and the rest of us might have made it too if Scar hadn't been so quick. Now she's offering to help us. She's not the person she's pretending to be to Petri and the rest."

They sat in silence for a while as they digested this.

"I think it could work. Seems to me like Petri has a personal grudge against you," Carrola said in the end. "That he'll want to do it himself, like Maitea says. Does that sound like him?"

"Oh yes. Pretending to be honourable Petri. We've never been friends. It sounds very likely."

"Well then, maybe she's telling us the truth, and we can use that. If you can piss him off enough, make a really good distraction."

"Oh, I can do that all right. I can piss people off without even trying."

She grinned a little lopsided grin, and Vocho went funny

inside, all sort of flip-flop. "Then maybe we've got a chance," she said. "Maybe the talents of Vocho the Great will get us out of this yet."

Maybe they would, but Vocho didn't rate his own chances very highly. He had to survive a duel against Petri, and he could barely stand up. He was going to be skewered in short order, by Petri bloody Egimont of all people. But he looked at Carrola, at her grey eyes smiling at him, and very uncharacteristically thought that it would be worth it if she made it out of this alive. He wouldn't last, but she would, and that was the important thing. He had just enough jollop for one last blast of fabulous, and he'd use it making sure she got out of this icebox even if he couldn't join her.

Instead of saying any of that, he gave her a grin and said, "Did you ever doubt me?"

Petri had no idea how long he lay in the snow struggling to breathe, how long it was before he heard Scar's voice, before the snow began to melt around him. When his eyes cleared, the first thing he saw was Morro's face, mouth hooked into a curl like Petri tasted bad.

He sat up and saw that everyone else was already out of the avalanche. He'd been an afterthought, and maybe Morro wouldn't even have bothered if not for the fact that letting him die would show his hand to Scar.

Scar herself hadn't waited around for Petri to be freed, but was directing her crew in their efforts to gather the horses together. Unsurprisingly, Kass's beast was nowhere to be seen. He recalled its whicker an instant before the avalanche had taken them, blown them downslope so that the boulders they'd stood next to were far above. Kass had been there, he was sure of it. But one look at Morro as he slid across the slope to Scar, who was gazing at him like he held all the answers, and he kept silent. Kept his mind from it too, just in case.

He must have been under the snow longer than he thought because the sun had slipped far past noon and was well on its way to dropping behind the higher peaks, the temperature plummeting with it.

"We must assume it's them," Scar said to Morro as Petri approached. She spared him a glance but no more. "And three of the horses are missing, including hers."

"Horses won't help them much in this," Morro said.

"Really?" Petri nodded back the way they'd come to the wide swathe of cleared snow. Morro had filled some of their trail as they went but had run low on blood, and now a clear path led at least halfway back to the camp. "I think you've given them a fine helping hand, not to mention a signpost."

"Get this arsehole out of my way," Morro snapped at Kepa, and the big man grabbed Petri's arm and threw him back down into the snow as Morro and Scar stalked off to the horses that her crew had managed to recapture.

"Kepa, what are you—" Petri struggled upright and stared up at a man he'd considered a friend.

"He says you talk too much." Kepa's ample brow furrowed as though he was struggling to remember. "Which sounds stupid now I come to say it, because you don't hardly talk at all excepting when you have to. But he says you're using us. Using Scar. That you want us to fail. He's going to get us everything – houses, food, beer. Respect. He's like us, see, no one wants him excepting us. Just a dreg, like we are. He's going to help us. He showed me."

"Showed you? On his hands?" Petri got up warily. Kepa wasn't the best with a sword, but with his height and reach he could be devastating, and Petri wasn't sure if he meant to be devastating to him.

"That's right. On his hands." Kepa nodded sleepily. "Showed me, showed all of us in the barn. Showed Scar too, oh he showed her lots, he did, when you wasn't looking." A lewd chuckle at that. "It's going to be grand, what he tells us. Grand. And warm too. I haven't been warm in years, it feels like. And there'll be food and beer and . . . It'll be grand. So you just keep your head down. I don't want to hurt you, even if what he says is true, but I can't let you spoil it. Just keep quiet and maybe slip off when he's not looking. Else you're going to get hurt."

Petri felt the ice inside grow. Cast out by outcasts . . .

Kepa rubbed at his forehead and frowned. "What was we talking about? Come on. We need to grab a horse if we don't want to walk home. Morro says that Kass woman's bound to head to camp now, and we'd best catch them up."

Petri followed him, his heart stuttering in fear. Morro had them, all of them, in his hands. All except Petri, and he knew it.

By the time they got back to camp, the sky was darkening towards a bruised purple. Petri hung far at the back, having been forced to walk, and watched Morro and Scar at the head of the line. Morro had got one of the crew to donate some blood and now rode with his eyes half closed, clearing the path ahead, closing it behind, often catching Petri in flurries of snow and ice that scoured his face, ruined side and not. Scar rode alertly, sending scouts out ahead, to the side, letting some lag behind. They found nothing, no one. But Kass was there, Petri knew it. He could feel the heat of her gaze on the back of his neck, even when he knew it was impossible, and couldn't work out how he felt about it. After a time he stopped wondering. It wasn't important, not compared to if he'd live through the night.

Finally, with nothing except bruises to show for the day, they made it back to camp. Scar stalked over to Petri, her eyes at dreamy odds with the energy of her walk. She hesitated when she reached him, some spark of her still alive behind whatever Morro had filled her head with.

"Are you with me?" she asked at last, a hint of the old Scar in her voice, wanting him to be her man when he hadn't been for some time. "Petri, are you with me or not?"

He reached out and took her arm, turned her so that he could see Morro behind her, keep an eye on the bastard. "I've always been with you, Scar, never against you. But—"

She slid her arm out of his grasp. "There are no buts, Petri. It's time, Morro says, and I agree. Time you showed me just whose side you're really on, because you've shown me nothing but dissent for a while now. I need – no . . . *want* – you with me. Or to know if you aren't, if you still hanker after *her*." Scar spat into the snow to show what she thought of Kass. "We've spent the day looking for her, and we'll keep searching, but there's some you don't need to find that we're keeping as bait. Some that in killing you'd sever every tie with her, for ever." Scar's voice was carefully level, her face blank. When he hesitated, her lip twitched the way he'd seen so many times before, just before she drew her sword. "I want you with me, but I need to know where your loyalties lie. Kill Vocho and I'll know for sure."

Petri looked towards the hut that held Vocho and the rest. No going back, not with Kass. He'd lost her a long time ago, and now he had other things to lose.

You are weakness.

Not in front of Scar he wasn't, not in front of the men and women who called this valley home. Who'd been seduced by a magician but were still his friends underneath. He had only this valley, these people. His own pride, mangled though it was. A poor thing, nothing like he'd once had, but all he had left. He would kill to keep it.

A glance up at Morro, at his lidded look, the hint of menace in the smile, showed him what else he had — this one chance or Morro would have them gut him like a pig. Balanced against that, killing a man whose death he'd often dreamed of. Be canny, be careful, be strong. Show the world what they passed by.

He strode towards the hut without another thought, sword in hand.

"What the hell is going on?" Kass gasped when they came to the final ridge.

Once the cleared path had given out, Danel had brought them by back ways and goat trails that Kass could barely even see, never mind follow. The horses had helped — Kass had been surprised how much she'd missed her great bastard of a beast — but it had still been hard going. They'd had to dismount often, and Kass had let her horse pull her up the worst bits, but the strain was starting to tell. Her whole chest ached, the dressing sodden again. Her head swam, and her stomach was a small hard knot inside her.

Now they stood on a tumbled escarpment above a valley dotted with huts. Scar, with help from a magician to deal with the snow, had obviously made it back before them. In a circle spreading outwards, torches went every which way.

"Looking for someone?" Danel said.

"Us, probably," replied Cospel gloomily. "Where have they got Voch?"

Danel pointed out a hut that stood apart from the rest, with a good assortment of people around it, gathered around a fire that would erase any advantage the shadows of the camp might give them. "There, or he was. And that over there, that's where the Skull lives with that Scar woman. She's right protective of him. As you may have noticed, miss."

She had. Petri lived with her. He hadn't wasted much time, had he?

"We have to get down there, get Voch out," she said. Her voice sounded vague and dreamy even to her.

Danel raised an eyebrow. "There's three of us and a lot of them."

"And most of them are not anywhere near that hut. If we're careful, we can get to it."

"If we're bloody suicidal, you mean."

"That's what she generally means by careful," Cospel said mournfully. "Got their own dictionary, see, her and Vocho. In their language, careful means suicidal, a bit stubborn means immovable to the point of stupidity, and 'Cospel!' means will you please do something suicidal and stupid."

"I am standing here, you realise that?" Kass looked down over the little village, one hand pressed to her throbbing breast.

A figure strode towards the hut that Danel said held Vocho. A familiar figure, a familiar walk, an unfamiliar un-face. Kass's hands were colder than ever.

Cospel swore under his breath. "Looks like it's now or never. You got your gun wound, Danel?"

"Nope, but won't take a moment."

"Good," Kass said. "Get yourself somewhere high."

"And shoot anyone who ain't us or left Kastroa with us," Cospel added. "Except Eder. I reckon you can shoot him."

Danel looked between the two of them, his cheeks wobbling. Being a mountain guard had probably never included this. "Anyone?"

Kass looked down at the figure advancing, familiar and not. Dead and alive. Loved and enemy. "Anyone, Danel."

He went, and Kass let herself sag. "I'm going to need that bottle."

"Thought you might. Don't suppose I can talk you into not . . . No, don't suppose I can." He sighed and handed it over. Nothing had ever tasted so sweet to Kass. Everything retreated except Cospel's reliable face and the bite of the air in her lungs. Breath came easy at last, and if her limbs were wobbling, at least they had some strength in them.

"Miss . . ." Cospel hesitated, which was very unlike him. "Miss, you want I should . . ."

She conjured a grin from somewhere. "No. No, this is one thing I should do myself. I might need a bit of help though."

"That's what you pay me for."

"Is it? I thought we paid you to thieve things and find things out and annoy Vocho."

"That too."

Petri was nearing the hut, his sword out, calling to one of the guards. From this side he looked no different to how he had been what seemed a lifetime ago. That man was still in there, but that man was also looking to kill her brother. *What seems good to you, Kass? I have no idea.* "Right. You got your tankard? Good. Come on, it's time you dented it a bit more."

*   *   *

Petri neared the hut. This was his chance to show his father, show Eneko, show everyone, once and for all that he was not a weak man, not a scared man. Strong as steel, harder than iron.

"Bring him out," he said to one of the guards, "and give him his sword."

Maitea stood by the guards, and it was she who opened the door to the hut. Vocho all but fell through, his face looking as though someone had slapped him. One of the other prisoners – Petri didn't know their names and hadn't cared to ask – helped him keep his feet and he nodded a thanks to her, slipping her a wink that was almost too Vocho.

Petri thought he might enjoy this.

Someone threw Vocho his sword, and he caught it, swung it, gave it that Vocho twirl that he thought was so impressive but was just ridiculous. The effect was marred by the fact he could barely move his bad leg, but that didn't stop his mouth working, more was the pity.

"Finally got up the nerve to finish the job, then? I wondered how long it would take you to get rid of that yellow streak all down your back and grow a spine. Actually, I bet good money that you never would, but that's a bet I'm glad to lose if it means I get the chance to put you on your arse."

Petri let Vocho shoot his mouth off, because nothing ever seemed to stop it anyway, and watched him. The blade went through a complex series of motions as Vocho loosened his sword arm and legs – thrust, block, attack, riposte, feint. Gimp leg or not, he would be a challenge. Petri focused his mind on that, letting nothing else in – none of the fear, none of the weakness. Beat Vocho and he would be strong, no one could deny that.

Finally, thankfully, Vocho ran out of words and settled into a modified stance that would allow him to fight even with that leg.

"Ready?" asked Petri in the drawl he knew drove Vocho round the twist.

"I've been ready to beat your arse for *years*," Vocho said and came for him.

Vocho gritted his teeth against the grind of the bones in his hip, the fire that lanced down his leg and up his back despite the last of the jollop, which he'd managed to swig before he'd come out of the hut. Not being able to pivot as he should, nor advance or retreat as normal, was hampering him more than somewhat as Petri came forward. But he was Vocho the Great, wasn't he? This one time he was going to have to be, gimp leg or not. He was going to die here, he knew that, die to save Carrola and the rest, but he was going to do it in style, damn it. He would die being great or not die at all.

With another opponent Vocho might have tried drawing him on, allowing him to stay in one place rather than risk his leg going and planting him on his face. It wasn't going to work with Petri today, he saw that from the off. Still, he had Petri's blind side to work with, and the fact that despite obviously practising with his off hand, he was still slower with it and clumsy when he extended.

Petri stood off, trying to get Vocho to move, and for a short time there was an impasse, but Vocho couldn't stand that for long, as Petri had probably calculated. Vocho risked a lunge that left his leg struggling to catch up. Petri deflected it with ease, following up with a cut of his own that forced Vocho back again, making his leg scream. Vocho didn't think he'd be able to keep this up for long. He hoped like crap Maitea would do as she'd said, that she was more her father than her mother.

He had to be quick before the jollop wore off and he seized up. A deep breath, a silent injunction to his leg to shut the hell up, and he went for a move that anyone would see as typical Vocho – a round cut that looked flashy but was slow, enticing Petri in for an attack. As soon as he did, Vocho changed his line, the blade dipped and came back up under Petri's guard on his blind side. But Petri was cannier than Vocho had ever given him credit for and had learned that guild rules were for suckers. An elbow crashed into Vocho's face, planting him firmly on his arse in the snow, to hoots and catcalls from the watching men and women. He couldn't be having that, no matter what his hip had to say about it, no matter what the plan had been.

Petri stood back as Vocho struggled up, an odd little grin playing about what was left of his lips. Supercilious bastard. Maybe he thought Vocho would go easy because of Kass, because of what she'd say or do if he sliced up her precious Petri, but he was dead wrong. Vocho caught Carrola's eye, tipped her another wink and spun towards Petri. His hip was bad, but with the last of the jollop not half as bad as he'd been making out. He caught the bugger by surprise in the top of the shoulder. Still his leg was bad enough, and the pain of it made his eyes cross as Petri leaped back.

But not for long. Petri's off hand whipped out, and he might not have been able to use the fingers but he sure as shit could use the dagger that Vocho could now see strapped to the wrist. Oh, bloody *perfect*.

A faint noise behind him, and Vocho came round in a quarter-circle, being flashy as hell and shooting his mouth off at the same time, dropping sarcastic remarks, drawing eyes his way, and not just Petri's. He hoped Maitea and Carrola would hurry up – he wasn't sure how much longer he could stay standing. A vicious attack by Petri, one that caught Vocho by surprise because the noble Petri Egimont would never have tried to slice his balls off. Only a leap back that twisted his hip saved him from never being able to father children, or even practise fathering them.

Unfortunately, it didn't save him from Petri driving forward with sword and dagger, forcing Vocho to move in ways that his hip was very vocal about. He parried and feinted, but the leg betrayed him at last and dumped him back on his arse, Petri's sword hovering in front of him backed by the unreal spectre of Petri's twisted half a face.

"I should have done this a long time ago," Petri said, but that was as far as he got because several things happened at once. Some of Scar's crew had now noticed Carrola and the rest's escape, ably covered by Vocho making as much fuss as possible during his duel, and were now chasing after them. Others lay, throats cut, in spreading pools of blood that melted the snow around them, Maitea close by, a knife half hidden in her skirts, before she disappeared into shadows. Lastly, a much-dented tankard flew out of the dark and bounced off Petri's head.

"Ah, Cospel," Vocho said. "Glad you could make it."

Kass seemed nailed to the spot. No matter the jollop, every limb froze as she watched Petri try his damnedest to kill Voch. No pretty swordplay this, no prancing and preening – OK, just a bit on Vocho's part because he couldn't blow his nose without preening, but now even that seemed forced. This was just one man trying to kill another. A viciousness in Petri she'd never imagined. And Vocho, what was he up to? His leg was paining him, plainly, but even so he wasn't fighting like he could or should. He was showboating. He was covering something up.

Petri had Voch on his back, but Voch didn't seem too worried; in fact he was grinning like a loon, like he'd just put one over on the whole world.

Cospel bobbed up from where they were hiding behind a stack of firewood; his tankard bounced off Petri's head, and Vocho said, "Ah, Cospel, glad you could make it," just as she realised. The crowd watching them had thinned, at least partly because Eder's last few guards captured with Vocho had made very good use of the distraction. Three of Scar's men lay in the snow in various states of actual or approaching death, and the hostages were evident by their absence. Except Carrola, who Kass could just make out lurking in the darker shadows behind the hut. She'd managed to get a gun, presumably from one of the downed men, and having wound it was taking a bead on Petri.

Kass wasn't sure what shocked her more – that Petri was willing to kill Voch or that Voch was willing to die to let the rest escape.

Carrola tightened her finger on the trigger, and Kass acted without thought. "Petri!'

He whipped round to face her as she stood revealed, and took a step back when he saw her. The bullet missed him by the width of a finger. He didn't appear to notice, instead taking a hesitant step towards her, mouth open and eye staring, before Scar came into view and said a few words behind him that made him start and turn away. Most of the rest of the bandits had scattered – chasing Carrola no doubt and Voch, who wasn't where she'd last seen him. Most, but not all; the rest were heading up the slope towards her and Cospel, swords and guns out.

Cospel grabbed for her arm and dragged her back behind the woodpile. "Come on, miss. Vocho's headed off for—"

She shook him off. The jollop was making her think in curves rather than straight lines. Vocho had escaped, for now, though the Clockwork God knew how safe any of them were. But Petri . . .

She was standing up again, mouth already open to shout something – she didn't know what – when a hand clamped over her mouth and a voice she recognised whispered in her ear. "It almost killed Vocho getting them all out," Dom said. "It'll kill him all the way if he has to come back for you, and you can't help Petri, not right now. This way. *Move!*"

The crunch of boots on snow penetrated then, the heavy breaths moving up the slope towards them, Scar's voice following, exhorting them to "Kill whoever's up there, and then bring me their head."

Kass moved.

Vocho staggered, fell, was pulled upright again by someone indistinct in the darkness and ran on as well as he could, which wasn't very well at all.

"Come on, come on!" Carrola muttered. He did his best.

The darkness was their friend and enemy. Their pursuers could see no further than their torch- and lamplight, but he and Carrola couldn't see where they were going. Vocho was dimly aware that it was just the two of them, the others having got separated at some point. Maitea was nowhere, disappearing as softly as she'd come.

Finally Carrola let him stop, probably because the sound of his breathing was so loud he was surprised they couldn't hear it in Reyes. He sank down and peered around.

"Where in hell are we? And where's Cospel? Didn't I hear Kass?"

"Don't know, don't know, and yes," Carrola whispered. "We came from that way."

Back the way they'd come, torches bobbed about, making shadow plays of people on the snow. Nowhere near far enough away, and one group was definitely getting closer. Vocho had the sudden and not entirely welcome thought that they might have dogs. Probably did up here, hunting and such. Would snow make it easier or harder for them to track? He didn't know, and he certainly didn't want to find out.

"Kass?" he said.

"I heard her, but . . . I don't know, Voch." Something odd in her voice, a strain that he couldn't put his finger on, over and above the more obvious strain of being hunted.

Vocho looked about, decided he really didn't like what he was seeing, and said, "Carrola, listen to me. Did you see, bugger, I forgot their names. The other two chaps from your troop. Did you see where they went? And Maitea, where's she?"

He dimly made out the shake of her head in the darkness. "They came this way, sort of, and it should be easy enough to find them, if they make it. Maitea came, helped us out and . . . went. Come on, up. I'll help."

A hand under his shoulder, hauling him up. He was far past refusing help and had the feeling Carrola would only snort in amusement should he try.

"Thanks," he said once he was on his feet. "Look, you've got the gun. Take my sword too, go and find the others and get the hell off this mountain. Back to Kastroa. Raise the alarm, tell them where we are. You can tell them too there'll be a whole lot less of Scar and Skull's men by the time they get here. Give them all the information you can; maybe they'll send some guards or something."

That did make her snort. "I doubt it. We'll have to send to Reyes if we want anyone to come other than the guildsmen you left in Kastroa. And what about you?"

"What about me?"

"You're intending to stay, I assume? Despite the fact you can barely stand up."

"Carrola . . ." What could he say? That he'd been expecting to die at Petri's hands anyway, that he'd be as great dying as he had been living, and now that he'd survived, well, Kass was here somewhere, and she'd been shot and she might have Cospel with her but then again she might not.

"You know, Eder was right about the guild, in a way," Carrola said.

"Hey now, that's not fair!"

"Quiet. Arrogant as they come, full of pride, thinking no one else can live up to their standards. Well, Vocho the supposedly Great, enough of your nonsense. You keep the sword; I've got the gun, and I am more than proficient in both of those should it be necessary, though I must say I prefer a gun. Now, let's go and find your sister. You're not the only one with a vested interest here."

"What do you mean, the 'supposedly Great'? I'll have you know—"

A hint of a grin in the dark, the flash of teeth and a quiet laugh. "OK, you were passable at executing an escape plan. Now shut up, and let's see if we can find your sister and get out of this mess. First, we've got to find somewhere to keep out of the way until all the hullabaloo dies down."

She led the way towards a place where an arm of the mountain fell away towards a steeply sloping field of scree that seemed the clearest path through the snow, and the least likely place to show tracks. Vocho lurched after her, muttering, "Passable? Passable!" and scuffing their trail as best he could behind him.

Petri watched silently as Scar barked out orders, as men and women rushed the place where Kass had been and came back empty-handed.

"Too many people running about," Kepa said. "Can't make head nor tail of the tracks."

Scar whipped at the snow at her feet with her sword. "Well then, we see where they came in, maybe where they went out of the valley. You know all the places, and there won't be tracks to muddle through out on the edges, excepting the main path, and we've had people there all night. Take all the people you need, find all of them and bring them back. In any state you see fit, I'm not fussy."

The burst of activity subsided until it was just Scar and Petri, him with his useless hand trying to staunch the thin stream of blood where Vocho had pierced his shoulder. Still he hadn't spoken, still she hadn't looked at him. She did now, a sidelong thoughtful look that ended with a twitch of her lip.

"Come with me," she said at last and stalked off, not even looking to see if he followed.

He went after her, unsure what else to do, what that call "Petri!" had done to him.

Scar banged into her hut and hurled her sword into a corner. Petri came in after, quieter, wary, even more so when he saw the hut wasn't empty.

Scar looked at him, her chin jutting in defiance as he saw Morro by the fire, a greased smile cutting his face in two.

A creeping feeling of dread stole over Petri, wormed its

way from the pit of his stomach to where bile stung his throat.

"Scar," he croaked, "don't you think—"

"I *think*," she spat, "that I can't trust you, that maybe you're as much a prize as Vocho was and that your head might suffice to warn Bakar."

He twitched at that, unable to stop himself.

"Don't think I've been blind, Petri. You kept my bed warm enough for a time, but I'm not as stupid as you seem to think, not as blind as you are. You left my bed, left me. You tell yourself that you don't care about her, about Vocho and the stupid guild, about Reyes and Bakar and the rest. You tell me that, but you're lying to us both. You couldn't even kill her brother to prove it to me, lost to a man who can't even walk properly. I thought you were better than that." A shrug, that hardness in her face again. "You taught my crew well and I thank you, but you're not the only asset at my command, nor even the most important. I have others who won't let hostages to my future fortune escape."

"They're close, both of them." Morro said. "She'll come, I know it as well as Petri does. She'll come, and we'll be ready for her. I have a spell or two in mind, and here, look, Petri is bleeding for me. So kind. She'll come and I'll freeze her so hard she'll shatter, and Petri will have made it possible."

Scar's eyes lit up at that, and she laid a gentle hand on Morro's arm, as she might have done with Petri yesterday.

Hate and want from both of them – from Scar and Kass – curdled in Petri's stomach until he couldn't be sure which was which.

"What good will it do," he said, "in the long run? They'll send more – more prelate's men, more guild, more everyone."

Scar came towards him, a smile on her face that he didn't

trust. He wondered what she'd done that he'd known nothing of, how she'd played him. How he'd let himself be played.

"And if they do? We have what we wanted, don't we, Silent Petri?"

She was very close now, her hand feather-gentle on his neck, a thumb stroking him. Trying to persuade him one last time, perhaps.

One word from Kass, that was all it had taken. One word, and every doubt came back, every remembered look, every shred of hope that he wasn't this man, that maybe, once, he could have been good and noble. That maybe he still could be.

What seems good to you? her voice asked in his head.

He didn't know, maybe he never had. He knew only how to survive the now, how to take all the iced rage in his gut and use it.

"Free," he said, his voice hollow. "That's what I always wanted."

"Good," she said. "And Morro is going to help with that. Shall we?"

She stalked out of the hut and Morro followed, offering a sly glance at Petri as he passed. They headed for the hut that held Eder. Scar banged open the door, revealing him on the floor, hands bound even though escape was impossible with his leg as it was.

Eder sat up straighter as they entered, set his face and stared at the wall.

"Well now," Scar said as she paced, "here's a pretty thing. My friend here has had the utter stupidity to let my hostages escape." The bitterness in her voice caught Petri's throat, roused him so that he would have bitten back, if not for the smiling Morro watching him.

"Distracted by that . . . that woman," Scar went on. "One word from her, and he goes to pieces. Isn't that so, Petri? No, you don't need to answer. But I'll want some answers from you, Eder. If you want to live to tell this tale."

Eder said nothing, moved no muscle.

She smiled so that her scar puckered. "If we catch them again I'll have to kill all of them. Even those who were with you, as well as the ridiculous Vocho and his sister. Morro has some very interesting ways he could use their blood, so he tells me. Of course that would make their deaths slow and agonising."

Eder opened his mouth and snapped it shut again.

Scar stopped her pacing and crouched in front of him. "Very slow and agonising. As yours will be. But you're the honourable soldier, aren't you? So honourable you shot your own ally for some bizarre reason of your own. Personally I wish you'd done a better job. But you can make amends and your guard will be safe. Or safer. Because have no doubt, we will find them. You weren't prepared for this mountain and what it can throw at you. What it *will* throw at them. Morro has seen and will see to that. They'll never make it down the mountain alive. So you might as well tell me what I want to know. Maybe, if you're very helpful, Morro here need not kill them at all, just use some of their blood. Maybe."

Eder blinked hard and finally turned to look at her.

"What assurance do I have of that?"

Scar stood up and slapped her thighs. "Not much. My word is all, and believe me —" here she turned to look at Petri "— I am loyal to those who help me and lethal to those who turn on me."

Petri couldn't meet her gaze.

She stared at him a moment more and then turned back to Eder. "Well?"

"Carrola, if you'd stay your hand there?" He looked from Scar to Petri and back again. "Please, I . . . Stay your hand there, and I'll tell you anything you want to know."

"I like loyalty in a man," Scar said at last, and her point wasn't lost on Petri. "Tell me what they meant to do."

Kass looked up at Dom in the dim light from the searchers' torches that just penetrated the little snow cave Dom had carved for himself and now sheltered four of them.

"Where the hells did you spring from?" she asked.

"From the same hut as Vocho," Dom said. "Only I escaped a little earlier, when some kind soul distracted the guards by shooting them."

"That was me. I was trying to get Petri to stop killing Vocho," Danel said.

"Well then, well done on both counts. I've been trying to work out how to get Voch out too, but it's been tricky. Apparently some damned fool got everyone stirred up looking for her, and consequently they're all being very vigilant. The vigilance of guards has been the death of many a good escape plan. And escapee. But my daughter and I managed in the end. She's very resourceful and as good at acting a part as her mother was. On the other hand, it's good to see you too."

Kass looked up at him. What in hells had happened to the graceful and pristine Dom she'd known, who Vocho had been so jealous of? This Dom was dressed, if it could be called that, in clothes most beggars wouldn't be seen dead in, albeit slightly warmer ones.

It didn't take too long to tell each other all they needed to know.

"I found my daughter," Dom said, but there was a tinge to the proud smile that came with the words. "But a magician found her first. Told her all sorts I would rather she hadn't known." He trailed off for a moment. "Still, she helped us all escape. She, well, you remember me saying youth makes us stupid? I begin to wonder. Maybe it's just age makes us jaded. Her mother had a kind heart once, before life got in the way." He shook his head with a puzzled smile, and his hands groped at nothing.

"Voch escaped like you say, and he had Carrola with him, but I don't know where they are," Kass said into the silence that followed, more to distract Dom than anything else. "Carrola seems level-headed. Maybe she'll stop Vocho doing the first damn fool thing that comes into his mind."

"I don't know," Dom said, seeming glad of the distraction. "He did well in that duel, given that he probably should have died in the first minute or two. I notice Eder got left behind. You, like the idiot you are, called out to Petri, not only alerting a horde of armed people to your presence, but informing Eder you are not as dead as he hoped. His officer's commission, any semblance of honour, any hope of getting back into Bakar's good graces – with you alive to tell the tale, he can kiss all that goodbye. He can probably kiss goodbye to his head too, unless Bakar has one of his fits of mercy. What's he got to lose if you're killed in the line of duty up here?"

"Nothing, I suppose."

"Exactly. Eder might well be even more dangerous now than he was before. Depends on whether Scar listens to him or not, and what he says." A short hesitation. "Depends if I can rely on my daughter doing what she said."

"Is she——"

A harsh look from Dom, one she'd never have expected of him, and Kass shut up.

"I don't know," he said in the end. "She's suspicious of me, maybe hates me, with good cause, but I think she hates Morro more. That may be our only hope." He cocked his head and looked at the blood on Kass's furs. "Is all that yours?"

She looked down and found blood was leaking through her dressing again. "Eder was pretty dangerous to start with."

"I could help with that," Dom said. She narrowed her eyes, and he blushed. "Ahem, on second thoughts, perhaps not."

"No," she said. "Perhaps not."

"How bad is it?"

She shrugged, only using one shoulder so she wouldn't cause any more damage. "No major organs destroyed, no broken bones. Lucky I have boobs really, or it might well have killed me."

"Uh, yes. Eder's certainly very determined, isn't he?"

"So am I."

"I've noticed that about you. What is it you're currently determined to do? Because while all this is terribly cosy, I feel we should really be making a plan."

"We came to sort out the Scar and the Skull. Then I came on to rescue Voch, but he's escaped and hopefully is in better shape than I am." She tried to think, but everything kept whirling in her head, not helped by the generous glug of jollop Cospel had given her. "Petri. I—"

"You can't save him, Kass. You can't. Why do you think we told you he was dead? Other than he asked us to, I mean." She shot Dom a look at that, but he hurried on. "You didn't do that to him, Eneko did. And before that,

Sabates. Not you. You can't save him from what he is now, who he is; only he can."

"And you couldn't save Alicia or your daughter, but it didn't stop you trying, did it?"

She regretted the words as soon as she'd spoken them, at the way his face shrivelled behind the beard and he stared down at his hands.

"I didn't mean—"

"Yes, you did," he whispered. "And you're right. But I made Alicia that way, Maitea too. *My* lies, *my* stupidity. My responsibility in the end. All you did to Petri was be too late despite every effort. The rest of it was his choice. You can't save him, Kass. You never could."

It's been too late for me for a long time.

She looked at Dom's worn face, the ragged beard, heard again the slight hitch when he'd said his daughter hated him. "You can't save Maitea, either, can you?"

Dom turned away with a frown that told her she'd hit home, and she wished she hadn't.

"What are we going to do then?" Dom said at last, as though he knew exactly what her answer was going to be.

"I can't *not* try to save him," she said. "And I don't think you can't either. If you want to, then you and me, Dom, are going to do what I came to do: put a stop to the Scar and Skull however we can."

Chapter Twenty-seven

A shout dragged Scar from the hut, leaving Petri with Morro, exactly where he didn't want to be. He made a move after Scar but the voice stopped him.

"Couldn't even do that right, could you? Couldn't even kill a man who is everything you despise. So much for the dread Skull. Your cowardice, your *weakness*, could destroy us all. Well, I for one don't intend to let that happen."

Against all his better instincts Petri turned. Morro had his gloves off now, the dark shapes swirling on his hands trying to catch Petri's eye. He kept it determinedly on Morro's smooth face, though he broke out in a sweat at the effort. Everything about those hands wanted to be watched, wanted him to see, was *made* for him to see. His own hand trembled, and he gripped the hilt of his sword for reassurance, for something solid to hold on to amidst the swirling smell of cooking blood.

Morro smiled, a smooth lifting of the lips, pure and unadulterated pleasure. "Scar believes everything I tell her now, and you know what I'll be telling her next? How I sadly had to kill you to defend myself. She might not have believed it before, but helpfully you've made sure she will now."

It came swift and sure, before Petri had time even to open his mouth to reply. Ice in his limbs, so that they felt as brittle as glass, that to move would be to shatter, leave sparkling parts of himself upon the floor. The cold grew – bred – in his bones down to the marrow. His heart stuttered with it, his lips blew breath that fogged, and Morro's smile grew, and with it the ice. Petri couldn't turn away, couldn't move without cracking, but if he stayed he was dead. A moment of weakness, and he saw the hands, saw snowflakes grow and fade all over them, icicles like daggers. Everything was numb except the pain of his heart struggling with the ice that now ran in his veins.

"She'll believe me because she already believes you betrayed her, that you want her place, or dead, or both."

More shouts, then Scar calling for Morro harshly and insistently, a shot that rang like a bell in the crystal-cold air. Morro turned for the door, calling for Maitea to "Keep an eye on our friend here" before he ventured outside into what sounded like chaos.

Maitea appeared out of nowhere, seemingly made of shadows that coalesced into her form, one finger on her lips for Petri to be silent. Her hand on Petri's was hot, hot enough to burn his fingers, melt the ice that coated them, break the frost-bound spell of it. Daughter of a magician, he thought, and apprentice to another. The warmth of her hand spread.

"We don't have to live the lives they tell us," she breathed into his ear. "Run. While you have the chance."

Petri broke – broke free, broke for the door. He didn't stop for anything, not to make sure Morro didn't follow, not to stop his magic if there was any stopping it. Fear and ice made him run, made him a coward again as he staggered out into the snow, afraid that he would shatter, that no matter how he tried he could never be the man he wanted to be.

He ran from the torches, from Kepa's startled face, from Scar's snarl, from Morro's hands and Maitea's whisper. Cast out from the outcasts . . .

He ran from everything and everyone.

Kass crouched in the lee of a hut, watching chaos unfold as Dom launched himself into a knot of bandits, sent three flying and was left confronted with the bald giant. He never hesitated, not for half a heartbeat, coaxing a grin even from her exhausted lips.

Scar was there, moulding everyone to her orders by sheer force of will. But where was the magician? Where was Petri? Kass moved silently from hut to hut as only an assassin could. Dom was making a marvellous distraction, but no Petri so it was useless. A shot behind her, a scream, and she turned, but Cospel's "Hah, want to shoot him in the back do you? Tough shit, sunshine" reassured her that he and Danel were doing their best to make sure no one brought Dom down until she'd found who she was looking for.

She managed to avoid a few stray crew members, ducked around another hut and there he was, running right in front of her, covered in a thin sheen of frost that glittered on the bones of his ruined face. He ground to a halt as he saw her.

They stood, both of them unmoving, unspeaking, for long seconds. There was too much she wanted to say for it to come out as anything coherent. All she could do was stare.

"Come to kill me then?" he said at last. "Go on, get that sword up. Run me through. Go on, Kacha the brave, Kacha the good, Kacha the saviour of fucking Reyes. Go on. I'll give you the fight of your life."

His voice but not his words. Not her Petri. Two men swam in front of her, overlapping, merging, drawing apart. *You can't save him.* One thing these men shared she could see in both their eyes. Terror. A look she knew of old, in the eyes of men before they died, before she killed them. She was two women to his two men, a killer sick of killing.

"I haven't come to kill you."

"What then? Gloat? Come to gawp at my new face like everyone else? Well come on then, have a good look. It's not like you'd have ever loved this half a face, is it? As soon as Eneko put that blade on me, my old life was dead, the old me and everything he ever dreamed of." The voice was a growl, the bare-bone half of his face glinting and gruesome in the flickering light, but he was still in there. She just had to find him.

"Oh, but I do love that face, even as it is," she said. "You just never gave me the chance."

His sword dropped away and he cocked his head as though what she said surprised him. Had he thought so little of her? Had so little of him really survived?

"I came to save you," she said into the silence. "I never left you, in my head. By the Clockwork God's cogs and gears, I swear I tried to be in time in Reyes, but I was too late, no matter how I tried, so I came to save you now. Or rather I came to save, not the Skull, but the Petri I'm in love with."

The frost on his face cracked as he laughed at that, a sound that ended in a wheezing growl that set all the hairs on the back of her neck quivering. He whipped his sword towards her, meeting hers with a clang. He laughed again and pressed towards her so that their faces were inches apart.

"The Petri you know is dead, sliced away by Eneko's knife."

"I refuse to believe that." With a heave she shoved him away, and he whirled off back into dancing snow that shrouded him in darkness, leaving her to hitch painful breaths, holding herself up on the side of the hut.

Petri's lips burned where he imagined she'd kissed them, burned with heat and cold and his own regret as he ran. Tears blurred his eye. There was no escape – from Morro, from Kass, from himself.

He turned a corner and suddenly could see clearly for the first time in weeks, in perhaps his whole life. Scar's crew were on the ground and bleeding, or trying to get close to Dom and his whirling sword as he played with Kepa. Scar was shouting orders, Morro approaching her back. A look of stunned dreaming in all their eyes but Morro's.

Petri looked down at the sword in his hand, not a duellist's but solid nonetheless. Scar had brought him here all that time ago to do a duellist's job, and here he was, running like the weakling they always said he was. He recalled Scar asking him if he was sick of running. And he was. Sick of running, tired of being weak. Even if Kass couldn't help him, he could do the one thing that would free them all from this nightmare.

It had begun snowing again, Morro's work, Petri thought, to shield them from who stalked them, make their guns useless from any distance. Soft feather flakes this time, swirling in a bitter wind. Morro could, would perhaps, make this winter last for ever. Petri walked through it, felt the flakes stick to skin, melt in eyelashes and hair until he could see them flowing in a whirl that centred on the magician. Morro was standing like he was king of the mountain, Scar watching him like she used to watch Petri, and the stab of that surprised him.

Further on Petri could make out the ring of sword on sword, a grunt here and a scream there as a blow told, but now he couldn't make out who it was, who was winning. Scar's crew, if the cat-smile on Morro's face was anything to go by. Petri crept closer, silent in the snow, Silent Petri, the old Petri and the new. Afraid but not going to give in to it. Weak perhaps but ignoring it. He screwed his courage to the hilt of the sword in his shaking hand.

He paused just out of striking range behind Morro. The magician's attention was all on the fighting, which was louder now, so that Petri could just hear the heavy breathing of a man spent, hear a muttered curse. A gust of wind, and the snow cleared for a brief second, revealing Kepa bleeding from half a dozen places. In front of him Dom, a ragged prince, taunting him.

Others of Scar's crew surrounded them, waiting for an order perhaps or just an opportunity. One of them waited too long — with a reverberating clong he went down as though someone had snuffed him out, revealing a hard-breathing Cospel with a gun in one hand and a dented tankard in the other. On the other side of the ring a second went down, screaming at the sudden hole in his leg, his cry mingling with the unmistakable sound of a gun going off at close quarters. A third man ended up planted face first in the snow and stayed there. Kass's face was just visible behind the curtain of snow for a second before she retreated into the darkness.

Dom and Kepa ignored them all, intent on their fight.

"You're not bad," Dom said breathlessly, "but can you do anything about this?" He let loose a flurry of attacks, feints, double-bluffs and cuts that should have carved Kepa into bite-sized pieces, yet only drew blood, didn't follow through.

Kass's face appeared again, blood running from somewhere in her hair. She looked straight at Petri. He saw clearly now, couldn't mistake that look. Don't let go of yourself. I believe in you. You're a good man.

No, he wasn't. But he wasn't a weak man either; he was never going to be weak again. Seeing Kass again had shown him that if nothing else. Once, in another lifetime, Petri had watched while Bakar had taken down a whole regime of magicians and their puppet king. Have an edge, he'd told Petri, and do it quick. They die like anyone else. He had his edge – Morro didn't know he was there, thought him slowly freezing to death or at least firmly under Maitea's gaze.

Petri Egimont, both of him, took a step forward, shut his eyes and thrust.

His blade met nothing but air.

When he opened his eyes Morro was there, but Petri never even saw his face. Only his hands, free of his gloves, gently steaming as falling snow melted above them. The markings caught at him, pulled him in. Death and ice, breaking swords and blood.

"You think I didn't know you were there?" Morro said, his voice barely audible over the whisper of snow. "You think I can't deal with the likes of you?"

The hands moved, and Petri's eyes moved to follow, helpless to do anything else. A scalpel appeared, a hand reached out, found an arm not its own, slashed and drew blood, drew out a scream that rang familiar in Petri's head. The scent of cooking blood became everything.

Other voices came, other screams, but so did the ice in Petri's hands, in his heart, freezing him, turning him to glass that might shatter.

"Weakness, Petri, that's what you are."

Chapter Twenty-eight

Vocho leaned on Carrola, past all shame. Torches moved jerkily below them, a scream rose out of the darkness beyond, and the snow fell. Vocho thought the snow might always fall.

"Can you see what's going on?" he asked. "Because that sounds very much to me like someone has met either Kass or Dom and is regretting it."

The sound of a shot, unmistakeable, and another scream.

"Come on," he said. "I'm buggered if I'm going to miss out on all the glory."

"Voch, you can hardly walk—" Carrola said.

"I can bloody well walk that far. There'll be no living with her if she does it all herself."

They staggered down the slope, a beast with two bodies and three good legs between it. By the time they reached the bottom they were both sweaty and Vocho was out of breath. The torches were patchy and made as many shadows as they did rings of light, but at least they had an idea where to go and a better chance of making it without falling over something. They moved, slowly and jerkily, towards the centre of the little valley. Snow hissed above the torches, whipping into Vocho's eyes, but he scrubbed them clear.

Dom, rags flying, was clearly playing with the bald-headed giant in a cleared area in the middle of the huts. Vocho could just make out Cospel flitting between shadows, until he settled in one, knelt down and took aim with a gun. A resounding bang, and a man fell to his knees with a scream and a splash of bright blood in the snow. Over at the back there was some sort of ruckus that seemed to involve Scar, the magician and Petri, but Vocho couldn't make it out clearly, except that Scar's arm was pouring yet more blood into the snow. Where in hell was Kass? There! Breathing heavily in the shadows, staring at Petri with a sword in one hand and a knife in the other, though both seemed clean of blood. Which was more than could be said for her — blood old and new covered her, but she was alive and upright and Vocho felt his knees sag a touch at that. He covered it by shifting his weight on Carrola, and was comforted when her arm grasped him more firmly.

"Petri!" Kass called out, her voice almost lost in the wind. "Petri, look at me. Me! Not his hands!"

Petri bloody Egimont, scourge of Vocho's life. A crabbed movement by one of the huts to his left, the one they'd kept Vocho in, caught his eye. A gun poked out of the door, next to a dead body. A hand wound it, pointing it at Kass all the while, who was so intent on Petri, as always, she'd not noticed.

Vocho let go of Carrola, ignored her shout and staggered towards the gun and the man holding it.

Eder lay in the doorway, his leg in its splint stiff before him, winding the gun until it clicked. Vocho lurched past the dead body – throttled from behind by a scarf, face purple and grotesque – and all but fell onto Eder.

Eder didn't even miss a beat. The butt of the gun cracked Vocho on the side of the head, making his eyes go screwy. Before he could catch his breath Eder was on him, punching, smacking with the gun. Vocho's nose broke and flooded blood over both of them. Vocho, blind with pain, still came on. He managed to get a hand to the gun, but Eder head-butted him, broke his nose again, it felt like, and his grip slipped.

The barrel swung towards him, and he didn't think, grabbed at it, grappled with Eder. Vocho kicked out with his good leg, caught Eder's broken one with his boot, and the gun went off right by his ear, his head ringing with the noise so that the rest of the world seemed silent.

Something that felt like a hammer hit his hip, and he was pretty sure he screamed, and then Eder's hot face was in his, spittle flying as he mouthed "Fucking guild, fucking guild" over and over. What was it with Vocho and lunatics? He seemed to attract them like jam attracts wasps. The gun butt came down again, knocking Vocho flat on his back, his bad leg twisting as he went. Eder stood slowly, propped himself against the door jamb, blood running from a cut lip that even now curled in distaste. He began to wind the gun again.

"I'm going to kill you," he said as it clicked home. "And then I'm going to—"

A bullet took him in the cheek, splattering bone and blood and brains all over the door jamb behind him. The eye that was left briefly took on a surprised expression before it shut, and his body slid down, boneless and breathless, to crumple over Vocho. The gun fell barrel first into the snow.

"I'm pretty certain that puts paid to any promotion," Carrola said behind him in a shaky voice. "I don't think they like it when you kill your captain."

She knelt next to Vocho and dropped the spent gun like it was hot. She looked sick to her stomach, much how Vocho felt.

"They may not," he said at last. "I, however, am pretty damned glad."

"Petri," Kass shouted, "look at me. Me! Not his hands!"

She headed for him, even now unable to believe he wasn't her Petri, that there wasn't something of him left inside. A shot went off close behind her, and she turned. Vocho lay under Eder, blood over both of them, grappling for a gun.

A glance back at Petri. Something happening to him, something the magician was doing. Icicles glittered over his cheeks, bone and flesh. His breath came out in a burst of ice crystals that tinkled as they fell.

She stood, torn. Brother or one-time lover? Petri was turning to ice before her eyes, but Voch was turning to blood behind her. For once in her life a decision didn't come easily. She wavered between the two, had just decided Vocho, no Petri, no definitely Vocho, when Eder's face disappeared in a spray of blood and bone. Kass didn't even stop to see who'd fired – Voch didn't need her now, but Petri, and maybe everyone else in this valley, did.

She headed for him, calling his name, hoping he could break free, but a figure stood in her way. Scar. She towered over Kass, blood pouring from a cut along her arm, but she didn't seem to let that bother her. A sword swung easily in the other hand as she settled into a low stance.

Morro murmured something which Kass didn't catch but

galvanised Scar into frantic action. She launched herself at Kass with a series of blows that she only barely parried, which numbed her arm, made pain shoot through her chest as the wound began to bleed again.

"You." Scar circled, looking for another opening, but Kass kept her guard up, did her best to make sure there wasn't one. "Petri would have been mine, would have followed me to victory, but for you. I loved him, but now I can't trust him, and he's going to die. Because of you."

Kass didn't bother with words of her own – there didn't seem much point. Instead she feinted, tried to turn it into an attack but the movement dizzied her. Too long since food, since she had all her blood in her body. The feint was clumsy, the attack off point and left her wide open to the punch in the face she received. Everything whirled, white snow and black sky, and she was flat on her back, one hand reflexively holding her sword up to ward off any follow-up. She scrabbled to her feet, shook her head to lose the blood that leaked from her eyebrow and tried again.

Scar was quicker, had her blade scything around at head height as Kass regained her feet, making her slip as she dodged. The blade missed, but Scar didn't stop, the blow flowing into another on the backstroke. The hilt of her sword caught Kass a stunning blow on her cheekbone as it passed. If Petri had been teaching them swordplay, he'd done far too good a job on Scar. Even so, on a good day Kass could have beaten her despite the other's size, but this was very far from being a good day.

Kass staggered back out of Scar's longer reach and tried to clear her head. Scar didn't give her a second to breathe but came again, a series of crunching overhand blows that had Kass on her knees desperately looking for a gap to insert her knife into and not finding one.

"Petri," she gasped out.

The sound of cracking ice and a wet sound followed by a thud stopped the pair of them in their tracks, and Kass risked a look.

Petri stood, bloodied sword in hand, looking confused and triumphant at the same time. The magician's body seemed to take an age to fall at his feet, his precious blood arcing out of him.

Two heartbeats of utter stillness as everything changed. The snow stopped falling on the instant. The wind dropped to near enough nothing and lost its knife-edge. Clouds boiled away to reveal the moon.

Scar launched herself at Petri, Kass forgotten as she brought her blade around. Petri didn't move, looked too stunned to care, but Scar never reached him. A fair-haired young woman appeared out of the shadows, a knife in hand. Scar roared at her to move, tried to bat her away, but the young woman sidestepped, was no longer there and thrust her knife into Scar's back, dropping her like a lead weight.

Behind her, Kass heard Dom swear in surprise. She flicked a quick look Vocho's way as he stood jerkily, Carrola under one shoulder to hold him up.

But Kass couldn't keep her eyes from Petri for long. The icicles melted from his face, leaving him looking pale and ragged but calm. Calmer than she'd ever seen him. He turned a cold eye on her. It was Petri, as she'd known it had to be, but not him. She would never have found her Petri standing over a body, the blood still dripping from his sword. Her Petri would never have rounded on her, that same sword coming for her, a snarl on what was left of his lips.

She stood her ground, heart hammering and with her

sword loose in her hand. She had to know if he had changed that much, if the man she'd once loved, maybe still did, was behind that ruined face. The sword came, and he was no slower than he'd been with his right hand, quicker than spit. The sword came so close that blood splashed her face, warm salty drops that seemed to shock Petri into pulling the blow at the last second. The sword tip hovered by one cheek, trembling.

"I didn't mean for this," Petri said at last, so quietly Kass only just heard it. The set of his shoulders, the way his hand moved on the hilt of his sword . . . there he was, the man she'd been in love with, still was. "I meant only to survive up here, with all the other outcasts. Find a bit of peace with myself." He looked down at where Scar lay dead in the snow. "She didn't mean for this either. She didn't; none of us did. We just wanted to be allowed our little space to live. Only Morro, the magician . . ." A quick glance at the fair-haired young woman who'd felled Scar when Kass couldn't, and it was Dom's daughter, it had to be, looking so like her mother. Petri and Maitea shared a look, a brief smile. "We couldn't do it again – live the life someone else chose for us."

He turned back to Kass, the two parts of him at war. "I wanted to be strong, do you see? I was weak in the head. Always weak, and I wanted to be strong for once, and I was. Until he came, and they all fell under his sway and . . ."

He looked at her, a strange kind of pleading in his one eye, and dropped the sword. "It was only by hating you I could make myself strong enough, with enough rage to keep me warm up here, find the steel inside. But it was me who betrayed, me who failed and paid the price. Not you."

"You were always strong," she said. "You just never knew it."

The realisation struck her that by saving him she would have ruined what little he had left of himself, would have made him see only his own weakness where she saw strength. He'd resisted a magician where the rest had not, had survived things which would have killed other men. She couldn't save him – Dom was right – not if she loved him. But she could help him save himself.

"And a pretty trap we're all in, even now," Petri said. "Whatever I do, Bakar will want our heads. The Shrive or the gallows, those are what my choices are reduced to now, but I'll come quietly enough."

"Unless the guild master makes your case. No gallows, no Shrive. Not for you, if I can help it. A chance, perhaps. But you have to save you."

"I—"

She kissed him one last time on his ruined lips, a kiss to end all others, and she felt his hand at her waist one last time as he pulled her in. A long sweet kiss like those they'd shared when they'd been happy before it all turned to blood and dust, a last kiss to pay for all. Then she turned away and never once looked back. The Petri she knew was dead, but it hadn't been her that killed him.

By the time Kass strode over to Vocho, the snow underfoot was starting to melt and Scar's men and women were regaining their wits. Vocho rather fancied not being around when they were fully alert. He mopped at his twice-broken nose.

Kass spared what was left of Eder a glance that paled her ashen face even further, absently wiped away a trickle of blood from her eyebrow and cocked her head at her brother. "Glad to see you're alive then."

"Glad to be alive. Quite nice to see you too."

But behind the banalities he could see it. She was his sister, after all, and he knew her better than anyone, could see how she tried not to shake, how her hands were determinedly still, her eyes dry as dust and her mouth pinched at the corners.

"Petri's dead," she said, and he nodded, knowing exactly what she meant. "And so is the Skull."

She took a deep, shuddering breath and gazed up at the stars, hard and bright in a sky clear of snow clouds, through air that was becoming rapidly spring-like. When she looked back down it was Carrola she turned to, and a glance passed between them that baffled Vocho.

"Voch," Kass said in a voice that sounded utterly unlike her, "I need you to do me a favour."

"Could I at least get rid of the blood first? Maybe have something to eat? Get away from these nice people who might still want to kill us?"

Kass scanned around as though only just realising they were standing in the middle of a battleground. "Oh, I don't think so. Not after what you're going to tell them."

He narrowed his eyes. "And what am I going to be saying?"

"You can start by saying that you'll arrange a pardon for them all, provided no more thieving, no more killing. And that Bakar will let them have No Man's Land. Imanol will have a fit, but he can go screw himself. You can tell him to think of it as a new trading opportunity. Maybe they can have a few of Kastroa's upper pastures too – this valley's not big enough, really. You tell them that, and that the guild will help get them going – livestock, seeds, that kind of thing. They can make this place their own. I think you'll find they become quite friendly."

"Maybe. But why am *I* going to be telling them?"

"Because I just quit, Voch. You're guild master now."

"Oh, hold on. You can't do that! It'll fall apart with me doing it — it almost did before! I mean, I'll probably kill a couple of the more annoying masters within the week and, and, burn all the paperwork again and, and . . ." His brain dried up. "Carrola, tell her she can't."

Carrola's frown was back, a thoughtful one. "I can't tell her anything."

"Voch, look at me," Kass said. "You can. You can appoint someone else when you get back to Reyes if you want, but for now you're in charge because I'm not coming back to Reyes." Kass had that look, the one he knew all too well, the one that meant she was going to do it whether he liked it or not. "I'm leaving."

He had one last try. "Please, Kass. *Please*. Reyes needs you." Then an admission that didn't come easily. "*I* need you."

"No. It's not the place for me. Not any more. And you don't need me any more either. Vocho the Great, and not just in his own head this time. I'll even pay a few bards to make up songs about you, if you like. How you risked your own life to let Carrola and the others escape. How you saved me from being shot in the back. You could be Vocho the Fabulous. You can be anything you like now, Voch. But I can't go back."

Vocho looked over at Petri, ready to hate the bastard, and saw him talking to his bald-headed giant friend, giving orders, making arrangements, before he crouched down by Scar's body and gently covered her. Nothing left for Kass in Reyes, or here, or anywhere. Vocho was a selfish sod, and he knew it, but even he'd not go so far as to drag her back to nothing just because he wanted it, because he couldn't live without what he got from Reyes. The adulation, the salutes, the comfort of being in streets he knew and loved. It was home, and where he belonged. His next words were the most painful of his life. "If you have to."

"I have to."

Funny, really. She annoyed the crap out of him at least half the time – he'd spent a major portion of his life alternately jealous of and competing with her – and here he was sniffling like a babe in arms. He was tired, that was all, and his leg hurt, and his nose was probably spread over half his face, ruining his dashing looks.

They sat for a while, truly brother and sister for one of only a very few times in their lives, until Kass stood up and wiped a hand across a suspiciously damp face.

"You don't need me, Voch. But if you want me, then I'll come running. I'll never not do that. You know what and who you are; I . . . I have no idea, yet. The old me has cracked like an eggshell, and I don't know who's underneath, but she doesn't belong in Reyes. Not any more. You can do this, Voch, if you try, but not with me there to pick you up when you fall. You have to do it on your own if you're going to be any good. And you will be. Better, you'll be great. Bet you a bull."

And then she left him with nothing but a sad smile.

Petri crouched by Scar's body, unsure how to feel. She'd taken him in, given him a reason to survive and then turned against him. He stood up and looked around. To one side Dom stood with his head bowed in front of something swathed in shadows – Maitea, Petri saw. Dom held her hands in his and their words were earnest and low, only for them. At last he dropped her hands, kissed her forehead and moved away into the darkness, and there were unashamed tears on his face and defeat in his shoulders.

Maitea stepped into the light, but it seemed even then that shadows were never far away.

"I thought you belonged to Morro in your head," Petri said.

"He thought so too, more fool him." She smiled, and Petri was struck again by how much she looked like her mother, but her father was in there too, in the shadows and secrets she walked with. "He wanted to train me. Scar said she freed me, but I earned my freedom a long time ago. Morro wanted to take that from me, make me a slave again, his slave, slave to the magic. I won't go back to being told what my life will be."

"But Dom . . . you said you hated him. Another lie?"

She grinned, more expression on her face than he'd ever seen, and looked more than ever like her father. "Yes and no. He was trying to help me, but then Scar came and . . . Morro wanted me to learn an important lesson in magic by keeping Dom here and twisting him to my own ends. My apprenticeship, in fact. An apprenticeship I never wanted."

"Why are you telling me this?"

A glance over her shoulder to where Dom had disappeared, before she looked back up at him. "Because I want to stay."

"You're a magician."

"I saved your life. Twice. I belong in the mountains. I've lived here all the life I can remember and I want to stay. Besides, you're going to need my help."

"Maybe," he said at last because she was right. "But you keep your gloves *on*."

She smiled again, and that was all her father, poised and secret, but Petri found he believed it nonetheless.

They stood for a time in the growing warmth, Petri savouring the feeling of having come home at last after a long and winding journey. Scar's crew were now looking to him for orders, for direction, most looking lost and bewildered as Morro's influence wore off. His crew now maybe, his family certainly. Petri sent some off to check who'd lived through the night, others to look in all the huts. Kepa wandered up, shaking his head and muttering to himself.

"What now?" he said to Petri. "What do we do now? They're going to know where we are, and without the magician there's not enough of us against all the prelate's men they're bound to send. We got to run, I'm thinking, all of us. Find somewhere to hide."

"Perhaps not."

Vocho stood on the edge of the ring of questioning people, propped up on a bit of wood for a crutch, blood all over his face. One of the other hostages hovered near him, glaring at Petri as though daring him to try anything. She had a wound gun in her hand and the look of someone happy to use it, if she must. Cospel stood on his other side, but Kass wasn't there. Petri got the feeling Kass was never going to be there again, and that twisted inside him but set him free at the same time.

Vocho limped forward, and the crew muttered and mumbled but no one said anything out loud.

"I'm not supposed to kill you," Vocho said, "but frankly I'm quite tempted. You've made a total bugger-up of a perfectly good life – mine – not to mention put a few holes in me, which doesn't incline me to be very well disposed towards you. And now I have to be bloody guild master and sort this mess out."

"We could just kill him?" Kepa said hopefully.

"Appealing," Petri said quietly, "but no."

"Shame. He's a right pain in the arse."

Petri looked around at all the men and women looking to him, to see what he would say, what he would do. His little band of waifs and strays. Maybe there was more than one kind of strong in the head. He turned to face Vocho. "What did you have in mind?"

Chapter Twenty-nine

Two days later Kass pulled her horse to a stop as the sun rose over the mountains and tipped the hills below in gold. The snow had gone and, barring the rushing streams full of meltwater that crossed and recrossed the track, it was as if it had never been. Instead of knife-edged winds and the sharp taste of snow, now there was a balmy breeze from the south and the smell of green things waking up. The promised thaw, at last, to match what was happening inside her.

She'd been taking it easy, resting where she could while she regained her strength – she'd lost a fair bit of blood. Now she sat for a while, watching, revelling in a dawn as she hadn't in months, maybe even longer, before she got the horse going again. She hadn't even had to try hard to find the bastard animal; he'd found her and had taken a small chunk from her arm in a friendly sort of way as a greeting. At least she had someone familiar to be with as she tried to work out what she had left, who was under the cracks in her life.

The day rose warm and willing, and she was, if not

content, at least hopeful. She'd made a decision, and now she had to live with it. She rounded a bend in the track and pulled up short, the horse snorting its displeasure at the sight of another rider sitting as though waiting for her next to a thundering river which would be gone when the snows finally gave up the ghost.

He took off his hat and turned his face up to her, and she wondered where in hell Dom had managed to find a razor to shave off the raggedy beard, not to mention a half-decent suit of clothes. Not quite up to inducing a fit of jealousy in Vocho, but smart enough. They sat and looked at each other for a while, and then she nudged her horse on.

"Turned out nice again," he said, getting his horse to fall into step with hers.

"I wondered where you'd got to. One minute you were fighting that bald giant, the next you'd gone."

"I like being mysterious. It amuses me. And good of you to notice."

"I wanted to say goodbye," she said and narrowed her eyes his way. "I intend to leave, no matter what you say."

An amiable smile. "I know. I thought I'd ride with you for a bit, that's all."

"I also intend to leave on my own." Then again . . . "How long a bit?"

He shrugged. "Until I get bored? Where are you going?"

"Don't know yet. This way."

"Ah, yes. I've been to Don't Know Yet. Periods of intense boredom interspersed with moments of sheer terror usually. Much like everywhere. Weather's nice though. No snow as a rule. I think I've had my fill of snow for a bit."

They rode in companionable silence until they reached a fork in the track. Right would take her back to Reyes, to Voch, to home and the guild and all the memories that went with it. Going back would be to sink back into them and maybe never escape who — what — she'd been there. Last chance.

"I've found," Dom said softly, "that the memories are always there. You can't escape them, but you can soften them, make the edges of them cut you less. And there's only one way to do that. Make new memories. Better ones, hopefully."

"Maitea?" She let the question hang in the air.

Dom stared off ahead before he shrugged. "A fine young woman. Just like her mother, and like her father too in many ways. Good with shadows and mystery. She helped us back there. But she doesn't need me, or want me. If I were to stay . . . No. No, it wouldn't work. And if she left, she might end up just like her mother too. She's decided to stay, and that's for the best. But I can't stay. Better memories await." His hands opened and closed on his reins, opened and closed like he was trying to hold on to something that would not stay held.

Kass looked down the road that led to Reyes. "Do you think he'll be all right? Voch, I mean?"

Dom looked at her from under the brim of his hat, his eyes shadowed and old and tired to the bone. "I think he'll be fine. He's got more sense than you ever give him credit for — he always had you to fall back on if anything went wrong. Down there, in that camp, he didn't have you or even know if you were alive, and he made a bloody good fist of it. Kept his head, mostly, if not his mouth shut. There's probably nothing in the world that can be done about that mouth."

"Probably not."

She turned left, away from Reyes, and Dom followed.

"OK," she said as they reached the crest of a rise, and the rolling and dipping plains of Ikaras opened up below them like an unfurling map full of unknown names and strange places, whole countries to get lost in. "Let's get a few things straight."

"Yes?" He sat up and looked more like the old Dom again, riding easily like he was on oiled springs, his whole body perfectly poised.

"If you're really coming too, then it's friends. That's it. Nothing else. I've decided I have terrible taste in men. Just in case you had any funny ideas."

His answering smile was rueful. "Your taste in men is better than my taste in women. Yours didn't orchestrate a war just to kill you. Did he?"

"I don't think so. Maybe. I don't know." She sighed. "Fine, you win."

"Excellent. Friends it is. No funny business; all will be deadly serious. Anything else?"

"Yes. For the sake of your ears, never let me have a gun."

He laughed, and the sound gave her the first hint of a lightening in her chest, the thought that maybe, perhaps, she'd be all right, that maybe they both would be all right.

"I've heard that," he said. "No funny business, no guns. Now that we have the rules out of the way, have you *any* idea where you want to go? People of our talents can find work wherever we find ourselves."

She looked down over a green plain that led towards the distant shimmer of the sea. For the first time in an age she felt at ease with herself, with the world. "I've heard Five Islands is nice this time of year."

Chapter Thirty

Vocho was once again cursing paperwork. At least he was in the warm now, beside a toasty fire in Kastroa with a bottle of jollop freshly made by Cospel in his tunic. He was still alternately swearing at Kass and missing her like hell. He kept finding his mind wandering, wondering where she was, where she was going, what she'd do when she got there. Whether he'd see her again. There was a big Kass-shaped hole in his side. Who was going to watch his back now?

He was also having a great deal of trouble with the wording of this particular bit of paperwork. Raised voices echoed through the door, rising to a crescendo that ended with a sharp rejoinder to someone to "Piss off" before Carrola came in, looking flushed and pleased with herself.

"You're doing an excellent job of keeping people away," he said.

"That's easy. Use a bit of logic, add some uncomfortable truth, wrap it up in sarcasm, hit them with it right between the eyes, and they don't know where to look. That Imanol is a sod, isn't he? Trying to charge us rent for this place, *and* he wants us to pay for the furs Kass didn't bring back. I told him to go to every hell there is and take it up with the prelate."

"Good. Don't think I could have managed him as well as all this. A report for the prelate. Apparently it's a must, so Cospel tells me, though I'm inclined to think he's saying that because he thinks it's funny. The Clockwork God may know what to put in it, but I don't. The worst part is going to be where I admit Petri's not only still alive and is the Skull, but never mind, I let him off. And just to top it off, I've promised the prelate will help them."

And admit he'd lost Kass along the way. He really wasn't looking forward to that part.

Carrola sat down next to him, so close that he went all flip-flop inside again. They'd barely had a minute alone since Kass had left, and he found he missed that almost as much as he missed Kass. Perhaps even more, because he'd have been quite happy just sitting and looking at Carrola, which is more than he had ever been able to say about his sister.

"I was wondering . . ." he said, then hesitated for perhaps the third time in his life, all caught up in looking at her. *Gird your loins, my lad.* "Um, I was wondering, seeing as you probably haven't a position in the guards any more—"

"No, the chief of the prelate's men here relieved me of my duties this morning. He gave me an honourable discharge though, so it could have been worse. Very apologetic about it too. 'Understand your dilemma', 'possibly only course of action in the trying circumstances' and all that, but in the end 'not a precedent we want to set'."

"No, I can see it might pave the way for a few murders. Anyway, I was wondering. Um. See, I quite like bits of the whole guild-mastering thing: everyone listens to what you say, mostly, plus they all stand to attention when I walk past, people think I'm important and of course the sheer dash of the title quite suits me. I like bawling out lessers when they cock up basic footwork as well, though I can live without the snotty noses. Only there are other bits I'm not so good at. Eneko used to have a sergeant-at-arms as his assistant. She used to terrify all the lessers and not a few of the masters as well. I was, um, wondering if you want the job? You terrify me quite often, so it seems it could be a good fit."

"You *need* terrifying quite often. Anyway, aren't I a bit old to join the guild? Shouldn't you appoint one of your masters?"

Vocho raised what he liked to think was an imperious eyebrow, though its only effect was to make Carrola giggle. "I hereby appoint you a master of the duelling guild of Reyes. I can do that, you know."

"Can you now? I'd just like to point out I left my last position when I decided my captain needed a shot in the face. You'd have to cut back on shitwittery, because I can do it again."

"Good point, good point. Consider it a thing of the past." A slight pang at that because that was half the fun. But along with the guild master's position and the adulation, came a lot of responsibility. It did, however, also mean he wasn't required to duel as often, and considering his hip . . . and he'd found over the last few days that he could do the responsible, even the heroic, just as well without Kass. Maybe even more so, because he didn't have her to rely on to get him out of whatever he got himself into. "I promise. On the Clockwork God's cogs and gears."

"Believe that when I see it. So what would my duties be?"

"Paperwork. And stopping all the masters bitching about each other to me."

"Anything else?" Her own eyebrow rose in a decidedly non-imperious but much more inviting way than his own. "Because I can think of more interesting things we could do as well."

He was blushing again; he could feel the heat of it working its way up his neck. "I'm, um . . . sure we'll come up with something."

"You better had, because you are irritatingly bad at picking up hints. I accept. As my first action as your sergeant-at-arms, I would like to give you this. It might help with that report."

She handed him a sheet of paper, roughly printed and a bit smudged.

"Local newspaper. Brought out a special edition after I talked the man with the press into it. Well, I say talked. More threatened. Best to get the story right first time, right? I told him everything and had him send a load of copies towards Reyes, just to get those bards a good head start, with none of your little extras. This story doesn't need any. I gave him the title too. What do you think?"

He looked down at the sheet and grinned from ear to ear. Right at the top, in bold type, it said VOCHO UPGRADED FROM GREAT TO FABULOUS. Under that, in slightly smaller type, "Heroically risks self to save prelate's guards."

It was the best newspaper he'd ever seen. He might have to frame it. He looked back up at Carrola, who was grinning as broadly as he was. "Is that one of those hints?"

"Yes, Vocho. Yes, it is."

And just in case he missed any more, she grabbed him by the front of the tunic and kissed him soundly. His insides went flip-flop for quite a long while.

extras

www.orbitbooks.net

about the author

Julia Knight is married with two children, and lives with the world's daftest dog that is shamelessly ruled by the writer's obligatory three cats. She lives in Sussex, UK and when not writing she likes motorbikes, watching wrestling or rugby, killing pixels in MMOs and is incapable of being serious for more than five minutes in a row.

Find out more about Julia Knight and other Orbit authors by registering for the free monthly newsletter at www.orbitbooks.net.

if you enjoyed

WARLORDS AND WASTRELS

look out for

BATTLEMAGE

by

Stephen Aryan

CHAPTER 1

Another light snow shower fell from the bleak grey sky. Winter should have been over, yet ice crunched underfoot and the mud was hard as stone. Frost clung to almost everything, and a thick, choking fog lay low on the ground. Only those desperate or greedy travelled in such conditions.

Two nights of sleeping outdoors had leached all the warmth from Vargus's bones. The tips of his fingers were numb and he couldn't feel his toes any more. He hoped they were still attached when he took off his boots; he'd seen it happen to others in the cold. Whole toes had come off and turned black without them noticing, rolling around like marbles in the bottom of their boots.

Vargus led his horse by the reins. It would be suicide for them both to ride in this fog.

Up ahead something orange flickered amid the grey and white. The promise of a fire gave Vargus a boost of energy and he stamped his feet harder than necessary. Although the fog muffled the sound, it would carry to the sentry up ahead on his left.

The bowman must have been sitting in the same position for hours as the grey blanket over his head was almost completely white.

As Vargus drew closer his horse snorted, picking up the scent of other animals, men and cooking meat. Vargus pretended he hadn't seen the man and tried very hard not to stare at his longbow. After stringing the bow with one quick flex the sentry readied an arrow, but in order to loose it he would have to stand up.

"That's far enough."

That came from another sentry on Vargus's right who stepped out from between the skeletons of two shattered trees. He was a burly man dressed in dirty furs and mismatched leathers. Although chipped and worn the long sword he carried looked sharp.

"You a King's man?"

Vargus snorted. "No, not me."

"What do you want?"

He shrugged. "A spot by your fire is all I'm after."

Despite the fog the sound of their voices must have carried as two others came towards them from the camp. The newcomers were much like the others, desperate men with scarred faces and mean eyes.

"You got any coin?" asked one of the newcomers, a bald and bearded man in old-fashioned leather armour.

Vargus shook his head. "Not much, but I got this." Moving slowly he pulled two wine skins down from his saddle. "Shael rice wine."

The first sentry approached. Vargus could still feel the other pointing an arrow at his back. With almost military precision the man went through his saddlebags, but his eyes nervously flicked towards Vargus from time to time. A deserter then, afraid someone had been sent after him.

"What we got, Lin?" called Baldy.

"A bit of food. Some silver. Not much else," the sentry answered.

"Let him pass."

Lin didn't step back. "Are you sure, boss?"

The others were still on edge. They were right to be nervous if they were who Vargus suspected. The boss came forward and keenly looked Vargus up and down. He knew what the boss was seeing. A man past fifty summers, battle scarred and grizzled with liver spots on the back of his big hands. A man with plenty of grey mixed in with the black stubble on his face and head.

"You going to give us any trouble with that?" asked Baldy, pointing at the bastard sword jutting up from Vargus's right shoulder.

"I don't want no trouble. Just a spot by the fire and I'll share the wine."

"Good enough for me. I'm Korr. These are my boys."

"Vargus."

He gestured for Vargus to follow him and the others eased hands away from weapons. "Cold enough for you?"

"Reminds me of a winter, must be twenty years ago, up north. Can't remember where."

"Travelled much?"

Vargus grunted. "All over. Too much."

"So, where's home?" asked Korr. The questions were asked casually, but Vargus had no doubt about it being an interrogation.

"Right now, here."

They passed through a line of trees where seven horses were tethered. Vargus tied his horse up with the others and walked into camp. It was a good sheltered spot, surrounded by trees on three sides and a hill with a wide cave mouth on the other. A large roaring fire crackled in the middle of camp and two men were busy cooking beside it. One was cutting up a hare and dropping pieces into a bubbling pot, while the other prodded some blackened potatoes next to the blaze. All of the men were armed and they carried an assortment of weapons that looked well used.

As Vargus approached the fire a massive figure stood up and came around from the other side. It was over six and a half feet tall, dressed in a bear skin and wide as two normal men. The man's face was severely deformed with a protruding forehead, small brown eyes that were almost black, and a jutting bottom jaw with jagged teeth.

"Easy Rak," said Korr. The giant relaxed the grip on his sword and Vargus let out a sigh of relief. "He brought us something to drink."

Rak's mouth widened, revealing a whole row of crooked yellow teeth. It took Vargus a few seconds to realise the big man was smiling. Rak moved back to the far side of the fire and sat down again. Only then did Vargus move his hand away from the dagger on his belt.

He settled close to the fire next to Korr and for a time no one spoke, which suited him fine. He closed his eyes and soaked up some of the warmth, wiggling his toes inside his boots. The heat began to take the chill from his hands and his fingers started to tingle.

"Bit dangerous to be travelling alone," said Korr, trying to sound friendly.

"Suppose so. But I can take care of myself."

"Where you headed?"

Vargus took a moment before answering. "Somewhere

I'll get paid and fed. Times are hard and I've only got what I'm carrying." Since he'd mentioned his belongings he opened the first skin and took a short pull. The rice wine burned the back of his throat, leaving a pleasant aftertaste. After a few seconds the warmth in his stomach began to spread.

Korr took the offered wineskin but passed it to the next man, who snatched it from his hand.

"Rak. It's your turn on lookout," said Lin. The giant ignored him and watched as the wine moved around the fire. When it reached him he took a long gulp and then another before walking into the trees. The archer came back and another took his place as sentry. Two men standing watch for a group of seven in such extreme weather was unusual. They weren't just being careful, they were scared.

"You ever been in the King's army?" asked Lin.

Vargus met his gaze then looked elsewhere. "Maybe."

"I reckon that's why you travelled all over, dragged from place to place. One bloody battlefield after another. Home was just a tent and a fire. Different sky, different enemy."

"Sounds like you know the life. Are you a King's man?"

"Not any more," Lin said with a hint of bitterness.

It didn't take them long to drain the first wineskin so Vargus opened the second and passed it around the fire. Everyone took a drink again except Korr.

"Bad gut," he said when Vargus raised an eyebrow. "Even a drop would give me the shits."

"More for us," said one man with a gap-toothed grin.

When the stew was ready one of the men broke up the potatoes and added them to the pot. The first two portions went to the sentries and Vargus was served last. His bowl was smaller than the others, but he didn't complain. He saw a few chunks of potato and even one bit of meat. Apart from a couple of wild onions and garlic the stew was pretty bland, but it was hot and filling. The food, combined with the wine and the fire, helped warm him all the way through. An itchy tingling starting to creep back into his toes. It felt as if they were all still attached.

When they'd all finished mopping up the stew with some flat bread, and the second wineskin was empty, a comfortable silence settled on the camp. It seemed a shame to spoil it.

"So why're you out here?" asked Vargus.

"Just travelling. Looking for work, like you," said Korr.

"You heard any news from the villages around here?"

One of the men shifted as if getting comfortable, but Vargus saw his hand move to the hilt of his axe. Their fear was palpable.

Korr shook his head. "Not been in any villages. We keep to ourselves." The lie would have been obvious to a blind and deaf man.

"I heard about a group of bandits causing trouble in some of the villages around here. First it was just a bit of thieving and starting a couple of fights. Then it got worse when they saw a bit of gold." Vargus shook his head sadly. "Last week one of them lost control. Killed four men, including the innkeeper."

"I wouldn't know," said Korr. He was sweating now and it had nothing to do with the blaze. On the other side of the fire a snoozing man was elbowed awake and he sat up with a snort. The others were gripping their weapons with sweaty hands, waiting for the signal.

"One of them beat the innkeeper's wife half to death when she wouldn't give him the money."

"What's it matter to you?" someone asked.

Vargus shrugged. "Doesn't matter to me. But the woman has two children and they saw who done it. Told the village Elder all about it."

"We're far from the cities out here. Something like that isn't big enough to bring the King's men. They only come around these parts to collect taxes twice a year," said Lin with confidence.

"Then why do you all look like you're about to shit yourselves?" asked Vargus.

An uncomfortable silence settled around the camp, broken only by the sound of Vargus scratching his stubbly cheek.

"Is the King sending men after us?" asked Korr, forgoing any pretence of their involvement.

"It isn't the King you should worry about. I heard the village Elders banded together, decided to do something themselves. They hired the Gath."

"Oh shit."

"He ain't real! He's just a myth."

"Lord of Light shelter me," one of the men prayed. "Lady of Light protect me."

"Those are just stories," scoffed Lin. "My father told me about him when I was a boy, more than thirty years ago."

"Then you've got nothing to worry about," Vargus grinned. But it was clear they were still scared, more than before now that he'd stirred things up. Their belief in the Gath was so strong he could almost taste it in the air. For a while he said nothing and each man was lost in his own thoughts. Fear of dying gripped them all, tight as iron shackles.

Silence covered the camp like a fresh layer of snow and he let it sit a while, soaking up the atmosphere, enjoying the calm before it was shattered.

One of the men reached for a wineskin then remembered they were empty.

"What do we do, Korr?" asked one of the men. The others were scanning the trees as if they expected someone to rush into camp.

"Shut up, I'm thinking."

Before Korr came up with a plan Vargus stabbed him in the ribs. It took everyone a few seconds to realise what had happened. It was only when he pulled the dagger free with a shower of gore that they reacted.

Vargus stood up and drew the bastard sword from over his shoulder. The others tried to stand, but none of them could manage it. One man fell backwards, another tripped over his feet, landing on his face. Lin managed to make it upright, but then stumbled around as if drunk.

Vargus kicked Lin out of the way, switched to a two-handed grip and stabbed the first man on the ground through the back of the neck. He didn't have time to scream. The archer was trying to draw his short sword, but couldn't manage it. He looked up as Vargus approached and a dark patch spread across the front of his breeches. The edge of Vargus's sword opened the archer's throat and a quick stab put two feet of steel into Lin's gut. He fell back, squealing like a pig being slaughtered. Vargus knew his cries would bring the others.

The second cook was on his feet, but Vargus sliced off the man's right arm before he could throw his axe. Warm arterial blood jetted across Vargus's face. He grinned and wiped it away as the man fell back, howling in agony. Vargus let him thrash about for a while before putting his sword through the man's face, pinning his head to the ground. The snow around the corpse turned red, then it began to steam and melt.

The greasy-haired sentry stumbled into camp with a dagger held low. He swayed a few steps one way and then the other; the tamweed Vargus had added to the wine was taking effect. Bypassing Vargus he tripped over his own feet and landed face first on the fire. The sentry was screaming and the muscles in his arms and legs lacked the strength to lift him up. His cries turned into a gurgle and then trailed off as the smoke turned greasy and black. Vargus heard fat bubbling in the blaze and the smell reminded him of roast pork.

As he anticipated, Rak wasn't as badly affected as the others. His bulk didn't make him immune to the tamweed in the wine, but the side effects would take longer to show. Vargus was just glad that Rak had drunk quite a lot before going on duty. The giant managed to walk into camp in a straight line, but his eyes were slightly unfocused. Down at one side he carried a six-foot pitted blade.

Instead of waiting for the big man to go on the offensive, Vargus charged. Raising his sword above his head he screamed a challenge, but dropped to his knees at the last second and swept it in a downward arc. The Seveldrom steel cut through the flesh of Rak's left thigh, but the big man stumbled back before Vargus could follow up. With a bellow of rage Rak lashed out, his massive boot catching Vargus on the hip. It spun him around, his sword went flying and he landed on hands and knees in the snow.

Vargus scrambled around on all fours until his fingers found the hilt of his sword. He could hear Rak's blade whistling through the air towards him and barely managed to roll away before it came down where his head had been. Back on his feet he needed both hands to deflect a lethal cut which jarred his arms. Before he could riposte something crunched into his face. Vargus stumbled back, spitting blood and swinging his sword wildly to keep Rak at bay.

The big man came on. With the others already dead and his senses impaired, part of him must have known he was on borrowed time. Vargus ducked and dodged, turned the long blade aside and made use of the space around him. When Rak overreached he lashed out quickly, scoring a deep gash along the giant's ribs, but it didn't slow him down. Vargus inflicted a dozen wounds before Rak finally noticed that the red stuff splashed on the snow belonged to him.

With a grunt of pain he fell back and stumbled to one knee. His laboured breathing was very loud in the still air. It seemed to be the only sound for miles in every direction.

"Korr was right," he said in a voice that was surprisingly soft. "He said you'd come for us."

Vargus nodded. Taking no chances he rushed forward. Rak tried to raise his sword but even his prodigious strength was finally at an end. His arm twitched and that was all. No mercy was asked for and none was given. Using both hands Vargus thrust the point of his sword deep into Rak's throat. He pulled it clear and stepped back as blood spurted from the gaping wound. The giant fell onto his face and was dead.

By the fire Lin was still alive, gasping and coughing up blood. The wound in his stomach was bad and likely to make him suffer for days before it eventually killed him. Just as Vargus intended.

He ignored Lin's pleas as he retrieved the gold and stolen goods from the cave. Hardly a fortune, but it was a lot of money to the villagers.

He tied the horses' reins together and even collected up all the weapons, bundling them together in an old blanket. The bodies he left to the scavengers.

It seemed a shame to waste the stew. Nevertheless Vargus stuck two fingers down his throat and vomited into the snow until his stomach was empty. Using fresh snow he cleaned off the bezoar and stored it in his saddlebags. It had turned slightly brown from absorbing the poison in the wine Vargus had drunk, but he didn't want to take any chances so made himself sick again. He filled his waterskin with melting snow and sipped it to ease his raw throat.

Vargus's bottom lip had finally stopped bleeding, but when he spat a lump of tooth landed on the snow in a clot of blood. He took a moment to check his teeth and found one of his upper canines was broken in half.

"Shit."

With both hands he scooped more snow onto the fire until it was extinguished. He left the blackened corpse of the man where it had fallen amid wet logs and soggy ash. A partly cooked meal for the carrion eaters.

"Kill me. Just kill me!" screamed Lin. "Why am I still alive?" He gasped and coughed up a wadge of blood onto the snow.

With nothing left to do in camp Vargus finally addressed him. "Because you're not just a killer, Torlin Ke Tarro. You were a King's man. You came home because you were sick of war. Nothing wrong with that, plenty of men turn a corner and go on in a different way. But you became what you used to hunt."

Vargus squatted down beside the dying man, holding him in place with his stare.

Lin's pain was momentarily forgotten. "How do you know me? Not even Korr knew my name is Tarro."

Vargus ignored the question. "You know the land around here, the villages and towns, and you know the law. You knew how to cause just enough trouble without it bringing the King's men. You killed and stole from your own people."

"They ain't my people."

Vargus smacked his hands together and stood. "Time for arguing is over, boy. Beg your ancestors for kindness on the Long Road to Nor."

"My ancestors? What road?"

Vargus spat into the snow with contempt. "Pray to your Lantern God and his fucking whore then, or whatever you say these days. The next person you speak to won't be on this side of the Veil."

Ignoring Lin's pleas he led the horses away from camp and didn't look back. Soon afterwards the chill crept back in his fingers but he wasn't too worried. The aches and pains from sleeping outdoors were already starting to recede. The fight had given him a small boost, although it wouldn't sustain him for very long. The legend of the Gath was dead, which meant time for a change. He'd been delaying the inevitable for too long.

*　　*　　*

Carla, the village Elder, was standing behind the bar when Vargus entered the Duck and Crown. She was a solid woman who'd seen at least fifty summers and took no nonsense from anyone, be they King or goat herder. With a face only her mother could love it was amazing she'd given birth to four healthy children who now had children of their own. Beyond raising a healthy family the village had prospered these last twenty years under her guidance.

Without being asked she set a mug of ale on the bar as he sat down. The tavern was deserted, which wasn't surprising with everything that had happened. On days like this people tended to spend more time with their loved ones.

"Done?"

Vargus drained the mug in several long gulps and then nodded. He set the bag of gold on the bar and watched as Carla counted it, but didn't take offence. The bandits could have spent some of it and he didn't know how much had been stolen. When she was finished Carla tucked it away and poured him another drink. After a moment's pause she tapped herself a mug. They drank in comfortable silence until both mugs were dry.

"How is everyone?" asked Vargus.

"Shook up. Murder's one thing we've seen before, in anger or out of greed, but this was something else. The boy might get over it, being so young, but not the girl. That one will be marked for life."

"And their mother?"

Carla grunted. "Alive. Not sure if that's a blessing or a curse. When she's back on her feet she'll run this place with her brother. She'll do all right."

"I brought in a stash of weapons and their horses too. You'll see she gets money for it?"

"I will. And I'll make sure Tibs gives her a fair price for the animals."

The silence in the room took on a peculiar edge, making the hairs stand up on the back of his neck.

"You hear the news coming in?" asked Carla. There was an unusual tone to her voice, but Vargus couldn't place it. All he knew was it made him nervous.

"Some," he said, treading carefully and looking for the trap door. He knew it was there, somewhere in the dark, and he was probably walking straight towards it.

"Like what?" asked Carla.

"A farmer on the road in told me the King's called on everyone that can fight. Said that war was coming here to Seveldrom, but he didn't know why."

"The west has been sewn together by King Raeza's son, Taikon."

Vargus raised an eyebrow. "How'd he manage that?"

"Religion, mostly. You know what it's like in Zecorria and Morrinow, people praying all the time. One story has our King pissing on an idol of the Lord of Light and wiping his arse with a painting of the Blessed Mother."

"That's a lie."

Carla grunted. "So are all the other stories about him killing priests and burning down temples. Sounds to me like someone was just itching for a war. A chance to get rid of all us heathens," she said, gesturing at the idol of the Maker on a shelf behind her. Most in Seveldrom prayed to the Maker, but those that didn't were left alone, not killed or shunned for being different. Religion and law stayed separate, but it was different for the Morrin and Zecorrans.

"What about the others in the west? They aren't mad on religion, and no one can make the Vorga do anything they don't want to."

Carla shrugged. "All people are saying is that something bad happened down in Shael. A massacre, bodies piled tall as trees, cities turned to rubble because they wouldn't fight. After that it sounds like the others fell in line."

"So what happened to King Raeza then? Is he dead?"

"Looks like. People are saying Taikon killed his father, took the Zecorran throne and now he's got himself a magician called the Warlock. There's a dozen stories about that one," said Carla, wiping the bar with a cloth even though it was already clean. "I heard he can summon things from beyond the Veil."

"I didn't think you were one to believe gossip," scoffed Vargus.

Carla gave him a look that made men piss themselves, but it just slid off him. She shook her head, smiling for a moment and then it was gone.

"I don't, but I know how to listen and separate the shit from the real gold. Whatever the truth about this Warlock, and the union in the west, I know it means trouble. And lots of it."

"War then."

Carla nodded. "Maybe they think our King really is a heretic or maybe it's because they enjoy killing, like the Vorga. Most reckon they'll be here come spring. Trade routes to the west have dried up in the last few days. Merchants trying to sneak through were caught and hung. Whole trees full of the greedy buggers line the north and southern pass. The crows and magpies are fat as summer solstice pheasants from all their feasting."

"What will you do?"

Carla puffed out her cheeks. "Look after the village, same as always. Fight, if the war comes this far east. Although if it comes here, we've already lost. What about you? I suppose you'll be going to fight?"

There was that odd tone to her voice again. He just nodded, not trusting himself to speak. One wrong word and he'd plummet into the dark.

"People like you around here. And not just for sorting out the bandits," said Carla scrubbing the same spot on the bar over and over. "You know I lost my Jintor five winters back from the damp lung. The house is quiet without him, especially now that the children are all grown up. Fourth grandchild will be along any day, but there's still a lot that needs doing. Looking after the village, working with the other Elders, easily enough work for two."

In all the years he'd known her it was the most Vargus had ever heard her say about her needs. The strain was starting to show on her face.

He settled her frantic hand by wrapping it in both of his. Her skin was rough from years of hard labour, but it was also warm and full of life. For the first time since he'd arrived she looked him in the eye. Her sharp blue eyes were uncertain.

"I can't," Vargus said gently. "It's not who I am."

Carla pulled her hand free and Vargus looked away first, not sure if he was sparing her or himself.

"What about the legend of the Gath?"

He dismissed it with a wave. "It was already fading, and me with it. There aren't many that believe, fewer still that are afraid. It's my own fault, I guess. I kept it too small for too long. It would only keep me for a few more years at best. This war is my best way."

Carla was the only one in the village who knew some of the truth about him. She didn't claim to understand, but she'd listened and accepted it because of who he was and what he could do. It seemed churlish to hide anything from her at this point.

He waited, but to his surprise she didn't ask for the rest.

"So you'll fight?"

"I will," declared Vargus. "I'll travel to Charas to fight and bleed and kill. For the King, for the land and for those who can't defend themselves. I'll swear an oath, by the iron in my blood, to fight in the war until it's done. One way or the other."

Carla was quiet for a time. Eventually she shook her head and he thought he saw a tear in her eye, but maybe it was just his imagination.

"If anyone else said something like that, I'd tell them they were a bloody fool. But they're not just words with you, are they?"

"No. It's my vow. Once made it can't be broken. If I stay here I'll be dead in a few years. At least this way, I have a chance."

Reaching under the counter Carla produced a dusty red bottle that was half empty. Taking down two small glasses she poured them each a generous measure of a syrupy blue spirit.

"Then I wish you luck," said Carla, raising her glass.

"I'll drink to that, and I hope if I ever come back, I'll still be welcome."

"Of course."

They tapped glasses and downed the spirit in one gulp. It burned all the way down Vargus's throat before lighting a pleasant fire in his belly. They talked a while longer, but the important words had been said and his course decided.

In the morning, Vargus would leave the village that had been his home for the last forty years, and go to war.